DANGEROUS THINGS

CLAIRE RAYNER

DANGEROUS THINGS

Michael Joseph
LONDON

MICHAEL JOSEPH LTD

Published by the Penguin Group
27 Wrights Lane, London W8 5TZ
Viking Penguin Inc., 375 Hudson Street, New York, New York 10014, USA
Penguin Books Australia Ltd, Ringwood, Victoria, Australia
Penguin Books Canada Ltd, 10 Alcorn Avenue, Toronto, Ontario, Canada M4V 3B2
Penguin Books (NZ) Ltd, 182–190 Wairau Road, Auckland 10, New Zealand

Penguin Books Ltd, Registered Offices: Harmondsworth, Middlesex, England

First published 1992

Typeset in Monophoto 11½ on 13½ pt Sabon
Printed in England by Clays Ltd, St Ives plc

A CIP catalogue record for this book is available from the British Library.

ISBN 0 7181 3549 0

The moral right of the author has been asserted.

The quotation on page 128 from 'This Be the Verse', from *Wintering Out* by
Philip Larkin, is reproduced by kind permission of Faber and Faber Ltd.

For Susan Watt
Guide, Philosopher, Friend
and
Ideal Editor

A little learning is a dang'rous thing;
Drink deep, or taste not the Pierian spring:
There shallow draughts intoxicate the brain,
And drinking largely sobers us again.

An Essay on Criticism, Alexander Pope

One

———————⟨∞∞∞⟩———————

Hattie pinned her list to the fridge door with a blob of Blu-Tack and then, to make sure, added a green and red wooden pig with a magnet in its bottom. Then she stood and glowered at it. She'd been through it three times already this evening: why drive herself mad? But all the same she started again. Just to make sure, she told herself, to make assurance doubly sure – Jessica's swimming gear. Check. Sophie's gym gear. Check. Spare pants for Sophie in a plastic bag; she didn't often have accidents nowadays, but she felt safer having her just-in-cases in the pocket of her school bag, so, check. Digestive biscuits for break for both. Check . . .

This time when she'd finished she made herself sit down at the kitchen table to drink her tea, even though it was half cold now. There was nothing more she could do to be ready for the morning. Yes, it would be a panic to get the girls up and breakfasted and dressed ready to be collected by Inge from Judith's next door at half past seven, so that Peter could drive them to school together with their Jenny and Petra on his way to the hospital, but she could manage that. Their clothes were laid out ready and she'd checked their school bags three times, for God's sake. What more could she do? Put tomorrow's supper ready by the microwave so that she could put it straight in when she came home herself?

She almost got to her feet to take the prepared dishes from the fridge and then made herself sit down again. Ridiculous. Leave room at food temperature for almost twenty-four hours – where was the sense? That way they'd get gastroenteritis, and then what would she do? Bad enough they had a working mother, poor little scraps, without having one who poisoned them with bad food. And she contemplated both her children getting horrendous symptoms, dying and being buried while all the neighbours, teachers and hospital staff stood around staring accusingly at her, and then shook her head at her own silliness. She really had to stop this. So she was taking a job! Lots of mothers had jobs and didn't flap the way she was. It would do the girls no harm at all to have her out and earning; do them good, in fact. Judith had pointed that out kindly, but without pulling any punches, warning her that she was getting a bit obsessive about the children.

'It's too much for them, Hatt,' she'd said. 'No kids ought to have a mother who frets over them the way you do. Too many of your emotional eggs in their baskets, ducky. Heavy for 'em. Time you got out and about a bit more. It's been a year since Oliver died, and if you don't try soon you'll turn into Queen Victoria and much good that'll do you or the kids. Come to supper on Friday. I've got a few characters coming you might like. Doesn't matter if you don't. It's getting out that matters. So I'll see you at half past seven and lend me that big silver platter of yours. I need it for the starter. Crudités, I thought . . .'

Thank God for Judith, Hattie thought, staring into the depths of her chilly tea. I'd have gone off my trolley without her. A year since Oliver died. It didn't seem possible. It was only a few days. It was a lifetime. It was both. And she drew a deep breath and made herself think about how it had been, exploring her memory gingerly in the way she'd use her tongue tip to explore an aching tooth. There had once been a time when there had been an Oliver full of energy and plans and ambition, but that she couldn't remember. She didn't want to remember. It made what came after so much worse. So she thought of Oliver ill, of the way he had sat curled up in his chair staring out of the window and doing nothing. The business had fallen to pieces around them, for how could a book-designing consultancy operate when the book designer stopped work? The doctors had told him he should go on working, told him the lousy way the drugs made him feel could be overcome if he put his mind to it, but he'd not believed them, and had just got worse and worse and then almost pettishly, she had thought at the time, died.

Oh, but she'd been angry! How dare he do that to her, leave her with the girls still little more than babies, with Sophie just five and Jessica a clingy seven? How could he have cared so little for her that there'd been so little money, so little concern for what it would be like to be a widow at thirty-five?

Her eyes filled with tears, and she put down the beaker of cold tea and sniffed hard. It still hurt. It ought to be better by now, surely? People said a year, once the first year and its anniversaries was over, it'd be all right. 'You're still young,' they said to her, as though that helped. 'You'll find someone else, of course you will.' And she wanted to hit them, because how could there ever be another Oliver? The one before the sick one she'd almost learned to hate, the one who'd left her alone and angry. To find such another wasn't possible; she wanted to shriek that at the well-meaning idiots who bleated at her. And one day she had shrieked just because she had to and not because of what someone had just said, and thank God it had been Judith she'd shrieked at. Judith had listened calmly and let it roll over her and then just hugged her and fed her hot soup, and chattered on about nothing much in the way she did usually, thank God, because if she hadn't Hattie would have got up and gone. Left the girls, left the house, left the misery, left it all.

Left the girls. Guilt filled her as the thought came into her mind. She couldn't have felt worse if she'd actually done it. They'd suffered so much, those two; they'd adored Oliver when they'd been very small and he'd been good with them, playing a lot, talking to them a lot, reading to them a lot. But then the leukaemia had sucked all that out of him and he'd sat and stared out of the window and pushed them away when they'd come to him; and they'd been bewildered and hurt and had gone away, to her, and that had made her hate him too. Oh, they'd been bad days, dreadful days, and she had actually thought of making it worse for them, taking herself away from them as well as their father.

She got to her feet abruptly and took her beaker to the sink to wash it and put it away, and then started to set the table for breakfast. She wasn't going to leave the children, not ever. She was theirs as long as they wanted her, and that was that. Tomorrow she'd phone Hilary Roscoe and tell him she'd changed her mind. She wouldn't be starting work with him, because small children shouldn't have working mothers, and –

She stopped, the muesli bowls in her hand, and stared blankly at the list pinned to the fridge. She'd been through all this before, *ad nauseam*. It would do the girls no harm at all if she had a job. It would do them good. Keep remembering that as long as she planned it right, made sure her support system was strong and intact, nothing but good all round could accrue. Peter and Judith had said so, her own commonsense told her so and Hilary Roscoe had made it possible for it to be so. She had to do it.

Hilary Roscoe. She thought more about him, and her lips curved a little. How Oliver would have laughed at him! So very urbane, so very good-looking, with his silvery hair and his deceptively young-looking tanned face and his so perfectly cut suits; just the sort of smoothie Oliver had always found most ridiculous. He called them slickers and had told her that publishers' offices were full of them, standing out like proverbial sore thumbs against the earnest young women in ethnic clothes and the rather battered young men in crumpled jeans who always looked as though they were about to burst into tears of anxiety. When Judith had introduced them with her usual garbled nutshell sketches ('Darling, this is Dr Hilary Roscoe, madly important, Headmaster of the Foundation, you know, down in Wapping, always on the telly talking about education and frantic most of the time about money and all the rest of it, you'll get on terribly well; Hilary, this is my darling friend Hattie who's a widow and used to be a Sister at Old East, you know, the hospital down the road from your place, and is about to go back to work now her children are off her hands at school. Now you two be cosy together while I go and look at the lamb. I daren't trust Inge not to overcook it —') she had remembered Oliver, and that made it difficult to warm to Roscoe.

But they had got on surprisingly well. He talked to her in the sort of concentrated way she liked, not constantly peering over her shoulder to see who was there who might be more interesting and not trying to overhear other conversations around them. She found him easy to talk to, and blushed when she realized she'd poured it all out: how Oliver had been such a splendid book designer for the sort of packagers who do those expensive coffee-table art books, and how he'd not bothered much with insurance except for the mortgage on the house, fortunately, so life was difficult though not impossible, but as for even thinking about where she should send the girls to school when they were eleven plus, well, forget it. It would have to be an ordinary comprehensive and that was that. There was certainly no money for school fees. Not, she said then, that she'd be able to send them to Dr Roscoe's school even if she could afford it, since it was a boys' school.

'Not entirely,' he said, and smiled at her and his face creased most charmingly, so that he looked, paradoxically, younger than ever. 'Not any more. I'm taking girls into the sixth form next term. It's an extraordinary thing for a school like mine to do, though I know many others do. But we're the *Foundation*! But there it is. It's fashionable, and I can't deny I'll be glad to get them, because it's getting harder and harder to make the budget balance. We get little enough choice when the cold winds of recession blow and they're blowing *very* hard right now, aren't they? So, girls in my sixth form next term!' And he shook his head in a sort of mock amazement and laughed, a pleasant, even musical, sound, and she liked him even more.

'It should be interesting for the school,' she said. 'Letting females into that monastic atmosphere.'

'A little too interesting, perhaps.' He looked less amused. 'Time will tell. I'd as soon not do it, of course. But how can I do otherwise? I'm competing with the likes of the City of London and St Paul's and Westminster, all of them in much more salubrious areas than we are. Taking girls was frankly the only option I had left.'

They were sitting at the dinner table by now, herded there by Judith who yapped at them in true sheepdog fashion, and he looked round the table with the amused expression back in position on his face. 'I must say that I'm amazed that we've found parents willing to give us a try. What they think their precious lambs will get from being with my boys I can't imagine. They're a formidable lot, my sixth form. I can see these more delicate blossoms wilting in their shadows. It's gratifying they want to take the risk, don't you think? Stupid but gratifying.'

Suddenly Hattie didn't like him so much, seeing his charming attention to her as patronizing, and his concentration on her conversation as the behaviour of the trained diplomat rather than the spontaneous generosity of the sort of man she'd hoped he was. And because by now she'd had one of Judith's generous gins and tonics and was halfway through her first glass of wine, she was reckless and launched herself into an impassioned defence of girls of sixteen. She told him sharply that they were far from likely to be in the shadow of his boys, since there was a good deal of research that showed girls were just as academically capable as boys and often more so, and pointed out with considerable heat that they were likely to have a distinctly civilizing effect on what were no doubt the usual crowd of hobbledehoys that were boys of that age.

And he laughed – actually laughed – and apologized. 'I bow to the superior knowledge of the mother of daughters,' he said and raised his glass at her and she glared back at him, nonplussed. He was still being patronizing, she was sure, and yet he looked so open and friendly and genuinely free of any rancour; and she lifted her own glass in response, almost without realizing she'd done it, and subsided.

But after dinner, when they were scattered around Judith's big comfortable drawing room with their coffee, he'd come to sit beside her and apologized again. And that time she blushed and told him she was sorry if she'd been rude; it was just that so often girls were put down when in fact they were –

'Yes,' he said. 'I got the message, loud and clear. Look, I rather think you could be the solution to a problem for me. My establishment is, as you pointed out, monastic. Staff as well as pupils. The only women around the place are cooks and cleaners and so forth and they don't count –'

She found herself responding with irritation again, but he'd seen it coming as she opened her mouth, and held up both hands in mock surrender.

'I don't mean they don't count as people, of course they do. It's simply that they aren't part of the teaching staff. So, I'll have a gaggle of schoolgirls in the place and not a woman anywhere to care for their problems as and when they arise. I can just see one of my masters trying to deal with a patch of pre-menstrual temper or –'

'It doesn't happen to everyone,' she said a little waspishly. 'Most times when women get angry it's for a good reason and has nothing to do with their hormones.'

'You see?' he said and set his head to one side almost winsomely. 'I can't know that. Nor can any of my staff. I'm going to need someone who can spot the real McCoy and help with it, and who can make sure any wrongs are put right and that the girls are generally mothered and so forth. One wouldn't want them to be unhappy at school.' He laughed again then. 'And to tell you the truth I have to keep their parents sweet. Imagine if one of them asked me what happened if her daughter got ill, and I had no satisfactory answer! So there you have it. You're the only person to solve my knotty little problem.'

She squinted up at him, a little confused. Not with the effects of the gin and the wine — which had already subsided, leaving her feeling sombre — but because she'd lost the thread of what he was saying.

'I am? How?'

'Why, by being my female member of staff! I've been looking for someone suitable, but even in these hard times suitable staff are hard to find. You seem to be properly qualified — some teaching of health and hygiene matters to the girls, and some first aid too. You can help the boys when they get battered at rugger and so forth — there'll be lots to keep you busy —'

'But what about the person who does the job now?' she'd protested. 'Won't it cause problems if I —'

'I told you, there isn't anyone.'

'So who bandaged the boys when they got battered at rugger last term?'

'Oh, mostly no one. We're quite a stoical lot, you know. Don't make heavy weather about a few grazes and bruises. And the physical education staff all have first-aid qualifications, of course. They can set a sprained ankle or whatever it is you do to such a joint at the side of the field and then go on to win the match.'

'Very commendable,' she murmured, but he ignored her irony.

'Won't you do it? This is really so fortuitous, meeting you tonight. I've tried so many agencies and to no purpose at all. They charge the earth and one never knows what sort of rag tag and bobtail'll turn up from them.'

'Perhaps I'm rag tag,' she said, and lifted her brows at him.

'Lawks-a-mussy me, it's a lidy if I never saw one.' His mock cockney grated a little. 'No, my dear girl, you're perfect. Any friend of old Peter and Judith —'

'You've known them a long time?'

'Ever since he took my appendix out a few years ago. Splendid chap. So, tell me you're interested.'

'I have two small children! I can't possibly –'

'You're not listening, my dear girl,' he said reprovingly. 'I am offering you a job in a school. School hours, school holidays and half-terms and all the rest of it. I know you use the State schools but I do assure you the holidays match! When they have holidays, so does the Foundation. Ideal, I would have thought –'

'Of course it is!' Judith crowed from behind Hattie's shoulder. 'Best idea in the world. She'll take it –'

'Here, hang on, Judith!' Hattie was alarmed, feeling the safe ground tremble beneath her feet. 'You really can't –'

'Oh, can't I!' Judith retorted. 'Just watch me. She can't do it for less than – oh, sixteen K a year.'

'Don't be absurd! The scale for a school nurse at middle level is £13,885 and I can't –' Roscoe protested but Judith threw her hands in the air.

'You said she'll be teaching hygiene and so forth, so that's got to be worth more than just a school nurse. Fifteen and a half K and that's my last offer,' she cried. 'Come on, Hilary. The Foundation isn't that broke.'

'You don't know the half of it! I can stretch another – oh, six hundred, I suppose. Fourteen and a half K, and there I must stick. We have money troubles, remember? Fourteen and a half K and the term starts on 6 September. Come and see us before that, of course. Get the feel of the place, but you're not needed till the day before the horrors descend on us.'

'I'll think about it,' Hattie tried to say, but neither of them had been remotely interested in that.

'She'll be there,' Judith assured Hilary blithely. 'I'll sort out the children and so forth. Best thing either of you could do. I congratulate you both.'

Hattie went on laying the breakfast table now, putting the chocolate hazelnut spread in front of Jessica's place and the Marmite in front of Sophie's and the remains of the Cooper's Oxford marmalade in front of her own. Would it be worth cutting bread now and setting it ready in the toaster? No, that would dry it out. But she'd have to be sharpish in the morning. There'd be just enough time if she really moved to get it all done and the house tidy and herself dressed and tolerably well made up before she had to leave at eight-fifteen. First day at school, she thought, and then laughed aloud. She was terrified, that was the truth of it; as scared as Sophie had been when she'd started at Ruggles Road Infants and Junior Mixed. Hattie had felt for her then; and now she felt even more keenly for herself.

She finished the table and then drifted about the kitchen until she found herself standing in front of the fridge again.

Oh, God, she thought. If I don't go to bed right now, I'll start checking that bloody list again. Tell me I haven't made a complete ass of myself taking this job. Tell me it'll be all right. Tell me it isn't going to be sheer bloody murder . . .

Two

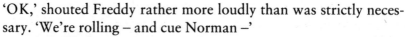

'OK,' shouted Freddy rather more loudly than was strictly necessary. 'We're rolling – and cue Norman –'

Dilly made a point of not looking at him, nor at the actor who was now walking slowly forward towards the camera, talking earnestly at it in a low tone, choosing instead to fix her eyes on the cameraman who was too occupied to notice her. That'll show him, she thought illogically. He can't push me around the way he pushes everyone else.

'But he can,' her inner voice whispered. 'What the hell else are you doing here if you haven't been pushed here?' And she scowled and shifted her gaze to the far side of the street where a little band of gawpers was staring at what was going on and clearly enjoying the spectacle of Important Director at Work with which Freddy was obliging them.

All this for a silly documentary, she thought scornfully. Who gives a piss about the Freedom of the City of London anyway? And across the other side of the road, as if in agreement, a plaintive baa-aa escaped from the van parked by the kerb and Freddy cursed and shouted, 'Cut!' and at once she felt better. To see Freddy so put out was balm, she told herself, to her wounded soul, and then repeated the words because they sounded so good. Balm to her wounded soul.

The afternoon dragged on, with the sheep who were there to act the part of a flock being driven over London Bridge – though since there were only seven of them they were hard pressed to look more than a disorderly gaggle – behaving as foolishly and messily as only sheep can until the pavements and roadways were slippery with sheep shit, and then it started to rain so the whole crew had to stop and Freddy was made to wait balefully till the light improved again.

The tea break came just as the sun returned, and that led to Freddy doing some fairly grovelling begging to get the crew to work on, or at least to get the stinking sheep in the can while the light let them film; they could hold over some of the scenes from today to tomorrow, but it would cost an arm and a leg to get those friggin' sheep out here again; and Dilly watched, highly amused, as the nattering and bartering went on. But eventually they shot the sheep and packed them back into their van to send them back to wherever they had come from, and Freddy called the break. And Dilly slid down from her place on the wall outside the pub on the corner and wandered over to the catering bus parked beside the road. She wasn't thirsty and she wasn't hungry but having tea was something to do.

'Having fun, sweetie?' Freddy called in his brightest voice as she passed him and his attendant knot of cameraman, sound recordist and actor, and she knew what was expected of her and managed to deliver it, baring her teeth in the most artificial grin she could conjure up and murmuring, 'Oh, yes, Daddy, lovely, Daddy, thank you,' and went on to the urn, pleased with herself. He knew now if he hadn't before. She only ever called him Daddy when she was livid with him. The politeness had all been an act for the others, who had been impressed by it, she had seen that clearly. And that meant he couldn't bawl her out for showing him up when he got her on her own, because she hadn't. He'd be in the wrong and she'd be in the right, and that maybe would give her the chance to try again to get him to see things her way. It was getting late, but it wasn't too late. She could still get back to Liverpool on the night train, and march into school next day as though it had all been arranged. They'd let her stay. They hadn't wanted her to leave in the first place; and as she took the strong black tea and clicked a couple of saccharin tablets into it from the tub in her pocket, she let her fantasy slide away agreeably.

No more stuck here in London with Freddy pretending to be a Marvellous Father, so-difficult-to-bring-up-a-child-on-your-own-when-you're-a-man-especially-if-it's-a-daughter-but-good-old-Freddy-he's-a-goer; no more being made to go to some ghastly school full of poncey boys who'd never seen a skirt on the premises before and wouldn't know how to treat a woman properly if their bloody lives depended on it; no more being so alone. She'd be back where she belonged, and she watched her imaginary self being surrounded by the people in Liverpool and fussed over deliciously, and then watched herself working marvellously well and not just getting her four A levels but getting them all with A grades and then setting off for university –

'Christ, but it's like pulling teeth to get any work out of these buggers,' Freddy said in her ear. 'Sorry it's a bit slow this afternoon, Tuppence. Thought you'd enjoy today's shoot – sheep and all –'

Dilly, who loathed above all things being called by her baby name, first scowled at him and then smoothed her face into a friendlier expression. She still had favours to ask, after all.

'It doesn't matter, Freddy,' she said. 'Listen, have you a moment? Because I've been thinking . . .'

He looked sideways at her and took a deep draught of his tea, noisily. She could have hit him for it.

'If you've been thinking about going back to Liverpool to that bunch of scouses you've got another think coming. You're going to the Foundation tomorrow and you'll love it.'

'Just because you did it doesn't mean I will,' she said, still controlling her temper. 'I'll hate it. It was great at St Aloysius. I liked it there. They liked me –'

'They'll like you at the Foundation too,' Freddy said. 'Listen, what do you want of my life, Dilly? I've got enough problems, haven't I, with your stinking – with your mother taking off like that? And a living to earn. I can't make it in Liverpool, that's for bloody sure. It's here I get all my jobs and Christ knows there aren't that many around even for a man of my record. I can't leave you in Liverpool –'

'Why not? I can look after myself.'

'You're sixteen and you can't. And if you think I can afford to pay for you to live there when I've a perfectly good flat here in London, think again. Grow up, Dilly, for the love of Mike. It's money that's the problem, and it's no good pretending otherwise.'

'But you're paying for this bloody school,' she blazed, unable to control her anger another moment. 'Use that to rent me a room in the 'Pool and –'

'No,' he said flatly and banged his thick white cup down on the ramshackle table beside them. 'It's not on, and there's an end to it. Anyway . . .' He hesitated. 'If you must know, the fees for the Foundation are being paid by your grandmother. She'd not pay for a room in Liverpool this side of Armageddon, so there it is. You're stuck, kid. Just the way I am. Like it or lump it. I'm going to shoot three more scenes before we wrap tonight, one way or another. Are you staying?'

'No,' she said sulkily. 'It's boring.'

'You're telling me.' He said it with real feeling. 'It's not my idea of making bloody *War and Peace*, believe me. Listen, Tuppence, let's not be bad friends over this. We've got to live together, so make it easy for us both – swallow the medicine. You can't do anything else.'

She stared at him, her face smooth and expressionless, and he stared back uneasily.

'I've told you all there is to tell you. I can't afford to keep you in Liverpool. Your mother's buggered off somewhere, and your grandmother's willing to cough up and send you to a decent school. It's not so bad, for Chrissakes! It could be worse. Just get off my back, will you? Go to school tomorrow. Give it a chance. You might like it. There should be a lot of talent lying around.' He looked as though he were about to produce a leer and then thought better of it. 'Like I say, there's not much else you can do, is there?'

She was silent for a while and then lifted her brows in resignation. 'OK. I suppose so.'

He hugged her fervently, and she could smell the faint sweatiness of him and feel the way his muscles seemed to shake with a fine tremor as he held her, and, as usual, her carefully built structure of anger against him crumbled, and after a brief hesitation she hugged him back. He wasn't all that bad, really, she thought as she watched him going back to the others with a little swagger in his walk. He's a silly show-off, of course, but what else do you expect of a man?

Stella stretched her back, pushed the last of the sports socks into the completed pile, and breathed deeply, waiting for the sense of virtue to overwhelm her. There had to be a reward for such a boring task, and usually it came in the form of that deep smugness which filled her after she'd managed to force herself to do something she loathed. Cleaning the oven was a good source of it, and so was doing the ironing – the most hateful task ever invented, in her opinion – and marking Genevieve's clothes for school should have been a very rich seam.

But it didn't come, and she picked up the socks again and began to separate them into pairs and then rolled them up neatly into balls, checking as she went. Socks, T-shirts, swimsuit, regulation blue one-piece – not that Genevieve was likely to wear it much; she always got out of swimming if she could – skirts, shirts, blazer. At least there wasn't as much of it as there used to be. Now she was a sixth-former she could wear her own clothes most of the time. She only needed full uniform, Dr Roscoe had assured Stella, for 'those school events when one wishes to inculcate a sense of community – Founder's Day and so forth – I know you'll understand.' And he'd smiled devastatingly when he said it, a fact that Stella refused to think about now. She'd liked him too well for that. Instead she contemplated the clothes in front of her; the whole lot would barely fill one shelf of Genevieve's wardrobe. Was that why there was less satisfaction in making sure it was all properly marked? When the boys had been at school, she'd had to sew those bloody name tapes on to great heaps of the stuff, and had cursed herself for not giving the boys the same initials. If they'd been called James and Jeremy and John or whatever she'd have been able to hand things down easily without all that laborious unpicking and resewing; but with a surname as colourless as Barratt initials had to be correct. There could be any number of Barratts in a school as big as the Foundation, after all.

Genevieve at the Foundation; Stella let her hands fall into her lap and stared sightlessly at the wall in front of her. Genevieve in the sixth form; it was ridiculous. Another few months and she'd be gone too, like the boys, and would she ever come back? She felt the cold fill her at that thought; it had been bad enough that the boys had never come home after university, but at least she'd had her baby girl to keep her busy and content. She had never let herself think of Jenny being grown up and gone, like the others.

But she'd have to soon. They both would, and she tried to imagine how Gordon would be when the time came, and felt colder than ever. He'd suffer even more than she did, so intensely was he attached to his daughter, and Stella at once made her eyes focus back on the pile of uniform. No sense in thinking about all that now. There was still a lot to be done before she could get ready to go out for dinner with them both tonight. That was the best bit of the last day of the holidays before the first day of term; they'd started the ritual of going out for a Chinese supper with the second boy, Peter, and continued it ever since. Tonight would be just another one, a lovely family event – and the last but one, a wicked little voice deep inside her head whispered, and she hated it. Why waste the present fretting about the future, for God's sake? That way madness lies, she told herself, and managed to laugh at her own foolishness.

Later that evening, watching Genevieve playing with her chopsticks and insisting she wanted to eat Chinese style, taking bits from the communal dishes rather than loading her own bowl, Stella felt the old worry come back. Was Genevieve all right? Was she happy? And she said suddenly, as with much laughter Genevieve managed to drop a carefully collected piece of sweet and sour pork back into its dish, 'Darling, you don't have to go to the Foundation if you don't want to. You could stay with the girls in St Monica's.'

Genevieve put her chopsticks down and looked at her, her head on one side, birdlike, and her face bright and inquiring. 'Oh, Mummy, do stop! We've been through it over and over! They've got much better facilities at the Foundation than they've got at dismal old Monica's and I know I can work better there. I'll never get the chance to get decent grades at the old school. Do stop worrying, darling.'

'Of course stop worrying!' Gordon said heartily and put his hand over Genevieve's. 'She'll be fine there. It's a great old school, great.'

'It was for you and the boys,' Stella said sharply. 'But they've never had girls before.'

'We're not creatures from another planet,' Genevieve said, and laughed. 'Darling, you sound so Victorian. Do stop fussing,' And she looked brightly at them both and took her hand away from Gordon's.

'Try some of this, Genevieve,' Stella said then, trying to sound light, casual. 'It's divine. Deep-fried seaweed – it's incredible the things they think of. I wonder who was the first Chinaman to fry the stuff? And why he thought it'd be any good?'

Genevieve looked at the heap of deep green shreds and shook her head. 'I've had masses of everything,' she said lightly. 'Enough, no more! 'Tis not so sweet now as it was before.'

Stella couldn't help it. 'You've eaten hardly anything. Daddy's had most of it, and I've had masses and –'

'Mummy!' Genevieve said warningly, and looked at her father and they both laughed indulgently and Stella looked at Genevieve's profile, with its small nose and the sharp line of her jaw over her polo-necked sweater – and why on earth did she put that on on a warm summer evening? – and then down at her delicate bird-thin wrists, and with every atom of effort she could make managed not to say another word, watching the waitress carry away the half-full dishes without a murmur. But it wasn't easy. The waste was dreadful; but that wasn't why she was so upset. She knew it, but she had to pretend she didn't. It was very difficult.

The man rolled over in bed and grunted, and then, with as much care as if he'd been a cat, stretched each limb one by one and then arched his back and yawned hugely. The boy beside him, who had drifted into a restless sleep, was still hovering on the edge of it and the man turned his head and saw him and then bent his knee and kicked him hard, and the boy fell out of the bed and lay blinking on the floor, his body very white against the deep crimson of the rug. He sat up and, moving awkwardly, scrambled to his feet, twisting his body a little so that he hid his genitals, but not very successfully. His body was thin to the point of scrawniness and that made them look even bigger, just as the pallor of his skin made them seem duskier. The man stared at his crotch with a thoughtful look and then yawned again.

'Get me something,' he said and the boy peered up at him in the half light, because the curtains were closed, and stared, not knowing what to do or say, and the man laughed.

'Don't sit there gaping at me like a bush baby, for Chrissakes! You heard what I said, get me something to eat. No, don't get dressed,' as the boy made a move towards the chair where his clothes were. 'Do it like that. Let me watch you. Open the curtains first.'

The boy stood still and the man made a small but clearly

menacing movement and the boy moved away, not quite scuttling like a crab, but giving that impression. He opened the curtains and then, his back to the bed, moved across the room to the far side where a half-wall separated the space to form a kitchen.

It was hot; behind him the window glowed orange with the late afternoon sun and the sky was a brassy blue that filled the room with its weight. If it hadn't been for the watching eyes from the bed, the boy would have been happier being naked. As it was, he felt as though he'd lost his skin as well as his clothes.

He moved about the kitchen, getting the food ready, very aware of the room behind him as well as the man in the bed. It was an expensive room, but squalid in its disorder. Papers were piled about and there were discarded clothes and half-eaten food and empty wine glasses and bottles, and dust greying the edges of the crimson carpet. But none of that took away the overall effect. The room was filled with furniture made of glass and chrome, or highly polished slender wood, obviously original art deco pieces, and a couple of sculptures of naked men in deep green alabaster and the creamiest of marble that, though small, were perfect, and fitted into mirrored alcoves on each side of the empty pink marble fireplace. The room should have felt light and cool, in spite of the September weather, for it was large and high, but it would have felt oppressive even if the sky outside had been filled with snow, for the ceiling was painted a deep crimson to match the carpet and the walls were papered with black, with a few silver flashes stuck on in a random pattern. It was a disgusting room in many ways and the boy hated it; not least because when he'd first seen it, in the days when the man had been so different, it had seemed to him the acme of elegance and sophistication.

He brought the food carefully, a grilled bacon and tomato sandwich, garnished with lettuce and mayonnaise, with a beaker full of black coffee set on a tray with legs, and he put it down carefully, managing not to shake and spill anything, and stepped back, grateful for his own steadiness, grateful that he'd learned to make the sandwiches exactly as the man liked, grateful to be out of his reach in case he managed to find fault anyway.

But whatever he did it was to be a bad day. He'd suspected it as soon as he'd arrived just after lunch and been shouted at for wearing jeans and a torn T-shirt and flipflops. How dared he, the man had shrieked, how dared he walk into his room looking like that? He ought to be whipped, whipped like a dog, and the boy had shaken, not sure if it was a game they were playing or real anger as the man had pulled the clothes off him and started to go through his usual ritual; and he still couldn't be sure. Because it had ended as it always did; and now the man lay there on the crimson satin sheets, swearing at him over and over again, and still he stood there, half turned away in a useless attempt to hide some part of his nakedness behind the jut of his hip, such as it was, and tried not to let his face show how he was feeling.

The swearing went on, as the man ate the sandwich and drank the coffee, managing not to miss a bite though the words never stopped; and then suddenly he shouted, 'Get the fuck out of here!' and gratefully the boy dived at the chair and scooped up his jeans and flipflops and T-shirt, and made for the door, knowing better than to attempt to dress in the room, and prayed no one would come by as he stood outside on the communal landing of the house, pulling them on with shaking hands.

But he was free at last, and went down the stairs and out into the evening streets, trying to burn away the shakiness in his muscles by moving fast, and at last it eased and he felt better. His throat still hurt, but then it always did, for a long time afterwards. That was because he'd complained once about it, and said he'd rather not do it. Now he always had to.

Oh, God, he thought as he waited for the tube train. Oh, God, tomorrow. How will it be tomorrow? It could be worse, and if it is, what shall I do? How can I manage, with A levels too? How can I cope?

There was no one at home when he got there, but then there never was. Would it have helped if there had been? He doubted it.

The body lay crumpled, twisted, collapsed in on itself, like a stuffed toy that's been left in the washing machine too long. The face was livid, the colour the thick muddy sort that is always disturbing to look at, and the groove round the neck was almost purple. The contrast with the torso beneath was sharp; the skin there was yellowish, beneath a dusting of gingery chest hair, and the lacy pink silk knickers with the frilled legs that covered the crotch had the sheen of a cream fondant. An altogether repellent sight, made even more disgusting by the orderliness of the room around it. Carefully made shelves of aluminium bracketing with the books on them arranged in size order, rather than alphabetically, matched the neatest of desks, built of veneered chipboard and with papers piled on it in perfect alignment. There were lead pencils on the tray, all carefully sharpened, and a complete set of coloured pencils arranged in graduating shades in rainbow order, placed with such precision they seemed to have been painted on to the surface. Above the bed there was a hessian-covered board which had been squared off with strips of red and green tape to make a chequer board and within each square there were lists and memos all written in the same cramped upright handwriting, but in the whole range of colours the pencils offered. Each piece of paper was set with perfect exactness next to its mates and had a ruled border decorated with coloured stripes. The bed beneath was as smooth as a shop-window display with just one painful incongruity: a battered Bendy toy, Ferdinand the Bull, leaning drunkenly against the slope of the pillow, its wide eyes staring out impishly at the body on the floor.

The young police constable who was standing looking down at the body on its arrangement of mirrors and pillows felt a little sick. This was the first body he'd seen since he'd come out of training and on to the job, and it was going to take him a long time to get used to being a copper if this was the sort of thing you had to look at right after you'd had your breakfast. Especially if you had to come out with someone like Sergeant Croxley who was pointing out the details to him with what the constable was sure was unnecessary relish.

'They always does that, see? The sort of knot that's supposed to slip, only sometimes they don't. Like this time. Poor bugger. The mirrors is a nice touch – see? He's got 'em set so you can see what's happening at every angle. Really something, that is – Oh, come on, take a look, for Gawd's sake! You're not goin' to be much good to the job if you can't even look at a corpse without your head twisted half off your neck trying to avoid it. The sooner you got used to this sort of thing the better. It's amazing what some fellas'll do to get it good and up, 'nt it?'

And he slid into an account of other cases like this he'd seen in his seven years in the Force, lavish with detail, and the constable first got paler and then began to sweat. But he managed to keep his face passive and even to speak.

'What's in it for 'em, then, Sarge?' he said, and though he sounded husky he was proud of his ability to say anything at all.

'What's in it for 'em? Christ, but you are green, aren't you? Never heard what happens to a hanged man? Gets the biggest bloody hard-on you ever saw. Well, some of 'em do. Not that I remember the days when they hung villains, of course, but I remember working with coppers what did and they told me. These blokes not only get a big hard-on, they blow off an' all – come like bloody magic, according to what I've been told. Not that I've ever tried it, you understand, but you can't help wondering.' He looked down at the body again and shook his head. 'Nor will I, not when I've seen this sort of thing so often, the way I have. It goes wrong, you see, so you end up deader than you might have expected. All because of sex.' He shook his head again and laughed. 'Or excitement, of course, though this one looks a bit young to have had a heart attack, eh? It's hard to say what happened when they're not around to be questioned, that's the thing of it. And I'm not about to try any experiments to see how it works, neither. Nor will you if you've any sense.' And he looked sternly at the police constable as though he'd suggested he was about to do just that. 'Not that you can help but be interested. I remember one case' – he looked consideringly at the young policeman – 'well, let's just say the fella hadn't been missed for a week, so by the time we got to him it wasn't pretty anyway, and a certain part of his anatomy – I'll go no further – a certain part had burst.'

The young policeman gave up the struggle. He blanched again and made for the door, leaving the sergeant highly amused behind him. But not for long. He still had the boy's mother to talk to – when she got home, which, according to the cleaner who'd found him when she'd come to do her usual day's work, would be in about an hour.

'Other side of London she is. That's why I have my own key, you see. So I just comes and goes as I need to, been doin' it for four years, ever since this poor little soul was a child.'

'How old is he?' the sergeant had asked, shepherding her out of the room, finding her matter-of-factness more upsetting than his constable's clear horror. 'Do you know?'

'Sixteen,' the cleaner had told him as she went back down the stairs. 'Had his birthday in the first week of the holidays. Going back to school to do his A levels, his mum told me. A levels – he'll not be needing them now, will he?' And the sergeant had watched her go and gone back to the room to upset his constable, needing to do that because of the way he was feeling himself. He'd never get used to this sort of thing, not ever, and it was bad enough when it was a grown man. A boy of sixteen was something else.

He sighed deeply and sealed the room with tape to keep it waiting for the CID team, not that they'd have much to do; it was an obvious case of misadventure as far as the sergeant was concerned. He'd be the one to do the worst part of the job, talking to the boy's mum.

Shit, he thought, and sat down at the kitchen table and pulled out his notebook and made a few headings, ready for the questions he'd have to ask when the mother got here. Name, Address, Next of Kin, School . . .

Three

The staff common room stank. There was no other word that would fit the unpleasant blend of elderly coffee and old shoes, pine disinfectant and cigarette smoke, and above all male sweat, and Hattie, sitting uneasily on the edge of a battered armchair, thought gloomily, I'll need clean clothes every day, or I'll smell as bad myself.

Outside the door she could hear the loud voices of boys on the move and thought, At least they're not as shrill as girls would be; and then felt guilty at her disloyalty. She'd have to be careful not to let herself get as misogynistic as the people who worked here, and she looked round the room unhappily.

It was untidy in a way that looked deliberate, as though its occupants regarded being neat as bourgeois and shaming; the newspapers piled in one corner, old *Times*es and *Telegraph*s, looked as though they'd been arranged in such a way that their mastheads could be clearly seen, and Hattie wondered what would happen if she brought in a few copies of the *Guardian* and set them there too. Uproar, she suspected. This lot were traditional Tories to a man, that was obvious. The armchairs that were scattered about over the threadbare carpet – had it once been red? It might have been. Now it was just muddy and nondescript – could have been throw-outs from a gentleman's club, so deep and soft and shabby were they, and the wall shelves where books were piled had the dusty look that only comes after months or even years of undisturbed rest. There were a couple of long low coffee tables made of cheap plastic-veneered board which had been burned all round the edges with cigarettes, a scattering of chipped glass ash trays and, on the walls, which were painted a dispiriting beige, curling old notices, cartoons clipped from newspapers and photographs of boys sitting in frozen clumps looking for all the world like waxwork dummies. The two long windows which gazed out on to the school's central quadrangle were uncurtained, and in the corners of the room were old bags, abandoned tennis shoes and sweaters and, for all Hattie knew, she thought wildly, a couple of dead bodies. It all looked too depressing for words and she contemplated the possibility of getting to her feet and walking out and just going home.

But she couldn't do that. She'd have to face Judith if she got home too soon, and sitting here waiting for God knew what might be to come had to be better than that. The harassed secretary in Hilary Roscoe's office had sent her here to wait 'till someone comes who knows what you're supposed to be doing and where you're supposed to be. No one's told me, I'm afraid, for Headmaster really has been too busy to think of the details you know,' so wait she would. And she thought a little wryly of her status as a detail, and sighed softly. Well, see today out, at any rate. She would think again about it all tomorrow.

The sound of shouting boys rose several decibels and she looked up as the man who had come in kicked the door closed behind him and cut out some of the din he'd admitted.

'Oh!' he said, startled, and stared at her blankly as she got to her feet. 'What? Can I help you? Did you want the Head's office? It's just along the corridor and –'

'No,' she said. 'The Head's secretary sent me here to wait. She said someone would know where I was supposed to be.'

'Miss Wheale said that? Oh. Then I suppose . . .' He stood undecided for a moment and then came further into the room and set a bulging briefcase down on one of the coffee tables. 'Well, I suppose she was right. I mean – um –' He unbuttoned the raincoat he was wearing and took it across the room to hang on a hook beside the bookcases. 'May I ask what – ah – who – ah – well, I mean –'

'I'm Hattie Clements.' She held out one hand. 'I'm starting this term as school nurse, and teaching some health subjects. Mainly because of the girls in the sixth.'

His face cleared at once. 'Oh, yes, yes, of course! We've got them this year, haven't we? Of course, of course. Well, who'd have thought old Roscoe'd have the wit to appoint a female to the staff? How splendid! I mean, I think so.' And he pushed out one hand. 'I'm Edward Wilton, English Department, third form master. I must say, I'm delighted we've got a few girls. Do the old place a world of good.' He shook hands for a long time, and Hattie had to pull away from him fairly firmly before he'd let go. 'Though I must warn you not all the others feel the same. So don't mind what some of 'em might say. Old Bevan, you know, he's not mad keen on the idea and –'

The door opened again and Hattie looked around. Three men came in together, all talking at once, or rather two talked as one listened with an amused expression on his face, and she looked at them hopefully. Two of them appeared to be a good deal older than Edward Wilton (who was, she thought, somewhere in his middle thirties), in fact well older: sixty or so, she hazarded; and the other – the listener – was a tall man with a good deal of grey hair which far from making him seem old was rather attractive. About forty, she thought, and liked the look of him.

The two older men stopped short as they caught sight of Hattie and the fatter of them, who was wearing a large-brimmed dark hat, stood and glared at her from beneath the shadow of its brim as the words which had been pouring out of him stopped as sharply as if someone had pulled out a plug.

'Good God!' he said loudly and then looked over his shoulder at his companions. 'Steenman, Collop?'

'Don't ask me,' one of them said and pushed past Hattie to go further into the room, pulling off his overcoat. He marched over to the hook beside the bookcases, peered at Wilton's coat already on it and then unhooked it and dropped it on the floor before hanging up his own in its place. 'I may be Roscoe's second deputy on paper, but don't ask *me*. You should know better than that.' His voice was thick with irony.

'Good God Almighty,' said the fat man again and pulled off his hat and threw it across the room so that it skimmed the coffee tables and landed neatly on top of the pile of newspapers. It was clearly something he'd done a great many times. 'I thought he'd have come to his senses by now. The craziest thing I ever –'

'Martin, this is Miss Clements,' Edward Wilton said to the last of the three, who was still standing just inside the door, and then went scurrying across the room to pick up his coat and hang it on an adjoining hook. 'She's our new, er – our new –'

'*Mrs* Clements,' Hattie said loudly and held out her hand towards the man Wilton had addressed as Martin. She was burning with fury; the rudeness of that horrible old man had left her almost speechless. Once she'd have bitten his head off for it, would have made sure he knew she wasn't the sort of woman to stand there and let stupid clods like him treat her so, but all she could do now was try to control the shake of anger that filled her and made her neck tremulous. Her hand shook a little too, she noticed, and hoped the man Martin would not.

He seemed not to, and took her hand and shook it, looking at her closely but not offensively.

'Mrs Clements? You're here to teach the girls in the sixth?' he said, and the fat man, who was now ensconced in the most battered and clearly comfortable of all the armchairs, produced a loud noise, half exclamation, half derisive snarling cough. Martin Collop lifted an eyebrow in his direction and said loudly, 'Bevan, do you *have* to be so disagreeable this morning? First day of term's bad enough without you giving us your all-too-familiar impression of Orson Welles on a bad day.' He looked at Hattie then and made a small grimace. 'You must tolerate Dr Bevan, I'm afraid. Every staffroom has to have its resident grizzly and he's ours, God help us. And God help the boys he teaches. How they ever get any geography into their heads I can't imagine. So, you're to teach the girls?'

'Not only that,' she said as crisply as she could. 'I am to be school nurse. I'm somewhat surprised you haven't had one here before.'

'I think we did once,' Martin said. 'Some years ago. I suspect she succumbed to severe Bevanitis. Anyway, she disappeared and ever since we've managed well enough without.'

'Welfare, that's what it's all about.' Edward Wilton had come back to stand beside her, almost scurrying in his eagerness. 'I wondered about that, you know, when the Head told us last term about taking girls. Who'll look after 'em? I wondered. Who'll understand the things that upset 'em? Girls being girls, you know, and not the –'

'Not the same as boys,' Martin said gravely. 'Absolutely, Wilton. Your grasp of essentials deepens with your experience of the world. You must have had a most interesting vacation to have come on so well since July. Girls are indeed different. So, yes, it's an excellent idea to have a woman around the place for them. Pity they aren't a few more –'

Again the odd noise came from Bevan who then lifted his chin and bawled, 'Where's the bloody coffee, then? Wilton, go and see where the bloody coffee is. Go on, don't stand there goggling at me like a half-dead codfish.'

Wilton reddened and opened his mouth to say something but again the door opened and a black woman in neat overalls came in with a tray loaded with cups and saucers and a coffee pot and a biscuit tin, and at once the room seemed to lighten. Wilton ignored his irritation and hurried to pick up the pot as soon as the maid had set her burden down and gone, ignoring Bevan pointedly as he began to pour for everyone else.

'We ought to do some more introductions, Mrs Clements,' he chattered. 'Yes, more introductions – is black all right for you? Are you sure? There's plenty of milk – well, there is at present, it might run out later.' He threw a glance of loathing at Bevan which clearly took a lot of courage and Hattie was amused. 'Some people hog it, of course, but right now – oh, Martin, you take yours black too, don't you? Yes, and there are a few biscuits, do help yourself . . .' And Wilton thrust the tin of Butter Osbornes at her.

A few more men had arrived now and seemed as startled by the sight of a woman in their staffroom as the earlier arrivals had been, but showed it – or hid it – in different ways, and Hattie began to enjoy herself. It was quite amusing to cause such a stir in such a very small pond and she took her coffee and sat down in one of the armchairs and watched them all as she sipped.

'Well now, as I said, this is Martin Collop, Mrs Clements.' Edward Wilton had clearly appointed himself her guardian and she accepted his concern graciously. Later perhaps he might become irritating – his tendency to repeat phrases and chatter nervously could clearly become tiresome – but at present he was helpful.

'Martin Collop is Head of English, you know,' Edward was gabbling at her, 'and the best Drama person; you can't imagine how good, but you'll see later on – this term, you know, very big for Drama it is, of course, and – yes, Head of English, my boss.

And then there's Gregory Steenman, the Mathematics department, all very esoteric there, don't you think? I always do. This
is Mrs Clements, Gregory, just starting today. And here's Richard
Shuttle from the French department and his friend, also in French,
he's George Manson, probably spent the whole of his holiday
locked up in the Dingdong somewhere. The good old Dordogne,
eh? You usually do . . .' The two in question looked at him and
then at Hattie, and showed no expression on their faces at all,
just holding out their hands to be shaken, but Hattie felt the
suspicion in them and said nothing, just smiling briefly. 'And
here's Sam Chanter, Biology, all those frogs and suchlike . . .'

She shifted her head at that. 'Biology? How do you do?'

Chanter, a bulky man with a good deal of untidy dark hair,
looked amused. 'A subject you like?'

'I trained as a nurse and midwife,' she said. 'So –'

'Oh, Christ Al-bloody-mighty!' cried Bevan in the armchair,
his voice dripping with disgust. 'All this mumsy chatter makes
me sick. Can't we have our coffee in peace for once?' And
Gregory Steenman snorted with laughter as Wilton raised his
voice to drown them both out. 'Oh well, yes, of course,' he
said brightly. 'You would be interested, wouldn't you? Yes,
naturally – oh, and here's our Tully, pride of the staffroom . . .'
And he giggled a little awkwardly as the door that had
crashed open to admit the newcomer crashed closed just as
noisily.

He was a tall thin man, with his head shaved almost to the
scalp, so that only a stubble of fair hair showed on its pinkness.
His eyes were a bright hard blue and looked even brighter because
the lashes that surrounded them were thick and long but almost
white, they were so pale. He was wearing what seemed to be a
tightly fitting catsuit of dark blue cloth, which reminded Hattie
of the blue calico that she had seen French schoolchildren wear,
and round his narrow waist was a wide and very heavy leather
belt with a brass buckle that showed a lion with its mouth wide
and snarling. It was difficult, Hattie found, not to stare at it.

'David, this is our newest member of staff, come to help us
deal with the girls. She's teaching some health things, but mostly
she's here for the girls. Which soothes my anxieties a good deal, I
can tell you. Mrs Clements, this is Dave Tully, and as I'm sure
you don't need me to tell you, he's the Art department. Most of

it on his own, aren't you, Dave? Now that young Matterson's gone, who used to help him . . . well, mustn't go on about that right now.' He looked uneasy suddenly, and a small silence fell on the room until Edward seemed to recover himself and hurried on. 'They don't think it's worthwhile here at the Foundation, having too many people to look after the arts. We have to be glad there are enough of us in the English department, hmm, Martin? Yes, we're not even sure of that sometimes, there's so much to do –'

'If you talked less you'd do a bloody sight more work!' Bevan howled from the depths of his armchair in a sudden access of rage, but Wilton paid no attention, considerably to Hattie's amusement, and nor did anyone else except perhaps Steenman, who threw a glance at him, but didn't do anything. Clearly he was rude to everyone and didn't just save it for women, Hattie thought, and turned and beamed a wide smile directly at him. It was a technique she used sometimes when angry male drivers objected because she overtook them or otherwise behaved as assertively as they did; she would blow them kisses in her rear-view mirror, and it clearly drove them almost to apoplexy. Now it worked again; Bevan stared at her furiously and reddened to an almost purple tinge and again produced his horrible snorting noise. Behind her Dave Tully laughed.

'Mrs Clements, if you can make old Bevan as annoyed as that, you and I are going to be friends!' he said. His voice was light and mocking and had a hint of a Northern accent. 'Won't that be nice for me, Dr Bevan?' And he put just enough emphasis on the 'Doctor' to make it offensive. 'Two of us to drive you up the wall. One of these days you'll get stuck up there and never come down.'

'Oh, leave him be, Tully,' Steenman said, and got to his feet. 'I'm afraid, Mrs Clements, that you may find the company here less than agreeable. I shall talk to the Headmaster about making better arrangements for you. A room of your own somewhere perhaps, so that you can be in peace –'

'Oh, no, thank you,' Hattie said and again smiled sweetly. Inside she was still furious but now she was beginning to feel better. She'd taken some of the initiative into her own hands. 'I'd hate to be quite alone. No way to keep in touch with all that is going on in the school, to be alone! I'll be much happier taking my place here in the staff common room with all the rest of you. Then you can tell me if there are any little problems the girls are having' – she smiled even more widely – 'and I can tell you if you're upsetting them. I'm sure that will be immensely useful, don't you agree?'

'Oh yes,' Wilton said earnestly, but no one else spoke and Hattie thought, That'll show you, you –

The bell rang so shrilly that she jumped convulsively and the fat man for the first time looked as though he was getting some pleasure out of the situation; but she gathered her wits quickly and looked at Wilton.

'We keep asking to have the bell put outside the door rather than in here – makes such a racket,' he bawled above the continuing shrilling. 'But you know how it is, always more important things to do than trying to please the staff, and so forth.'

The bell stopped at last and she took a deep breath as several of the men put down their coffee cups and gathered up piles of books and made for the door.

'Should I be leaving now too?' she asked. 'Isn't it' – she scrabbled deep into her memory of her own schooldays – 'assembly now, or whatever?'

Wilton shook his head. 'Not on the first day of the autumn term. Everyone changing their forms, you see, and there are new bugs to look after and so forth, and all the timetables and suchlike to fix. The first day's always a bit of a time-waster, to tell the truth. You don't do any real work, you just tell the little blighters about the work that's coming up, and fiddle with these Godforsaken timetables and people's dental appointments and music lessons and all the rest of it. I have to go. The third'll be committing mayhem –'

The room had emptied now and as he reached the door she cried after him almost despairingly, 'Where do I go now, then? I don't know the –'

'Sorry!' Wilton smiled anxiously at her and shook his head. 'So sorry, Miss – Mrs Clements, madly sorry, just no idea. Go to the sixth-form room perhaps? I imagine the girls'll be there and they're why you're here, so I'd try there if I were you. I'm sorry Staveley wasn't in here this morning – he's the sixth-form master. Yes, that's what you should do. Go to the sixth-form room – it's just at the far end of the corridor . . .'

And then he too was gone, leaving Hattie staring at the door as the last of the clattering footsteps of running children faded and left her in the middle of the self-conscious squalor of the staffroom. Which, she thought savagely as she gathered up her bag, still stinks. In every meaning of the word.

Four

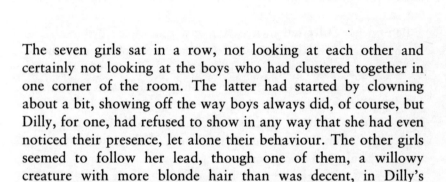

The seven girls sat in a row, not looking at each other and certainly not looking at the boys who had clustered together in one corner of the room. The latter had started by clowning about a bit, showing off the way boys always did, of course, but Dilly, for one, had refused to show in any way that she had even noticed their presence, let alone their behaviour. The other girls seemed to follow her lead, though one of them, a willowy creature with more blonde hair than was decent, in Dilly's opinion, had shown signs of being interested in the display; but even she had subsided when the other girls continued staring sternly ahead of them and now sat a little slumped and bored at the end of the row. Now the boys sat and waited too, talking a little but offering no more horseplay.

On the wall ahead of them, over the long benchlike desk that stood there, was a plaque of dirty brass on which words had been deeply engraved, and Dilly, for want of something better to do, began to read them.

'Dame Alice Nollys, Her School for the Children of Freemen of the City of London. Erected 1558 in Memory of Alderman Richard Nollys of the Worshipful Company of Scriveners. Requiescat in Pace', and below that a later piece of engraving: 'They Gave Their Lives That We Might Live, 1914–1918', and then in even more recent script, '1939–1945', followed by lists of names. She read them, trying to see behind the blankness of the Johns and Archibalds, Edwards and Henrys, to the sort of boys they might have been. Young, certainly; old people don't get killed in wars, they just start them going, Dilly told herself. Young people have to do what old ones make them do, like me sitting here. I hate old people. All of them.

The door banged open and the boys at the back straightened up and the girls stiffened a little as a square man with an aureole of iron-grey hair brushed high over his head came in, his elderly and very rusty black academic gown streaming behind him in the wake he had created.

'Good morning,' he bawled, not looking directly at them, and dropped the little pile of books he was carrying on the table with a small crash, and then, with what was clearly meant to be a lissom leap but looked rather more effortful than that, sat on the edge of the high desk. 'And for God's sake, man, sit down. If I needed a chair I'd ask for it.'

Behind her Dilly felt rather than saw one of the boys subside, letting the chair he'd been about to carry to the newcomer clatter to the floor, and stared at the man in front of her. His face was round and fat, like an angry baby's, she decided, and he drank a good deal. She'd seen that red-eyed soggy-lipped look too often before not to know it well. Whoever he is, he'll be unpleasant, she thought, and felt the familiar sense of dreariness that the thought of alcohol always created in her.

The master caught her eye, looked angrier than ever and then flicked his glance to the back of the room, talking over the girls' heads loudly.

'Well, I haven't much time to waste here, I've got better things to do than talk to you lot. Haven't even got time to get my morning coffee, but there it is, I've got to welcome you to the sixth form, God help me, of which I am master. I don't have to tell those of you who *belong* to this establishment this fact, but I have to do so for those who are here for the first time today. It will not have escaped School's notice that we have been invaded.'

He makes us sound like cockroaches, Dilly thought, and scowled at him, wanting to get up and shout back that she for one wasn't here of her own choice; but of course she didn't.

'Nor will it come as a surprise to those who *belong* here that I for one think this is as stupid an arrangement as could be devised for the Foundation. Not that anyone listens to what I have to say, despite my seventeen years in this Godforsaken hole. It takes people of sense to do that, and we are not, by and large, greatly blessed here with such persons.'

There was a soft movement from the boys behind and a breath

of laughter and Dilly sat grimly staring ahead. She wouldn't give the bastard the pleasure of seeing how she felt; and please don't let any of the rest of you do it either, she shouted inside her head at the row of girls beside her. Don't, don't, don't –

'I must take minor exception, sir, to your comments.' The voice was a silky one, deeper than Dilly would have expected from a boy of sixteen or so. The accent was odd too, very precise and clipped, and she tried to work out in what way she found it odd. But the voice was going on.

'For my part, sir, I find this invasion, as you regard it, a highly agreeable one. Can you not consider the possibility that some of us are of an age to relish the company of well-reared young females?'

The man sitting on the desk looked sourly at the source of the voice and then sniffed loudly. 'Are you still talking in that ridiculous way, Forster?' he demanded. 'It was boring last year. This year it's likely to prove stultifying.'

'My dear sir,' the silky voice murmured, 'would you have me speak in the common manner? Surely not.'

This time there was real laughter from the rest of the boys and Dilly felt the other girls turn round to look and allowed herself to move slightly on her chair and turn her head unobtrusively. To go on being intransigent about it would be daft, she decided. There were useful things to be found out, clearly.

Leaning against the wall in the far corner she saw the boy she had noticed briefly on the way in: tall, very slender but clearly muscular, his hair thickly springing and arranged in neat dreadlocks. He was smiling widely at the man on the desk, and his teeth looked incredible, like a television advertisement, in his very smooth and handsome face. His eyes were wide and dark beneath a high broad forehead, his nose was an elegant prow that jutted from his face with great authority, and he was black. It was an extraordinary face and Dilly thought she'd never seen anyone quite so beautiful.

He moved then and came to the front of the room, and Dilly smiled a little. He moved as well as he looked, smoothly and with a spring in his step that made him seem to exude energy. 'Now we're sixth-formers, it is my understanding that we may enjoy a modicum of additional freedom. That being so' – and he smiled even more widely, making it clear he had no intention of waiting for any rejoinder – 'I take some of that freedom upon myself to greet our fair newcomers with the appreciation that they must surely regard as their just due.'

Beside Dilly the girl with the cloud of blonde hair giggled shrilly and nudged her neighbour on the other side, who was staring at the tall black boy with her mouth half open. The boy saw her, and bowed a little ironically. 'You find my mode of speech amusing, ma'am? I beg you will not. It is my crusade, you must understand, to bring back the elegance of a vanished age. It is not good enough to speak as sloppily as some of my friends here –'

'Oh, belt up, Harry,' one of the other boys called. 'Give the rest of us a chance.' And he too moved forward until he was standing right behind the blonde girl's chair, and at once the rest of the boys moved forward too. The man sitting on the edge of the desk said nothing, just watching, and Dilly looked at him, nonplussed. If anyone had behaved like this under a teacher's eye at St Aloysius, they'd have had a boot up their backsides by now.

The boy Forster moved to stand beside the master and beamed at the rest of them. 'Well now, ladies, let me take over from our esteemed usher here. A man highly regarded by us all, I do assure you, for all his apparent – ahem – bellicosity.' He turned his head and looked at the man beside him with such a gleam in his eye that Dilly couldn't help producing a giggle of her own, and the boy looked at her and sketched a wink. 'Permit me to introduce our revered Head of History and author of what will undoubtedly be *the* definitive textbook of British Military History *when* he finishes it. Mr Michael Staveley.'

'Shut up, Forster, and stop showing off,' the man growled, but he was clearly not at all annoyed, and Dilly stared at him, her puzzlement growing. How could a master be so easy-going when someone was being so insolent to him? Or couldn't he tell it was insolence? Surely he could. No one could be that thick, not even a schoolmaster as old as this one.

Forster sketched his ironic bow again and said solicitiously, 'Are you sure I can be of no further help, sir? I would not wish you to tire yourself unduly –'

'I told you to shut up. Now, you lot, let me get on with the business. This year there are twenty-three of you. Would have been twenty-four but, as I dare say you heard, Matterson met with some sort of accident . . .'

There was a little intake of breath but no one said anything and Staveley looked up and said, 'You'll send a card or some such, Forster?'

'Already have,' the boy said. 'Fixed it as soon as I saw it in the paper.' The accent had coarsened slightly and Dilly risked another look at him. Now he was no longer performing. He looked back at her, catching her eye at once and she jerked her head back, feeling her face redden. 'I sent flowers to the funeral too. I'll collect from you lot later.'

There was a little flurry of words then, as the boys began to mutter and ask questions but Harry Forster said loudly, 'Later! I told you, later,' and they subsided. He's quite something, Dilly thought, and this time didn't turn her head.

'Very well. We can forget that, then. I've got the timetables here. If anyone has any problems with them, don't bother me. I've got enough on my plate already without getting myself in a lather over what you lot want. Sort it out between yourselves. I'll leave it to you, Forster, to sort out the rest of it all. You're Form Captain and so forth? Yes. Well, I've got to sort out the Cadets right now. The only bloody thing worth dealing with in this whole bloody school. Forster, five sharp this evening, you hear me?' And without waiting for an answer he was gone, slamming the door behind him so hard that a little spurt of dust lifted from the floorboards in front of it.

'A charming creature, is he not?' Harry Forster was back in character now, and came to the front of the room and with a wicked mimicry of Staveley's attempts to be lissom lifted himself on to the desk as easily as if he'd drifted there. 'Now, my dear young ladies, let me introduce us all, hmm? You must then introduce yourselves. You can have no idea with what eagerness, not unmixed with trepidation, we have looked forward to this day. To have females amongst us in this cruelly misogynistic place – it promises us so much! And now we have had the chance to observe you, why, our trepidation vanishes like a puff of wind and we are left all eagerness. You are precisely what the apothecary ordered.'

'He'll burst if he goes on like this,' someone said. 'Listen, don't you think you should tell us your names? Then we'll know where we are.'

The blonde opened her mouth eagerly but Dilly got in first.

'I'd have thought it was better manners for you to tell us who you are first,' she said waspishly. 'Seeing we're the new arrivals. And seeing we've been fairly thoroughly insulted already and it's not half past nine yet.'

'The lady speaks aright!' declaimed Harry. 'Oh, all right, all right!' as someone aimed a kick at him. 'I'm Harry Forster. English, History and French. President of the Drama Society, clarinet in the school jazz combo, Captain of Cadets and all round young marvel. These twits are Richard and Robert Carter, the unholy twins, same subjects as mine but utterly repellent with little in their heads apart from rugger in the winter and cricket in the summer. A real load of balls, believe me. This is Vivian Botham, who is –'

'Arse, Arse, Arse!' several of the other boys chanted and Dilly looked over her shoulder at the boy beside whom Harry was now standing, with a hand on one of his shoulders. He looked back at her with a face quite smooth of any expression and Dilly managed to nod at him and smile. He was a very small boy, she decided, and then realized that half the problem was that he was standing beside Harry, who had to be at least six foot two. He's about five six, she thought. Shorter than me. Poor little devil. Arse – no wonder, with a name like Botham. This time she did smile at the silent Botham, embarrassed by her own thoughts, but he stared impassively back and said nothing.

'I'm Gillian.' The blonde girl got to her feet and moved away from the others to stand with her back to the big desk, leaning slightly backwards. She's not just endowed with bloody hair, Dilly thought irritably, gazing at her, she must be a 38D if she's an inch. And no bloody waist to speak of. I hate her. 'Gillian Brownlow. I'm doing English, History and Music. I do hope we're all going to be friends.'

The room seemed to rearrange itself as everyone in it began to move and start talking; several of the boys made for Gillian, who stood and smiled at them and said very little, just looking from one to the other contentedly, and the girl on her other side, who had long sleek dark hair, and, now Dilly could see her face clearly, was obviously an Oriental of some kind, made for the twins as Dilly herself stood and watched them all, her face a little twisted.

Harry came and stood beside her. 'And you are?' he said invitingly.

'A female,' she snapped. 'So get your patronizing over nice and quick, hmm? Then I can get on with what I'm here for.'

'Ah!' he said softly and smiled even more widely. 'At last! Someone I can relate to. Another of a beleaguered minority! Welcome to Chauvinist Towers, my dear girl. They've had a great time so far with just a couple of niggers like me and a handful of Asians and Jews. Now they can get to work on you women too; it'll take the heat off the rest of us, perhaps? A delicious thought!'

She looked at him. 'If it's that sort of place then why do you stay?'

'Because I'm not the sort of person to run! My dear, they can sneer till they're blue, but they can't touch me. I've got more charisma than any other chap in the school, don't you know?' Again his accent changed subtly and she stared at him, fascinated in spite of herself. 'The Head's madly grateful to me – wheels me out whenever the Labour brass comes sniffing round from the Town Hall, proving to 'em he's as liberated as they are by having me here, and half the school's in love with me even if the other half wants to bring in the Ku Klux Klan to lynch me. But those little ones in the third and fourth!' He gave a deep theatrical sigh. 'My dear, *such* a burden and *such* a responsibility! But one does one's best!'

She stared at him. 'Do you ever stop putting on an act?'

'Hardly ever,' he said. 'So boring to be ordinary, don't you think? I do. What's your name?'

'Dilly Langham,' she said after a moment. 'If it's any of your concern.'

'It's easier to say than "hey you",' he said a little absently. 'Dilly – an odd name.'

She reddened. 'I can't help it. It wasn't my choice.'

'Oh, I don't know. One can always change what one doesn't like.'

'Oh, yes,' she said bitterly. 'Just like that. Try it on my father.'

'Point taken. Parents are hell. So what are you doing? Let me have a go: not the sciences, I don't think, you wouldn't be here if you were interested. We've got the lousiest labs this side of the Mile End Road and you can't say worse than that. English? Yes. Art – you look bad-tempered enough to be one of the arty lot. And History, I'll bet. Eng. History. That's why you looked at poor old Staveley like he was a heap of shit. Don't worry. He's not as bad as he tried to pretend. Just the average sort of ass, really. Am I right?'

'Not completely,' she snapped. 'I'm doing French too.'

'Four As! There's posh!' He sounded Welsh now.

'Why shouldn't I? Does it put you out in some way?'

'Oh, not i' the world, ma'am, not i' the world!' he said airily. 'I'm glad you're here. You could be worth fighting with. Got a bit of muscle. The rest of 'em don't look too promising. Except perhaps the Malaysian piece. Another beleaguered minority. Better and better.'

'You're a bloody offensive bastard,' Dilly said with a sudden flare of anger. 'Where do you get off calling people names?'

'Names? When did I call anyone a name, for God's sake?' He looked genuinely bewildered. 'I know it's tough coming to somewhere new, but you don't have to come on quite so bitchy.'

'She's not a piece! She's a girl, for God's sake,' Dilly snapped.

He looked blank and them made a small grimace. 'Thou speak'st aright, I was indeed in error. *Mea culpa, mea culpa* –'

'Oh, piss off,' Dilly snapped and moved away from him. 'I've got better things to do than play your stupid games. If you want to talk to me, talk properly. Then maybe I'll be interested.'

'Oh,' he said and stood and watched her as she went over to the desk to look over shoulders at the timetables Staveley had left for them. And then moved quietly away. She felt him go and was absurdly pleased with herself. What a dickhead, she jeered inside her head. Completely.

Beside her the Oriental girl murmured, 'Are you doing sciences or arts?'

'Arts,' Dilly said. 'You?'

'Maths and Physics.' She was gloomy. 'I told my father it was stupid sending me here. You ought to see the labs – diabolical.'

'So I've been told. I'm Dilly Langham.'

'Bonnie Ching.' She held out one hand. 'I thought this party ought to be fun, for sure. Not too sure now. That Staveley . . .'

'Yeah. Bad news. Have to see how it goes.'

'No women staff either?'

'I don't know. Haven't seen any.'

'Christ,' Bonnie said feelingly. If there was just one woman in the staffroom it'd help. Can you imagine how it's going to be?'

'I knew before I got here. But they never listen, do they?'

Bonnie knew at once. 'Parents,' she said heavily.

'Yeah. Parents.'

There was a little silence and then Bonnie said, 'That poor devil – imagine being called Arse.'

'Sort of thing boys would come up with,' Dilly said, and glared over her shoulder at one of the boys who had pushed past her a little more roughly than she thought he should. 'Can't keep their minds above their bloody navels.'

'Or ours,' Bonnie murmured. 'I like the look of Harry, though. Did you ever see anyone so gorgeous? Sort of a cross between Richard Gere and Eddie Murphy. Nearly as funny too.'

'And doesn't he know it,' Dilly said. 'I'm blowed if I'm going to fall for that one. Pretty or not.'

Bonnie nodded, her face alert and smiling. 'I thought you liked him.'

'I'm going to look around. I've got a free period now, according to this timetable. What about you?' Ignoring any talk about Harry Forster seemed the best thing to do.

'Got to go to the Physics lab to get equipment sorted out. See you later, maybe.'

'Yeah.' Dilly turned for the door.

'You're doing Art as well,' a breathless voice said in her ear. 'Do you mind if I stick with you for a bit? Don't know anyone, you see . . .'

Dilly looked at the girl who was now standing with one rather hot hand on her arm. 'None of us does,' she said a little sharply. 'You can if you like.'

'Oh, thanks. It's so awful being on your own. I – it bothers me and you look sort of – and you're doing Art and French as well as me and –'

'Yes, well, I suppose. Look, I'm going around the school now for a look around. I'll be back later. Talk about it then –'

'I'm Genevieve Barratt,' the girl said quickly, not letting go of Dilly's arm, and peering up at her anxiously. 'Please call me Jenny. And please, don't make me wait here on my own. I really don't think – I mean, it's a little bit – isn't it?'

Dilly stopped and stared down at her, frowning. The girl looked harmless enough, if a bit of a wet, and maybe she'd turn out to be worth knowing; but right now, Dilly had a deep need to get away from all of them. The noise in the sixth-form room was loud and getting louder and she needed some air as well as comparative quiet.

'Oh, well, if you must,' she said then. 'We'll find the library for you, all right? Then I'll go and look around a bit and you check out the books there. Then we can compare notes.' The idea grew on her and she became a little more cheerful. 'Yeah, that's what we'll do. Compare notes. Come on. This place is driving me bananas.'

And she pushed out of the form room as a loud bell rang in the corridor outside and the sound of running feet signalled that the day had started in earnest for the Foundation and its seven hundred pupils.

Five

What a wally, thought Dilly disgustedly. First day here, and so far she hadn't seen anyone worth talking to. Except perhaps Harry Forster; but that was a thought not worth thinking, she told herself fiercely, so she wouldn't think it. Instead she glared at the man and told herself again, What a wally. But she knew she was kidding herself. Really the Headmaster was gorgeous. Tall and sleek with the sort of hair that shone grey but was thick and springing like a child's even though he wore it brushed back hard, and a face that looked like a real-life version of the drawings of the heroes in the comic books they all used to read when she was in the fourth form at St Aloysius. Not that she'd read them herself, of course, perish the thought; but she hadn't been able to help seeing them when everyone else read them. And here she sat staring at a man who looked just like the Kevins and Nigels and Malcolms in the cartoons, only older and more intense, with a square chin with a cleft in it and a strong jawline and deep dark eyes, the whole bit. He had to be a wally.

He was standing now looking round at them all with a hint of a smile on his face and she noticed the way his glance lingered on Gillian and was even more disgusted. Wasn't it bad enough the whole bloody sixth form had fallen into instant lust with Gillian? Did he have to look at her like that, as though his eyes were dribbling over her? Sickening wally, not just an ordinary one. A sickening one.

'You can't imagine how excited everyone is,' he said, and his voice was gorgeous too. Rich, but not heavy, almost like the way Harry Connick sang, only English of course. 'This school is four hundred years old and you are the first women to set foot over the threshold. As pupils, that is.'

Clever sod, Dilly thought, trying very hard to dislike him. Calling us women. And she saw Bonnie Ching beside her relax and look admiringly at him and knew she herself would be the next to slide under his spell, unless she was very careful.

'Now, it won't be easy for you. We – the men here – will need time to get used to having you around and I dare say some of us'll behave oddly until we do. Not sure whether to fuss over you or ignore you.' He smiled devastatingly, looking directly at Gillian again. 'So please be patient. Eventually we'll all learn to regard you as people first and as women second. Though I doubt we'll ever be able totally to ignore your femininity. I apologize in advance for that to the more – um – severe of the feminists among you . . .'

This time he caught Dilly's eye and she tried not to scowl at him, working hard on keeping her face looking ordinary, and she must have succeeded because his gaze moved on to Bonnie. 'But thus the world wags and why should we here at the Foundation be any different? Feeble men, all of us . . .' And the smile appeared again and this time everyone laughed, and Dilly thought furiously, Tittering idiots!

'Now, we do want you to fit in as just a normal part of the school, but we also realize that as women you do have a few special needs. Not least of which is someone of your own sex to talk to from time to time, apart from each other. So, let me introduce you to another new arrival at the Foundation, Mrs Clements. She's your own particular member of staff here to advise and guide you on anything that worries you.'

Mrs Clements looks all right, Dilly thought, staring at her judiciously. Tall, well-cut dark hair, just enough make-up to look like a person without going over the top, a good suit in a rich russet that went well with the yellow shirt she wore under it, and a friendly face. About thirty-fiveish? Probably.

Mrs Clements was looking at the Headmaster in some alarm. 'Er, Dr Roscoe,' she began and he lifted his brows at her and she reddened slightly. 'Headmaster, may I just make the point that I don't yet know all there is to know about the way the school is run, so I might be a bit of a broken reed at first –'

'Not to worry,' he said and smiled at the girls. 'You may not know all the answers, but you know a man who does.' And again the girls giggled. 'Treat me like the AA man in the advertisement, Mrs Clements. If one of the girls has a question you can't answer, then refer to me. Between us, we'll take excellent care of you all. Now, I'll leave you to Mrs Clements, and remember, you're a valued part of the school even though you're girls, so don't allow yourselves to be upset if some of the people here are less charming than they should be at first. You'll soon tame them – us – I'm sure.' And with another of his incredible smiles, which Dilly decided sourly he probably practised in a mirror, he went, leaving Mrs Clements leaning against the long desk and looking at them a little nervously.

There was a silence when the door closed behind the Headmaster and then Mrs Clements said, 'I have to tell you I'm not in any sense a teacher. This is my first job in a school. You're entitled to know that, I think. I'm a nurse and a midwife with a good deal of experience in looking after children and young people. I've been appointed as a sort of welfare officer for you. So, the problems I'm best able to help with are those to do with your health, both physical and psychological and any, well, social difficulties you may have. Problems to do with work or exams and so forth' – she held her hands out to show helplessness – 'I'd be useless. But I can promise you that if you have any difficulties with any of the teaching staff you can use me as a go-between.' She nodded, suddenly forceful. 'Yes, indeed. That may well be a useful thing I can do for you.'

'Are they that bad?' Dilly asked, and Mrs Clements looked at her and made a grimace.

'Oh dear, did I show it that clearly? Well, I have to say it's early days yet, of course, but I've met a few of them. And I'm here to tell you there are one or two definite dinosaurs. You'd think the devil in a skirt had gone into their staffroom this morning, the way they reacted to me!'

Dilly felt her shoulders relax. This was better! She leaned forward eagerly and said, 'Tip us off which ones?'

Mrs Clements laughed aloud. 'No, of course not! That'd be making prophecies for you – self-fulfilling ones. I could be quite wrong. The people I'm thinking of could have taken a bit of a scunner to me personally, and'll be positive angels to all of you, so –'

'I'll bet not,' Bonnie said. 'You can always tell the difference between someone who doesn't like you because you're not his sort of person and someone who doesn't even try and hates you just because of what you were born. A woman or a different race or whatever. Believe me, I know.'

There was an embarrassed silence and then Mrs Clements said, 'Yes, you could be right. And if you get anyone starting on you because you're from the Far East, let me know and I'll –'

'I'm from the Far West, actually,' Bonnie said. 'My family have been in Bristol from yonks. My great-grandfather settled there. See what I mean?'

Mrs Clements went red. 'Oh, blast,' she said. 'I'm sorry. Fair enough. But all the same, let me know if you have any problems. I'll murder 'em!'

The girls were relaxing rapidly now, no longer sitting upright on the uncomfortable chairs, but sprawling a little, some with their legs stretched out, and Hattie, looking at them, felt better. She might have put her foot in it with the Chinese child, or whatever she had been before her great-grandfather reached Bristol, but in essence they had a rapport. It was like the old days when she'd come into a new ward of children and had to get their trust and attention on the first morning; she'd learned how to do it then without actually thinking about it, and the old skill was still there. And that was a comforting thought which made her relax too.

'All right. Let's get to know each other. I've got a list of names here but they mean nothing till I put faces to them. Sing out as I call each name and then we can see where we are . . .'

The rest of the morning moved smoothly. It had taken some time to get in to see Dr Roscoe to find out what she was supposed to be doing (only to be told charmingly but very firmly that here in school she was to address him as Headmaster at all times and never by name, a command she had difficulty remembering) and then the girls had to be collected from the various parts of the building to which, it appeared, they had scattered, and brought back to their form room, from which the boys were temporarily excluded, so that she could be given her first taste of what her job would be. Now, as she worked her way through the register and moved around the room shaking hands with each girl as she answered her name ('Always touch children when you talk to them, nurse,' her Sister Tutor had instructed her when she'd first gone on duty on a children's ward. 'It comforts them.' It had then, and it still did, she discovered happily), she felt better. Her collision with the masters in the common room had almost persuaded her to see to it that this first day at the Foundation would double as her last; to hell with Judith and her nagging, to hell with the need for a job, she wouldn't stay here to be insulted. But by twelve-thirty and lunchtime her opinion had been almost completely reversed.

She had been told that there was a staff dining room, but the thought of that removed all trace of appetite. Sometime, eventually, maybe she'd brave that, but the possibility of seeing the fat and horrible Dr Bevan again, and the unappetizing smells of heavily boiled cabbage and strongly fried onions that drifted through the hallways combined to send her out of the building in search of whatever refreshment she could find elsewhere.

She came out by a door that took her into the central quadrangle and stopped when she got there, staring round. It was beautiful; the old warm red brick and grey stone of which the buildings had been put together over the centuries glowed in the September sunshine above a lawn that someone clearly loved dearly. It was as green and striped as a 1930s advertisement for weedkiller, and against each of the four buildings that flanked its perfection were borders filled with glowingly flowering plants, chrysanthemums carefully tied up to stop them straggling and gaudy dahlias and drifts of Michaelmas daisies, blue and green and misty against those old stones.

She took a deep breath of sheer pleasure and lifted her face to the sun and stood for a little while with her eyes closed; it felt good and she felt good. And I didn't think about Jessie and Sophie all morning, she thought then and opened her eyes sharply, filling up with a mixture of guilt and exhilaration. It was, surely, a major step forward to be so involved in what she was doing that she could manage not to think about her children. And she shook her head at her own confusion and hurried across the grass towards the main gate which led out into the street.

By the time she got there a man was standing at the edge of the path glowering at her, his hands folded threateningly over a high paunch, with the brass buttons of the uniform he was wearing glittering malevolently.

'And 'oo do you think you are, walking on the grass like some – well, I won't say the word what comes to mind. This place is out of bounds, lady, 'ooever you are, so don't you come sneaking in here again, do you 'ear me? And then walking on the grass!'

His voice was high and thin but none the less truculent and she looked at him a little wearily. Another of these bloody men to deal with.

'I am Mrs Clements, I am a member of the staff, I am here to look after the girls in the sixth form. I did not know the grass was sacrosanct, and I won't walk on it again. Are you happy now?' she said with considerable belligerence and he blinked at her.

'Go on, there ain't never been no women on the staff here —' He stopped then and shook his head. 'Girls in the sixth! They got to be bleeding mad. Never 'eard of such a thing!' and turned his back on her and went marching into the little cubbyhole beside the street gate and slammed the door behind him. And Hattie, feeling as childish as her behaviour, stuck her tongue out at his retreating back and went out of the gate and into Nollys Street and then on to Cable Street.

The contrast was startling and she needed it. Here were the squalid buildings she had known ever since she had first joined the nursing students at Old East all those years ago as a hopeful eighteen-year-old; here were the shabby streets she'd hurried through when they'd run the Home Care scheme for sick children and had so many severely ill children to look after on the district that they'd never had any off-duty time; here were the cheap shops that were almost more familiar to her than those around her home in Hampstead; here was the noise of the market at Watney Street, with its raucous yells and the eternal blare of pop music from the record seller's cheap old record player; the stench of traffic; the shrieking of the gulls from the river; and the distant smell of water over all, and she took a deep breath, relishing it. Whatever happened at the Foundation with its artificial atmosphere of overwhelming maleness, this was real and comfortable and salutary. It was hard to feel sorry for herself or confused here.

She went for lunch at a doner kebab restaurant in Cable Street, not too far from Shadwell station, comforted by the familiarity of its smell, that queasy mixture of roasting lamb and armpitty cumin seed and newly baked pitta bread, and ate a salad with a bowl of hummus and a vast cup of coffee, and went through her register, which she'd brought with her, trying to fix the girls in her mind.

Most of them were run-of-the-mill enough, she thought, but there were some interesting ones: Dilly Langham, the tall girl with the untidy light-brown hair and the sulky expression, could turn out to be worthwhile, and she thought that she had come across people like her before, so determined to hang on to what they regarded as their individuality that they repelled everyone who came near them. It would be hard work to make a friend of Dilly but worth the effort. A challenge anyway.

Gillian Brownlow: nothing exceptional there, an ordinary type, really; fizzing with sexuality and not much on her mind apart from the demands of her own hormones. Pretty in an obvious way with all that bouncing yellow hair and her old-fashioned trick of peeping up at people – especially men – with her head tucked down to show the delicacy of her chin for all the world like a television advertisement for shampoo or whatever. Even Roscoe – Headmaster – had found her provocative. She'd need some watching.

Bonnie Ching: a nice girl but rather like a Jamaican girl Hattie had trained with, with a chip on her shoulder set there by other people's behaviour to her. She'd need protecting rather than watching.

And Genevieve . . .

Hattie sighed and swallowed the last of her pitta and hummus and pulled her coffee closer. If she stuck it out at the Foundation it would be mostly because of Genevieve Barratt, she decided, as she sat with both hands cupping the hot coffee and her eyes staring sightlessly out into the hubbub of Cable Street. She was so typical it was almost a textbook case: the voluminous sweater, even on a day as warm as this, the full skirt gathered so beauti-fully over her hips, the fragile birdlike wrists and ankles and the faintly downy look of the narrow cheeks. Anorexia nervosa, all set to starve herself to death given half the chance. Hattie had spent the toughest year of her professional life as staff nurse in charge of a ward full of them and had sworn she'd never spend another moment with people as intransigent, as devious, as self-centred and as thoroughly miserable as they were. But she'd got hooked then because they were so . . . well, so *interesting*; and now she was halfway hooked again. At least she'd have to find out if anyone had realized that the girl was ill, whether anyone had done anything about getting help for her.

She went back to the school the long way round, going to Watney Street market first; she had time, and it had always been a fun place. It still was, with its hubbub of stalls filled with vegetables, from the most homely of potatoes and onions to the most exotic of eddoes and yams, and the rails filled with cheap cotton shirts in vivid colours and jeans which, at the price being asked, had to have escaped from the backs of various lorries. And above all there were the people who argued and shrieked, laughed and talked and ate non-stop, people of such a mixture of colours and eye-shapes and languages that it felt like being in the middle of a whole world in miniature. Just walking through the market made her feel good, just as it had in the old days before she'd ever met Oliver, before she'd ever been the mother of two small daughters, the days when she'd been free and hopeful and –

She moved south then, heading back to the school, and came back to Nollys Street and the high stone walls with their ornate iron gates and looked around at the other houses that faced it: the elegant eighteenth-century and perhaps earlier façades sadly crumbled and battered now, but surviving not just the Luftwaffe's 1940s Blitz but the property developers' 1970s one; and sighed. It was a ridiculous anomaly, this school, not just physically in its building, but in itself. A boys-only school admitting girls for the first time in four hundred years; a staffroom seeing its first woman ever – it was dismal and she was being absurd herself being here. But it was interesting too; and she thought of Genevieve and her bright – too bright – eyes and fragile bones, carrying her self-inflicted disease on her face to those who knew what to look for; of the luscious Gillian asking with the look on her face to get herself into complicated sexual disarray in this hotbed of male hormones as clamorous as her own; of the sulky Dilly and the watchful Bonnie with her smooth oval face and handsome slanted eyes; and sighed again. Just one day here and she felt as much a part of the place as if she'd been here for months. Ridiculous.

She stopped on the corner waiting to cross, holding back for a rumbling lorry to pass and then saw them, at the other end of the street, walking together with their heads down and very close together, and she paused. The taller and older of the figures was unmistakable; there couldn't be many men who went about in tightly belted blue calico catsuits. The other figure was slight and somehow tremulous, even at this distance, and she stood in the shadow of the wall watching them come towards the gate that stood between herself and them, not quite sure why she was watching, or why she found it best to hold herself against the wall in the shadow of one of the buttresses that lifted itself there. But she did and was glad she had when the man looked up and round swiftly and then bent and kissed the boy on the mouth so hard that he seemed to stumble backwards, and then Tully smacked him lightly on the rump and turned and broke into a jogging run which took him away from the gate back towards the river end of Nollys Street. The boy stood for a long moment with his head down, then shuffled his feet and walked quietly into the school through the big gates.

The bell started producing the shrieking clamour that she now knew punctuated all the affairs of the Foundation, and she shook her head slightly and made for the gate herself. It wasn't surprising, surely, that in a school like this there should be liaisons between male and male; a little worrying they should exist between master· and pupil, but even then, the master couldn't be much older than thirty-five or so and the pupil wasn't wearing uniform so he had to be a sixth-former – sixteen then, at least. Pretty grown up.

None of your business, Hattie, she told herself as she made her way back to the sixth-form room, carefully skirting the grass and using the cindered paths. None of your business. Even though you are supposed to be the school welfare officer. But all the same, she thought as she made her way up the green and cream painted staircase, all the same I'm going to watch out. I wonder who the boy is? And whether he's happy? It would be interesting to find out.

Six

'A *what*?' Hattie said, and looked at the poster Edward Wilton was pinning to the cluttered board in the common room. 'You can't mean it!'

'Can't mean what?' Wilton said uneasily, and peered at the poster. 'I thought I'd got it right – the Autumne Charity Fayre. Friday 27th at 2 p.m., two weeks tomorrow, stalls and –'

'It's the spelling,' Hattie said. 'Fayre – ye Gods, I thought only little old ladies with whiskers who organized church bazaars ever called 'em that.'

'Well, you have to make it attractive ...' Wilton said and again gazed unhappily at his poster. 'We have one every September and we've always spelled it that way; it adds a sort of charm, don't you think?'

'No,' Hattie said firmly, and turned away to find an armchair that wasn't cluttered with other people's things, so that she could put her own on it. 'I can think of nothing I'd more gladly stay away from than an Autumne Fayre.' And she deliberately enunciated the superfluous letters. 'Putting an "e" on the end of autumn, no – honestly, Edward! And you a member of the English department!'

'No one's ever objected before,' Edward said huffily and went to get some coffee from the tray. Hattie grinned at his back, and settled down in the chair she'd freed for herself by the usual means of putting the things that had been left there on to the floor. It was too easy to torment Edward and be rude to him the way the other men were; he'd been kind enough to her, after all, and she mustn't let herself be infected by the common room's usual sardonic tone. The fact that the rest of them – with of course the exception of Dr Bevan – were getting used to her and being friendly mustn't be allowed to dull her sensitivity or encourage her to play up to them.

So she said kindly, 'Oh, I dare say it's just my prejudice. It's like those tea places that call themselves Ye Olde Tea Shoppe; I won't go into them on principle, however thirsty or in dire need of cream cakes I am. Ignore my nagging and tell me all about it. Do we all have to go?'

'Don't *have* to, but I'd be grateful if you would,' he said, immediately beaming at her. 'I mean, it's such a hell of a thing to organize but we have to do it. Headmaster likes it, you see, it pleases the Council people, they always come swooping around the way they do every chance they get, and we have to make sure we've got stalls for African Famine and Equal Opportunities and so forth as well as for our own fund-raising. Can I put you down for a stall?'

'Not a stall,' Hattie said hastily. 'I wouldn't have time for that.' Indeed she wouldn't, not if they were like the ones that she had had to look after at Old East's charity events, when they so effortfully raised money to buy essential equipment for the Baby Units or the Geriatric Wing. 'I'll help with things on the day – teas and that perhaps?'

He brightened visibly. 'Oh, yes please, that'd be great, really great. We've had the boys do it other years but to tell the truth they ate more than they sold and people always complained at what they did sell. Perhaps you can get some of the girls to help you, hmm? Then I know it'll be run properly and we might make a few bob on it.'

She nodded and sipped the coffee he'd brought her and marvelled a little that she was so at home here now. That first uneasy day seemed an eternity away now, and she stared back over the term, a little amused. She'd thought at first she wouldn't have enough to do, but it was amazing how busy she had become. The word had gone round among the boys very fast that they could talk to Mrs Clements just as the girls did, if they wanted to, and, in the little room she'd been allotted, near the Headmaster's office but not too close to it, she had set up some simple first-aid gear and had got into the practice of being there each morning when school started and during the lunch hour, because so many of the pupils came to her then.

There were grazed knees and torn fingers to dress, and sometimes wrenched ankles or knees, especially on Thursdays and Fridays when the sports people were at their most active, but the boys came for other reasons too. Those with spots – and there were a very large number of them – soon learned the value of the supply of skin-peeling creams and lotions she had bought out of the small float she had managed to extract from the Headmaster's secretary, and they would sit enthralled as she reassured them that it wasn't their fault they had acne, that they hadn't brought it on themselves by eating chocolate or hamburgers and chips, but had it like hordes of others because they had healthily active hormones, and then relax visibly.

Poor little devils, she would think as yet another went away with an obviously lighter step, what was it like in the past for them, with no one here to help them? And now and then, if the boy looked approachable and sensible, she would talk lightly and very elliptically about other things, trying to imply without putting it into as many words that they needn't think they had their spots because they masturbated either; that every boy who ever was did that and it was nothing to worry about, indeed, a necessary part of growing up. But she soon stopped doing that. The ones she had tried to talk to had shown at once by the crimsoning of their necks that they knew perfectly well what she was on about, and made it equally clear by their rapid departure from her little room that they had no intention of talking about it, not ever, and certainly not to her; and she had sighed and packed away her lotions and creams ready for the next time and was glad she had daughters. So much easier to deal with, daughters.

'The parents come as well of course,' Edward said. 'It's as bad as those damned Open Days, I'm afraid. They pin you in corners and want to know how their little darlings are getting on, and it's always the ones with the stupidest and laziest little darlings who get you first and you have to try and say something that won't send them off in a huff and yet not tell lies because they'll catch you out at the real Open Day. It's really all very tiresome,' he ended plaintively.

'Then why do you do it?' Hattie said and then shook her head. 'No, don't tell me. Headmaster likes you to. Do you ever do anything because you want to and not because of him? I know he's the boss and all that, but he needs you as much as you need him, if you see what I mean. More, probably. What happens if you stand up to him and say you've got something else to do on the twenty-seventh? Would he fire you?'

'Oh, it's not that he'd do that. It's just that he'd . . .' He wriggled his shoulders uneasily. 'It's just that you tend to do what he wants you to do. It's really easier. Don't you?'

'Don't I what?'

'Find it easier to do what he wants you to do?'

'He doesn't seem to care much what I do,' Hattie said, and set down her coffee cup. 'Seems happy enough to let me get on with what I'm here for. So what with the sessions I hold for the boys to patch them up and the times I've got with the girls – they've got free periods at all sorts of times, of course, because they've all got such different timetables, so I only get to work with two or three at a time, but that's fine with me. I can have discussions into this and that with them and they seem to like it – I don't have much time left over. And he seems happy to leave it to me what I do.'

'Nice to be you,' Edward said gloomily. 'I wish he was the same with us. Mind you, it's because we're the English department, I suppose. It was his subject when he taught so I dare say – well, there it is . . .'

'I still don't see why you have to be lumbered with the charity thing if you don't want to be,' Hattie said. 'I'll do the teas because I said I would and anyway, it might be quite fun. I can bring my daughters, I imagine, and –'

He looked alarmed. 'Little ones?'

'Quite little.'

'Oh!'

'You don't want them here?' Hattie said, and her eyebrows were up and she stared at him very directly.

'I don't mind,' he said hastily. 'Not me, personally, but –'

'I know. Headmaster mightn't like it. Well, blow that, I'll bring 'em anyway.' She got to her feet. 'I'm getting out of here before the mob arrives. I'm in no mood for listening to Tully torment Bevan –' She stopped then. 'Does he turn out for this thing?'

'Tully? Oh, yes. In a big way.' Edward sounded enthusiastic now. 'He organizes a stall where his A-level boys do fast portraits of people, and then he does them too and they're very good and of course they get all excited, the parents, you know, and it's usually worth at least three or four to him. Often much more.'

'Three or four what?'

'Commissions.' Edward was at the door now. 'I think it's the only reason he works here. He gets his hands on the parents. Some of them are really stinking with it and Tully likes that sort best –'

The door opened and almost pushed him over.

'What does Tully like best?' He was wearing crimson corduroy trousers today, cut low on the hips in a way Hattie thought rather dated, but which suited his leanness very well, and over them a black polo-necked silk sweater which set off his shaved head elegantly. He looked more than usually pleased with himself.

Wilton had started to sweat and his face was patched with colour. 'Uh – just – I was just explaining to Mrs Clements about the Charity Fayre, you know, and how there are stalls and you and the A-level Art boys do portraits and . . .'

'And what do I like best?' Tully said again and looked at Hattie with almost invisible eyebrows raised.

'Rich parents,' Hattie said, and sat very still, staring at him as directly as she could, determined not to let him force her to break eye contact. Ever since that first day when she had seen him with whoever it was – she had looked out for the boy afterwards but hadn't been able to identify him among the horde – she had been suspicious of him. It was none of her business what the boys and masters did, she knew that. And who was she to make judgements? If girls of sixteen were considered to be at the age of consent for heterosexual relationships – and lesbian ones, come to that – why shouldn't a boy of the same age be equally capable of making such choices for himself, no matter what the law said? So she had told herself, trying not to be censorious about Tully, but she hadn't succeeded. She found him a thoroughly unsavoury person, unpleasant to be with; a man who made her feel deeply uncomfortable, as though she had been caught wearing just a shirt and no pants or skirt. A horrid feeling. Now she sat and stared at him, head up, and didn't at all hide her lack of warmth for him.

'Oh, really?' Tully said and looked sideways at Wilton. 'What am I supposed to do with them, mmm, Wilton? Knock 'em down and take their wallets?'

'Oh, shit,' Wilton muttered and escaped, and Tully laughed and came across the room to the coffee pot.

'Christ, if he were any wetter he'd turn into a patch of mildew and that'd be that. I suppose he told you I only work here so that I can get my hands on rich parents in order to screw commissions for portraits out of them?'

'Yes,' she said, still staring at him.

'Then he told you the truth. That is why I'm here. And for one or two other things, of course.' Again his eyes slid sideways at her, mocking her, daring her to ask.

So she dared. 'Like what?'

'Oh, the hell of it,' he said, and took his coffee cup and went to lean against the wall near her chair, so that he could stare down at her. 'It amuses me to torment the likes of Bevan. I like having a go at some of the boys too – nasty sprigs of middle-class idiocy who wouldn't know a decent bit of painting if it bit their ears and who have the brass nerve to make comments on *my* work. Oh, I put them through one hell of a hoop.' Still he stared at her, daring her to object.

'No boy, however stupid, could possibly be upset by anything you said to him, I imagine,' she said steadily. 'You're such a poseur he surely has to see you for what you are.'

'Which is what?'

She took a deep breath. 'Not very pleasant.'

There was a silence and then he smiled widely. 'Do you know, there's more meat on your bones than I'd thought. Got a mind in there somewhere, have you? A bit more than a womb on legs, trembling with compassion for the poor little girlies trapped in this evil morass of masculinity? Who'd have thought it, looking at you –'

'Don't you dare patronize me!' she flared and again he laughed.

'Patronize? It's the in-word for your sort these days, isn't it? It's what all women accuse men of doing, as though the men are likely to give a shit what women think – those who can think, that is. Patronize? My God, if I wanted to patronize you you'd really know it. But I don't want to. You're really quite entertaining, aren't you?'

'Thank you for nothing,' she snapped, and got up and collected her little pile of books together. She'd promised to get copies of a new publication on assertiveness training for three of the girls and she had the copies with her now. He looked down now and saw the covers, and laughed.

'Assertiveness training? For those madams you've got there in the sixth? That'll be the day. I've seen 'em, through a man's eyes remember, I've seen 'em. The one with the lank blonde hair she keeps flicking at everything in trousers that's as high as her shoulder, wearing the thinnest clothes she can find to show us what pretty titties she's got – what do that sort need with assertiveness training?'

She looked at him and then, not knowing quite why, began to laugh, and for the first time he looked taken aback. She let the laughter continue, made the most of it.

'Oh, you poor thing,' she said. 'Scared of them, are you? Well, well. So that's why you're here in a boys' school. Because you find women alarming. Well, I'm kinder than you. What was it you said? Oh yes, I'm trembling with compassion for you. So I won't patronize you. I'll just say that your secret's safe with me.'

And she walked up to him, reached up and tweaked one cheek between her thumb and forefinger, pinching hard. Her grandmother used to do it to her when she was a child and she'd hated it. Now she took a delight in doing it to him.

She walked out of the room steadily enough, letting the door bang behind her, and got down the stairs and along the corridor halfway to her own little room before reaction set in, and set in so hard that she had to perch herself on a window sill, waiting for the trembling to ease off. Her legs, her back, every part of her shook with it and she felt slightly sick for a moment.

But exhilarated too. Maybe he'd go to the Headmaster and complain of her bad behaviour and maybe the Headmaster would tell her to go because he wanted peace and tranquillity at the Foundation, not nasty brawls of this sort, but even if he did – and her commonsense told her that was exceedingly unlikely, even if Tully complained to him, which was more unlikely still – it would have been worth it. She could still see the look of incredulous fury in his eyes when her pinch on his cheek had made them water with the sharpness of it, and she let her head droop forward and giggled softly. That'll show the bastard, she thought, and then took a deep breath as suddenly the bell, that hateful raucous bell, shrieked the time over her head.

She stayed where she was, as the tide of boys erupted from form rooms and began its usual hammering way along every corridor in the school as people changed classes, and she watched them go, glad that one or two of them smiled at her as they charged past, and waited. And then, as the first couple of sixth-formers came into view, marked out by their lack of uniform, sharpened her scrutiny. Now she was more sure than ever that the boy she had seen with Tully that first lunchtime was not a willing participant in whatever there was between them. She could still see in her mind's eye the way the boy had stumbled back under the impact of the man's kiss, and she tried to convince herself it had been dismay that had caused that recoil, rather than a loss of balance. It had to be; no boy could possibly want a relationship with a man as hateful as David Tully, of that she was sure; and she watched the boys as they passed her, trying to see some likeness in their shapes to the one in her memory.

But it was an impossible task. That had been her first day, before she'd set eyes on any of the sixth-form boys. She knew most of them now at least by sight – or almost knew them – but then he'd just been an anonymous boy of sixteen or seventeen or so, in a sports shirt and grubby grey trousers; there had been no highlights she could fix in her memory.

Well, she thought as the flow of boys receded and she could go on her way to her own room, I'll just have to watch Tully, then. And brightened.

The ill-spelled autumn fair, that surely was the place where she'd be able to see what was happening? The boys would then be able to be with whom they liked, because, although it was a school event, it was happening outside normal school hours, and if one of them particularly liked to be with the repellent Tully she'd be able to see for herself. And if Tully made a set at one of the boys, surely she'd be able to see that too.

And she lifted her chin and hurried on, as though moving fast would bring the autumn fair date nearer. Because now she really was looking forward to it.

Seven

The Friday of the Charity Fayre was traditionally a half-holiday which no one at the Foundation took. Some of the boys risked sloping off well before four in the afternoon and the occasional master had been known to develop a mysterious allergic ailment that kept him away, but generally speaking the school turned out in force, a fact which everyone drummed firmly into Hattie as the newest recruit to the staff.

But she didn't mind being there in the least because of her own feelings, quite apart from her still lingering curiosity – or was it anxiety? She wasn't quite sure – about David Tully and his involvement with the boys. She wanted to bring the two halves of her life, home and the Foundation, together. She didn't know why it mattered that she should, just that it did.

So she had arranged for Judith to bring the girls straight from school when they came out at three o'clock, and she was absurdly excited at the prospect of showing them where she worked, and even more of showing them off to some of the people she worked with. She could imagine the girls of the sixth cooing over Sophie in particular, for she had Oliver's dark curly hair and ridiculously large and shining eyes with very long lashes, but Jessica would get her share of attention too, for she was a pretty child even if she lacked some of her sister's more obvious charms. Thinking about how it would be when they arrived greatly enlivened what would otherwise have been a day of considerable drudgery for Hattie, because she and the sixth-form girls had been told firmly that their task was to feed the multitude, and that meant the making of vast numbers of sandwiches and the arranging of even vaster numbers of small iced cakes bought cut-price from a bakery in Watney Street market.

That the girls had been furious was inevitable. 'Why do these bloody men always shove us into kitchens?' Bonnie snapped when she was told what they were expected to do, and Dilly Langham had flatly refused, until Hattie had pointed out that offensive though it might seem on the surface to be treated as 'little women' and made to act as feeders and carers, it would be infinitely more agreeable than having to work with the boys who were making heavy weather and a great deal of noise over putting up the various stalls and amusement booths for the afternoon.

'We'll be able to do what we want to do in our own time,' she said, and the girls had seen at once what she meant and stopped fussing. Even Dilly agreed it was worth being a mere sandwich-maker to avoid the company of the male mob, and they settled to a pleasant enough if effortful session of boiling and mashing eggs, slicing cucumbers and chopping watercress into cream cheese, chattering contentedly as they worked.

By the time they had finished, their tea room, which was in one of the biggest tents set in the corner of the quadrangle, looked very attractive. Long trestle tables had been fetched from the school dining room and set up all round the canvas walls and draped in white plastic cloths on which their trays of sandwiches, plentifully strewn with mustard and cress, had been displayed. The cakes were set with equal care on white paper lace doilies in a row behind the sandwiches, and between each plate stood a cup in which chocolate fingers had been arranged by Bonnie. There were piles of paper plates and stacks of plastic beakers and three great chrome urns borrowed from the school kitchens, and quantities of cardboard cartons full of irradiated milk and tea bags stood ready behind each urn.

'Look at it,' Dilly said disgustedly when they'd finished checking the small tables and chairs that had been arranged in the middle of the space, and were looking at the results of their handiwork. 'Doesn't it make you sick?'

'Oh, come on, it's not that bad,' Bonnie said. 'I didn't lick my fingers once when I was making the egg sandwiches and they're my favourites.'

'I don't mean them,' Dilly said. 'It's that artificial-looking stuff. Plastics and irradiation – ugh! Whatever happened to real china and real milk?'

'Luddite,' Hattie said amiably. 'It's called convenience, this way. And don't tell me you'd rather have to struggle with the sort of milk that goes off on afternoons as hot as this and that you want to wash up heaps of china cups and saucers instead of stuffing them dirty into plastic sacks.'

Dilly grimaced and said no more, but she still looked surly and Hattie looked at her uneasily. She'd been snappy all day and particularly sharp with Genevieve who had worked with more enthusiasm than Hattie had ever seen her display, making twice as many sandwiches as everyone else and going to a lot of trouble to arrange the cakes, which were iced in particularly virulent pinks and greens and yellows, with finicky care. If Dilly doesn't lose her temper with someone before this afternoon's out, Hattie thought, I'll be a – And Genevieve; if she eats anything after all the trouble she's gone to to make it ready, I'll be another whatever it is. If she doesn't – and I'll watch her all the time – then I'm going to talk to her parents about her. If I get the chance. Because I'll know I'm right about her.

On the dot of two the groundsman, now almost incoherent with fury over the state of his lawn, opened the big gates and people poured in. Most of them were parents, dragged from all corners of London by sons who knew their form masters would make their lives hell if they didn't turn out, and who themselves had only put on the screws because the Headmaster was harrying them, but there were also a few local people come to see what there was to be had. The Headmaster wanted them to show the visiting Council dignitaries how egalitarian they all were at the Foundation, but not so many that they would overwhelm the parents who were likely to look sideways at too many scruffy clothes and punkish hair styles. It was a matter of some pride to him that somehow each year he managed to get the balance just right, by inviting people from local churches and old people's clubs to come in, and bribing his gatekeeper to turn away others on the grounds that they were too late and the place was full.

Within fifteen minutes the quadrangle was alive with people. Hattie, standing at the door of the refreshment tent and looking at it all, had an odd sense of unreality. It was like being inside a 1950s Ealing film; there actually were women in shady hats and floaty dresses mixed up with men in the darkest and neatest of city suits and boys in well-brushed school uniforms and masters in their gowns; the occasional scruffy local managed to look like a country yokel circa 1955 rather than a Shadwell citizen of 1991. I'll have to be careful, she found herself thinking. I could get as locked into the past as any of them. Because she now knew that was the engine which made the Foundation run. It clung to its anachronistic state as a dying man to a raft, the Headmaster most of all. Watching him now as he moved among his guests with so much urbanity he looked as though he'd been sprayed with gloss, she found herself pitying him. He looked so self-assured, so certain that he had a right to his position of eminence, when in fact he was just a shadow, a faintly ridiculous reminder of something that had once been important in England but had long ago ceased to matter in any real sense. Schools like the Foundation had significance only to those people who played parts in the charade. To the councillors and the Mayor, who had just arrived and were being purred over by the Headmaster and Dr Bevan, who was looking unusually affable as he hovered by the Head's side being every inch the Deputy Head, the whole thing must seem a nonsense. They certainly looked bemused and on one or two of their faces there was a hint of scorn. It was almost as though Hattie could hear them thinking: What possible value can four hundred years of tradition have to the people who live in the surrounding streets and sprawling ugly blocks of flats and whose children have no possible hope of a place here? None, decided Hattie, and went back into the tent to check that the urns were boiling ready to make the teas that would soon be demanded by the wandering crowd outside. Better to keep herself busy than to think too deeply about what she was doing working in such a place.

She found that most of the girls had gone, seeking out their parents to show them round and to encourage them to spend money at the stalls ('It's an important charity thing, Mum, for heaven's sake spend a bit more than that. Don't show me up. It's for Kurdish refugees and all that . . .'), except for Dilly, who was sitting on a chair behind one of the urns, reading. The chair was tipped back precariously as she sat with her feet up on the table and as Hattie came up to her she scowled and then, ungraciously, took her feet off the table and let the chair down with a little thud but kept her head down over her book.

'Your parents not coming, Dilly?' Hattie said as casually as she could. It was difficult not knowing the family backgrounds; there was always the risk of saying the wrong thing and as she saw the colour creep into the back of Dilly's neck she knew she'd done just that. And decided to deal with her tactlessness head on. It was the only way.

'If you don't have parents and you want to tell me to mind my own business, fair enough,' she said as lightly as she could. 'I really shouldn't have asked.'

Dilly still kept her head down, but she closed her book. 'Natural enough, I suppose,' she muttered.

'But rude,' Hattie said. 'Sorry.'

'Not really.' Dilly looked up at her and seemed more relaxed. 'It's what teachers always do. They ask about parents the way parents ask about teachers. It's like we don't exist in the middle, you know what I mean? We're just there to give you all something to do.'

Hattie laughed. 'I do know what you mean,' she said, and perched on the edge of the table, pushing back some of the cakes to make room for her bottom. 'I turn up at my children's school as much to be seen by their teachers to prove I'm a good caring mum as to see the children's work. That's important, of course it is. But I do have this ridiculous thing about wanting to please the teacher. At my age!'

Dilly smiled suddenly and Hattie felt a warmth move into her. She was really quite good at this job she'd found herself pitched into.

'You do try hard, don't you?' Dilly said. 'Wanting to be a real mate to us, are you? You can't, you know. Not when you're one of the staff and we're not. It can't be done.'

The warmth vanished immediately and Hattie stared at her, nonplussed, and Dilly smiled more widely than ever. Clearly she felt better.

'Oh, it's all right,' Dilly said. 'Don't look like that. It's just a –' She shrugged. 'I never wanted to come to this bloody school and now I'm here I still don't like it much. But I've got no choice but to be here.'

'Well, give me some credit for something useful,' Hattie said. 'Tell me about it.'

'Here we go!' Dilly was derisive. 'Let me welfare you . . .'

'It's up to you. I put my foot in it to start with, and I don't want to go on doing it. Talk if you like. Don't if you'd rather not. It's really up to you.'

'Oh, I'm sorry,' Dilly said after a moment and then got up and went over to the entrance of the tent to peer out. 'I shouldn't take it out on you, really. Not your fault. It's all his –'

Hattie said nothing. She'd learned that much at least.

'And even that isn't really true.' Dilly came back to her chair and flopped into it. 'Poor bugger. Does his best, I suppose. It's just that he's so stupid and gets it all wrong all the time.'

Still Hattie said nothing and Dilly shot a glance at her. 'You're good at this, aren't you? Oh, well, what the hell?'

'What am I supposed to say to that?' Hattie ventured after a long pause, and Dilly shrugged.

'Nothing. Look, it's nothing all that special. My mother went off with someone else. Left me with my dad. We used to live in Liverpool, Mum and me, but after she went I had to come here to live with him. He can't work anywhere other than London, he says. Film director.'

'Sounds interesting,' Hattie said as Dilly stopped and again seemed to have dried up.

'Mmm? Oh, not really. He thinks it's madly glamorous, of course. But it's just a lot of tatty ads and second-rate TV things. Nothing all that good. It's like this place. You'd think it was something special, the way the Head and the masters go on, but it's only special because they think it is. It's a dreary dump really, but they think it's great, so to them it is. Freddy's the same. He thinks he has this madly exciting life, so he does. To me it's a load of crappy rubbish, but what can I do? I can't do what I want yet.'

'What do you want to do?'

'Go back to Liverpool. Get my A levels there. Go to university there.' Dilly made it sound as though she were talking about Shangri La. 'Liverpool's great. It's really great. I'd do anything to stay there but' – she seemed to flatten as some of the excitement that had lifted her ebbed away – 'it can't be done.'

'Really can't? A pity,' Hattie said cautiously and then added, 'Isn't there anyone you can stay with while you do your A levels? A friend's family, maybe?'

'What with? Peanuts?' Dilly said roughly. 'Someone's got to pay my bloody board and lodging, haven't they? And Freddy can't – and yes, I know about the fees here, but he doesn't pay them. My grandmother does and she won't let me go back to the 'Pool so I'm bloody stuck here, aren't I? And he's out there somewhere showing off to them all because he was a boy here way back in the olden days when life was really worth living, oh, but the sixties were wonderful, and all that shit. And he needn't think I'm going out to look for him. Because I'm not.'

'We'll need refills of the sandwiches once the crowds are let in here,' Hattie said after a long pause. 'I left enough stuff in the kitchens to make a new batch. We could just as easily start them now as later.'

Dilly looked up at her and pushed her hair off her face with both hands and slowly grinned.

'Yeah,' she said. 'Yeah, we could, couldn't we?'

'If anyone comes asking I'll tell 'em you're busy, shall I?'

'You do that.' Dilly got to her feet and made for the back entrance of the tent, the one that led back towards the school buildings. She stopped as she reached it and looked back over her shoulder. 'You're all right, you know,' she said. 'Sorry if I was a bitch.'

'You weren't,' Hattie said, and smiled at her. 'No more than generality.'

Dilly made a face and escaped, and Hattie sighed softly and made for the other entrance. She'd round up the girls and open the flaps of the tent to invite would-be tea-drinkers in. Her own children would be arriving at about four and she'd like to be free by then to give them some attention. Starting serving teas as early as two-thirty would help speed things up a little, even if it did reduce the attention paid to the stalls – which would irritate Edward Wilton considerably. But she'd risk that.

Outside the light seemed painfully bright and she squinted through the crowds, trying to find the girls, and in consequence almost butted into the official party. The Headmaster put out a restraining hand and she blinked up at him, startled.

'Ah, Madam Mayor, may I present my newest member of staff? Mrs Clements, looks after our sixth-form girls, you know. Organizing teas this afternoon, a most vital job. And Mr Akenshield, Mrs Rusting, Miss Greenlees . . .' He murmured his way through the whole party, faultlessly recalling every name, and Hattie stood and nodded and grinned awkwardly at them, feeling like a first-form child and wanting to escape, but they were murmuring at her, asking her about the girls: Was it working well, having girls in just the sixth form and didn't she think the school would be more normal if there were girls all through? And she nodded and smiled and managed to produce inane answers that said nothing very much, painfully aware of the Headmaster's eyes on her, and he seemed pleased enough and at last shooed his party onwards and she took a deep breath and then turned to continue her search for the girls. But again someone was in the way.

'You handled that rather well,' Sam Chanter said. 'Kept the Headmster happy and almost convinced those oiks you were saying something useful.'

'Why oiks?' Hattie was angry suddenly. 'Just because they're Council people? And, shock horror, Labour Council at that?'

'I joined the Party twenty years ago,' Sam said mildly. 'The fact I work here hasn't got a thing to do with my private or political feelings, you know. I called 'em oiks because that's what they are. Look at them, for heaven's sake! The most boring farts this side of the river.'

She followed the jerk of his head and looked again at the Headmaster's cluster of people and found herself smiling against her will. They were really very dreary-looking, all five of them; the women drab because they didn't know how to be anything else, rather than because they were making any sort of feminist statement, and the men self-satisfied, oily, dull.

'I suppose you're right,' she said and then looked at him again. 'Did you say you were a member of the Labour Party?'

'Lapsed. I joined after I left the C.P.'

She laughed at that. 'You weren't really a Communist!'

'At twenty you're a fool if you're anything else. Isn't that what they say?'

'No. What they say is that if you're not a socialist when you're twenty you've got no heart, and if you're not a Conservative when you're forty you've got no head. Or something like it.'

'Right. Well, I had my share of heart when I was twenty. Now I've got no heart left. And not much head. So I work here and take life easy.'

She looked at him curiously. 'I wouldn't have thought you that sort. Lazy, I mean.'

He grinned widely. 'I'm not. I'm working on a book. It fits in better with working here than in a State school. So I'm using the capitalists to suit my own socialist ends. How's that?'

'I like it,' she said. 'It's got class.'

'I might just as well ask what you're doing working here when you're obviously more in sympathy with the Council people than you are with the Headmaster.'

'It's a convenient job,' she said, 'for a widow with young children. I'm not entirely comfortable about it, and I won't pretend I am. But a job's a job – and this one gives me school holidays.'

'I knew all that. Wilton told me.'

She shook her head. 'That man seems to know everything about everybody.'

'Not everything. Have dinner with me sometime and I'll tell you what he hasn't told you. And you can fill in the gaps in what he told me about you.'

She blinked. She'd hardly spoken to the man before this; he'd just been part of the common room, like the rest of them, one of the pleasanter sort; certainly he'd shown no interest of this kind in her before today and she almost shrank physically from him as she contemplated the enormity of his suggestion. Go out to dinner with a man? She couldn't. There was Sophie and Jessica and Oliver and –

She shook her head sharply. 'It's really very kind, but the children, you know, and babysitters and –'

'Not an insuperable problem, I imagine?'

'Well, I'm not sure – really. I can't – well, it's kind of you but . . .'

He stood and looked at her as the crowds pushed past and the smell of crushed grass and popcorn from one of the stalls washed over them and after a moment he smiled. 'Oh well,' he said. 'Just thought I'd ask. Another time maybe.' And he nodded at her and turned and vanished into the crowd, leaving her feeling a great deal more irritated than she would have thought possible.

Eight

The children's appearance at the fair was every bit as successful as Hattie had hoped it would be. The girls fell on them with coos of delight and the children were equally enchanted with them and showed off outrageously while contriving to eat a great many more of the garish iced cakes than Hattie felt was good for them. But she let it happen, content to see the children having so much fun, and also because she was so busy; it was amazing just how much effort was needed to serve tea and sandwiches and cakes to large numbers of well-behaved people on a hot afternoon. They pushed and shoved, grabbed and nagged, and she shovelled food on to paper plates and money into the old wooden cigar box that did duty as their till until she was sweating.

But she still managed to be aware of what was going on around her, and absorbed information about who was talking to whom and how they reacted to each other in a way that quite surprised her. She had forgotten just how well trained she had been in her nursing days in the art of unobtrusive observation.

To start with she was very aware of Judith, who had brought her own two children, Jenny and Petra, as well as Sophie and Jessica (and both of them were having as much fun as Hattie's pair) and then gone on to spend the afternoon giggling and flirting with any of the men she could get to listen to her. It was ridiculous to feel, as Hattie did, slightly shocked. There was no harm at all in Judith and undoubtedly she adored her Peter, but she still enjoyed measuring her femininity against every man who came into range. First of course the Headmaster, who let her dimple at him and pat his arm in a proprietorial fashion for at least five minutes before he offloaded her – a congé she accepted cheerfully enough – on to Richard Shuttle and George Manson, with whom she began to chatter in rapid and very ungrammatical French as soon as she discovered that was the subject they taught. Hattie watched her from the corner of her eye and almost caught herself sniffing in disapproval. And then made herself stop watching, because it was so silly to pay any attention to something so very unimportant. Her efforts succeeded and she managed to transfer her interest to other people; first a stocky man in tight and obviously expensive jeans and an open-necked white shirt – so open-necked that it displayed sparse chest hair in which a rather old-fashioned-looking gold medallion nestled – who was holding noisy court in one corner of the tent. Several of the boys clustered round him, clearly fascinated by what he was saying, and Hattie managed to listen above the hubbub that surrounded her.

'David Lean always told me that . . .' came floating through first, and then, '. . . no use at all for the Michael Winners of this world, damage the industry for all of us, self-indulgent garbage . . .' And she looked at him with sharpened interest. Dilly's father? Perhaps; and then Dilly herself came pushing in through the back entrance to the tent bearing another pile of sandwiches, caught sight of him and scowled; and Hattie applauded herself for her successful identification. And watched him some more.

He was very relaxed, laughing a good deal rather loudly, throwing back his head boyishly to display very white teeth (Crowned? Hattie wondered. Probably) and looking into the boys' eyes as they talked to him. He was clearly one of the world's touchers; he slapped their backs and punched their shoulders American-style when one of them said something he liked, and left one arm draped negligently around the shoulders of the boy who was nearest to him and she thought, Is he like Tully? And then shook her head at her stereotypical thinking. There was, after all, Dilly. And even if that meant he was, as one of the cruder surgeons for whom she had once worked had been given to saying when they had a patient of doubtful sexual identity, someone who didn't know if he were Arthur or Martha, what was it to do with her? She'd been at the Foundation only a matter of weeks and already she was obsessed with male attachments. Ridiculous, she told herself, as she dragged her attention away. It's not as though he were even part of the school. Just a pupil's father.

Dilly tried to ignore him, attempting to slip out of the tent again, but he saw her and waved eagerly at her, and unwillingly she put down her tray and went towards him with a lumpish sulky gait that told the world how little she wanted his company. But he seemed quite oblivious and beamed at her delightedly and hugged her unresponsive shoulders and chattered at her and the surrounding boys – who now looked uneasy and tried to back away – in a way that even Hattie found embarrassing. How Dilly must be feeling she could well imagine. He was clearly a deeply shaming parent to have, so over-the-top and so anxious to please that he resembled nothing so much as an over-eager outsize puppy.

She slid her eyes away, looking for others to spy on; and then let her lips quirk. The word had come into her mind of its own volition and she should be ashamed of it, really, but she wasn't. She was spying on people and where better to do it than in the middle of a busy tea tent? It was like the old cliché about hiding things in the most obvious position you could. Here was a good place to spy and she enjoyed it, and why not? Anyway, she told herself as she went on piling sandwiches on plates and watching the people around her, it's part of my job. How can I understand what's going on here if I don't keep my eyes well open?

She saw Genevieve then and stepped back to let one of the others – Bonnie as it happened – take over her place. She'd take a short rest, and she moved even further back so that she was behind the girls who were busily serving, and stared shamelessly at the group in the corner.

They'd managed to get themselves a corner of a table to sit at, and were huddled there, Genevieve and two people who were clearly her parents. Her mother looked like a larger blurred copy of Genevieve; the small clearly defined features that made Genevieve appear vulnerable and birdlike were on her mother merely pointed and sharp and gave her a peevish expression; the thinness that was so much a part of Genevieve under her usual high-necked sweater and bulky skirt, was in her mother a sort of thickening, yet lacking in form. Looking at her was like looking at a wax doll that had been left out in the hot sun so that its limbs and trunk had melted and become misshapen. The bones were still there, easy to see, but shadowed by unpleasant dimpled flesh. Her clothes were depressing; she had clearly made a great effort to look as a mother should look at a school event; a fine see-through fussily printed fabric dress over a darker slip, and a hat that should have looked rather cheeky but managed only to look silly were accompanied by perfectly clean white gloves of the sort no one ever wore any more, and a pair of high-heeled shoes that must have been agonizing to walk in on the soft ground of the quadrangle. There was a line of pain between the woman's brows that suggested just how grateful she had been to sit down.

But it was at her husband Hattie looked longest. A man of equal neatness to his wife, in a dark grey suit and a shirt of such blinding whiteness it was almost blue, the obvious effort to dress up which looked faintly foolish on her was in him somewhat intimidating. His shoes shone so aggressively that it was hard to believe there were feet inside them, the crease lines on his trouser legs looked as though they'd been drawn with a set square, and the line of shirt cuff above each soft white hand seemed to threaten to cut them off by the sharpness of their edges. He was sitting with one of those hands set lightly on his daughter's, and his head was close to hers as he ate steadily, pushing egg sandwiches into his neat little mouth, and all the time watching Genevieve.

She wasn't eating at all. Hattie watched her pushing a piece of sandwich about on the paper plate in front of her, and went on watching as she seemed to raise pieces of it to her mouth, but so obviously – to Hattie the trained observer who had spent a full year dealing with anorexic deviousness – not allowing a crumb to pass her lips, that her own lips tightened. This girl was sick. Very ill, and clever with it. She was watching her father eat, her eyes fixed on him whenever he looked up from his plate, and he was happy and relaxed and didn't see what she was doing at all. Hattie flicked a glance at the mother then, and felt a sudden jolt. The woman was staring at her husband with her eyes so wide and dark that it was as though she were shouting something at him that he refused to hear, and Hattie moved sharply, pushing past Bonnie to get out, and went over to them. She had to.

'Hello, Genevieve.' She managed to sound very bright as she came alongside them and Genevieve looked over her shoulder at her, her face very pale in the greenish shadow thrown by the walls of the tent.

'Oh, hello, Mrs Clements,' she said after a long moment and then very deliberately turned back to her parents, making no effort at all to introduce them.

And that made Hattie angry. She didn't know what at; being snubbed was not so awful, after all. And anyway, maybe the child hadn't meant to be rude and just lacked the social grace to know how to behave. Hattie pushed the anger down inside her and smiled widely.

'May I introduce myself? I'm Hattie Clements. I look after the girls' welfare here, while they're in the sixth form, and I'm also the school nurse. The Headmaster appointed me specially, since he had no women on the staff. He felt you, as parents, would prefer to know your daughters had a woman to talk to, if necessary.'

The woman looked up at her eagerly and her hat shifted slightly on the back of her head rather ludicrously, and Hattie thought, She doesn't wear that often. She dressed up especially for today. For the school? For her daughter? For her husband?

'Oh,' she said breathily. 'How do you do?' And she got to her feet and held out one hand.

The man beside Genevieve said nothing, but he stopped eating, just sitting there with his hand over Genevieve's and staring up at Hattie from beneath lowered brows.

'How nice – Yes, very sensible of the Headmaster – very kind, I mean, who can know, yes . . .' And she shook Hattie's hand. Her glove felt damp and thick under Hattie's fingers. Unaccountably the woman giggled and looked nervously at her husband and daughter.

'Er – my husband – Genevieve's dad – used to be a boy here, you know. Still on the Governors – Both our sons were – Yes – Gordon, dear? Mrs Clements?'

It was definitely a question and for a moment Hattie thought he wasn't going to answer; that he was going to look away and ignore her, and go on talking to Genevieve who had kept her head turned well away from Hattie throughout. So Hattie didn't give him the chance.

'Hello, Mr Barratt,' she said cheerfully, even effusively, and without waiting to be asked moved past them to the back of the table where a chair was pushed well beneath the edge for lack of space to be pulled out, and tugged at its back. Unwillingly Gordon Barratt got up and nodded at her.

'How do you do?' he said and then stared at her owlishly.

'May I join you for a moment or two?' Hattie said brightly. 'It's so exhausting serving tea. I've been on my feet for hours, it seems. I do hope you're enjoying our efforts.'

The chair was pulled out at last so she could wriggle in and she sat there opposite Genevieve, between her parents, smiling from one to the other.

'I do hope you are,' she said. 'It would be too miserable if after all our work you didn't like what we'd made for you all.'

'They're very nice sandwiches,' Mrs Barratt said eagerly. 'Very nice. Aren't they, Gordon?'

He didn't look at her. He was sitting staring at his daughter again. 'Very nice,' he said after a pause just long enough to be insulting.

'You too, Genevieve?' Hattie said, determined now to carry it through. She'd come across this stonewalling before. They had to be got at, had to be hauled out from behind their damned defences.

'Me too what?' Genevieve said after a moment and Hattie laughed. 'At least I'm not teaching you English,' she said and could have kicked herself for it. There'd been no need for that. 'The sandwiches. I wondered what you thought of them.'

Genevieve looked down at her plate. 'Very nice,' she said woodenly.

'Oh,' Hattie said and smiled even more widely. 'Are you sure?'

Genevieve looked up. 'How do you mean, sure?'

'I wondered how you could know they were nice. You've only been pretending to eat, you see. I've been watching you.'

There was a sharp silence between them, highlighted by the roar of chatter and laughter going on all around them and then suddenly and horribly Mrs Barratt began to sniff and tears rolled down her cheeks. She made no effort to control them. Just sat there sniffing.

'Stella, shut up,' Gordon Barratt said softly. 'You're making an exhibition of yourself.'

'Dad, I'd better be on my way.' Genevieve began to get to her feet. 'Got to go and see if the girls need me to take over.'

Hattie had reached for her at her first movement and had her by the elbow and now, gently but firmly, pulled her down so that she had to sit again. 'No, Genevieve, I really think you should stay and hear me. Because I have to talk to your parents about you and I don't want to do it behind your back.'

'There's nothing to talk to them about,' Genevieve said, but there was no fight in her voice. She spoke faintly, as though it didn't really matter whether anyone was listening to her or not.

'Genevieve, there is. I suspect you've lost half a stone more since the beginning of term. It can't go on like this, can it? Someone in your family has to face up to what's going on. I've been watching you, and – well, this mayn't seem the best sort of place to discuss it, but it's the place we happen to be in. Someone has to talk to you and your parents about the way you're starving yourself. Maybe even to death.'

She said it very deliberately, not taking her eyes from Genevieve's face but very aware of the two adults flanking her. 'I've tried to talk to you about it already this term, haven't I? Since you got here, really. I saw it the first time I met you. You're ill, love, and someone has to do something about it, if you won't.'

'She's not ill,' the man said and his voice was as flat as Genevieve's had been, but there was menace in it. 'Not in the least. This is a lot of nonsense and I'll thank you to confine your interest in my daughter to school hours –'

'This is school hours,' Hattie said, and looked at her watch. 'For another five minutes, anyway. And you're here. I'd have felt it best to come to your home to see you if you hadn't happened to be here.'

He seemed to stiffen at that, and she turned her head to look at him, for Genevieve was now sitting with her head bent and her hands clasped in her lap. 'You can't come to our house just like that!' He sounded amazed, as if she'd suggested he strip off and dance naked in the middle of the tent. 'I never heard of such a thing! We come to the school as and when it's necessary, and that's as far as it goes. This is a day school, in case you hadn't noticed, not one of those all-in places.'

'And Genevieve is a sick girl attending it, and I have responsibility for her while she's here. For her health and welfare, that is. I'd be failing in my job if I didn't point out to you that she's ill.

She has a condition called anorexia nervosa. I don't usually go around making diagnoses, prefer to leave that to doctors. But I have a lot of experience in this condition and I know I'm right. Aren't I, Genevieve?'

She leaned forwards and reached for Genevieve's arms and, tugging on them, managed to bring her clasped hands up on to the table and to hold them. They felt thin and dry beneath her fingers. 'Not only don't you eat, and not only are you as thin as a scarecrow in consequence, but you've got a downy skin – look at your cheeks in the mirror, Genevieve, and turn your head to the light and you'll see it – and you're restless and tense and your periods have stopped –'

On her left there was a sharp hiss as Gordon Barratt took a breath and she looked at him and he said in a slightly higher voice, 'Really, this is disgusting. To talk of such things in public and in front of her father.'

Hattie frowned fleetingly. 'That sounds very, well, outdated of you, Mr Barratt. It's been a long time since periods were something never talked about –'

'Not in my house it hasn't. We still keep a decent home, never mind what people like you do.' He got to his feet abruptly. 'Genevieve, come on. We're going home. It's time we left anyway. I'll see you to the underground and then I'll come back for the Governors' meeting. I'll deal with this matter then. Come on now.' And he went, pulling Genevieve behind him like a small child, and Stella Barratt stood up and stared after them, her tears drying on her face and her expression flat and empty.

'There, you've done it now, haven't you?' she said, and turned and looked at Hattie. 'Talking about that in front of him. He's very squeamish, you see. Can't deal with it.'

'I'm sorry,' Hattie said. 'I didn't mean to cause . . .' She was shaking now inside, aware of how badly she'd mismanaged the whole business, and suddenly Stella Barratt amazed her, for she smiled, seeming to know, to understand.

'It's all right. He'll get over it. He always does. These things come up and there's all sorts of fireworks and the next time you speak to him, it's like it never happened. Never says another word about it. He won't at the Governors' meeting either. I wouldn't worry. And you're right about Jenny, of course. But what can I do? It's them against me. I worry about it all the time . . .'

And then she too was gone, threading her way out through the crowd and leaving Hattie standing staring after her. And slowly becoming aware of someone tugging at her skirt and saying with increasing urgency, 'Mummy, Mummy, I want to do a wee – Mummy, a wee, *now*.'

Nine

The only place to take her was the boys' cloakrooms. To reach the staff loo would mean a trek through long corridors, not very practicable with a child who was now urgently clutching herself in an effort to prevent her bladder emptying, and Hattie hurried her there, praying silently the place would be unoccupied. A small girl among schoolboys could cause considerable upheaval.

It seemed to be and she breathed a sigh of relief as Sophie, even more relieved, at last pulled up her knickers, flushed the lavatory and emerged.

'Where can I wash, Mummy?' she asked virtuously, peering around her with great interest, and Hattie, eager to get her on her way, said hastily, 'I'll find you a wet flannel when we get back to the tent, darling. This loo's for boys and it'll upset one if he comes in and finds we're here as well. Come on now.'

'There's one here already,' Sophie said conversationally as obediently she followed Hattie towards the doors, and Hattie stared over her shoulder at her.

'What did you –?'

'I saw. Under the walls, you know? I always look along when I'm at my school, just to see how many feet there are.' She giggled. 'It looks so funny, lots of feet with knickers round them. These feet didn't have knickers though. Boy's feet, with trousers.' Hattie lifted her head and listened, but there was only silence and she stood uncertainly, frowning. If there was a boy here when they came in, why didn't he make his presence known? Why be so particularly quiet? To have made some sort of sound would have been the natural thing to do, surely. Or was he shy because he'd realized the new arrivals were females? Or – and here she bit her lip – was there some sort of naughtiness going on? Smoking perhaps? She sniffed. No tobacco smoke. Well then, what? She wasn't exactly one of the boys' invigilators, and yet she was one of the adult staff. Which meant that she had a responsibility to make sure all was well. Usually there was a staff member around the boys' cloakrooms when they were in use, to make sure there was no mayhem, but now she was the only member of staff, and didn't that mean she should check all was well with whoever was hidden away?

She heard a sound then, a sort of thick gulp, and she thought, Someone's being sick. Now I really will have to check up.

'Darling,' she said softly to Sophie. 'Can you find your own way back to the tent? See, just down the corridor there to those doors and then turn to the left, that way. You'll see the quadrangle and the tent quite easily. Go and find Auntie Judith and ask her to get a wet flannel from one of the girls for you. I have to see everything's all right here.'

Sophie went off with alacrity, delighted to get the chance to be on her own in this exciting new place, and as the big double doors sighed and closed behind her after she had pushed her way through them, Hattie went back into the cloakroom and stood quietly, listening.

Whoever it was must have assumed the interlopers had gone, because now he was sobbing, a soft, irregular gulping sound that made Hattie's throat tighten. The sound of others' distress had always disturbed her too much. It had taken her the most part of a year of her nursing training to learn how not to cry herself when she saw someone else doing so. Now, at the end of a long hard day and with her defences down, she was startled at the strength of the old response in her, and it made her sharpen her tone and she called loudly and peremptorily, 'Who's there?'

There was an immediate silence and she could feel whoever it was holding his breath. She wasted no more time, but marched along the line of cubicles, each with its wide gap at the bottom of its door, and its narrower one at the top, pushing on them, hard.

The one at the end wasn't locked, but there was resistance to her push and she thought, He's holding it, and stopped her own pushing at once. There was the sound of a bolt being slid home and she sighed and said firmly, 'Look, I won't come in if you

don't want me to. No need to hide, though, if you're feeling ill.
It's Mrs Clements here. Remember? I'm a nurse. If you're ill I
can help you. What's the matter?'

There was silence again and that irritated her and she almost
shouted, 'Open this door at once!' and shook it. And the authority
her anger gave to her tone seemed to work, for now the bolt was
drawn back and the door opened and a boy came out.

He looks sick, she thought, very pale and sweating, and he
was shaking so much it was impossible for him to hide it, and
her anger melted at once. She set her arms across his shoulders
and half pushed, half led him to one of the benches in the middle
of the cloakroom, below the rows of hooks bearing assorted
coats and school bags, and sat him down there.

'Here, you poor old thing!' she said, slipping easily into the
briskly informal note she used to use with anxious patients. 'You
do look under the weather! What's the matter? Feeling naus-
eated?'

The boy managed to shake his head and she looked closer at
him and recognized him. 'You're Botham, aren't you?' she said
and the boy, still shaking, opened his mouth as though he wanted
to speak and then closed it, and tried to nod. But the shake in his
neck was so powerful that all that happened was a sort of
waving motion and he looked at her with a face so filled with
misery that again she could have wept for him.

'You're terrified,' she said, almost under her breath, realizing
at last what the problem was. 'All this shaking and breathless-
ness – What on earth happened to make you feel this way?'

Again the boy tried to speak, and this time managed to get a
few words out. But it was difficult and his voice was husky.

'Nothing,' he said. 'Nothing at all – got a bit of asthma –'

'Not at all,' she said strongly. 'This isn't asthma! You're not
wheezing. You're just in a panic state. Come on now, do as I tell
you. We can get you out of this. Lean forward – that's it. Now,
slow deep breaths with me. In, out, in, out; that's the way,
deeper. No, don't pant, in, out, in, out –'

It took fully five minutes to get the rhythm right and she
wished heartily that she had the statutory paper bags about her
person to use to help him rebreathe his own air, a technique that
would have shortened the process of calming him down very
considerably, but even without one at last her efforts worked

and the shaking began to ease as the boy went on breathing more slowly. She let him lean back against her arm and sat and watched him, still sitting with her arm about him. Some of the colour had come back into his thin face now and the sweating seemed to have eased. Certainly he looked far less ill than he had, and she nodded at him in some satisfaction.

'That's better,' she said. 'Now, tell me. What upset you so much? That was a panic attack, a real textbook job. You were overbreathing, the lot. What brought it on?'

He shook his head wearily. 'Nothing. It just – it happened.'

'Does it happen often?' she pressed him as he sat silent again. 'Does it?'

'No,' he said at last. 'Sorry.'

'No need to apologize.' She was brisk again. 'Better to sort out what caused it and see if we can prevent it happening again. Panics can turn into habits unless you deal with whatever triggers 'em early. Now, did someone say something to you, do something to you –'

'No!' His voice was so loud that it was almost a shout and she jumped. 'Sorry,' he said again, in a quieter tone. 'No, I mean it's nothing. I'll be all right now. Please may I go, miss?'

'How are you feeling?' She looked at him thoughtfully. His colour was now almost normal and the desperation she had seen in his eyes had gone, to be replaced by a sullenness that she recognized as habitual in him. This was how he usually looked as he went scuttling around the school with someone or other sure to spot him and shout loudly, 'Wotcha, Arse! Want something to wipe yourself with?' or something equally felicitous. Poor Arse, she thought. Born to be a victim, by the look of him. Even now, concerned for him though she undoubtedly was, she could have shaken him in frustration at the wooden way in which he sat slumped in front of her with his eyes down and no evidence of any response in him.

'Botham,' she said. 'What's your first name? Calling people by their surnames the way you all do here is dreadful. Vivian, isn't it? Yes, Vivian. All I want to do is help you. I'm not into dishing out detentions or order marks, you know. I'm not a member of the teaching staff. I'm a nurse here to look after the girls and to give you boys whatever help you might need. Now, obviously you were feeling really rotten there, and I'd like to help you avoid feeling so bad again. So, tell me what it was that alarmed you so much.'

He looked up at her now and though his eyes were still as opaque as pebbles she felt a warming to her in him, and she waited hopefully to see what he would say; but the moment passed and he stood up, shakily, but managing to hold himself to a sort of attention, and said only, 'Please, miss, I'm fine now. Can I go?'

She shook her head, sitting staring up at him in the poor light of the dusky cloakroom, and sighed. 'Oh, I suppose so. But you are silly, you know. I could be useful to you, if you'd let me. It's obvious someone or something scared the living daylights out of you, and the least you could do is tell me what it was so that I could stop it upsetting someone else, even if you'd rather deal with it alone for yourself.'

She waited, hoping his natural altruism would rise to the bait, but he made no response and she shrugged and got to her feet.

'Oh, all right then. Go. But remember I'm here if you ever want to talk to me. As I said, a tendency to panic attacks needs to be dealt with fairly firmly, fairly quickly. Otherwise it gets to be a lifelong habit. And I doubt you'd want that.'

He looked at her again with what she thought for just a moment might be a willingness to talk at last, but the moment vanished as fast as it had come and he just nodded awkwardly and turned and half scuttled, half slithered out of the cloakroom, and she followed him to see him going along the corridor towards the exit to the quadrangle as though he were being chased, feeling flat and angry. If she couldn't get the confidence of a child who was obviously feeling as dreadful as that boy had been, what use was she to anyone?

But then her commonsense pulled her out of that and she followed Arse to get back to the quadrangle herself. She'd have to leave it to the boy now. If he wanted help he'd come for it, no doubt, but meanwhile she'd keep a wary eye on him. No more. Just an eye, she told herself as she ducked in under the tent flap to find Judith and the children. He's a pathetic scrap and it'd be pleasant to be able to help him. The time would come.

On the underground, going home with Judith as the children rushed from one side of the carriage to the other to peer out of the windows at the blackness and the swooping dust-laden cables which were all there was to be seen, whooping as they went, she and Judith talked about the afternoon. Or at least Judith did. Hattie contented herself with listening and throwing an occasional hush at the children in response to the noisiest of their sallies.

'What an incredible afternoon, darling,' Judith cried above the rattle of the train wheels. 'I never *saw* such dodos, did you? The woman in the frilled georgette or whatever it was, the one you were talking to, made me think of the one in the poem, do you remember? "Why do you walk through the fields in gloves . . . O, fat white woman whom nobody loves." Not of course that she was fat, rather scrawny really, in a saggy sort of way. Stepped straight out of one of those awful black and white movies you get on the box on Saturday afternoons in the winter. And those masters, darling, *how* you must laugh. I talked to all of them, I swear. Made up my mind I would, though they're bent as corkscrews, some of 'em. That French teacher . . .' She giggled. 'What a waste of a face, that tall one, what was his name – Richard? – yes, Richard, quite fanciable, I'd have thought, but there you are. If he's one of *those* there isn't much you can do, is there? Then I talked to Wilton, when I could pin him down – what a worry guts! I can't recommend him. Too anxious for words. He'd drive you bonkers. Then there was a perfectly hateful fat man who cut me as dead as mutton, and I think he's bent too; well he must be, he was so off me, and I didn't even start with the chap in the purple scarf. Does his haircut with hedge clippers, I dare say. I know his type. Not so much a man-lover as a woman-hater, I'll bet you. As far as I could tell the only piece of real talent around is the bushy one. The one with all the hair, you know? I couldn't get round to finding out if he was married or not – you'll have to ask some leading questions, darling – but if he isn't, well, I'd make a bit of effort in that direction if I were you . . .'

Hattie hadn't been listening properly, letting the words flow over her and thinking about Genevieve and Arse in a confused sort of way, but now she stirred herself and said, 'What did you say?'

'I said the bushy one – I thought I heard someone call him Sam – he's worth a bit of an effort, I'd have thought.'

'What sort of effort?'

'Oh, sweetheart, don't be coy, for heaven's sake! One of the reasons I was so heartset on getting you to work at the Foundation was because it was all so butch there. Crawling with men! Now I've had the chance to give them a good looking over, I'd have to disqualify quite a few, but it's not all hopeless. As I said, the bushy –'

'Judith!' Hattie said wrathfully. 'If you think I'm there to manhunt, you can just think again! I'm not even remotely interested in men and –'

'So you say,' Judith said with a highly sapient air. 'But I know you better than you do. Or at least I know better what's good for you. It's high time, ducky. Oliver was, we all know, the greatest man who ever lived, he really was. But ever lived is the key word. Or words. It's been a long time since he died and really you –'

'Stop it, Judith!' The tone in Hattie's voice was dangerous, and Judith shot her a sharp little glance, no longer laughing. 'I won't have any match-making going on. Not now or ever. Do you understand? I'm just not interested.'

'Then why did you ask me to bring the girls to school, if not to look over the available scenery?' Judith opened her eyes wide. 'Darling, it never occurred to me I'd upset you if I said – well, I mean, I thought you wanted an opinion.'

'You thought nothing of the sort.' Hattie got to her feet as the train slowed ready to pull into Charing Cross station where they had to change to the Northern Line. 'I wanted to let the children see where I worked. I thought it'd help them to be, well, more comfortable with me having a job if they could see where I was when I wasn't with them. That was why I asked you to come, and that was it. Nothing more. The rest you made up. You know you did.'

'Well,' Judith was laughing again now. 'I meant it kindly. I do adore you, you know. You're such a lovely mix of up-front and stuffy, you know what I mean?'

'No,' Hattie said shortly and she shepherded the children off the train.

'Well, take it from me, you are. Someone one day is going to be very lucky to get you, though he'll have his work cut out to get rid of the stuffy bits. No, not another word. What is it, my angel? No, not a comic, not now. That man only sells evening papers, not comics. When we get home perhaps, if you're good. We'll see. Come on! They're signalling an Edgware train! Run for it —'

So Judith wasn't someone Hattie could talk to about her confusing afternoon. It would have been comforting to share her anxiety about Genevieve and her parents, and to talk about the way that poor boy Arse had behaved; but Judith, who couldn't keep her mind above the level of a very mediocre soap opera, Hattie told herself with some acid, wasn't the person to provide that comfort. All she could do was keep her mouth shut and her eyes and ears open and watch what went on at the Foundation. And maybe, somehow, intervene in a useful sort of way when necessary.

Up-front and stuffy? she thought then, as they settled the children in their seats to complete the journey to Hampstead in the stifling air of the deep tube train. What sort of a description is that, for heaven's sake?

At first he made up his mind not to answer the phone. No matter what, he wouldn't. It had to be him ringing. He knew that he was alone on Friday evenings, that she went out on Fridays and left him to do his dinner in the microwave. He'd told him that almost at the beginning of it all, pleased and excited, thinking it would be fun for them both, a chance to be really alone, and at first it had been. Now of course it was different, and he sat at the kitchen table, the steak and kidney pie from M & S congealing on his plate in front of him, and listened to the phone, feeling the shaking start again deep inside.

But then he had to answer it. It could be for her, after all, and if he didn't answer it and whoever it was told her afterwards, said, 'Where were you when I phoned on Friday? No answer,' then she'd come and go on at him about where he'd been and why he hadn't answered it, and it'd be no good saying he was in the bath or something like that, not now they'd got the new sort of phone you could take with you –

'Oh, shit, shit, shit!' he shrieked at it, and picked it up from the tablecloth and pulled up the aerial and answered it. And knew at once he'd been right the first time. Because there was only silence to hear at first.

'Well, well,' the voice said at last. 'Well, well, well, well. So

you are there. And here's me thinking you'd popped off with someone else. "He's left me-ee for another,"' the voice sang and then giggled. 'Not that you'd do that to me, would you? No, of course you wouldn't. So what's the time then? Half past eight? Gives us a couple of hours, at the very least. Make sure everything's ready. And don't forget to make certain the lights are out this time, or you know what'll happen.'

The phone clicked and died and he sat there with it held to his head, his hands sweating so hard that it was slippery, and began to cry again. There was nothing else he could do.

Ten

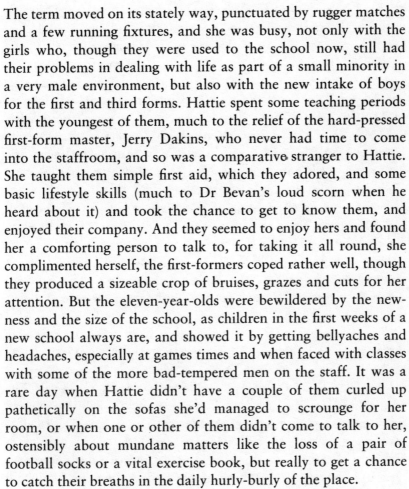

The term moved on its stately way, punctuated by rugger matches and a few running fixtures, and she was busy, not only with the girls who, though they were used to the school now, still had their problems in dealing with life as part of a small minority in a very male environment, but also with the new intake of boys for the first and third forms. Hattie spent some teaching periods with the youngest of them, much to the relief of the hard-pressed first-form master, Jerry Dakins, who never had time to come into the staffroom, and so was a comparative stranger to Hattie. She taught them simple first aid, which they adored, and some basic lifestyle skills (much to Dr Bevan's loud scorn when he heard about it) and took the chance to get to know them, and enjoyed their company. And they seemed to enjoy hers and found her a comforting person to talk to, for taking it all round, she complimented herself, the first-formers coped rather well, though they produced a sizeable crop of bruises, grazes and cuts for her attention. But the eleven-year-olds were bewildered by the new-ness and the size of the school, as children in the first weeks of a new school always are, and showed it by getting bellyaches and headaches, especially at games times and when faced with classes with some of the more bad-tempered men on the staff. It was a rare day when Hattie didn't have a couple of them curled up pathetically on the sofas she'd managed to scrounge for her room, or when one or other of them didn't come to talk to her, ostensibly about mundane matters like the loss of a pair of football socks or a vital exercise book, but really to get a chance to catch their breaths in the daily hurly-burly of the place.

It seemed to Hattie sometimes that life was more tense now

than it had been when she'd started at the Foundation two months ago. The Headmaster became an ever more remote figure, rarely available to talk to any of his staff, but spending a good deal of time in meetings outside the school.

'Fund-raising,' Edward Wilton said when she commented on it to him one afternoon. 'The talk is that unless he raises enough dosh in the next twelve months the Council'll be able to close us down.'

'Could they do that?'

'Of course they could. Why not?'

'Oh, I don't know.' She was embarrassed by her own ignorance. 'I mean, the place has been here for years, and I imagine it's got a fair amount of money. The land and buildings have to be valuable and then there are bursaries and legacies and so forth, aren't there, that people have left, old boys and so on?'

Wilton laughed at that. 'This place is mortgaged to the eyebrows! It ought to be worth a bomb of course, on this site, but it's all listed stuff, so no one wants to buy it. All anyone could do is start a different sort of school here and that's what the Council wants to do. And of course you have to remember we're under the supervision of their Education Department. We get local government grants and so on; there are some assisted places. If we don't come up to scratch all that money's withdrawn, so we need enough of our own to fill in our shortfall and still satisfy the demands of the Education Act. It's not easy. That's why the Head's so involved in fund-raising and why he keeps a watchful eye on the Council. They'd jump in so fast if they got the chance you wouldn't see their wake. They're dead opposed to decent schools like the Foundation, of course. Want to make 'em all into State ones –'

'There are decent State schools, for heaven's sake. It's not only this sort of place that –' Hattie began hotly but Edward shook his head.

'Oh, please, don't let's get political! I couldn't bear it. The atmosphere in the staffroom these days is hellish enough, everyone biting each other's heads off. Don't let us start. Just take my word for it. If the Headmaster doesn't get some extra money soon and if we don't manage to improve our exam pass rate and the science teaching in particular, then the Council'll close us down. So we've all got to push like mad. Is it any wonder the place is tense, as you say? Not that I'd noticed particularly, I must say, much too busy, of course. Not like you, hardly any teaching to do, just those girls to fuss over.'

With which acid and uncharacteristically unpleasant shot he went and she sat on in the staffroom alone, irritated and upset.

The quiet time she was enjoying at the moment was far from usual; she'd started a series of regular sessions for the girls on living skills, which included dealing with all sorts of education material the girls never got from anyone else, like the workings of their own bodies and the various ways there were of dealing with relationships, and that in addition to her usual activities filled her day as full as any master's. But she couldn't argue with Wilton. As he had said, it was bad enough that everyone else was so tense without her adding to the pressure.

She had pressures of her own, anyway, worries that would not go away. She had not forgotten the episode with Arse and made sure to keep an eye on him, but there was nothing to see and that in itself concerned her. He slipped around the school in his usual quiet fashion and showed no signs of ever being ready to talk to her, though she would greet him with cheerful smiles whenever she could (to which he never responded, being careful never to make any eye contact with her) and no one in the staffroom ever said anything about him. And that was significant, because they talked endlessly about the boys and their behaviour. However much the boys might gossip about their masters – and she imagined they did – it was as nothing to the way the men talked about the boys. But though she listened with sharpened awareness, no one ever seemed to add anything at all out of place about Arse. She hated the way she found herself listening for sexual innuendo in their conversation, but it couldn't be helped. Her doubts had been alerted, especially now, about Arse, and it wasn't possible for her to quell them.

She worried, too, about Genevieve. The girl dodged her whenever she could, either cutting Hattie's sessions altogether, or sitting silently and uncooperatively well at the back of the room, and Hattie didn't push herself at her any more than she did at Arse. But she noticed all the same; noticed her skin get both downier and more translucent, and noticed her clothes get more voluminous and disguising – and it was easier for Genevieve to increase their enveloping effect as the weather sharpened – and she fretted over her. Soon something more definite would have to be done. However alarming, indeed intimidating, her father might be, the fact was that Genevieve was getting thinner and thinner, and no one but Hattie seemed to know or care, she sometimes thought. But still she said nothing. Until the girl was willing to give Hattie her confidence, there was nothing she could do. So she watched and waited for the chance to approach Genevieve again. The time would come; it would have to. And it would prove to have been well worth waiting for when it came, of that Hattie convinced herself. Thinking that way at least helped her to feel less guilty about her inaction.

Late in October, almost accidentally, she accepted dinner from Sam Chanter. It was just after half-term, and she was alone at home. This year it had worked out that the school Sophie and Jessica and Judith's children attended had their half-term break the week after the one at the Foundation, and Hattie had been in a great lather of anxiety over that and how she'd manage. Judith, however, had solved the dilemma in her usual scatty fashion by accepting the offer of a visit to a villa in Northern France owned by a friend of hers.

'We're driving there, darling, taking the ferry, three cars and hordes of mums and children, such bliss – Peter says he'd die rather than come. I wish you could, but I know it's not on, what with your job, so let me take the girls. They'll adore it and Jenny and Petra'll have no fun unless they're there to play with. So it's all settled. You can have a blissful week painting your toenails after work and having long, long baths . . .'

And to Hattie's gratitude she said nothing at all about having the time to go out with someone. She'd been very circumspect ever since that journey on the tube, and had said nothing at all about a new man for Hattie, a piece of self-control on Judith's part for which Hattie gave her full credit. And perhaps it was that which diminished her guard.

Whatever it was, on the Monday evening she was actually loitering on her way out of school, instead of rushing off to get home in time for the girls as she usually did, and Sam Chanter caught up with her as she stood beside a patch of late dahlias in a protected corner of the quadrangle, revelling in the way their rich rubies and crimsons, golds and purples splashed against the stone walls.

'I'm used to seeing you with go-faster lines, legging it for the tube,' he said. 'So, what can ail thee, lady-at-arms, alone and palely loitering? That's the only bit of poetry I can ever remember. How kind of you to give me the chance to misquote it at you.'

She laughed. 'It is a luxury to take my time, I do admit. My children are away on holiday with a friend. Gone to France.'

'Lucky them. And the weather's good, too.'

'Mmm,' she grinned. 'I read the French weather forecast before the English one. It's lovely for them. I miss them though.' She reddened then. 'I'm sorry. I shouldn't have –'

'Why not? You're allowed to be a person with feelings, you know, even here at the Foundation. Allowed to have children you miss.'

'I don't want to turn into one of those people who do nothing but talk about their home lives and problems all the time.'

Sam Chanter laughed. 'Like Steenman. We all know about his old mother. She has these attacks every year or so. We get used to listening to him whingeing on and on about her.'

'I wasn't meaning to criticize him –'

'I was. So, clearly, tonight's the one we can have dinner. Since neither of us is in a hurry. There's a concert at the Barbican you might like, and there's a restaurant there that isn't marvellous, but it isn't that bad either.'

'Oh!' She blinked. 'I don't know much about music . . .' she said, knowing it to be an absurd response, and he greeted it with the dismissal it deserved.

'Gershwin you don't have to know about. Just have to listen. Come along. I dare say I'll be able to get another ticket somewhere in the house, and then we can do a swop with whoever turns up to sit next to one or other of us.' And she took so long trying to think of something to say to refuse him that wouldn't seem rude that they were halfway to the underground before she could come up with even the lamest of excuses. By which time the moment seemed to have passed.

She enjoyed the concert greatly, and the food was, she told Chanter, marvellous. 'If only because I didn't have to think about it. It was just there and I ate it. I'd forgotten just how agreeable that can be.'

'I know precisely what you mean, and I hope we can do it

again. No, don't look like that. You can pay for yourself if you've got a hang-up about that. I just like pleasant company that talks enough but doesn't overwhelm me with chatter. You're an excellent companion for such an evening as this, and I hope we can do it again.' And he managed not to sound patronizing, though his words could have been so construed.

He said goodnight at the tube station with no unseemly fuss about seeing her home and just nodded a goodbye and that helped her relax and be comfortable the next time he suggested they go out, this time to the theatre, and made it possible to accept him.

After the half-term respite, when the children came back, she got into the habit of getting a babysitter in on one night a week; not Judith (or her Inge) who would have been altogether much too interested in where she was going, why, and above all, with whom, and indeed she didn't get round to telling Judith she was going out with Sam Chanter at all. She just murmured vaguely to her about the school's Christmas play and how she'd have to be around for rehearsals, and hoped that would cover her absence from home. It was none of Judith's business anyway – and besides, she was bound to jump to foolish conclusions. And there were none to jump to.

Which was quite true. She learned a little more about him on those evenings; that he too had been widowed, soon after marriage, and preferred not to talk about it, so she didn't; and that he had no intention of staying at the Foundation any longer than he had to.

'Once the book's done and I can get a home for it, and a commission for the next,' he said cheerfully, 'I'll be off to my garret to live the life of a creative type. Not that I am, particularly, but I fancy the idea.'

'You must be creative if you're writing a book. Unless it's a textbook you're doing.'

'I wish it were,' he said. 'You can earn a fortune from textbooks. Once they're on the list for a set syllabus you're laughing. No, I'm not writing a textbook.'

She said nothing, just looking at him expectantly, and he smiled at that.

'Well done you. Any other woman would ask questions.'

'You'll tell me if you want to. You won't if you don't. Why waste breath?'

'Admirable commonsense. All right. It's a thriller.' He sounded a little defensive.

'Fun,' she said. 'What sort? Alastair MacLean? Freddy Forsyth?'

'You read thrillers?'

'I read everything and anything. It's the only thing that kept me sane these past months.'

'Yes,' he said, and looked over her shoulder, into the past. 'I did that too.' There was a little silence and then he said, 'No, it's not a modern sort at all. More like – well, nearer Jules Verne.'

She was enchanted. 'I adored those stories! They were marvellous. Lots of physics and chemistry, of course – is that what you mean? Science-fiction-type thrillers?'

'Perceptive of you. Yes. Mine obviously deals with biology because it's what I know about.'

'Tell me about it.'

'I don't think so. I'll never write it if I talk too much about it. Better to put the words down on the page.'

'I suppose so. When do you work on it?'

'When I can. Evenings. Weekends. Early mornings.'

'You still sleep badly?' It was as though she knew what his life had been like; their shared experience of widowhood sat easily between them, undiscussed but recognized.

'Sometimes. Not as often as I used to.'

'I feel a little wicked now,' she said then. 'You're wasting an evening with me when you could be writing.'

'Don't be so arrogant!' There was amusement in his tone which took any sting out of the word. 'I need a night out from time to time. I'd rot if I didn't. It's more agreeable with good company than on my own. Not that I couldn't cope on my own, of course.'

'Of course,' she said gravely, and he laughed.

'Enough about me. Your turn.'

'I'm not writing a book,' she said. 'Nor likely to.'

'Glad to hear it. There're already too many competitors. What do you want to do eventually?'

'Do? What I am, I suppose.'

'What, even after your children have left home? They won't be around much longer. How old are you?'

'Thirty-six.'

'Then in another dozen years or so you'll still be under fifty. Will you still be paddling around at the Foundation?'

She reddened. 'I'm hardly paddling now.'

'Oh, of course you are. You're certainly not in deep water, striking out to keep yourself afloat. You're capable of much more than you do there.'

'Oh, I see what – Thank you. Well, yes, I suppose I am finding the job easy enough. It just happens to suit me at present and –'

He brushed that aside. 'So what do you want to do when your kids are at full-time school and old enough not to need you there to mop up tears and so forth when they come home? You can be back at full-time work in another four or five years, you know.'

'I haven't thought about that.'

'You should.'

'Why?'

'You'll rot if you don't.' He got to his feet and she perforce stood too. They'd finished their meal and he was holding the slip of the bill, to be paid for at the door on the way out. 'I've seen it happen to too many people.'

'I'll take that risk,' she said sharply. 'I'm staying around at home at the times my daughters are there until they're well past their teens. They might need me. Things happen to kids left alone too much.'

They had reached the cashier and she took the bill from his hand and looked at it and began to dig into her bag for her share. It had been accepted by them both that their nights out were Dutch treats; it was much easier that way.

He was silent as they came out of the restaurant into the chill of the November night, and then he stopped on the pavement and looked at her. His face was an odd colour in the sodium light thrown by the lamp over her head and she looked at him and thought, I wonder how I look to him? And then pushed the thought away in embarrassment. That was the sort of thing Judith would be worried about. She should know better.

'You could be right,' he said. 'To stay at home when they're in their teens, I mean. If poor old Matterson's mum hadn't been out all the time, maybe he'd . . . Well, your two have each other, of course. And you'd never just leave them alone even if you couldn't be there, would you?'

'Of course not.' She started to walk and he fell into step beside her. 'Anyway, it doesn't arise. I'm not going to do it. Who's Matterson?'

'Mmm?'

'People have said his name a lot, and they always sound so odd when they do. Who is he?'

'Was,' Sam said. 'A sixth-former, last year. Bright boy. Marvellous watercolourist. Extraordinarily gifted.'

'Sixth form. Sixteen? And dead?'

'Yes. He was going to do four As, poor bastard.'

'What happened?'

'It's a nasty story.' He seemed curiously unwilling to go on and she was suddenly irritated by that. It was as though he were trying to protect her, and that was not to be tolerated.

'I'm not a child, you know,' she said tartly. 'Not some sort of fragile blossom who can't be told nasties. I was at Old East for enough years, in Casualty and Theatres much of the time. I don't shock easy.'

'He died by accident, they said at the inquest. Strangled by a ligature while seeking sexual gratification. There are tricks males can use to give themselves extra-powerful – sexual arousal, and sometimes fulfilment. They have almost to hang themselves for it to happen . . .'

'I see,' she said steadily. He'd clearly found it difficult to talk about and she gave him full credit for being as direct as he had. 'I seem to have heard of such things.'

'Have you?' He said it almost savagely. 'Well, lucky old you. Most people, thank heaven, never find out about it. Let alone how to do it. It's one of those things experienced men have to teach the less experienced.'

'Yes,' she said and her steps slowed a little. 'Yes, I see that. You think this boy – that someone else . . .?'

'I doubt he picked up the knowledge from a book,' he said, and his voice was still hard. 'This is information passed on by word of mouth and demonstration, believe me. I'd never heard about it until Matterson died, for Christ's sake, yet he was sixteen.'

'You think someone showed him how?'

'I think someone shared it with him and then left him to it, frankly. The evidence at the inquest was a bit – well, I wasn't satisfied. They were and they left it at accidental death, but I still think there was more to it than that. If the kid had had another person in the house with him, it wouldn't have happened. Not in his own home, would it? It wouldn't have been so easy for someone to walk away and leave him.'

Now she stopped walking and turned to look at him. 'You think that Matterson was killed, then?'

'Oh, not deliberately. It wasn't someone doing him in to please himself. We're not talking deliberate murder. But I do think someone was around when it happened and could only be there because the kid was on his own. And when it went wrong, whoever it was left him to it. Or maybe got a kick out of seeing it go wrong? I've heard of men like that.'

'And he was a Foundation boy,' she said. 'Like Arse.'

'What about Arse? Poor little sod, what's he got to do with –'

She started walking again. 'Oh, it's silly, I suppose, but I just – well, I'm concerned about him. He's such a little misery. And then, well, at that autumn fair thing . . .'

She told him then what had happened, and it was comforting to be able to share it. He listened and said nothing until she'd finished and then nodded.

'You think someone at the school could be getting at young Arse? Dammit, we ought to call him by his name.'

'I know.' She felt herself redden in the darkness. 'It's just that no one else does.'

'I know. And it suits the poor little bugger. I suppose you could be right and there was someone at the school that afternoon who scared him. Or it could just be that he had a panic attack.'

'I think there was a reason. I don't know why – I know they can happen out of the blue, but it wasn't quite like that. Someone had scared him badly.'

'You think it's one of the staff.' It wasn't a question, and she took a deep breath and nodded.

'I wondered about Tully,' she said, amazed at her own lo-quacity. Why tell this man all this? Because he's the first agreeable person you've met for ages, a secret voice inside her answered. She ignored the private conversation and went on and told Sam about her first lunchtime at the school and again he listened in silence till she'd finished.

'I doubt it's Tully,' he said at length. 'I doubt it very much.'

'Why? It could be! To behave like that —'

'Precisely. If he were up to some sort of secret villainy he wouldn't be so outrageous in public. Tully does what he does for effect. He doesn't ever want to hide anything. He probably saw you that day and kissed the boy expressly to shock you.'

She stared at him blankly in the dim light, and then was furious. Not with him, but with herself for being so foolish. He had to be right, of course he did. She'd been naïve in the extreme.

He seemed to know her thoughts because he started to walk again, and said cheerfully, not looking at her, 'Don't feel bad. It's easier for me to understand the man. I've known him for years, heaven help me. You've only been in the place a matter of weeks.'

'However short a time it is, I should have thought it through more sensibly. I feel stupid.'

'Well, you're not. But I wouldn't think too much about Arse. I'll keep an eye on him too. He's in one of my sets. Will that make you feel a bit better?'

'Yes,' she said. 'I think it will.'

And it did.

Eleven

Dilly sat at the back of the gym, leaning against the wall bars as comfortably as she could, watching them with as clear an expression of scorn on her face as she dared put there, wanting everyone to know that she had no desire to be involved, that she was there only because Mr Staveley had been so unpleasant about the people who hadn't volunteered to be a part of the whole stupid nonsense from the beginning and most of all because Freddy had insisted.

'It'll make a nice little film,' he'd said in what Dilly regarded as his most oily of patronizing tones. 'Young people working together for the good of their school and for charity. Could get it networked with a bit of luck and a following wind.'

'Bollocks,' Dilly had said as nastily as she dared. 'You're always saying that about those poxy little films you do and none of 'em ever get on network TV except at the sort of times no one worth fourpence is watching. Nine-thirty on a Sunday morning, that last one was! Big deal.'

He had lost his temper then, so spectacularly that he had surprised himself as well as Dilly, and had played the only card he had that could make her do as he wanted, albeit sulkily.

She had sat there at the kitchen table at home as he'd roared and shouted, marching up and down and generally making what she told herself with some glee was a complete prat of himself, and then had told her he'd give her no pocket money for the rest of the term until she not only apologized but agreed to be a part of the show he was to video; and the thought of being completely without a cash source had pulled her furiously into line. There was little else she could do, anyway. Staveley was being perfectly hateful about it all, almost as bad as Freddy.

'This bloody play-acting's the only alternative you've got to the Cadet force,' he told the sixth with some smugness. 'Headmaster's rules. Some of you can do both, but you can be very sure all of you are going to do at least one. Which means that all you girls have to be in the play. So, there it is. Like it or lump it, love it or hate it, do it you will.'

That man Collop, she thought, staring at the master who was sitting in lone splendour at a table set in the middle of the hall facing the stage, that man Collop's a bastard. Her face was set in a more venomous scowl than ever as she thought it. He ought to be walled up in a room without any doors or windows, and no lavatory; she let her mind slide away into devising horrible experiences for Collop, to whom she'd taken a strong dislike. He taught one of her A-level courses and though she was one of the better students and drew little of his fire, she hated his use of sarcasm as a controlling mechanism for some of the other people in her set. Poor old Arse in particular got more than his fair share of attacks with that clever tongue which produced words that sounded so elegant in the silky tones he used, but which made Arse's neck redden painfully. Collop's about as yukky as they come. And she looked to where Arse was sitting hunched against the wall bars, much as she was herself, and considered briefly the possibility of going across to join him. And then dismissed the notion. She was too much of a misery herself right now to seek company, and he didn't look miserable. Later perhaps, when they'd escaped from this damned gym and were free, she'd suggest a coffee down at the trailer that was parked near the market. That could be agreeable. Arse hadn't a lot to say for himself, but what he did say matched her own opinions very comfortably.

She saw Mrs Clements then and let her shoulders relax a little. Dilly liked Mrs Clements; you could talk to her like a person, because that was how she talked to you. There was none of that awful business of putting on a special voice just because you were a pupil and she was staff. Most of the men here, Dilly thought, considered all the pupils to be children when there were in fact very few of them, only the first forms. After that, they were all adults really, locked into the ridiculous world called school. University would be different, of course. Lectures that you could cut if you chose to, setting your own work schedule . . .

She let her mind drift off into a beatific set of images of university life in which she, Dilly, was surrounded by congenial people who were as witty as she was herself, and no one was ever bored or broke or lonely –

'Could we have the girls over here, please.' Dilly blinked and tried to hunch herself into a smaller bundle as Collop's voice lifted effortlessly to fill the big gym and then, realizing how silly that was, got sulkily to her feet. On the far side she saw several of the others moving forward with alacrity, especially Gillian, and that made her angrier than ever. Stupid bitch'd probably get a decent part, leaving the rest of them to be boring old maids or ladies-in-waiting or something, she thought, and then was aware of her own illogicality, for she didn't want a part in the poxy play, did she? All of which left her feeling scratchier than ever.

'We're not going to cast according to gender,' Martin Collop said, as the girls came up in a straggle. 'If we did that, two of the best parts in the play'd be lost to you lot. Anyway, I've always thought Katherina should be played by a boy. It's written that way. But Bianca's up for grabs if anyone's interested in trying out. For the rest of you, ladies-in-waiting, though one of you can play the Widow, if you're up to it. Otherwise a boy'll do it perfectly well.'

'What about the Hostess?' Dilly said sharply, not sure why she bothered; she didn't want a part, of course she didn't. 'She's got two or three lines, hasn't she?'

Collop looked at her and was clearly annoyed at her display of knowledge. 'We're not playing the first two scenes, the Christopher Sly stuff. Hardly anyone ever does. Want to try for the Widow? I imagine you're after a part.'

She lifted her chin at him, ignoring the implied question. 'Why not Bianca? I could read that all right.'

'You're not the type,' he said. 'She's pretty. An empty-headed doll, but pretty.' He swivelled his gaze at Gillian. 'You can read for Bianca, if you like. You look well enough.'

Gillian dimpled delightedly. 'Yes, please,' she said. 'It'd be great fun.'

'No doubt you think so,' Collop said. 'But it's damned hard work and no fun, as you call it, at all. And you're not cast yet. I'll try several of you. Come on.'

He took them up to the stage and, as the rest of the boys

stopped their private conversations at last, put each one of them in turns through the lines, and Harry Forster, who had been sitting on the floor with his back to the stage mounting, turned on his haunches and stared up at them with his face alight with laughter. Gillian looked down at him and stumbled, and Harry laughed even more, though still silently.

'Good sister, wrong me not,' fluted Gillian, and tossed her long blonde hair, untied now that classes were over, so that it floated over each shoulder, 'nor wrong yourself, To make a bondmaid and a slave of me —'

'You might do better if she did,' Collop said, interrupting her with no attempt to be civil. 'An actress she'll never make you. Here, you, at the back there — what's your name? You have a go.'

Genevieve moved forward, uneasily, but there was an elegance about her movements and for the first time Collop looked grudg-ingly approving. 'You could play it, got that fragile look. Let me hear you . . .'

'Yea, all my raiment, to my petticoat, Or what you will com-mand me will I do, So well I know my duty to my elders —' read Genevieve, and her voice had an agreeable husky tone to it that made Collop nod even more approvingly.

'Next to Robert Carter, you'll look well enough,' he said. 'Learn the lines by the end of the week or I'll raise hell.'

'I'm not sure . . .' Genevieve began and Collop, who had turned away, looked back at her and snapped, 'What did you say?'

'I've got a lot to do,' Genevieve muttered, her voice huskier than ever. 'And my father mightn't like me to —'

'To hell with your father!' Collop said. 'He's not running this Drama group. I am. Why are you here if you didn't want to work on the play?'

'Because they were told they had to be.' It was Hattie, moving closer to the table now. She'd been on the far side of the gym, talking softly to some of the younger boys, but now she was watchful, and Dilly, who'd been sunk in her own anger, became a little more aware of what was happening. 'If it isn't possible for Genevieve to fit in the rehearsal time, then there it is, she can't. She might manage the rehearsals for attendants and servants and so forth, but if you want her for a principal and she can't spare the time —'

'I could ask him,' Genevieve said then, looking at Hattie with pebble-hard eyes. 'Dad. He might say it's all right.'

'How kind of him!' Collop said and stared at her for a long moment in a way that was deeply insulting, and Genevieve flushed.

'It's a matter of her work load more than anything else,' Hattie said, moving a little closer to Genevieve. 'Right, Genevieve? That would be what might worry your father.'

'Yes,' murmured Genevieve, still staring at Collop. 'Yes, it would be. But I could ask.'

'Then you're worrying over nothing, aren't you, Mrs Clements?' Collop said and turned away. 'Let me know by tomorrow first thing. Otherwise, I'll take it you're my Bianca. Forster! Come here. You're trying for Petruchio. Let me hear you.'

There could be no question but that he'd be cast, Dilly thought, listening to that rich honey-gold voice full of laughter curl itself through the wall bars and into every corner of the big gym. And it'll be interesting to see a black Petruchio with Carter being so fair and buxom . . . She found herself thinking more about the play and the way the various characters interacted and wanted suddenly to be playing Katherina. It could be fun with Harry Forster for her Petruchio. Only without the last scene where the stupid bitch chickened out and let the men win. Oh, but she'd show them how to do it if she got the chance . . . and she slid into another reverie about how she'd rewrite *The Taming of the Shrew* once she got to university and how she'd do a pastiche version ending the way it ought to with Katherina a right-on woman, not climbing down but winning triumphantly, and stupid Bianca finishing up as a dreary drab –

Which isn't fair, she thought then, watching Genevieve as she moved across the polished floor towards the corner where the girls had left their coats and bags. Bianca needs Katherina's help. She's so bloody submissive she makes you sick; in a proper version of *The Taming of the Shrew*, Bianca would end up as assertive as Katherina. Less powerful, but at least a proper woman standing up for herself.

'All right then,' Collop was saying. 'The rest of you, servants, ladies-in-waiting and whatever. I'll plot the scenes you're in and pin a schedule to the Drama board. Make sure you get the dates down in your diaries. I do nasty things to people who turn up late for rehearsals, let alone those who miss 'em. That means you too, madam.' He was staring at Dilly. 'If you could bear to stop dreaming of some pimply youth and concentrate on the matter in hand I'd be grateful.'

Dilly went scarlet. 'I was thinking about the play, actually,' she said in a tight voice. 'It's a stupid play and needs rewriting.'

Collop, who had started to make notes in the big notebook in front of him, looked up and stared again. 'You – Now, listen, everyone! We have one of your sixth-form ladies who thinks she can rewrite Shakespeare! Before breakfast, I imagine? It shouldn't take you long, not with your superior knowledge and intellect.'

Dilly didn't care. 'I didn't say I'd rewrite it,' she snapped. 'Just that it should be. It's stupid. It ends all wrong.'

Harry Forster had got to his feet and come to lean against the side of the stage where Dilly was standing. 'A hit, a very palpable hit!' he murmured. 'My Lord?' and looked owlishly at Collop.

'Oh, I see! You don't like the fact that at the end Katherina is put in the place where she belongs and chooses to knuckle under to Petruchio?' Collop said, and slowly the boys who had been scattered about the big hall again returned to cluster behind him. There were smirks on some faces; they knew when a row was brewing, and when it was safe to enjoy it. This one ought to be good; one of the girls and old Collop? Not to be missed.

'It's not the place she belongs in! It's the place she's been put in by men,' Dilly said. 'It's only because men think women are here on this earth just to – just to service them that the world's such a rotten place with wars and cruelty and –'

'Aha!' Collop's brows were up as he sat perched on the edge of his table with his arms folded. 'So it's all Shakespeare's fault that there are wars, is it? And cruelty? It hasn't occurred to you that the man was a brilliant writer who saw the world as it really was and set it down on paper? Hmm? Or are you so bemused by all this liberation crap – liberation nonsense – that you think Shakespeare was really the Virgin Queen and the more virgins there are the better?'

'You're cheating!' Dilly flared and leaped down from the stage. 'I'm making a real point and you're just – you're just –' She shook her head and stopped. Tears were very near the surface now and she was more grateful than she could ever have imagined being when Hattie took her by the elbow and said loudly, 'Mr Collop, I really think we'd better get on. All this banter is no doubt fun, but my girls need to get away soon, so if we could just get on –'

'Ah, I see! Your *girls* have to be protected against us tough men? Poor little girls! I can't imagine how the Foundation ever got on before we were honoured by their presence in our sixth form.'

There was a little titter and Dilly, her eyes now very bright with tears, concentrated all her efforts on preventing them spilling over. She wouldn't give him the pleasure, she wouldn't, she wouldn't –

'I certainly can't, either.' It was Harry Forster who spoke. He had followed her down from the stage, and put one arm across her shoulders. 'It's my firm opinion that they've improved the place no end. Three cheers for a little feminine influence, say I. Hip, hip –' And because the boys nearly always did what Harry wanted of them, a ragged cheer of sorts went up and it was Collop who reddened this time, and Dilly felt her tears slide back beneath her lids as gratitude to Harry almost choked her.

'I really think we must be hurrying up now,' Hattie said with a strongly practical note in her voice. 'Genevieve, perhaps you'd like to fetch Dilly's things for her as you're going. And if you don't mind, I'd like a word with all of you in my room as you leave. Bonnie, Bridget . . .' Almost like a sheepdog she worried them all into a group and on towards the door, and Collop looked after her and called with a savage note in his voice, 'Am I able to count on the return of your charges to future rehearsals, Mrs Clements? If they're not going to be reliable because of their emotional problems, better to tell me now than later. Then I can do as I always have done most successfully in the past and cast entirely from the Foundation boys.'

'They'll be here,' Hattie said grimly. 'Right, girls?'

Dilly looked over her shoulder at him and called loudly, 'Definitely! And I'll try for the part of the Widow. She at least does try to stand up for herself a bit.'

'Yes. A tiresome character,' Collop said and turned away. 'Well, I'll think about it. Next Tuesday then. Don't be late.'

When Hattie had seen the girls off the school premises, after assuring them all she'd do her best to be at as many rehearsals as she could to make sure they had a defender if they ever needed one, she went straight back to the gym, marching there with as much noise as she could get her heels to make, slapping them down on the stone corridors to give herself the courage she needed to top up her anger. How dare he treat her girls so? She wouldn't allow it, not now or ever; and she went straight into the gym, her chin up and her face set.

Collop was still sitting at the main desk, working his way through the casting of Gremio and Hortensio, and the boys were, as before, scattered about the available space, one or two of them even trying to smoke a cigarette without being noticed by the absorbed master, blowing the smoke out through the open doors.

She walked past them for once, ignoring their behaviour even though she was determined to stop people smoking wherever she could, and stopped directly in front of Collop.

'I think you owe my girls an apology,' she said in a low voice. 'There was no need to be so very nasty, was there? It's hard enough for them being part of a very small minority here –'

'And a fairly feeble minority at that,' murmured Collop, not lifting his head from the notes he'd been making. 'Or its representative is.'

'What did you say?' she said more loudly because she was even angrier now. '*What* did you say?'

'Look, Mrs Clements.' He put down his pen and looked up at her with an air of bored weariness that was exceedingly insulting. 'The only reason those wretched females are here is because the Headmaster needs them to maintain his position in the school and the school's position in this borough. The only reason you're here is because they are. The only reason I'm tolerating them and you here in my Drama group is because I've been told to. But I don't have to like it. This was a civilized place when it was what it was founded to be: a male enclave. I find it less so since this obeisance to some of the more tiresome notions of our times.'

A soft movement came from the boys and Hattie recognized it for laughter, and knew how choked Dilly must have felt only a few minutes earlier. He had a way of making his words, even those that could have been construed as civilized enough, sound like the most offensive of insults. He shouldn't be allowed to speak to me so, she thought furiously. He shouldn't; but all she could say was, 'Surely this is hardly the place for this sort of discussion –'

'I didn't initiate it,' he said and bent his head again. 'Better if you keep out of this group, Mrs Clements. I had thought at first when you arrived in our common room you and your girls might be an asset to the place. That was the triumph of foolish hope over wiser experience. Now I know the whole scheme can't be anything but a crashing bore. That's our bad luck, I suppose. But at least leave us in peace.'

'I'll be at every possible rehearsal I can,' she said, keeping her voice as low as she could, and almost hearing the ice crackle in it. 'Because the girls have to be. And I'm here to take care of them. And if someone pushes you off the stage and breaks your neck, don't expect me to offer any first aid. I'll be too busy cheering you on your way to perdition.'

Twelve

'I wanted to thank you –' Arse said and then shook his head. 'Not exactly that. I mean usually it's me he has a go at. With you there, it's not so bad.'

Dilly looked up at him and nodded. 'I know.'

'Anyone sitting here?'

'No.' Dilly slid along the bench a little. 'You can, if you like. What are you having?'

'The vegetarian,' Arse said. 'I usually do.'

'Me too. Not because I'm mad about animals, mind you. I get through a lot of hamburgers. There's a lot of sentimental rubbish talked about animals. Like that fool Gillian. It's just that I loathe the meat here so much. It's like eating dishcloths.'

'Is it?' Arse said and began to pick at his Spanish rice. It was coloured a fiery yellow and didn't look very appetizing. Dilly's half-eaten plateful had been pushed to one side; now she was eating an apple, though with small signs of any enjoyment.

'Someone ought to poison that bastard,' she said and Arse looked sideways at her and his lips curled.

'Don't think I haven't thought of it. I thought ground glass might do. Easy to get hold of. Just grind it up in the woodwork room. But it's not all that good. Doesn't always work.'

She looked at him, her eyes wide over her apple. 'Are you serious?'

'Why not? It's always useful to find out things. I do it a lot. Get an idea and then try to see if it'll work.'

'Christ,' she said and then laughed. 'Well, if he keels over good and dead one afternoon, I won't remember a word of this.'

'Thanks,' he said and went on eating his rice, pushing it neatly into his mouth and swallowing it almost immediately, seeming neither to taste nor chew it.

There was a silence between them as the big canteen increased its roaring and clattering because the second lunch sitting of the first two forms came thundering in to push the first sitting out of the way. Here at the sixth-form table, one of the privileges the older people of the Foundation were permitted, there was ample room and a pretence of peace; most of the others had gone, though there were a few people from the Geography set at the far end of the table, their heads down over some project they were involved with, and Dilly stretched and turned her head to look at the staff tables set behind a row of bamboo screens on which plastic ivy was entwined, and laughed.

'Just think, if ground glass really did work, you could fill all their water jugs with it and kill off the lot.'

'I don't think you can put it in water,' Arse said seriously. 'I think you'd be able to see it. There's a refraction problem or something. I haven't tried. Anyway, I wouldn't want to kill all of them. Just Collop. Probably. Maybe later . . .' His voice drifted away and he looked at Dilly and smiled and she thought, He's really quite nice. His face changed completely when he smiled, losing the pinched, empty look it usually had, and his eyes were a rich green colour she rather liked. He was a bit short for her, by an inch or so, but so what? She'd never been the sort of person to choose her friends by their looks. It could be pleasant to make a friend of this chap. She'd kept her distance from the girls, apart from Bonnie perhaps, who was a cheerful soul and good enough company here at school, but even she Dilly didn't see out of school. It was a bit lonely sometimes, even though most of her time was taken up with her course work and revision of some of the earlier stuff; it could be good to have someone to go around with, see a flick maybe, go to a concert.

'I'll have to think of something else,' Arse said, and pushed his plate away. It was quite empty. 'I dare say something'll come to mind.'

'I'd be careful who I said things like that to. Someone might take you seriously?'

'Who says I'm not? Anyway, I'm all right with you.'

'How do you know?'

He looked at her and smiled again. 'I am, aren't I? You wouldn't do anything to stop me.'

She was suddenly uncomfortable. 'Look, what you do is none of my business. But you'd make it bloody hard if you'd told me all sorts of stuff and then some sort of accident happened.'

'There aren't any accidents,' Arse said. 'Only things people do. Everything that happens to you is partly your own fault. You make it happen. No accidents.'

'Oh, don't be daft! How can it not be an accident if you happen to be on a train and it crashes and breaks your legs? That can't be your fault.'

'Who pushed you on the train? If you get on a train or a bus or anything you take a chance that it won't crash. If it does, and you're hurt, it's because you made the wrong choice.'

She shook her head. 'That sounds awful. It's like –' She stopped and tried to get the thoughts clear in her head. 'It's like you can't ever stop being careful. You have to think all the time about what you do and who you do it with.'

'That's right,' Arse said and got to his feet. 'I'm going for a Coke. Do you want one?'

She hesitated and then nodded. 'All right. Where?'

'By the market. Are you sure you've made the right choice?' Again he produced that disarming smile. 'I mean, if a motorbike runs off the road and ploughs into us while we're there in the street, it'll be because you were there to be ploughed into. You're choosing now. Taking a chance there's a motorbike on its way.'

'Yeah? Well, I'll take it. The odds are ridiculous anyway.'

'Tell 'em that when you wake up in Old East.' And this time he actually laughed, and Dilly got to her feet and followed him out of the canteen. She hadn't felt as relaxed with someone for ages, she thought. Absolutely ages.

'You really must stop sulking at me, Mrs Clements,' Martin Collop said, and stood back to let her into the staffroom from which he'd been just about to emerge. But he turned back to follow her into the room. 'That really was the most frozen of stares you gave me then!'

'It was meant to be. And I don't sulk. I just choose the people I want to speak to very carefully.'

'And you don't want to speak to me. All because I got irritated with your dear little girls. But really, you know, the first day, casting a new play – it's always a pretty fraught affair. I apologize. There! Does that help? I hope so. I really can't do with having you sitting at every rehearsal glowering at me like a *tricoteuse*. What do you think I'm going to do to your little ewe lambs? Rape 'em?'

Hattie looked at him and lifted her brows. 'I don't think about you at all. I just do my job here, looking after the ewe lambs.'

'Well, they're safe enough with me, I do assure you. We've been rehearsing for weeks now, almost at the end, and I haven't laid a finger on one of 'em.'

'You've used your tongue to good effect,' she said with a certain tartness of her own.

'Ye gods, what do you expect? Constant If-you-pleases and Do-you-minds? There isn't time for that. They get no worse than the boys do, and I thought you women were all into equality these days.'

She opened her mouth to lash back at him and then closed it. It would be a waste of time and very boring, much as the past few weeks had been. Afternoon following afternoon had been spent in the cold but stuffy gym as *The Taming of the Shrew* took some sort of form, and although it was a play she'd always liked, now it irritated her beyond measure; she'd come to share Dilly's view of it as having the wrong ending for modern women, but it wouldn't help to say as much to Collop. There he stood, his head on one side, smiling his patronizing oily smile; she could have hit him.

'Let's just leave it that as long as the play's in rehearsal, I'll be there to keep an eye on the girls. And not for anything else. No pleasant conversation with you to pass the time. It's bad enough I have to be there; I don't need to bore myself stupid into the bargain,' she said, and picked up the coat she'd come to fetch and marched out, leaving him staring after her with his face white with temper. She felt better; she'd managed to be very rude without even trying very hard, and it had hit home. That would be enough to keep her warm all through a long dull evening at home, after the girls had gone to bed.

'No,' Genevieve said. 'I don't want to.'

'What you want and what you'll do are two very different

things, young lady,' Gordon Barratt said, and leaned back in his chair and smiled at her. 'You might as well give in. You always have to in the end. Don't you?'

There was a long silence and then Genevieve said softly, 'No, I don't.' And sitting in her armchair on the other side of the room, her shoulders hunched, so that she was smaller, less visible, Stella felt colder still, though already it was as though her inner parts were crackling with ice. Just listening to them talk made pictures form in her mind, horrible pictures; it took all her concentration to keep her attention on the words they said so that she didn't have to look at the images.

'You will this time,' Gordon said and got to his feet. 'Do you hear me? You'll drink that chocolate and then you'll drink another cup, if I have to pour it into you with a funnel. And don't think I wouldn't.'

'Try it,' Genevieve said, still very softly. 'I'm not a little girl now, am I? It wouldn't be so easy now, would it?'

'You look like a child,' he said and there was a whip in his voice that made Genevieve redden for a moment. But it faded fast and she smiled back at him, sweet as ever.

'Yes,' she said. 'Yes, I suppose I do in some ways.' She looked at Stella then, who, caught unawares, found herself making eye contact and felt sick, flicking her eyes away, not wanting to look at her daughter, not that way at any rate.

'So, do it.' He sounded rough now, angry, and that seemed to make Genevieve even stronger.

'No,' she said. 'You can't make me. Just try it!'

'Don't think I won't,' he said. 'Stella, she's to drink it, you hear me? I won't be back till eleven, but if she hasn't had it by then, and the other one as well, believe me, I'll pour it into her. And if you try to cheat, throw it away, any of that nonsense, I'll know. I always do, don't I?'

Stella said nothing and he repeated it, a little louder. 'Don't I?'

'Yes,' Stella said, and then with a sudden spurt of animation, 'I want her to drink it even more than you do.'

'Well, then,' he said with an oddly triumphant note in his voice, and went, leaving the door open behind him so that they could see him in the hall, winding his scarf round his throat, tying the belt of his overcoat in the old-fashioned trendy way, with the buckle dangling, pulling on his gloves. Neither of them said a word.

He came back to the living room to stare at them both.

'I'll know,' he said. 'Don't forget that. I'll know!' And turned and went. And they listened to his footsteps on the crazy paving of the path and the creak of the gate and the footsteps again as he went down the road. He never took the car when he went out to his committee meetings. Stella had asked him once why not, but she'd long ago forgotten the explanation he'd given her. There'd been one but it had been pushed out of her memory, like so many other things.

'It'd be easier if you did drink it,' Stella said after a while. 'You know how he is.'

'I know better than you do,' Genevieve said. She was sitting at the table now, her revision books spread around her. She had put the radio on and it bleated softly at them. Melody Radio, where music comes first. No talk, just music. It's like us, Stella thought, and wondered what would happen if she reached out and switched it off or changed the channel. Gordon would have done that. Of course she didn't.

'All the same,' Stella said after another long pause, 'I wish you would, darling. You really are – I mean, now there are other people who are talking . . .'

'Other people?' Genevieve didn't lift her head from her books.

'That teacher, nurse, or whatever she is. At your school.'

'She doesn't matter. I'll deal with her,' Genevieve said. 'Look, I've got work to do here. Do you mind? If you chatter I can't do it.'

'You've got the radio on.'

'That helps,' Genevieve said, and turned it up louder.

'You've got to drink it. For peace and quiet.' Stella tried again, desperate now, and this time Genevieve lifted her head from her work. 'And for your health.'

'You don't really mean that,' she said.

'Of course I mean it!' Stella cried, and sat up more straightly. 'You know I worry about you, darling. You really do need to get a little more vitamins and so forth into you. It's winter. It's unhealthy to be so – well, you are rather thin –'

'It's unhealthier not to be thin,' Genevieve said, still sitting staring at her mother. 'You know that.'

'You'll never be really fat,' Stella said, hopelessly, knowing she was going to lose the argument. 'Not to be *fat* . . .'

'Bigger than I am would be unhealthy. Why don't you let me explain it, Mum? You never let me explain it.'

'Because it's all too silly!' The tears were starting in Stella now, deep inside. She could feel them gathering somewhere around the level of her bottom ribs. They'd gather into a pool and that would rise and rise, until it could climb up to her chest and then her throat and then she wouldn't be able to talk at all and it would just – She shook her head as though that would help. It didn't, of course.

'Well, if you think it's silly,' Genevieve said, turning back to her books. '*Silly* . . .' And she said no more at all however hard Stella tried to persuade her. And after an hour Stella gave up and took the cup and drank the cold chocolate herself. He could always tell if the cup had just been emptied into the sink rather than drunk from. Then she went into the kitchen and made another cup because he always knew how much milk there was and how much cocoa powder, and drank that too, though they both made her retch. But it was worth it. Better than the row there'd be if he came in and thought they'd not done as he said.

Genevieve was already in her room when Stella went upstairs at half past ten. 'I looked after it all, Jenny,' she said, standing outside her daughter's bedroom door. She had never liked to meddle, even when Genevieve was little. 'They need their own space,' she'd tell her friends, who admired her good sense, wishing they could be as restrained themselves with their own children. 'The cup's still on the table, so he ought to be all right.'

Again that silence, and this time Stella felt the hostility in it. 'I won't say a word,' Genevieve said eventually. 'Not a bloody word. You needn't worry.'

So that was another day it was all right, Stella thought, and went to sleep very quickly. It was always the best thing to do.

Harry's party ended late. There was no reason why it shouldn't; the parents wouldn't be home until the small hours, Harry assured them all cheerfully, and even then they'd hardly be likely to fuss.

'They leave it to me, mostly,' he said when the Carter twins nagged about it. 'There's much too much going on in their lives to let them get over-involved in mine. Which is a consummation devoutly to be wished by you all.'

He had beamed round at them all and they had stared owlishly back at him; there was little more they could do because they really were pretty far gone.

Richard and Robert had brought a full bottle of vodka, and a couple of the others had supplemented that with Martini and Southern Comfort. They preferred it to the joints that Harry and Dave were sharing, with Richard taking an occasional turn.

'Oh, I don't know,' Robert said. 'It's not so much fun if they don't try and get involved. I like putting one over on the old man. He thinks he knows what we're doing and the poor cretin hasn't a clue.'

'If the father of the Carter twins, the estimable Carter père, who probably managed to achieve the existence of this ineffable brace of youths only because he stuttered, is a cretin, what does that make the Carter twins? Their share of wit and wisdom and general ability will have been diluted as well as attenuated by being passed on ... One frets and concerns oneself over the future welfare of the Carter twins.' Harry beamed at them and they beamed back. 'You'd agree, my friend?' And he prodded Dave, sitting next to him.

'Agree about what?'

'My opinion of the Carter twins.'

'I have no opinion of the Carter twins,' Dave said and cackled delightedly at his own wit, and Harry sighed.

'You've taken in too much of your own Ketema resin, my friend,' Harry said. 'That was a very old joke. Positively bewhiskered with antiquity.'

'None the worse for that,' Dave said. 'And who says I've taken too much?'

'Just have to look.' Harry leaned over and slid one long black finger into the soft leather pouch on Dave's knee. 'That was, as I recall, a somewhat plumper pochette. I like that. Very alliterative. Plumper pochette, plumper pochette ...' He went on repeating the syllables dreamily until they sounded like nonsense in his own ears.

'Some bugger helped himself,' Dave said after a long time, seeming to wake up a little. 'Would you believe it? Right there at school. Makes you sick, little buggers helping themselves.'

Robert Carter managed a giggle of his own. 'Should have asked in Lost Property.'

'Very funny, oh very witty, cretin divided by a half,' Dave said savagely. 'Was it you that took it, you bastard? You and that shit of a –' He lunged forwards and Harry pulled him back.

'Paranoia, side effect of hash as well known to the cognoscenti,' he said to no one in particular. 'Dave's been complaining of being robbed ever since I first knew him. Probably you are, dear boy, but there's nothing you can do about it except hide your stash more carefully. Have some orange juice. You'll need it in a minute if you don't already.'

'I'm dying of thirst,' Dave discovered and took the bottle and upended it into his mouth, splashing it on his scarlet shirt and not seeming to care. 'Roll another, Harry.'

'Might as well,' Harry said, and reached for the pouch. 'While you've still got it. Could be someone *is* pinching it, you know. Better find somewhere else to hide it. It's been discovered.'

'Yeah,' Dave said, and yawned, caring now. 'Yeah. Better think about that. Sometime.'

'Might be one of the staff,' Harry said as his fingers worked expertly with paper and shreds of tobacco culled from a filter-tip cigarette. 'You never know.'

'They'd have shopped me by now if it was. Anyway, they don't come into my room, do they?'

'How do you know?' Harry sounded very reasonable. 'Might do. Perchance they creep on airy-fairy pointed toe to search among the pots for pot –' He smiled round then. 'Now that really is witty. If accidental.'

'No, it isn't,' Dave said, scowling at him. 'Gimme that joint, for Chrissakes. How long does it take, a week? No one looks around in my room without me knowing.'

'Someone did. You said the little buggers did,' Harry said reasonably, and handed over the fresh joint after lighting it with great care, holding his head back to avoid the flare of the paper. 'So maybe you'd better find a new place.'

'It's you!' Dave said and glared at him and Harry laughed. 'You bastard –'

'You're not just stoned, you're boiled,' he said cheerfully. 'Talk about it tomorrow. Listen, I've got a couple of Gerry Mulligan records here. Sound fabulous when you're well away. Listen to this.'

So they listened to Gerry Mulligan and didn't think any more about the stolen pot. Not that night, anyway.

Thirteen

The dress rehearsal had started very well; 'Too well,' opined some of the cast who believed fervently in every theatrical superstition they could set tongue to, working hard at not whistling in dressing rooms or wishing each other good luck and so forth, and who were therefore certain that a good dress rehearsal meant a disastrous first night. The costumes had worked out better than anyone had hoped, since Martin Collop had decreed that they would eschew the obviously Elizabethan and wear instead simple outfits of black tights and close-fitting black sweaters; the boys' enlivened where necessary by such additions as crimson ruffs, red feathered hats and swords, and the same of the girls apart from the addition of white tulle skirts and, occasionally, crimson collars and cuffs. The set was little more than crimson drapes with swathes of white tulle to dress the back and to mark out various seating areas, and the total effect of black, red and white was really remarkably interesting. Or so Hattie thought, though she wouldn't have told Martin Collop for the world. He was already far too pleased with himself, in her settled opinion.

As far as *The Taming of the Shrew* was concerned, however, he had every right to be: a fact she had to admit, much to her chagrin, for, apart from the look of the piece, he had managed to fire his cast with enormous speed and energy. He had bullied, shouted, nagged, sneered and hectored at them, frequently reducing the girls to tears and making most of the boys – with the exception of Harry Forster – almost incoherent with rage and frustration at times. But his technique had worked, and Hattie sat at the back of the hall, watching with genuine delight as

Shakespeare's misogynistic play unpleated itself before her, and laughed aloud more often than she would have thought possible.

In spite of some hold-ups for technical reasons – the boys handling the lights were less deft than Collop required them to be and were told so with such force that one of them almost walked out altogether – Act Three was reached by six o'clock and Hattie relaxed a little. She'd arranged with Judith's Inge for babysitting, but she knew the girl got restless after ten o'clock. That was when she went out to meet her boyfriend – 'A jazz trumpeter, no less,' Judith had crowed proudly, as though such a person having an attachment, however tenuous, to her household added lustre to her own importance – and Hattie had promised Inge she'd be home as close to ten as she could. At this rate, she told herself, sneaking a look at her watch, she'd be well on her way by half past eight, or even earlier. Marvellous.

'Fiddler, forbear,' bawled Lucentio from the stage as the music jangled wickedly – a most useful contribution from one of the boys in the fifth form with a gift for composing – 'you grow too forward, sir. Have you so soon forgot the entertainment Her sister Katherina welcomed you withal?'

Someone at the back of the darkened hall had opened the big main door to slip out and left it partly open, and Hattie hugged her coat around her a little closer, for in spite of the very hot lights beating centre stage, the hall was a great cold echoing space, with its high vaulted ceiling and the overhanging balcony that trapped what heat there was up there in the dust and refused to return it for recirculation. A draught whistled round her ears and she sank her head into her neck to protect them, and then lifted her chin sharply, as the faint smell drifted into her nose.

Was one of these wretched boys smoking? It had become one of her personal campaigns, the stopping of smoking among the boys. Many of the masters closed their eyes to it, as heavy tobacco users themselves, but Hattie had spent too many hours nursing people dying of lung cancer, watching them drowning in their own self-inflicted disease, to be so tolerant. So she stared around the dim hall, trying to see the tell-tale glow that would pinpoint the miscreant so that she could bear down on him.

'Preposterous ass!' cried Lucentio, in high feather on the stage, 'that never read so far To know the cause why music was ordained!' And Hattie tried to ignore the smell, and to concentrate on a finely tuned performance from a lively fifth-former. But she couldn't. The smell of smoke was stronger and it wasn't, she now decided, due to a cigarette.

The rehearsal went on smoothly, the warring suitors on stage dancing their way round the blissfully happy Bianca, and she couldn't interrupt that; but she was alarmed in a way she remembered well. Fear of fire had been dinned into all of the nurses in her year, because there had been a disastrous and badly mismanaged one in the summer before they had entered the nursing school, which had resulted in the death of several patients. So she had never been able to rid herself of the edginess that filled her at the smell of smoke and she stopped trying to do so now.

No one noticed her go out of the hall; they were all intent on Bianca's attempt to circumvent the Latin of her wooing scene ('Now let me see if I can construe it. "*Hic ibat Simois . . .*"') and she let the door close softly behind her and stood for a moment in the empty corridor outside, sniffing.

It was stronger now, a definite if distant smell of burning wood, and she felt the tight clutch of fear and wanted to run back into the hall to cry the alarm; but had a sudden vision of Collop's face – and behaviour – if she created such an interruption. Almost before she knew what she was doing, she was half walking, half running along the corridor, her head up as she sniffed the air like a dog.

The smell got thicker as she moved towards the fourth- and fifth-form blocks in the Victorian part of the building, still called New School by everyone, and she stopped trying to control her fear and ran, pushing open the double doors that had been set at intervals along the long corridors to act as firebreaks, reckless of any danger. There were children here, her mind was shouting at her, a hall full of children, and there might be other boys still around in other parts of the building; at six o'clock there were still music lessons, club meetings –

The last pair of double doors opened to send a wave of heat on to her face which would have been welcome when she'd been sitting frozen in the hall; now it made her feel sick. She was in the fourth-form block, facing the Art Room, and on the other side of the glass door she could see a faint flickering glow and stood for what seemed like an eternity of a second while she tried to decide what to do. And then remembered her training in the old days.

The fire extinguisher was an antiquated one and she suspected it hadn't been checked for years, but it worked at first blow as she thumped it down on the floor and aimed it at the blaze which was small and indeed cheerful, busily burning away under a long table on which a large number of paintings and canvasses seemed to have been piled higgledy-piggledy. She'd done all the right things so far, she told herself over and over again as she played the jet of the heavy extinguisher on the outer edges of the blaze. She'd closed the outer doors in the corridor. Opened the Art Room door to the minimum needed to get in and then closed it again. Had the fire extinguisher ready and used it at once. Now all she needed was for the damned thing to last long enough for the fire to be put out; there was one of them outside every classroom, she knew, but how long it would take her to get to the nearest classroom for a replacement and back again, she couldn't be sure. The whole building could have caught by then, and all its occupants –

The blaze drew in on itself, lowered what had been a proud and even beautiful orange head and sank into a skulking crimson glow and then the hissing created by the foam became louder than the crackling that had been so terrifying, and finally the thing subsided with a disgruntled sigh, leaving behind it a heap of sodden grey mess. She stared at it for a long moment, marvelling that something that had been so malevolent should now look so pathetic, set down the fire extinguisher which seemed to weigh more now than she did herself, and leaned against the table behind her, trying to catch her breath.

She was shaking, every muscle that she had seeming to dance to its own piper, and gingerly she let herself slide down the corner of the table until she was sitting on the floor, leaning back gratefully against the heavy wooden leg. Ahead of her and almost at her eye level the remains of the fire lay sulkily, a few wisps of smoke still rising from it, and she stared at it almost sleepily, amazed at her own success. There'd been a fire and she'd put it out; and suddenly she was filled with a great surge of delighted joy and she lifted her chin and let out a yelp of relief and pleasure and excitement, all mixed up into a shrill high sound; and somewhere on the other side of the room it was echoed, but not joyfully. More of a whimper, rather, and Hattie turned her head and peered around her, looking further.

From this angle the room looked strange, much larger and certainly dirtier. There was a drift of paper around and wood shavings under what seemed to be a wood-carver's bench and pots and tubes of discarded paint as well as dollops of hard clay. Somewhere at the back of her mind she thought, Christ, I've been lucky. Another little while and all this would have been burning too. I'd never have managed to put it out.

She went on looking and then saw, right in the corner, what seemed to be a bundle of clothes or discarded school uniform, and she shuffled herself on her bottom over towards it. Would it have been easier to get to her feet and walk over there? Perhaps. But she wasn't going to try it. Her muscles were still shaking and she doubted she could trust her legs.

The little sound came again, a low choked yelping sort of sound, and she leaned nearer to the heap of clothes and poked it, and the bundle leaped convulsively and moved away from her.

'Are you all right?' she asked and was surprised at how husky she sounded, and coughed to clear her voice and then tried again. 'Are you all right?'

This time there was only silence and, suddenly angry, she reached forward and took a firm handful of the bundle of clothes and tugged, and it came towards her, and unwound itself, and she sat and stared at the face that was now close to her, a boy's face, very young and smooth, eyes swollen with weeping, sitting glaring at her.

'Who are you?' she said, peering at him, for the light was poor here under the tables. The overhead lamps sent great shadows everywhere and anyway he was sitting with the light, such as it was, behind him.

The boy seemed to consider for a moment and then went sliding away from her, half crawling and half slithering on his belly across the floor towards the door, and she caught her breath in surprise and pain as one foot in the heavy school shoe skidded over her hand and caught the knuckle.

It was the pain as much as anything else that galvanized her and she was on her feet and running across the room to the door to cut him off before she knew she was doing it, and then, as he reached the door a matter of a second after her, stretched out and grabbed his shoulder.

'Listen, you little ass! I asked you what your name was. You don't have to go kicking me from here to Christmas for that. Who are you?'

He shook his head and whimpered and lifted his hands to his eyes to push his knuckles into them and she thought with swift confusion, Poor little devil. He's worn out. He was very pale and swaying a little and almost instinctively she leaned across and set one arm round his shoulder and the other hand against his cheek, so that she could lead him to a tall stool beside one of the tables. It was all she could see to put him on and it was awkward lifting him into place, but she managed it and then stood there, her arm still around his shoulder, and her other stroking his cheek.

They stayed there a long time, it seemed to her, though it was probably barely longer than a minute or two; and then he stirred and said, 'It wasn't my fault, miss.'

'Did I say it was?' she said, and put a hand beneath his chin to turn his face towards her so that she could look at him. 'I only asked you who you were. I also asked how you were. You didn't answer either question, so let's try again. How are you?'

'All right, miss.' It came automatically, as though that were his answer to everything.

'Try again, I said. Have you been burned? Hurt yourself in any way? Or just very scared? Like me?'

He looked at her then and seemed about to say something and then stopped and said only, 'I'm all right, miss. Can I go, miss?'

'You most certainly cannot!' Hattie snapped with a spark of anger. 'I find you in a room with a blaze going merrily and you hiding in a corner and you think I'm going to say, "Oh, fine, OK, no problems. Just cut along then"? Be reasonable! Why didn't you raise the alarm? I only smelled it because I'm neurotic about fire and notice it long before anyone else does.' She lifted her head then and looked at the door. 'Though, come to think of it, you'd think someone else would've noticed by now.'

The boy yelped again and she hugged him closer, almost without thinking.

'It's all right. I won't let anyone hurt you −' She frowned briefly, as the thought struck her. 'Is there any reason why anyone *should* hurt you?'

He sat there lumpishly staring down at his feet and this time she noticed his hands, which were dangling limply between his knees, and reached down and picked up one of them.

'Here, are you hurt, you silly child? Why didn't you say so? Those are burns, I should be treating them. Come on.' And she dragged him off the chair towards the big butler sink in the corner of the Art Room and began to wash the hand beneath cold running water, scolding him all the time as she did it, to distract him from the discomfort.

'Yes, I know it hurts, but it's no good flinching like that. Burns hurt much more when they aren't dunked in cold water than when they are, so you'll just have to put up with it. How on earth you managed to –'

She stopped then and stared down at the hand which was cleaner now and showed the broad red cicatrice that spread across the thumb and forefingers and the back of the hand.

'I think, you know, we really have to talk sensibly about this,' she said, turning the tap down to a trickle so that it went running over the injury though less strongly, and held him fast. He couldn't have got away, however hard he tried, and whether it was awareness of this fact or sheer exhaustion that held him she didn't know, but he remained still.

'Did you start that fire?' she said, keeping her tone conversational. Silence.

'Other people will ask the same question, you know. It'll be easier if you tell me first. I could be on your side. You could tell me why. I think you did, you see. If you hadn't you'd be denying it like mad. Added to that, this burn is the sort you get when you put a match to something that's soaked in meths and flares back on you. I know. I've done it on barbecues. I'm not very good at barbecues. So, let's have another go, shall we? I know you set that fire. Now tell me why.'

He took a long shaky breath and then said in a high frightened voice, 'I couldn't think of anything else.'

'How do you mean?'

'It's the end-of-term things. Tests. I couldn't think of anything else to do.'

'You lit a fire under a table in here because of the end-of-term tests?'

'I didn't know what else to do.' He sighed, a long soft sound of the sort made by a child who has been crying for hours and is at last beginning to calm down. 'There wasn't anything else. I tried getting ill but they always know. I thought I could take poison, only I couldn't find any, and then I thought, If there's a fire they'll have to wait till next term to do them and maybe, in the holidays . . .' His voice drifted away and then strengthened. 'Not that it'll make any difference. I can't do it, no matter how long I take over it. I never can and I never will . . .'

'You started the fire because you wanted to avoid the end-of-term test?' Hattie said, staring down at him. 'Are they that bad?'

'Yes,' he said simply.

'Have you told your form master you're worried?'

The boy lifted his chin and looked directly at her and now she could see him clearly for the first time. A rather plain face, long and horsy, an effect heightened by the huge front teeth of the new adult, grey eyes very narrow and bloodshot between the puffy lids and a face that was slightly spotty. He looked, Hattie estimated, thirteen or fourteen. A fourth-former.

'Mr Tully's my form master,' he said. 'He doesn't know what it's like with Maths and English Grammar and History . . .' His voice drifted away again and he stared into the middle distance, his eyes blank. 'And Geography. And French. All of them. You can't tell people it's all of them, can you?'

'Your parents? Have you told them you can't cope? Maybe this isn't the school for you.' She could have wept for him. The boy was sunk in despair; it showed in every line of his face, the way his shoulders slumped and his mouth drooped open.

'My dad says it *is* the school for me. He says I've got to go to university. He never did, so I've got to –' The boy began to weep, big oily tears that slid down his face unchecked, and Hattie leaned forwards and held him close, rocking him a little. It seemed the only thing to do.

They heard it at the same time, the boy stiffening in Hattie's arms as she lifted her head to listen. Footsteps outside, a clatter of voices, doors opening and closing. And then Dave Tully was there, staring round at his room, as some of the fifth-formers clustered behind him, peering over his shoulder.

'What the fuck's going on here?' he said loudly, and one of the boys behind him sniggered.

'There was a fire,' Hattie said in a loud tone. 'I put it out. No need for any worry now.'

'You can smell it for bloody miles.' He pushed his way into the room, looked about him and then headed for the pile of grey mess beneath the laden table. 'Is this it? Christ! Not much of a mess to make a stink like that.'

His eyes moved, saw the surface of the table, and slowly his face reddened. It was almost funny to watch it, Hattie thought, still sitting with her arm round the boy's shoulders. He looked as she imagined a turkey cock would.

'These are some of my canvases!' he roared. He picked them up one after another, peered at them, and set them on edge on the floor, leaning against the table. 'Christ, if these had gone, I'd have –'

He whirled then. 'What are you doing here, Spero? What the fuck are you doing sitting there like a great baby cuddling his mummy with my canvasses on a table over a fire? Did you do this? Did you? Because if you did, I'll murder you. You hear me? I'll bloody murder you –' And he hurtled his way across the room towards Hattie and the boy, and she sat there and watched him coming and couldn't move at all.

Fourteen

'You had no right to go, you know,' Hilary Roscoe said. 'You took rather more upon yourself than was required.'

'I don't see it that way,' Hattie said, and looked down at her hands which were folded on her lap. I will not behave like a child in trouble, she thought fiercely. I will not let him do this to me. I will not let him bully me. But it didn't help. She felt just the way she had when she was twelve and had committed some minor peccadillo. 'The child was deeply distressed, and I had some understanding of his situation. His parents needed to –'

'His parents needed to know nothing!' Hilary Roscoe said. 'The matter would have been dealt with here and there need have been no trouble at all.'

'No trouble at all?' She lifted her head to stare at him. 'How can you say so when a child was so desperate that he –'

'A boy,' murmured Hilary. 'A *boy*.'

'I don't care what his sex is! At barely fourteen he's a child and he was distressed and so I –'

'Here at the Foundation, Hattie, we treat our pupils as the young men they are and will eventually have to be in greater strength. That's what's wrong with so much of the education offered at the comprehensives, you know. They provide the soft option all the time, make it too easy for the people they deal with to loaf around and make themselves useless. We have a different ethos here. We could have dealt with Spero and you should not have involved the parents as you did.'

'He couldn't cope! He couldn't talk to his form master. He got no help at all from the subject masters who taught him. He was desperate enough to try to hurt himself!' Hattie cried. 'How can you say his parents shouldn't be told, given the chance to take him away somewhere he'd be happier, better able to cope?'

'My dear Hattie.' He was suddenly all charm. 'I can't run this school successfully if I let the *boys* decide whether or not they can cope! They have to learn how to cope. Their parents send them here at considerable expense to make something of them and it costs me a great deal in effort to ensure they get their money's worth. If members of my staff take it upon themselves to run to parents and advise them to take their boys away, how long do you suppose we can keep going? Of course the boy's a dullard, I knew that from the start! But his father's doing very well for himself, wanted something better for his lad than he had himself, so he sent him here. He's been a considerable benefactor so far.' He sighed. 'Now I've had to expel the boy, since you let the story out, so that'll dry up. I really must ask you never to behave so – shall we say impulsively – again. Come to me. Let me deal with these matters –'

'You've expelled him?'

'I had to, much to my regret. As I said, the story's outside the school. If I didn't expel him, *pour encourager les autres*, you understand, future parents would be fearful. Had it remained in house – well, no point in dwelling on that. And I have to say we'd have made some sort of a fist of getting him through, you know. I have ways of dealing with these lazy dull boys and –'

'He isn't lazy,' Hattie cried. 'Just overstretched. He was desperate!'

'Boys can't be overstretched,' Hilary said, implacable as ever. 'Only the reverse. Well, there it is. He's gone and his father's potential support with him. Now someone else'll benefit. I dare say the man'll find a crammer to take him and any cash he's got to spare'll go to some other establishment. Pity . . .'

'And what about the boy? What about his situation? You've *expelled* him. That was an awful thing to do . . .'

He lifted his brows at her. 'Hattie, my dear girl, do be logical. Here you are complaining he couldn't cope, that you wanted his parents to remove him, and now you're fussing because I expelled him? I know women and logic aren't exactly the closest of bedfellows, but really –'

She brushed that aside, refusing to be distracted. 'There's a hell of a difference between getting the boy's parents to understand that they're pushing him too hard and too far and persuading them to let the child leave and go to a school where he could cope and might even be happy, and chucking him out like a – a useless unwanted bit of rubbish. His self-esteem's on the floor as it is. Now you've made it infinitely worse! His father'll give him a dreadful time. I've never met anyone so – so *stubborn*. He couldn't see what Daniel was feeling at all, couldn't understand it was misery that made him do what he did and not wickedness. All the same, I believe I'd made a bit of an impact on him. But now you've expelled Daniel, he'll go back to his old ways of thinking and probably punish him more. How could you do it to him? Poor little scrap . . .'

He shook his head, watching her with amused eyes. 'Thank heavens I've only got a dozen girls here. Imagine how life would be if I had more, and therefore more women on the staff. This place would be a shambles.'

She still refused to rise to the bait he was trailing. 'It could be a better place. Not so much unhappiness and –'

'This is getting silly,' he said, suddenly seeming bored. 'There isn't that much unhappiness here, and well you must know it! Of course some people get battered by the rush and tumble of the day; that happens everywhere. We're not running a haven for the helpless, you know. We're trying to educate boys to make them the sort of men who'll achieve something in life, who'll repay the investment in them their parents have made, and you can't do that by treating them all like infants in need of coddling. These boys aren't sick, you know, not hospital patients. They're boys who have to grow up to live in a hard harsh world.'

'It's got to be a dreadful world if the only way you can prepare boys for it is by driving some of them to make their own funeral pyres,' she said bitterly. 'Daniel Spero wanted to *kill* himself in that fire. You know that? Of course it was a dreadful thing to do, of course he could have killed God knows how many others, but he wasn't thinking about that. He was too far driven to think about it or about anything else. He just wanted to die. It's got to be a rotten school that does that to the children in its care.'

'Far from rotten,' Hilary said, and a part of her was amazed at how silky he sounded. She was being incredibly rude to him; she knew that perfectly well, and was beginning to wonder how far she'd have to go before he threw her out of his office and out of his school. Part of her wanted to be thrown out; it would be easier than deciding of her own free will she wanted to be away from these boys and all their miseries (and the girls and theirs too, come to that, she thought fleetingly, remembering Genevieve). But how could she go and leave them all to the sort of adult attitudes they laboured under at present? Somewhere deep inside her was the conscience that had always made her life so uncomfortable in so many ways. It had been that conscience which had sent her to talk to Daniel Spero's parents in their very handsome flat overlooking Regent's Park, and had kept her sitting there, amid the deep cream pile of the carpet and the crumpled white leather sofas and glass-topped tables that spelled money wherever she looked, long after she knew they didn't understand how desperately unhappy their son was and were concerned only with what people would think of him and therefore them; and it was that conscience that would keep her here at the Foundation unless this elegant man, sitting now and looking at her with that same amused look over his clasped hands, could be goaded into losing his temper with her.

'We may not be the best of the boys' schools in London,' Hilary said then. 'Our standards have fallen academically over past years – before I arrived here, you must understand – which is why the Daniel Speros of this world are pupils here at all. They can't get into any of the others, so they have no choice: it's us or the State system, which is the last thing their ambitious parents want. But we've got potential, and it's that I'm working on. I'll lift this school till it really is in competition with the big ones and then there won't be any more problems like young Spero because we'll be in a position to turn away the dullards the way all the other big schools do. Our entrance exam's a laugh at present, you know that? Everyone knows it in the trade and everyone thinks it'll go on like that for always. Well, it won't. Once I've got enough cash to keep me safe against the local authority and its hostility, I'll shake this place up – just you wait and see! We're not very good yet, but we will be.'

'There's a lot of unhappiness here,' Hattie said. 'Don't you care about that?'

'Oh, of course I do, what little there is. I deny it's that major an issue. Anyway, I've appointed you, haven't I? You're the carer here. You're the one who'll deal with the tears and tantrums. I've seen how things have gone and I'm really most impressed. You came because of the girls, but the boys are finding you very helpful too. It's splendid that, splendid.'

She shook her head in puzzlement. 'Then you aren't throwing me out? After the things I've said to you this afternoon? After my going to see the Speros and –'

'Throw you out? My dear girl! Why on earth should I do that? You must understand you're needed here. I repeat, you're the caring face of the Foundation, a warm reassurance to those parents who worry about such things.' He smiled even more widely then. 'Mostly mothers, I have to say. No, I wouldn't dream of letting you go. You behaved wrongly, and I've said so and there's an end of it. Leave it at that. Don't do it again and –'

She lifted her chin: 'I will if I think it's necessary,' and she remembered Genevieve again and wondered whether this was the time to tell Hilary that she'd already spoken to her parents about her and would do so again, almost certainly. But what was there to tell? The conversation of the autumn fair hadn't really gone very far. So she pushed the thought away. 'I won't compromise on that. I couldn't.'

'Well, perhaps a small compromise is possible.' He smiled charmingly. 'At least do me the courtesy of coming to tell me what you're doing before you do it. I can't stop you, I know. Short of locking you up here and I wouldn't do that! But at least you can do me the courtesy of warning me. The Spero affair came as quite a shock – having that man come roaring in here as he did was not very agreeable. And after all, I might have information you don't have.'

She thought for a moment and then said a little unwillingly, 'That sounds reasonable enough, I suppose.' And then suspicion filled her and she went on sharply, all the same. 'Any other man who'd been spoken to as I just spoke to you would have chucked me out neck and crop.'

'But I'm not any other man,' he said, and now he made her think not of silk but of a purring cat. 'I'm the man you see, who has great plans for a great old school which has potential for a great new future.'

'What sort of a boy were you?' she said suddenly, not sure whether she hoped to catch him out or whether she genuinely wanted to know, but deciding it was the latter, and tilted her head to stare at him. 'Can you remember? Was it easy being you, when you were fifteen or so?'

'Aha! A little light parlour psychology, is it? Well, forgive me, Hattie, but I really haven't time for that. At present. Some other day, perhaps. Over dinner at Judith and Peter's possibly . . .'

'Another amnesiac,' she said, pushing at him again, wanting to crack that carapace of charm and good manners. 'That's the trouble with every one of the people in this school as far as I can tell – well, most of them,' she amended, suddenly seeing an image of Sam Chanter in her mind's eye. 'They've forgotten what it feels like to be a boy.'

'Parents forget too,' Hilary said, and got to his feet. 'That's what being a parent's all about. Shall I quote Philip Larkin at you?'

'You will whatever I say.'

He laughed. 'You begin to understand me. I shall bowdlerize for your feminine ears. "They muck you up, your mum and dad. They may not mean to, but they do. They fill you with the faults they had and add some extra, just for you."'

Hattie, who had heard it before, stood up. She had to; he had gone over to the door and was holding it for her courteously.

'It's bad enough that "They fuck you up, your mum and dad",' she said clearly. 'Which was what Larkin actually wrote. Why do teachers have to do it too?' And she went out of the room and he smiled at her as she passed the secretary's desk and already his eyes had the vague look that comes of thinking of the next appointment, and she wanted to hit him; a rare impulse in her because she was not generally violent. But this man was enough to make anyone violent. And she went slamming out of the room and along the corridor, her face hot with anger.

So much so that she didn't see Sam Chanter coming towards her, and not until he put a hand on her arm and pulled her round to face him did she focus her eyes properly.

'What on earth's happened? You look as though you've had the devil of a shock or something.'

'I've had the devil of a row.' She let her shoulders relax, hoping that would stop the shaking in her muscles. She hadn't spoken more than a few monosyllables to Sam since the last evening they had spent together at a concert and eating supper;

she'd spent so much time at the *Shrew* rehearsals and he had been in a flurry of end-of-term tests and marking, so it was not surprising. Now she was a little startled at how comforted she was by his presence beside her, large and crumpled and calm.

'Have you now?' he said and laughed softly. 'Surprise, surprise. Or rather not. I imagine that happens to you a good deal.'

'Of course it doesn't,' she said hotly, 'I don't go around –' and then stopped and managed a smile of her own, albeit a weak one. 'Well, I do go off a bit half-cocked sometimes, I suppose. It's just that when I get upset or angry about something I'm not very good at keeping it in.'

'I had suspected something of the sort. Having seen you comport yourself in the staffroom.'

'Old Bevan, you mean? Well, he was being ridiculous. Huffing and puffing because I was already sitting in that chair when he came in! He doesn't own it, for God's sake.'

'As you made very clear. Now, tell me about this one. You don't usually look quite so ruffled.' He bent his head to look a little closer. 'Nor, I imagine, do you usually get so shaky in reaction. You must have drummed up a lot of adrenalin.'

'Indeed I did,' she said grimly, and then closed her eyes and winced as the bell for the end of afternoon school began to shriek its clamour above her head. As soon as it stopped he said, 'Time to have a cup of coffee or something; tell me about it?'

'I have to get home,' she said. 'I can't keep dumping the kids on Judith. I use her Inge too much as it is, with the play in rehearsal –'

'You can't go home to them in this state,' he said calmly. 'Do them no good at all. You go and phone, I'll pick up my gear and your coat and bag and see you at the main entrance.'

'There's a plastic bag from Sainsbury's too. Tonight's supper,' she said, and he nodded and left her and she rubbed her face a little wearily and turned and went to the gate porter's cubbyhole, which was behind her at the end of the corridor which held the Headmaster's office, grateful to be told by someone else what to do. It was curiously comforting to be gently bullied that way, and she phoned Judith's Inge, and then stood warming herself at the rickety electric fire while the gate porter ostentatiously ignored her, and waited for Sam.

'I think something a little better than coffee,' he said. 'You need a calmer-downer rather than a stimulant. So a small gin and tonic.'

'At this hour of the day?' She was scandalized. 'I couldn't.'

'Yes, you can,' he said. 'I recommend it.' And he helped her into her coat and then hooked her bag over her shoulder and turned her firmly towards the open door. 'On your way. Here you are, Edwards.' And he handed a key to the gate porter who took it with a surly grunt. 'I don't want anyone to have that key but me,' he said. 'If one of the sixth-form set are early tomorrow and want it, say no. I've got some delicate experiments set up there and I'm taking no chances. Goodnight.'

'Is this the one to the big biology lab, then? Or the little one?'

'The little one, of course. We gave up locking the big one ages ago. No need. But that small one's out of bounds unless I'm there. So don't let any of the eager beavers get in.'

He looked than at Hattie. 'I'm growing some interesting yeasts, and some of them produce an alcohol. I don't want anyone helping themselves to a sample and doing mischief with it. It was bad enough the year before last when someone set up a still in the big lab. They can't do that any more and I'm not letting them even think about what they could do with the sort of yeasts I've got growing. Goodnight, Edwards. Come on, Hattie.'

He took her to a dark brown fug of a pub just off the Highway and she settled herself in the corner seat he found her with her head resting back against the richly engraved glass behind her, her eyes closed, as he fetched their drinks. He brought the gin and tonic and a plate of ham sandwiches too.

'I'm hungry, so I assume you are too. Food is what people eat when their companion's missed his lunch. Today's lunch was more than usually repellent.'

Hattie, remembering the very salty and clearly elderly fish that had been put in front of them, agreed, ate the sandwiches gratefully, and felt a lot better.

He nodded at her approvingly. 'That's more like it. Now you look like yourself again rather than a harridan who's been crossed in hate.'

'Charming!'

'You didn't see yourself.'

'Well, I was angry. It was like talking to a jellyfish, or a cloud on legs. You can't get hold of him.'

'Ah! All is as crystal. The Head, our esteemed Lord and Master.'

'I thought he'd give me the push, you know.' She was feeling better by the moment as the gin lowered in her glass. 'If he'd had any sense he would have.'

'Dear me, what can you have done?'

She giggled. 'Told tales out of school. Literally.'

'Am I allowed to know what they were?'

She told him, waxing more and more angry as she did so. 'I know everyone on the staff was asked to keep quiet about what happened, and I know we agreed. I mean, the last thing we want is a spate of copycatting, which we might get if all the boys knew that Daniel Spero had done it on purpose. And I have to say it was impressive the way he handled it. No one apart from the boys who were with Tully seemed to have the remotest idea that anything at all had happened and even they didn't seem to realize it wasn't just an accident. But it was all so . . . I don't know, I was livid. And worried. No one was doing anything about Daniel, you see. He got a hell of a telling off and Tully made his life misery for the rest of the week and then – well, nothing. It just wasn't good enough. Someone had to help the poor lad. I tried to get out of him what he wanted but it wasn't any good, so I asked him if I could talk to his parents, get them to take him away, send him somewhere better suited to him.'

He drew a long soft breath. 'Now I see why the Head and you had a set-to. You went to see them?'

'Daniel was so – I had to. He thought I could do it. Persuade them, I mean.' She stared down into her glass, broodingly. 'He – after that evening, when I pulled Tully off him and everything – well, he seemed to think I was all right.'

'Got a crush,' Sam interpreted, and she flushed.

'Something of the sort. I had to do something for him, didn't I? And I thought his own parents – I can't imagine I'd knowingly put either of my two through that sort of hell if I knew how they felt about it. I couldn't believe they'd be the way they were.'

Sam made a twisting movement of his lips. 'I'm never surprised any more by the parents who use this school. Some of them are – oh, just as they should be. The sort I'd be, given the chance, I hope. Interested in their kids first and foremost. But there are a hell of a lot of them who make me want to – well, I'm not surprised, shall we say, that you met a pair who were less than agreeable.'

'Agreeable! Absolute bastards, both of them. Well, maybe she wasn't that bad, but who could tell? She said she had to leave it to him, she'd agreed it was something his father knew most about, and went away to make coffee. And didn't come back.' She shook her head. 'I can't imagine being like that.'

'Stop using yourself as the yardstick for everyone else. You'll just get confused.'

'I did get confused! All his father could go on about was what it might have cost him if the fire had taken hold and what people would say if it got out, and how he'd have to give the boy a lesson he'd not forget and – oh, it was awful. I got him to say he'd think again about keeping Daniel at the school, since he was so miserable, and I said it'd help him, Daniel, I mean, to talk to someone, a counsellor, maybe, or a doctor, but he just showed me out and the next thing I know is the Head's sent for me, and isn't at all happy. And it's *still* nothing to do with Daniel or what he needs or how he feels. It's all how much the school's losing in cash from Spero senior, who's been a benefactor, I gather, and how the Head had to expel the boy as the only way of dealing with it, now I'd let the cat out of the bag. I ask you!' She ended indignantly. 'How can anyone be so stupid?'

'In his shoes it wasn't at all stupid. It was a very clever thing to have done. Now he'll tell the school,' Sam said slowly. 'Poor little devil. Everyone'll know – it'll probably even get to the local papers, and the Authority'll be in on it – poor little sod! It would have been better if you hadn't gone to the parents, you know, Hattie –'

'Don't you start!' she flared. 'I was thinking of *Daniel*, dammit. Daniel, Daniel, Daniel! No one else seemed to give a damn for him –'

'I know. But I have to say it won't be any easier for him now. The Head'll tell the school he was a bad boy and had to be expelled and they'll tell their parents who'll be very approving and see Roscoe as very good news – the smack of firm Government and all that stuff. That'll put a spoke in the Town Hall's wheel, too. He'll come across as brave and wise, damn his eyes.'

'Oh shit,' she said, and he laughed and put a hand over hers.

'Don't sound so dispirited. You did the best you could. You

were right to try, from the boy's standpoint. Write to Daniel or phone him, why don't you? Tell him direct how to get the sort of help he needs. You can get him to see someone and talk about his problems, can't you?'

She lifted her chin. 'I think perhaps – yes, I could do that. Will he go, though, that's the thing.'

'He's got a crush on you, you said.'

She reddened. 'Well, yes, I suppose he would. All right, I'll do that. Thanks. I feel better. Not a lot, but better.'

'It's a free service,' he said lightly. 'Any time.' And he took his hand away, and that made her suddenly uncomfortably aware of his physical presence, and she couldn't look at him.

There was a little silence and then she said, 'I must go. Those hamburgers'll be thawing and the girls will want their supper.'

'And I had you down for a sensible vegetarian lots-of-fibre-and-fresh-fruit sort of mother,' he said lightly and she grimaced.

'On paper I am. In practice, hamburgers fill in a hell of a lot of holes.'

'Don't I know it. I'll see you to the station. No, don't argue. You've got more than hamburgers in this bag. It's heavy.'

'Potatoes and corn,' she said a little absently and got to her feet. 'I should stay here, shouldn't I? At the school, I mean.'

He looked startled. '*Has* he fired you? You didn't say –'

'No. He should have. I was dreadfully rude. If I'd spoken to any of the people I'd worked under at the hospital that way, I'd have been crucified, let alone sacked. He seems to like it though.'

He nodded sapiently and held open the door of the pub to let her out into the dank thin fog of the dark Highway. 'I can understand that. With you there as his token someone to look after the little darlings, he's safer.'

'I can't stand that.' She stood still in the street and stared ahead of her. 'It's hateful.'

'Of course it is. But think of the alternative. No one like you at the Foundation.'

She looked at him, glad it was dark so that he couldn't see her face clearly, because she knew she was pink again. 'You think that would matter, then?'

'I do. To a lot of people.' He paused and then said deliberately, 'Including me.'

'Oh dear,' she said. 'I really must go. It's getting awfully late.'

Fifteen

———————⟨⟨⟨⟨⟩⟩⟩⟩———————

Christmas came and went in its usual flurry of too much of everything, and Hattie enjoyed the chance to be with the children all day and every day, though somehow it wasn't as absorbing as it had been in the old days when they'd been small. Then she had needed to hurry through housework in order to play with them a good deal, working out complex daily itineraries involving parks and swings and ducks, but they'd become a great deal more sophisticated in the last term at school. Now it was a case of wanting to go to the library for more books, to a friend's house for a chance to see some megabrill videos (and that involved Hattie in tactful checking with the relevant mothers that the videos were the sort she'd be happy for Sophie and Jessica to see; megabrill could mean anything) and filling their own home with visiting friends. There would be coteries of shrill little girls in the children's bedrooms or the living room, all squealing and hooting over the doings of various of their number, and Hattie listened and watched and was a little melancholy. Oliver would have enjoyed this stage of their lives, she found herself thinking, and was then struck with remorse, for she had hardly thought of Oliver at all for weeks.

So she set herself to a strenuous round of cupboard- and drawer-cleaning and rearranging that left her exhausted and irritable and annoyed the girls so much they chose to spend more time next door with Judith's Petra and Jenny, leaving Hattie alone and lonely. She found herself welcoming the start of the new term at both the girls' school and the Foundation with far more warmth than she would have expected.

Not that she hadn't enjoyed her first term at the Foundation.

She had, in spite of the way it had thrown up unexpected problems, had been harder work than she'd imagined it would be and disappointing in terms of relationships. It had been one of the good things she'd hoped to get from the job, new friendships with new people, and in the event the misogynism she had met had been disagreeable. But for all that she had ended the term happily enough in a flurry of school parties and sherry drinking in the staffroom; and of course, there was Sam Chanter. But again, she wouldn't let herself explore the way thinking about Sam Chanter affected her, and she still wouldn't. However, she was more than happy to drop Sophie and Jessica off at their own school, where they were swallowed into their mob of equally shrill little girls with every sign of delight, and go on to the City on her own. This term, surely, should be easier. She was an established resident now, after all.

There was no fuss at all when she went into the staff common room this time. The people who were already there, and who included Ian Bevan, paid no attention to her whatsoever, treating her as invisible, and that was a comfort. Much less strenuous than fighting, she told herself philosophically as she stacked her few books and register into the cubbyhole she had managed to win for her own use. This term she had decided she would try to run for the boys similar classes to those she had initiated for the girls, on living skills and similar issues, and she had prepared, with considerable optimism, a full term's syllabus. She put her notice offering the sessions during the lunch breaks on the main notice board, and prowled the school looking for extra chairs and stools to spirit away to her own small room to accommodate the comers she hoped to get. A dozen wouldn't be bad, she told herself hopefully, and arranged her room accordingly.

And was delighted to find that she had almost half as many again. There was some ribaldry and guffawing as the boys shoved at each other and nudged and pushed, but the important thing was they came and she used the first session very carefully, determined not to lose them. A modicum of talk about sex, she decided, and a good deal more about them as people, should bring them back eager for more; and she settled down on the first Friday of term to see how she'd cope.

They were mostly fourth-formers who came, boys of fourteen or so, gangly, often touchingly fragile about the wrists and ankles, which were all too apparent in outgrown clothes, or gawky in too-large clothes bought by parents determined to get a little more for their uniform pounds. They were all battered, of course, clearly going to considerable length to look the same as each other, only more scruffy; and she sat in the small room which was already taking on a distinct smell of boy, so very different from the faintly Body Shop fruit and floweriness the girls gave off, and looked round at them in their shabby blazers with an apparently casual glance but which missed little.

'It helps to know something about you all,' she said as easily as she could. 'Not just names and ages, but more interesting details. Sport for example. Who does what?'

That helped a lot. She flushed out a couple of hearty footballers and a fencer as well as several swimmers and was fulsome in her praise of their healthy lifestyle.

'There's some evidence,' she said offhandedly, 'that exercise of the sort you do take on regularly strengthens bones and increases body size in general. Not fat, of course' – she carefully didn't look at the rather plump boy who was sweating gently in the back row – 'but the bits that count. Muscles across the shoulders and so forth. Buttocks and things.' She risked a look up at them and a grin. 'The sexy ones.'

A loud guffaw greeted that and she took courage. 'Do you know which bit of a man women notice first?' she said. 'Someone did some research. It certainly surprised me, and I'm a woman and supposed to know.'

'Faces,' someone said, and a more daring voice from the back murmured, 'Crotches,' and she laughed.

'Not faces. Not crotches. Bottoms.'

There was a loud, 'Whay, hey!' from all of them and she looked round and grinned even more widely.

'It was a great comfort to me,' she said. 'I thought I was a bit of a freak till then.'

The group visibly relaxed and she stretched her own shoulders slightly and thought smugly, I haven't forgotten how. There had been times in the past, on the wards, when she'd had to work very hard to get the trust and attention of a group of young ones. She'd learned a lot then and still had the old skills.

'Right then, a few more questions. How about alcohol? Can we talk about that?'

There was an uneasy silence and she smiled. 'My tipple's gin and tonic. Bit old-fashioned I suppose . . .'

'My mum likes that,' someone said. 'Rather well,' and laughed a little awkwardly.

'Well, it's what women go for, isn't it? That and sticky lickers. There's a ghastly concoction of advocaat and cherry brandy my mum likes. Sweet as all get out and looks like pus and blood. When I say that she gives me hell.'

There was a murmur of approval and someone else volunteered, 'If you put that advocaat with brandy and whip it up with cream it's fantastic. It's called an Alexander. It's sweet, but I like it.'

They settled into a happy discussion of various drinks and Hattie listened and registered and said nothing. But it was depressing to see just how knowledgeable they were about the various alcohols that were available and how obvious it was that they got through a good deal of it, especially at weekends.

'Getting rat-arsed on Saturdays,' as one of them said, 'is what it's all about.'

She stood leaning on the desk and said then, 'What about smoking? Got any views on that?'

'Oh, no you don't!' This was a boy in the middle of the group, tall and rather more self-confident than the rest, possibly because he still had some of the prettiness of his younger years, and was weathering through it on to adulthood less awkwardly than some of the others. 'The word's gone round, you know. You're dead anti cigarettes.'

She put her hands up in mock self-surrender. 'I can't deny it. I can't help it, it's my experience, you see.' And she looked up at them under her lids and went into a graphic account of the people she had looked after with lung cancer, ending with a most sanguinary tale of a man who had suddenly suffered the puncture of a major artery in his throat from a tobacco-induced cancer of the larynx, which had sent a great jet of blood shooting up into the air, and who had ended up as white and flaccid as a piece of elderly tripe. She spared no details and they listened in silence and when she had finished still remained quiet, not looking at her.

It was again the boy in the middle who broke the silence. 'For my part, I'm not into cigarettes,' he said with a heavily casual air that alerted her at once to the fact that this was something important. 'But I'm interested in the matter of risks. How does tobacco compare with other things as a killer? Like alcohol, say?'

She obliged with what facts and figures she could, trying to lull him into thinking she took his question at face value, but knowing there was more to come. She'd seen that sort of elaborately relaxed air before in someone who was bursting with a question he didn't quite know how to ask.

He managed it. 'And what about cannabis?' he said. 'You know . . . pot. Is that as risky as tobacco?'

They all seemed to hold their breaths, and she looked up with her face as smooth and relaxed as if they were discussing the weather.

'Cannabis. Interesting stuff. I have to say there's a lot less evidence around about it than there is on tobacco. I haven't any facts or figures here, but I could get them for you if you wanted them.' I'll have to phone Barbara Davis, she thought almost frantically, her mind going like a whirlwind behind her placid expression. She'll know. 'Not that it really matters, does it?'

'Well, I'd have thought it was quite important,' the fat boy said. 'I mean, the way people go on and on about it. You'd need to know if it was true, all the things they say, wouldn't you? If you were to make your own mind up.'

'But it's illegal,' she said. 'So isn't that the end of it?'

'It's illegal to park on yellow lines, but I bet you do it,' someone said, and she shook her head.

'Don't drive. But I take your point. There're a lot of things that people do that are illegal. Still and all, I wouldn't have thought this was the sort of lawbreaking that ought to be encouraged. What do you think?'

Silence, so she tried again.

'People who deal in cannabis often deal in other drugs as well. Heroin, amphetamines. Very nasty, those. Isn't that the risk of using cannabis?'

'I go to Harrods to get my socks and shirts,' the good-looking boy said, and smiled winningly at her. 'But I don't buy girls' knickers just because Harrods sells them too.'

There was another guffaw and she laughed too. 'Fair enough. Maybe you wouldn't. But some might.'

'If you worry all the time about what some people might do,

you'd never do anything yourself,' said the fat boy, and then the bell outside began to shriek and there was a concerted scraping of chair legs on the floor as they got up and pushed towards the door.

'I'll get those facts if I can by next Friday,' she said as they went. 'And some rather good stuff on sex. So far that isn't illegal.' And in the general laughter they left her leaning against her desk and thinking hard.

It didn't take a great deal of nous, she told herself, to work out that there were people using cannabis here. The big fair boy, for a start, and she looked down at her list of names and picked him out: Jeremy Dalrymple; and she laughed. He looked just the sort of person to have such a name and she could imagine his parents all too easily; probably living in Kensington and weekend-ing in the country and using the Foundation because none of the boarding schools or London day schools would have him. He looked far more interested in his personal affairs than in any school ones; his clothes, uniform though they were, still looked more expensive than any of the others', now she thought about it. I'll have to look into this. It shouldn't be impossible to find them, if they're using the stuff here in the school.

She didn't think at all about what she would do if she did find any smokers, which was, she was later to realize, rather a problem.

It took her only the first three days of the week to discover them and at first she was cock-a-hoop with her own prowess. She had started in the easiest way possible, simply walking about the place, looking as though she were going somewhere purposeful, while she was in truth looking with all the care she could into every corner she passed. It was at the end of the first day, when she took herself off to the underground station with legs aching and feet crying out for rest because she'd been on them so long, with only the time needed to eat lunch spent sitting down, that she gave the matter systematic thought, and realized she'd got it all wrong. There was no way these boys would smoke their pot inside the busy parts of the school buildings. The smell would give them away, and anyway there were far too many people about. It had to be somewhere quiet, unobserved, and above all, where smells would not be noticed. I can't be the only person, she reasoned, with an acute sense of smell. There would be others who'd identify it if people were smoking where they shouldn't. And smoking pot.

The rest of the establishment was of course less easy to investigate. The staff, and especially she as the only woman member of it, was not likely to spend time in the basement where the antiquated boilers which heated the buildings sat lowering like deities waiting to be fed, so she had to be careful. If anyone – and especially surly Edwards, who tended the boilers like a goblin acting as acolyte to said deities – saw her there, suspicion would be great. And she could hardly tell Edwards or anyone else that she was hunting for pot-smokers. That really would create an uproar. So, she would have to be even more devious in her behaviour than she had been already, a thought which depressed her. It was disagreeable to be such a snoop; but she was convinced it was necessary, so she went doggedly on, thinking and planning how she'd search the underpinnings of the old buildings. Tuesday was a difficult day because she had a special session with the girls that day, but on Wednesday she had a free period which ran into the lunch hour and that had to be the best time to investigate.

It was on Wednesday, still trying to be casual, and careful to be unobserved, that she made her way down via the steps which ran behind the gym and led to the storage areas where the big karate mats and the Indian clubs and other assorted athletic detritus were piled. Beyond that was the black dampness of the cellars, reaching away into darkness, and she went on into them gingerly, feeling absurdly like a child. This was the sort of thing the heroines of the story-books she had devoured at the age of ten had done, only they'd been looking for harmless things like burglars or lost treasure or foreign spies, not pot-smokers. She wanted to giggle but managed not to.

There was a tangle of new piping and some fairly fresh off-cuts of new timber piled in front of her, and she made her way round it, and then worked out, much to her own pleasure at being so successful a detective, that this lay beneath the area where one of the old lavatories had been converted into a washroom and lavatories for the girls, and she moved on beyond it, wishing she'd brought a torch. She wouldn't be able to go much further without some sort of light, she thought, and was annoyed at her own lack of foresight. There were electric lights of course, but she couldn't switch them on. That would warn the boys to keep away if their hiding place was indeed down here. Anyway she had no torch at the school, only at home, which would mean having to wait for another convenient day on which to search, and she wouldn't have one with a free period like this before lunch – she worked it out – for another week at least. 'Dammit,' she whispered. 'Dammit, dammit, dammit –'

And then lifted her head as the smell came to her, stale, tired, and a little damp, but familiar all the same. Old wet cigarette ends, the drift of long-ago-exhaled smoke, and she felt a lift of excitement that again made her feel childlike, and pushed on recklessly now, not so worried by the dark as her eyes adjusted.

And then she saw it, a pile of old timber this time, but so arranged that there was an open end through which it was possible to slide without too much difficulty – though it had to be easier for boys, she thought irritably as she caught one breast a sharp blow on a piece of wood, since they lacked such protuberances – and there it was. A pile of old cushions. A slab of timber, probably a discarded door, which had been set firmly on a few bricks at each corner to make a sort of table. Candle ends. She could just see the pile of magazines in the corner and a couple of ash trays on the table, and that was all. But she was in no doubt she'd found what she'd been seeking.

Question, she said to herself. Will they come today? Or will I have to keep coming back and hoping to find them here? They're sure to have someone looking out, so I can't just come down at lunchtime and see if they're here. They'll never be caught that way. I have to be here before them. Which means finding somewhere to hide.

'Oh, shit!' she said aloud, no longer feeling the excitement of the child on a detective game. This was horrid, this was spying. And she turned and came out of the cubbyhole and began to move back up the basement towards the light that showed where the steps were that would lead her back up to a civilized normal world where adults didn't hang around trying to catch adolescents in minor crime and –

But it's not a minor crime, she thought. Whatever they say about cannabis, there is that bit about people maybe using other stronger stuff once they start on it. I have to take this seriously.

And anyway, how can I help or decide what to do if I don't know exactly what's going on? I have to stay and spy, like it or not.

She went back to the cubbyhole and then on beyond it and chose a spot for herself behind one of the arches that dissected the space at this end of the cellar. She found a wooden box she could upend, put her handkerchief on it in the faint hope of keeping herself tolerably clean, and settled down to wait. It might be a waste of time; maybe they only came occasionally and this wasn't one of those times. But the smell had been strong, even though it was stale, and that told her that someone had been smoking here very recently. It would have faded within a week, surely. And she sighed softly and her lungs filled with the smell that had brought her here, and also the thin dampness of the sweating stones and the acrid rasp of the boilers and the rather chewy smell of the anthracite that was used to feed them. Not too nasty, really; but cold . . .

She leaned against the archway and slid into a half-sleeping state. It was agreeable and restful, and when she heard someone moving she wasn't at all surprised nor agitated. She just opened her eyes to exchange inner darkness for the outer kind, and waited a little dreamily to see what would happen.

There was some giggling and soft speech, though she couldn't pick out any words, and then a scuffling sound and after a moment a match was struck. She smelled it as well as heard it, and saw the glint of light and thought, somewhere at a deep level, The air down here carries smells much too easily. Then there was laughter and the striking of more matches.

She waited until the scent of fresh tobacco smoke – and with it, she thought, a hint of the smell of burning hay which she knew was cannabis – reached her, and then sighed again and got up and dusted herself down and walked purposefully to the pile of timber and stood there. She made no effort to go through the gap into the sitting space they'd made for themselves, but stood there as prim as a housemaid and coughed and said loudly, 'Gentlemen? I think someone had better come out and talk to me about what is happening here. All of you, for choice, at once. It certainly will be easier than trying to hold back, I think.'

There was a little silence and then someone said loudly, 'Oh, fuck!' and blew out the candle.

Sixteen

'Yes,' Judith said. 'You have put yourself in a tight spot, haven't you, ducky? Too awful for you.'

Hattie stared at her a little hopelessly. She'd come to talk to Judith because there was no one else she could think of to tell of her discovery who wouldn't turn the whole thing into a nightmare. What had seemed like such a good idea when she'd started out was now a huge problem. It would have been so much easier to remain in ignorance of what went on beneath the surface at the Foundation. She'd been the most stupid kind of meddler; the sort who never looked ahead to work out the effects of her prying. Now she had to act on the facts she had uncovered, and she knew that whatever choice she made of those that seemed to present themselves, it would be the wrong one. If she told the Headmaster, what would he do? Throw the boys out, the way he had Daniel Spero? That was highly unlikely, with his views on the importance of keeping the fees coming in no matter what. He'd only hush it up, she thought gloomily, for fear of other parents hearing about it and panicking, and that'll leave the boys thinking no one cares what they do and that they can get away with anything, which will do them no good at all. It has to be taken seriously.

'I'm really hanging by my fingernails,' she said. 'If I tell the Headmaster, it's odds on he'll do nothing –'

'You mean he won't do what you think he ought to do,' Judith said.

Hattie flushed. 'I'm not being that dogmatic, am I? I didn't think so. It's just that I don't think he'll take it really seriously. If I could hope he'd deal with it by being very tough on the boys but keeping them at the school, I'd not worry. But I think he'll keep 'em at the school but he won't do anything tough.'

'Hilary likes to be liked,' Judith said. 'He can't bear it unless everybody thinks he's the most wonderful, the best looking, the cleverest. He won't do anything tough, I agree with you there.'

Hattie looked at her, surprised as she always was when Judith said anything that was sensible, which was unjust because she could do it quite often when she chose. 'Which means there's no sense in telling him. But I can't just leave it there like that, when I made such a point of finding them out. There were six of them. All puffing away like engines. And with those unpleasant magazines as well . . .'

'I wouldn't have thought a few porno magazines would worry you,' Judith said. 'You never struck me as a prude.'

'I'm not. It's just they really were rather nasty. Not just porn, I mean, not the ordinary kind.'

'No? What then?' Judith was suddenly avid. 'Do tell, darling. Something way over the top? Peter and I'd love to see something new, most of them seem so boring now. No, don't look all pursed up like that. It doesn't suit you. Tell me what they were – frankly gynaecological and so forth?'

'Anything but.' Hattie didn't look at her. The magazines – and she'd only had a glimpse of them – had upset her more than she'd have expected.

Judith's face sagged a little in disappointment. 'I should have expected that, I suppose, in a boys' school. What a pity. I'll never understand why it is that so many good-looking chaps turn queer. Such a waste of faces. I suppose I should be grateful Peter's so hideous.'

'People don't turn queer, as you put it,' Hattie said irritably. 'If they're homosexual, it's just the way they are. It's not a matter of choice. Anyway, that's beside the point. What the hell do I do, now that I know? *That's* the point.'

'Tell 'em not to do it again,' Judith said and reached for the coffee pot. 'Some more, ducky? You look as though you could use it.'

'No thanks. Say that again.'

'Say what again?'

'What you just said.'

'I said more coffee – Oh, before that? I said tell 'em not to do it again.'

Hattie laughed and pushed her cup forward. 'I will have some more after all. You're a star, Judith, you really are.'

'I'm glad to hear it.' Judith cocked a glance at her and then giggled. 'Tell me what I said that was so starry and I'll try it on someone else. Peter for a start. He's a mean bugger, you know. I wanted to take the girls skiing at half-term and he just mutters on and on about the recession till you could scream. So, what did I say?'

'It's all so obvious. I'm a fool not to have thought of it,' Hattie said jubilantly. 'I tell the boys that I'll keep my tongue between my teeth as long as they behave themselves, stop their smoking and generally clean up their act. They'll breathe again because they won't realize the Headmaster won't do anything, will they? They'd expect big trouble, so they'll be grateful as all get out and I've avoided the hassle. Oh, really Judith, I sometimes think you're wasted just being a wife and mother and using all that energy only to get money out of Peter for extra holidays.'

'I don't,' Judith said.

'Ma'am,' Harry said. 'You're a star, if I may be allowed to say so.'

'I can hardly stop you,' Hattie said dryly. 'Considering it's what everyone's calling everyone else these days.'

'Fashion, ma'am, fashion,' Harry said solemnly. 'Let me rephrase it, then. It was not a felicitous construction after all. I and my – er – fellow miscreants are grateful to you for your forbearance –'

'A little less gratitude and a good deal more listening,' Hattie said briskly. 'You can save the fancy talk for someone else. First of all, you and the rest of them will turn up for my lunchtime sessions on living skills every week.'

Harry gave the impression of blanching, despite the high black gloss of his skin. 'But I'm a sixth-former, Mrs Clements.'

'Too bad.' She was implacable. 'Those are my terms and I hold all the trumps. You come to my sessions and you bring some of the other sixth-formers with you, and you all learn a bit. I'd like to see –' She stopped as though she were thinking though she knew precisely what she was about to say. 'Let me think – the Carter twins from time to time. I think they could benefit from a little of what I have to offer. And young A–' She stopped and swallowed. 'Botham, I'd like to see him. He's a shy sort of boy and I think he'd find benefit too. So you use your influence for good and not for bad, right?'

'If that's the first thing, what's the second?'

'A bit of genuine concern for the younger people in the school,' she said. 'I know you've got your prefect system and all that, but as far as I can tell it's used more to frighten the lower formers than to take any sort of care of them. So, I want to be sure that there's no more smoking in this school and that includes tobacco as well as anything else.'

'You're pushing your luck, Mrs Clements.' He'd stopped performing now and was looking at her curiously. 'Why bother? A place like this, it's full of bad shit. You can't clean it up all on your own with a few classes in living skills and making us all into nice caring prefects. People do the most amazing things in this place and, frankly, the less you and the rest of them know about it the better. You'll find it makes life easier.'

'That's the way the Foundation runs, isn't it?' She stared at him, her head up, no longer seeing him as a boy in need of punishment and training, but as an equal. He was certainly as big as she was, and had a striking presence that made it easy to overlook his age. 'Let anything go on as long as it happens in the dark. Like woodlice under a stone. Well, I've turned one of the stones over and I want to see you all scurry.'

'Power,' said Harry, regaining his flippancy. 'It's a heady drug.'

'Power nothing.' Hattie was crisp. 'It just makes me mad to see healthy people ruin their bodies. It's against everything I stand for. So take it or leave it. You do it my way or I start such a stink with the Headmaster that —'

'That he'll do nothing at all and go on encouraging parents to pour out more buckets of money, because that's really all that matters when you get right down to it,' Harry said. 'I'm not as impenetrable of mind as I am of skin, Mrs Clements. I can see what he's like as well as you can. That's why you're dealing with this yourself instead of shopping us. What'd you do if I called your bluff?'

She drew in a sharp little breath through her nostrils, needing to regain control of herself. Her pulses had begun to race uncomfortably. This was getting frightening.

'It's not bluff,' she said steadily. 'And don't underestimate Mr Roscoe. He has ambitions for this place. He wants to see standards raised and the quality of people coming here raised too – scholastically, that is. There's nothing wrong with the quality in any other way.' Why did I need to say that? she thought. In case he thinks I'm racist? Oh, God, but it's getting complicated.

He seemed to be aware of her thinking because he smiled slowly and said, 'Well, ma'am, I sure thank you for that,' and sketched a bow as though he were a caricature of a black servant in a 1930s Hollywood movie.

'So don't think it wouldn't make any difference if I told him,' she went on doggedly, doing all she could to hold on to her control over the conversation she had started. 'Because it would.'

'I can't take the risk,' he said. 'I've got a career to think of, a university to think of. So you're right. You hold the cards. I'll do what I can.'

He turned to go and then came back into the room. 'Those magazines . . .'

This time she couldn't control it. She went a bright red. 'They're none of my business. People's sex lives are their own affair. I have no interest in them. You must read what you choose. I'm no censor.'

He looked at her curiously, and then said, 'It's only cannabis and tobacco that worries you? Oh, well, I suppose that's what I should have expected.'

'If you expected me to be the sort of – of prude who makes judgements about people's sexuality, then you've badly misjudged me.'

'You saw the sort of magazines they were?'

'I wasn't all that interested.'

He laughed. 'I love it when people say that. So lofty. It's funny, because no one can help it. When there's stuff like that lying about you can't help but be interested. Your eyes behave like iron filings and the magazines are your actual pole.'

'It was dark,' she said unwillingly. 'Of course I looked; as you say, it's impossible not to. But I couldn't see much –'

'Leather and whips?'

'I don't want to discuss it,' she said and now she was angry. 'I told you, I make no judgements on people's sexual needs, whatever they are.'

'Boring or fancy, straight or gay . . .' He said it in a dreamy sort of tone, still looking at her with that half-amused gaze he'd kept on her face almost throughout.

'I told you. I'm neither a prude nor a censor. I believe everyone has the right to choose his or her own sexual style, as long as –'

'Yes I know. I've heard all the liberal claptrap before.' He sounded angry suddenly. 'As long as no one's hurt, as long as there's no coercion, as long as it's consenting people in private, da de da, de da de da, sing the old song.'

'It's the fact that you and your friends were smoking an illegal drug that concerns me. I've told you where I stand. I won't involve the Headmaster or the police or anyone as long as I have your assurance that you and the rest of the boys involved will make sure it stops. It's all that matters, as far as I'm concerned. The rest of your interests are your own affairs.'

'Very well, Mrs Clements.' He was suddenly different again, and she was bewildered. Now he was all schoolboy, obedient, a little shamefaced, subservient. 'I'll tell the others. We'll be at the next learning-to-live class, then, and thank you, Mrs Clements.' And he was gone, closing her door behind him carefully, and she stood and stared at it nonplussed. Bloody boys, she thought then furiously. I'll never understand them. Thank God for my two girls.

'You'll do as you're told, Jer. And you'll like it,' Harry said softly. 'So don't damage my ears filling 'em with bullshit. Anyway, she's not that bad. You went to her first class without too much fussing.'

'It's one thing to go because you choose to, another to do it because you're being bullied,' Dalrymple said, and winked at the fat boy, who was sitting wheezing gently beside him and looking glum.

'Yeah,' the fat boy said and squinted at Harry, who ignored him.

'I thought it might be some good dirt we'd get,' Jerry went on, looking sulky now. 'But all she really goes on about is –'

'I know what she goes on about.' Harry was getting irritable and it showed. 'And I couldn't care less for any opinion you might have of it. You go to her bloody classes for the next four

Wednesday lunchtimes. And forget about being bullied. You're not. You're just being told.'

'So what's the worst she can do?' Jeremy was feeling argumentative. 'Tell on us? Much that dickhead'd care! The less he knows about what's going on with us the better he likes it. Can't afford to have any nasty scandals, so it's easier to pretend everything's lovely. He wouldn't take any notice if she took him an ash tray full of roaches —'

'He gave Spero the push,' Harry said and there was a little silence between them, underlined by the shout that was coming from the lower form's play area. The fat boy gazed gloomily at the scratch football that was going on at the other side of the playing field between people from the third and fourth forms and then opened his mouth to speak, saw the look on Harry's face and closed it again. Then Jeremy stretched, looking as insouciant as he could.

'It'd suit me.'

'It wouldn't suit me,' Harry said softly. 'You understand me? It wouldn't suit me. So we'll see you there at the next class Wednesday lunchtime, right?'

Jeremy looked at him and then let his eyes slide away. 'Load of shit if you ask me,' he muttered. 'Oh, don't look like that! I'll be there. Might as well be if everyone else is —'

'Oh, they'll be there,' Harry said. 'They'll be there, never doubt it. You needn't worry about that.'

'Everyone except Tully,' the fat boy said suddenly and giggled shrilly. 'I'd like to see that, him sitting there listening to talk about women fancying men's arses, wouldn't you?' And he nudged Jeremy who slid a glance sideways at Harry and then giggled too.

'You know something, Burchill?' Harry said. 'You're so stupid you oughtn't to be out without a minder. One more word like that and you won't have a tongue left to talk with. Do you believe me?'

'Only joking, Harry,' the fat boy said uneasily and nudged Jeremy again. But Jeremy took no notice and slid off the bench they'd been sharing and moved away as the bells began their raucous shrieking again to mark the end of the lunch break. 'Only joking. Won't say another word —'

'You're bloody right you won't,' Harry said with an affable

air and grinned at him, and then walked away with Jeremy close beside him, moving in a diagonal line towards the small group of girls who were standing watching the football. Genevieve was standing a little to one side of it, and as Harry approached moved with apparent casualness so that he came up to her. Jeremy looked at Harry sleepily, seeking cues, and clearly got them, because he moved away, leaving the two to talk. But the fat boy hardly noticed. He stood disconsolately kicking the grass; he'd never learn when to say the right things, he thought mournfully. Yesterday he'd said something about Tully and they'd all laughed. Why hadn't they laughed today? He'd never understand.

The notice went up on the common-room notice board not long after half-term, and Sam Chanter stopped to look at it over her shoulder and laughed.

'That'll be a first for you, won't it? Oh, you'll love this!'

'Why? What happens?'

'Oh, such goings-on! Such rushings-around and carryings-on and eatings and drinkings and general drive-you-maddings! It starts with the procession, of course. That really is something, you must have heard about it. Our Founder's Day procession! It makes the TV screens every year, God help us.'

She frowned. 'Red tunics and white stockings?'

'You've got it. Yup. What the modern young man wears, a scarlet surtout, matching breeches with white hose and buckled shoes, full lawn sleeves – it's a travesty, it really is.'

'A travesty of what?'

'You may well ask. Of education. Of what life's all about, if you want to wax philosophical about it. We're supposed to be here to rear these kids to be good European citizens for the first half of the twenty-first century and how do we do it? Why, by encouraging them to dress up in the clothes of Elizabethan charity children to march through the streets to be gawped at.'

'It's tradition,' Edward Wilton said, coming in and pushing past them towards the coffee pot. 'And it's only once a year. I don't know why you're always so rude about it, Sam. I rather enjoy it, you know. I mean, it's so very English and so splendidly historical –'

'Historical my arse,' Sam said and reached for his own coffee.

'It's got about as much to do with real history as Anne Hathaway's cottage embroidered in chainstitch on a tea cosy. It's nostalgia run rampant. Enough to make you sick.'

'Sick again, Chanter?' Dave Tully had come in and was standing scowling at the place where the Headmaster's secretary had pinned yet another of her despairing appeals about the proper use of the small car park. 'You've got the queasiest stomach of anyone in the place, one way and another.' Sam's face was suddenly mottled with angry red patches and Hattie stared at him, startled at the sudden change in him. He was looking at Tully with such an expression of anger and loathing that she felt cold for a moment.

Sam said nothing but turned away with obvious contempt and Tully grinned. 'No more lectures for me, Chanter?' he said loudly and Wilton, after one worried look at the pair of them, scuttled for the door. 'No more teaching your grandmother to suck eggs?'

'I've said what I have to say,' Sam said, still not looking at him. 'I'm not interested in adding anything more.'

'How kind of you!' Tully said and winked at Hattie who also reddened and looked away. 'To think that I might be allowed to know my own business best – such a treat for me. I'm much obliged to you, Mr Chanter, sir, Mr Chanter ever-so-sir –'

'One of these days someone'll cut your throat for you, Tully,' Sam said and suddenly laughed. 'And no one'll cheer more loudly than I will. I don't know why I let you irritate me the way you do. You don't matter enough, after all.'

'Don't I? Well, we'll see,' Tully said, clearly feeling himself the victor in the exchange, and peered into the coffee pot. 'This stuff looks like shit, I'm going to pinch some of the Headmaster's. Interested, Mrs Clements? I'm much better company than Little Lord Fauntleroy here,' and he leered at Hattie so absurdly that she laughed, uneasy though the spat between the two men had made her.

'I'm not that desperate for caffeine, thanks,' she said, and Tully shrugged.

'Please yourself,' he said and went and there was a little silence behind him.

Hattie stole a glance at Sam. He looked his usual self again, calm and relaxed, and she wondered for a moment if she'd imagined the sudden spurt of cold fury that had been in him; and then, as he caught her eye and smiled, pushed it all to the back of her mind. Tully was always an irritating person; clearly there'd been some disagreement over something unimportant and Sam had for once let his annoyance show. It was no more than that, she assured herself, and smiled back at him.

'Bloody Founder's Day.' Collop had come in and was scrabbling in the battered leather holdall he carried everywhere with him. 'As if I hadn't enough on my plate, I've got to revive the *Shrew* for it.'

Sam laughed, genuinely amused. 'Oh, that'll be a joy! You'll never get the little bastards to get that together again, will you?'

'You watch me.' Collop sounded grim as at last he found the bottle he was looking for and began to unscrew it. 'I'll murder them if they don't and they know it. It's a fact that I find works like aqua vitae on a midwife.'

He tipped his head back and held the bottle high and they all watched silently as the stream of liquid from the bottle ran into his mouth and he swallowed it, splashing not a drop. It was his party piece, a trick he'd learned years ago in Spain when he'd worked in bars and restaurants during the long vacs from university, and he was proud of it, and when he'd finished, he screwed up the bottle again and wiped the back of his hand across his mouth.

'That'll get me through the first period, I hope. I've got the fourth, I ask you, the fourth! A bigger bunch of halfwits I have never had to suffer, even here, and if I had my way I'd get the lot of them sweeping the quadrangle or something. It'd do them more good than listening to me elucidate the inner meanings and hidden delights of *Silas Marner*. But what can I do, with Staveley off sick and someone having to hold the fort for his bloody sixth years? As if I hadn't enough to provoke me —'

'They're not that bad,' Hattie heard herself saying and could have bitten her tongue off. It was never clever to say anything at all to Collop; ever since the rehearsals for the play at the end of last term they'd been on the coolest of terms, but she had an affection for the boys in the fourth who were, it often seemed to her, the most bewildered of all the bewildered young ones in the place. The thought of their suffering Collop for the afternoon had made her wince. Now she braced herself for the acid of his reply, whatever it was.

But he ignored what she had said and only looked at her owlishly and said, 'I'll need your precious ewe lambs again. Am I to enjoy the pleasure of your company at all the rehearsals? Again?' And there was enough of an insult in the way he said 'again' that made her furious and she snapped, 'Of course!' without stopping to think. And then was even more furious, but this time with herself. She had enough on her plate with her girls at home and her own work here to want to sit it out again at late afternoon and early evening rehearsals.

But the die was cast and she had to accept it, like it or not. She was to be as much a part of Founder's Day at the Foundation as anyone else. March 6 would be hectic for all of them, with the procession and church parade to the City in the morning, and the Open Day in the afternoon, an Open Day which, she was told with gloom by Sam Chanter, included gymnastic displays; a series of demonstrations by the Cadet Corps ('It's the only thing Michael Staveley lives for all year,' he said. 'He'll be happy, at least'); shows put on by the boys in the computer group; several recitals by boys in the Latin and Greek classes ('Readings from the poets,' Sam said. 'Sheer bloody hell'); and various efforts made by all the rest of the school. The performance of the *Shrew* was to be the same night, and Sam shook his head as he explained it all to Hattie at length.

'By the end of it, none of us'll know whether we're on this earth or Fuller's, to quote my good old granny. Just you wait and see. It'll be murder, one way and another.'

Seventeen

'The place'll be like a morgue all morning,' Hattie said, stopping to look out of the common-room window that overlooked the quadrangle. 'Rather nice, really. No bells, and a chance to get ourselves braced up for the afternoon.'

'Not a bit of it.' Sam looked over her shoulder to where boys were gathering in a great chattering flurry like a cloud of scarlet and white jays. There were some of the rather small barely pubertal ones in a cluster just beneath the window and Hattie looked at their smooth young faces and the way their hair curled against the pleated white ruffs that were set over the scarlet surtouts and felt a wave of tenderness, which she tried to suppress. It was the sort of sentimental knee-jerk response some people have to choirboys; she should be ashamed to be so soggy. But it wasn't easy to be cool about the way they looked. Long white legs over black buckled shoes were very seductive. 'The place'll have humming with people. They don't all go to the parade, you know.'

'Oh! I assumed they did.'

'What, all seven hundred of them? The police'd never agree, even if we had the gear for all of them. No, just a hundred go. The rest stay here getting the Open Day stuff set up.'

'I should have realized,' Hattie said as a sweating Edwards, looking particularly resplendent in a crimson and black outfit loaded with gold braid which made his belly seem even larger than it was, tried to line the boys up in size order with the smallest at the front, but not until the Headmaster appeared in his flowing academic gown and crimson and black mortar board did any of them pay the least attention. Then as obediently as sheep they formed into lines of four, ready to move off.

On the far side of the quad there was a little group of men with cameras and microphones on sound booms and Wilton, who had come to join them, said, 'What's going on down there? The men with cameras –'

'What it looks like.' David Tully had come in and was staring out at the quad with them. 'The Head fancies a film to use as a fund-raiser at City dinners and he's got some self-important little shit to do it. Shushing you out of the way when you walk past – what a wanker! Carries on as though he owns the place. I'll have him before the day's out, see if I don't.'

'I know him,' Hattie said, peering and recognizing him. 'He's been filming the play. He's Dilly Langham's father.'

'And what might Dilly Langham be when it's at home?'

Hattie wouldn't look at him. 'She's one of my sixth-formers.' And then in a sudden flush of anger added, 'You know perfectly well who she is. She's in one of your sets for A level!'

'I pay no attention to the girls at all,' Tully said. 'Waste of time and energy. They do what the hell they like. And do it very badly.'

'No you don't,' Sam murmured in Hattie's ear as her muscles clenched so that she could turn on Tully, and, knowing he was right, she obeyed. But it wasn't easy.

'You ought to see what goes on when the outfits come up from the storage people,' Sam said loudly. 'It's a circus. They've got just the hundred, had them for years. Replaced after the last lot, which were fifty or so years old then, had been blitzed, and they're threadbare. Well, they would be after almost fifty years. It's amazing how they can keep on laundering and mending them. But they do, and they bring them here in huge baskets, all starched up and ready, and then sort through the boys to see who fits them. Not the other way around, choosing the boys to parade and then fixing the gear. Nothing so simple. It's the shoes that give the most trouble. I'd have plenty of blister plasters ready for when they get back for lunch. Which, by the way, is rather good news for us.'

'It is?'

'Mmm. One of the traditions that I rather like. Switzer's Oyster Bar in that alley just off Leadenhall Street, do you know it? Old as the hills, but nicely modest about it. They've got a history of over a hundred years of sending up a barrel of oysters and two of porter for the teaching staff on Founder's Day. The owner at some distant past time was a Foundation Scholar –'

'So, bread and cheese for you, lady,' Tully said as he pushed past them towards the door with what Hattie regarded as deliberate rudeness. 'Since you're not a teacher, you get no goodies. Not that you need oysters. Widow, aren't you?' And he looked at her with his head tilted and his lips curved in a malicious grin and then vanished, slamming the door behind him.

It was a moment or two before she understood what he meant and then hazy recollections of tales of the aphrodisiac effect of oysters on females came back to her and she went a mottled and rather ugly red.

'If you pay any attention to that, then you really are a fool,' Sam said calmly. 'Come on. I've got a demonstration to set up in my small lab and you've got the tea tent again, haven't you?'

She was still angry but she managed to follow his lead, aware now of the malicious and amused stares of some of the other men in the room, particularly Ian Bevan. 'Once a mug, always a mug,' she said as cheerfully as she could and he squeezed her arm in approval with the hand that the others couldn't see, and she felt a good deal better.

For a while. But as the morning wore on and she and the girls went through the boring routine of sandwich-making again, just as they had for the autumn fair, she found herself feeling oddly desolate. Why was so much malice directed at her? What had she done to these men that they should treat her so? Not all, of course. Sam was good news; and Wilton, though he had his tiresome moments, was all right. Most of the rest of them were harmless enough, but there was still this cold heart of hatred in Tully and Bevan and, to an extent, Collop, though he sometimes seemed to be amiable enough. Why should they feel so about her? And then one of the girls said something that made the others laugh and she pulled herself out of her own thoughts and joined in the chatter and found herself thinking, Well, the kids like me, at least. And then wondered if that was what was wrong. By and large the pupils of the Foundation, boys as well as girls, did like her; she knew that and she had a sudden memory of Judith saying sapiently, 'Hilary likes to be liked. He can't bear it unless everybody thinks he's the most wonderful, the best looking, the cleverest . . .' Was there an element of that in the way those men behaved? Did they crave the sort of popularity among the children she'd earned so easily? Well, maybe not; but it was pleasant to think so, so think it she would.

The weather seemed to be willing to indulge Founder's Day. The chilly rain of the morning cleared by the time the parade started, sent off with ironic cheers by the rest of the school, walking a little sheepishly in the middle of the road surrounded by policemen. The man in charge of the camera and the sound equipment busily leaping around where everyone could see him do so made loud appreciative noises about the thin sunshine that trickled through to light the wet roads to a bright gloss, and the bobbing scarlet surtouts and the glinting brass buckles on the shoes made a brave display. Hattie, to her shame, felt a little wave of emotion, made up of tears and pride and sheer pleasure, as she watched them go, and again was irritated. It shouldn't be so easy to manipulate people's emotions, she thought, and then saw Hilary Roscoe, striding along at the rear of his boys, about ten yards behind them, with the tassel on his mortar board bobbing and his gown billowing most magisterially, and could have given him a rude cheer herself. He was positively preening, she thought as the few passers-by there were stopped to stare. He loves it all. Silly man. Dangerous man because he's so silly. And vain.

But that was ungenerous of her, she decided, and went inside again to get on with her work, and refused to think at all about Hilary or his staff or the theatricality of the morning. This afternoon, with so many assorted outside visitors coming to see the school put on a different and much better sort of show of its own abilities and efforts, would be much more fun.

After swallowing their oysters and porter (and Hattie made a point of doing her fair share of work with the former, though even to spite Tully she couldn't cope with the latter), the staff climbed into their academic gowns and caps and she felt a little awkward at first as the only one in ordinary clothes, although what she was wearing, a dark amethyst dress cut to fit very well indeed and worn over black tights and shoes which gave her a severe and, she secretly thought, rather sexy look, was perfectly suitable; then Sam said approvingly, 'Very nice,' when he saw her all ready to face the fray and that cheered her greatly. She didn't need fancy dress to be part of the afternoon's events, after all.

The same people, it seemed to her, who had been at the autumn fair arrived at two sharp to be part of the Open Day. There was the same set of well-upholstered City men and their equally well-turned-out wives, the same look of unease on parental faces as they dealt with scowling sons who were clearly mortified at having to be seen by their friends and villains-in-arms as having anything to do with such awful people, the same air of money spent ostentatiously if not always well. Freddy Langham this time was very lordly, very visible, with his camera crew collecting footage of parents eating and drinking the afternoon tea Hattie and the girls had organized (and she was very amused to notice more than one man making a very definite effort to keep well out of range of the cameras; what did they have to hide? she wondered. School fees paid out of undeclared income, or as a tax dodge? She wouldn't be at all surprised) and Dilly in consequence hid herself inside the small form room that had been set aside to be used as a bakery/kitchen for the tea tent. And Hattie couldn't blame her.

Once the tea service was running smoothly (and it enjoyed this time the assistance of some of the women who worked in the school kitchens and was less dependent on Hattie and the girls), she was free to wander and look about, and she took the chance happily, glad now not to be clearly identified as staff by the wearing of academic dress. She could have been just a parent, anonymous and uninteresting to all the other parents, and that made her feel free and relaxed.

The computer groups had set up a game involving the catching of mice by cats which scurried across the screen in a highly enjoyable fashion in response to pressing of the various keys, and she spent a good deal of time in the first of the two rooms devoted to the subject, and only went into the second out of a vague sense of duty, doubting she'd find anything more interesting than that she had already been playing with. She found the room was very quiet: just three boys were there with a couple of parents, and the only unoccupied boy was Arse.

She remembered just in time. 'Hello – ah – Vivian,' she said. 'I didn't know you were a computer boffin.'

'I'm not.' He didn't look at her. 'Just doing a few things to help out. It's better than the Cadets.'

'Anything would be better than the Cadets,' she said warmly and this time he did look at her.

'Don't you like to see them marching up and down with their little guns?'

'I most certainly do not. I hate to see war and killing made into some sort of game. I won't be watching, and don't know how anyone can.'

'Oh, they can make 'em feel safe. Lots of nice soldiers all ready to get themselves killed if the stock market plays up over oil or whatever it is they think is worth killing soldiers for.'

'Well, I'm not one of them,' she said and perched herself on the edge of one of the desks. 'I'd be a conscientious objector if there were a war.'

'There's always a war on somewhere,' Arse said. 'Only most people don't bother to notice unless it's costing them money. Do you want to see this computer game?'

'If you want to show me.'

'Not really. It's just what I'm here for, so I thought I'd better ask.'

There was a little silence between them broken only by the chatter of the parents being shown a game by the other two boys in the room, and then she said, 'Are your parents here?'

He looked wooden. 'No.'

She considered leaving it at that but chose to push a little. 'Too busy?'

'Not interested.'

She looked at him nonplussed and then said, 'There's no answer to that, is there?'

'None at all. So I don't think you should try to make one. And don't feel sorry for me or anything like that. I'm a sight better off without having people hanging around here than some of the others.' And he looked over his shoulder to where a woman was giggling in a high-pitched cascade of sound as the computer game, this time involving a cat and some fleas, defeated her, and Hattie laughed.

'Well, I see what you mean. Parents can be hell. I remember how I used to feel about mine when they got out in public. Mortified, most of the time. Mind you, it was amazing how they improved as time went on.'

'I know,' he said sardonically and put on a pompous voice. 'Let us quote Mark Twain: "When I was sixteen I knew I had a fool for a father. By the time I was twenty I was amazed at how much the old man had come on in four years."' His voice reverted to normal. 'They're always quoting that one at us.'

'Sorry.'

'No need. You weren't going on, I don't suppose. Well, if you don't want to see that game –' He stopped and she flushed, aware that he was inviting her to leave, and got to her feet.

'If I'm in the way . . .'

'Oh, no. I just thought you'd be bored.'

And then he lifted his chin and looked over her shoulder towards the door and it was as if someone had switched on a light inside him. The heavy flat expression he'd worn throughout melted into a smile and he looked his age for the first time instead of like a rather well-preserved middle-aged man.

Hattie looked over her shoulder too, and saw Dilly peering round the door and she too looked alive and happy, and Hattie thought, Well! That's all right then. He's going to be fine. And she smiled at Dilly warmly.

'Hello, Dilly. Escaped the dreaded bread-spreading detail?'

Dilly seemed to become aware of her for the first time and came into the room, changing her expression as she moved from the excited one that had wreathed her face to a watchful closed look. 'Well, they didn't need me any more.' She looked at Arse. 'Wondered if you'd like to come to see the parade,' she said. 'They're marching and then there'll be some shooting practice. Targets.'

'The Cadets? Why should I go and –'

'I just thought you might like to,' she said quickly, carefully not looking at Hattie. 'We can be at the side where they won't notice us.'

'Oh.' He looked at her and then at Hattie. 'Oh, I see. All right. If you don't want to see anything here, Mrs Clements . . .'

'Nothing at all,' she assured him. 'You're free as far as I'm concerned.' The other people finished their game and, chattering loudly about how ridiculous it was that so much could be done with such a small set-up, went out of the room. 'Though I thought you said you wouldn't want to see the Cadets do anything.'

'Oh, I didn't think I actually said that.' Again the wooden expression cloaked his face and she was suddenly annoyed with him.

'Well, it's nothing to do with me what you do. I just had the impression you agreed with me that schoolboys playing at soldiers – the sort who kill – was a repellent concept.'

'I do,' he said. 'Dilly does too, don't you, Dilly?' He flicked a glance at Dilly who was standing staring at Hattie with a watchful look on her face. She said nothing. 'But that doesn't mean there mightn't be a case for watching them do it. They might do it badly, you see.' And suddenly he laughed as though suppressed glee had been too powerful for him. 'You never know your luck.'

'Come on,' Dilly said with sudden urgency, pulling on his arm, and he nodded at Hattie and followed Dilly with alacrity, and Hattie stood in the empty room staring after them, puzzled. They were up to something, she found herself thinking. They're just like Sophie and Jessica when they've done something outrageous, like the time they filled the bath with all the soap powder in the house, and turned on the taps so that the bathroom exploded into foam. It was the same look. They've done something involving the Cadets; and she got to her feet and made for the door purposefully. I think it might be worth watching the demonstration after all.

Eighteen

The sun had strengthened as the afternoon had worn on, and though the grass was still very wet and the earth beneath soggy, so that best shoes with high heels sank into little bore holes and white pumps became grass-stained, there was a sprightly air about the proceedings in the small playing field that lay at the back of the main school buildings. It was a long, narrow area, because much of the original acreage had been sold off piecemeal over the years to make money, but it lent itself well enough to a military type of display. At the far end there was a low dais on which Michael Staveley, looking absurdly pompous in the uniform of a major, was flanked by some of the sixth-formers in the uniforms, as far as Hattie could tell, of lieutenants, while numbers of boys from the fifth and fourth forms marched around in front of them to the tinny sound of a military march played by a record player over a loudspeaker system in a van parked in the far corner of the field, just by the gate that led out to Ratcliff Street.

By the time Hattie arrived it was clear the demonstration had been going on for some time. Most of the marching boys seemed to have got what they were doing right, though there was one group towards the rear who seemed to be thoroughly flummoxed and out of step in spite of the bawlings of the boy who was supposed to be directing their drill, and Hattie was amused to see how magisterially Staveley managed to ignore them. But within a few minutes the drill display came to an end, to scattered applause from the parents lined up watching at the end of the field opposite Staveley's dais.

Hattie found herself a spot to stand in reasonable comfort,

leaning against the brick and wood wall of the storage sheds which had been put up in one corner of the field, and settled to observe what she could. She tried to see Dilly and Arse, but they were lost somewhere in the crowd though she could see Freddy Langham, still very active with his camera, and wondered with some amusement just how long his film was meant to be. He could have been making *War and Peace*, he'd shot so much.

The next display involved four boys on motorcycles and it was rather embarrassing, even a little pathetic. She'd seen the sort of things that teams of such cyclists could do, but usually on television there were a dozen or so of them. These four made the best job they could of weaving in and out of patterns and getting closer to each other than would normally be countenanced, and when they'd finished the applause was louder than it had been for the drill, probably out of gratitude it was over, Hattie thought, as well as out of sympathy for its overall feebleness, doing her share of hand-clapping as much to warm her chilly fingers as for any other reason. But then she became more alert as some of the boys came on to the field tugging various contraptions with them, and began to set them up. They were the targets for shooting practice, with silhouettes of shoulder-hunched men pinned to them, and she looked at them with loathing. Why couldn't they settle for the sort of familiar archery targets that wouldn't have been so explicit? The use of the human form as something to aim at made her feel almost sick.

Some of the boys came down to the watching parents and started to shepherd them to a safer area and Hattie watched, amused, as Harry Forster, looking unbelievably handsome in his lieutenant's uniform, bowed at some of the women who were clearly unsure of how to react to a black skin wrapped in the sort of clothes that demanded obedience, and sent them to the other side of the field to the one where they were standing.

They went cheerfully enough and then Hattie saw that some of the staff were there too; Bevan, looking disgruntled and leaning heavily on his stick, stood immovable at a place where there was some gravel and Hattie could hardly blame him for refusing to be budged. That stick with his weight on it set on this wet earth would be worse than useless. Harry seemed to shrug and left him there, and, after a moment, one or two other members of staff strolled over to join him. Hattie could see Martin Collop and

Gregory Steenman and, a little to her surprise, David Tully. There was little amity between him and Bevan; she'd have expected him to keep his distance. But there he stood, leaning against the fence, very visible in the particularly artistic outfit he had chosen to wear today beneath his academic gown; a cherry-red velvet jacket with a matching cravat in silk and cream and shirtsleeves which were so exaggeratedly frilled at the cuff that some of the fabric fell halfway down his fingers. Hattie had seen a few of the puzzled and disapproving stares some of the fathers had thrown at him and enjoyed them; Tully was an unpleasant man to deal with but he did give people a run for their money.

She stayed where she was, well out of the way, and no one came to disturb her. She wasn't surprised. Here she could not see the targets that had at last been set up to one side of the field. There was a curve to this side which hid them, and that suited her well. It was not the targets she was interested in, but Dilly and Arse, for she could now see them clearly, standing not too far away from the knot of masters on the gravelled area. The rest of the audience, largely parents, though there were some of the younger boys with them, were clustered where they could easily see the targets at which the boys who were to display their prowess were already staring from their own places halfway up the range.

They had boxes with them and were wearing battledress rather than the dress uniform of the boys who had drilled, and they looked rakish and clearly pleased with themselves. Fifteen- and sixteen-year-olds, Hattie thought bitterly, liking to be seen strutting in camouflage battledress, wanting to shoot at cut-outs of human forms. Can't they see what it means? Can't they see how hateful it all is?

But clearly they had no thoughts at all apart from enjoying themselves, and she watched as they unloaded their boxes, pulling out rifles, loading them, settling themselves on their bellies behind stand-up baffles that were there to represent their hiding places as they played at being snipers.

There was a shout from the far end, where Staveley still stood on his dais, now with a pair of binoculars hanging importantly round his neck; then he lifted one arm and shouted the order to fire, and it began: the cracking of the shots; the shouts of some of the boys as they scored hits and knew it; the calls of the boys who had been set to collect the used sheets of target paper and replace them with new ones for the later-comers.

After about fifteen minutes of it, Hattie decided it was really rather boring. The boys came up to the butts in groups of four, and then retired to dig into their boxes to reload their guns, and she could just see them, for their place at the rear was within her line of vision. And she could also see that Dilly and Arse were watching them too, avidly, so she fixed all her attention on the same point that they did.

So much so that when it happened she wasn't at first aware of it. There was another crack of guns being fired and further shouting, but this time it was more urgent, and then there were other louder cries, more like screams, and still Hattie stared at the boys reloading their guns, wanting to see whatever it was Dilly and Arse were waiting for; but then there was another cry and a piercing shriek, and she had to turn her head to see the direction it came from; and saw there was a knot of excited people milling around on the gravel where the masters had been standing. Someone was lying down flat on the grass on his or her front and as Hattie stared two more threw themselves down in the same way, and, puzzled, she began to move towards the group. There was another shout, this time from the other side of the field where the dais was, and a couple more almost dispirited shots from guns and then the firing stopped and she saw Michael Staveley come lumbering over, waving one arm over his head, and Harry, who had been walking up to one of the targets, lifted his head and came sprinting across the field too.

She moved automatically, not thinking at all, just letting events happen around her in an unsurprised sort of way; she wasn't even particularly startled when she came up to the group of masters just as old Ian Bevan turned away from whatever it was he had been staring at and faced her, his cheeks mottled and blueish, and then with a sort of hiccup vomited. She just pushed past him and stared down at the ground like everyone else.

David Tully was lying on his back, with both arms flung above his head in the way that babies sometimes lay when they slept, and at first she thought absurdly that he was asleep. But something was wrong and she stared, and again the thoughts that came into her head were ridiculous: his cherry-coloured jacket had slipped upwards and covered half his face. But of course it hadn't. The cherry-red area *was* his face, not a covering at all, and she caught her breath as commonsense came back with a thump and she thought, He's bleeding, got to stop bleeding, keep airway open, and found herself on her knees beside Tully without being quite aware of how she'd got there.

They stepped back, all of them, seeming to bow to a greater authority and to be grateful it was there. Even Staveley halted at the edge of the crowd and watched as she reached forwards and with one hand pulled down Tully's jaw and with the other hooked one finger into his mouth to pull his tongue forward.

'Handkerchief, someone,' she muttered and one appeared over her shoulder and she used it to grab the tongue more firmly, because it was slippery with blood as well as saliva, and then lifted the chin so that the tongue couldn't fall back again.

One side of the face seemed to have collapsed. There was just a pool of red, lots of different reds; cherry like the jacket, but scarlet too, and rich crimsons, and bright shreds that seemed to have some blue in them, and she leaned forwards, hearing her lecturer's voice in her mind's ear: 'Look first, don't touch, look and assess; don't rush to touch, you do more harm than good that way . . .'

The cheekbone was shattered and half the nose with it; the airway was going to be the major problem and again she checked that the mouth was clear and that the chest was moving. He was lying with his eyes half open, staring blankly upwards, as though all this was really rather boring and he was damned if he was going to pay any attention to it; and tentatively Hattie pinched his tongue through the handkerchief with which she held it, hoping for a reaction. If he responded to pain he wasn't too deeply unconscious. The tongue jerked beneath her finger and she held on, hard, and thought, Not too bad, and then knew that was stupid. With an injury like this to the face the likelihood that he had escaped brain damage was small; there had to be some major injury there and that could mean – well, anything. That he would die; that he would survive, but mindlessly; that –

'Steady on,' she whispered inside her head, aware again of the people watching her so trustingly. 'Think about what to do. Deal with the breathing, then deal with the bleeding . . .'

He seemed to be breathing well enough. The chest rose and fell evenly if rather rapidly and she reached for a pulse in the neck on the uninjured side. That too was very fast and a little thready, but steady, and she bit her lip. He had to be bleeding as well as shocked; was the blood running down inside into the bronchii and on into the lungs? Couldn't be; his breathing would have been affected –

'Can I help?' She became aware that Steenman was kneeling beside her. 'Done some first aid. Just tell me what you want done.'

'I'm concerned about bleeding,' she said. 'There doesn't seem to be any arterial loss, though there's a lot of free blood there, of course, but no obvious pulsing. Has someone sent for help?'

'Forster's gone running. Fastest man we have. Shouldn't be too long. Look, let me hold the tongue. You see to the wound.'

Someone had brought a first-aid box and set it open on the ground beside her. She looked at it and then reached in for a piece of lint, and moving with all the delicacy she had set it over the bloody mess that had been the right side of Tully's face and watched as the redness blossomed against the fuzzy surface, spread and overtook the whole of the whiteness. It took several more pieces before she could see what was going on beneath and then she looked at the way the shreds of bone showed creamily in the depths, at the pulpiness of the whole area, and murmured, 'Can't put pressure on that,' and beside her Steenman grunted.

'It's amazing it's not an arterial bleed. Aren't there any big arteries there?'

'Can't remember – Oh!' She lifted her head as the sound came floating across the field. 'Isn't that a siren? It is, oh, thank God for that. I'm out of my depth here.' And she looked over her shoulder at the people behind her. 'Someone go and see where they are. Open the gates at the end of the field, maybe let them in that way. The quicker we get them here the better.'

Several people turned and started to run across the field and the others, seeming relieved by the action, began to talk, jabbering and exclaiming so that Hattie's head seemed filled with it like cotton wool that was pressed hard against her ears and made her head ache.

'What happened? I didn't see – did you see?' 'I thought it was something that . . .' 'He just seemed to jump in the air and then go over on his back.' 'It must have been one of the guns, but they were firing way off from us, weren't they?' 'Someone must have stepped on a gun or something.' 'I always said these boys shouldn't have real ones . . .' 'It's blanks they use though, isn't it? Not real ones. Blanks, must be blanks . . .'

'Quiet!' she shouted, unable to bear it any longer. 'I can't hear myself think. Shut up, please!' And behind her the voices stopped, and someone coughed and a few people moved away. She could feel them go and was glad of it.

And then at last there were other people there, people who knew what to do, big men with loud voices who leaned over and took the lint piece she was still holding over Tully's wrecked face from her fingers, and tutted loudly in her ear.

'Oh, nasty, very nasty. How did that – Well, never mind that now. Let's be having some space now, if you please, that's it, well back there, if you please, you too, sir, *if* you don't mind . . .'

Steenman got to his feet and one of the men reached over and with expert fingers slid an airway into Tully's mouth and then the other one was there, with a stretcher, and they unfolded it and had Tully off the wet grass and strapped into it as deftly as she remembered ambulance men always did do things, and she was so intensely grateful to them she could have hugged them; and one of them turned and winked at her in the old familiar way and said, 'Not to worry, miss. We'll take over now. Anyone coming to Old East with him? Relatives or –?'

'I'll go.' It was Harry, and Hattie looked at him as he came over to look down on Tully's face. 'I'll phone back to say what's what.' And then he followed the two men and Tully to the ambulance and they all stood and watched them get the stretcher in and follow it themselves and remained there as the white bulk of it went slowly lumbering across the field to the far gates, which someone was holding ready for them, and said nothing.

It wasn't until the gates had been closed behind them that someone said to her, 'Are you all right?' And she looked up to see who it was and laughed aloud. Edward Wilton, his face so crumpled and concerned that he looked like a battered teddy bear, and she tried to regain her composure and only managed to hiccup.

'It's hysterics,' a voice said behind her. 'I've heard of that happening, hysterics afterwards, when people have been all right up to then, all very –'

'No,' she said aloud. 'I'm fine. Thank you, Edward. I need a

wash though.' And she looked down at her hands and saw that
her skirt had blood on it too, and felt sick. But an image of the
way Ian Bevan had opened his mouth and vomited as she had
come across to see what had happened somehow managed to
stop the impulse and she swallowed and took a deep breath and
said again, 'I really must wash.'

'I'll take you over, Mrs Clements.' It was Dilly. Hattie peered
at her and nodded gratefully, and they turned and went, Dilly
with one hand under Hattie's elbow in a way which gave her no
support and indeed was uncomfortable, but which for all that
made her feel better. She needed some sort of direct physical
contact.

She washed in the boys' cloakroom, neither of them paying
any attention to the sign on the door, neither of them seeing any
need to cross half the school to reach the only girls' cloakroom
there was, and as Hattie rubbed at the blood on her skirt with
wads of lavatory paper, leaving a great wet patch, Dilly knelt at
her feet and did the same for her shoes, and Hattie let her,
lacking the energy to protest. She felt very weak and shaky now.

Dilly seemed to become aware of that and went away to come
back with a chair and Hattie sat down gratefully, letting her
head droop forward to deal with the dizziness that had arrived
now, and after a while she felt better and able to sit upright.

'That was awful,' she said. 'What happened? It seemed to me
to be – well, I didn't realize anything was wrong at first.'

Dilly was very pale. 'It was a gun, I think. I think he was
shot.'

Hattie stared at her. 'Shot? By one of the target-shooters?'

Dilly said nothing. Hattie frowned, trying to concentrate.

'But they weren't in line – no – I mean, to have hit him
someone would have had to be shooting right off the target.'

'Someone did,' Dilly said and then closed her mouth as though
she were afraid to say more and Hattie looked up at her and
remembered.

'What were you doing?'

'Doing?'

Hattie closed her eyes wearily. 'Not now, Dilly. He might be
dead for all we know. It was a dreadful injury. You and Ar –
Botham. What were you doing?'

Dilly took in a sharp little breath that seemed to echo in the quiet cloakroom and then she said, 'It was pepper. I swear to you, only pepper.'

'Pepper?'

'It was me. First. I said how much I hated the Cadet thing, every bit of it, and Arse said he did too and we thought, well, we thought pepper in one of the bullets so that when it fired it would go back in the gun and hit the chap who'd pulled the trigger. Don't ask me how it worked. Arse did the science. He's very clever like that. Me, I just got it into a box.'

'Got what into what box?'

'The kits they carry.' Dilly sounded impatient, almost normal. 'The ones with the rifles. They're called 303s and they have special ammunition. We got hold of some in a pub in Kilburn and Arse did things to it to make it fire pepper in the face of the person who pulled the trigger. It could have made them very – No one would have been killed or anything, or even blinded. I made sure of that. I told Arse I couldn't do it if – anyway, he said it wouldn't. Just be so horrible and like aversion therapy, no one it happened to would ever pick up a gun again. And people who saw it happen, they might get an aversion too. It was worth trying. It was our Open Day stunt, you see. The Cadets did theirs, and we did pepper. And now this . . .'

She was white and her eyes were wide and staring for the pupils were greatly enlarged and Hattie could almost smell the fear in her and reached out and took her hand.

'Don't panic. What happened to Tully was nothing to do with pepper. I saw that injury – that was a bullet. It had to be. I thought they only fired blanks . . .'

'Not always,' Dilly said drearily. 'I found out. Asked people. Anyway, you can get live bullets easy. Pubs. Irish pubs. There's always someone who'll – Honestly, it wasn't meant to do big damage. It was just pepper, freshly ground black and some cayenne –' She stopped then and giggled shrilly. 'Sounds like a recipe for cooking chicken, and all we did was cook Tully. Oh, Christ –'

'Shut up,' Hattie said loudly and Dilly, who had started to breathe very fast, stopped, gasped and stared at her, and then, very deliberately, clearly making a great effort, began to breathe more slowly and easily. Hattie nodded in approval.

'No need to say anything to anyone about this at present.

About you and your pepper. I'll let you know when and who to talk to. All right?'

'Yes,' Dilly said.

'You trust me?'

'I've got to,' Dilly said drearily. 'What else can I do? Oh, God, I wish I'd been shot. I wish it had been me.'

Nineteen

'Have they gone?' Hattie asked and Wilton looked over his shoulder for all the world like a conspirator and said, 'I think so.'

'No need for them to have been here in the first place,' Steenman said. 'Accident like that – no need for police. Not for accidents –'

'Accidents with guns don't happen too often,' Sam Chanter said, and got to his feet and went over to the window to stare out. The last of the parents and boys were leaving now, moving slowly past the two uniformed policemen at the gates who were collecting names and addresses. 'If Tully dies, it could get to be a very complicated business to sort out.'

'Isn't it complicated enough?' Martin Collop said. 'It certainly looked it to me. That face was –'

'We don't need any descriptions,' Wilton said quickly. 'Enough of us saw it. Hattie, will he survive?'

They all turned to look at her then and Hattie stared back, very aware of her own inadequacy, even more of the way they took it for granted she had knowledge they lacked. A major shift in the balance of power, that's what this is, she thought absurdly, and, even more absurdly, wanted to giggle. But only for a moment.

'I don't know,' she said. 'I'm not God.'

'You can make a more informed sort of guess than most of us,' Steenman said.

'Much good it'll do you, but all right, if you must. It depends on the amount of brain damage. If he gets his consciousness back then it'll be a good sign. If he stays unconscious then it's a matter of anybody's guess. And even that's not a very scientific assessment, only one of my own. It's just that in my experience of the people I looked after, those with head damage who come round fairly soon do better than those who don't. But he had awful injuries.'

'Won't be so pretty any more, will he?' Steenman said abruptly and then turned away to the window. 'Knowing Tully, he might prefer not to come round.'

'I've seen worse,' Chanter said unexpectedly, and then as they all looked at him added, 'Dog bites. Last year. There were films and pictures all the time about facial injuries. They can put a lot of them right with the newer cosmetic techniques.'

'I can't see any sense in this conversation at all.' Ian Bevan hauled himself from the depths of the big armchair where he'd been sitting with his eyes closed, but clearly not sleeping. His voice was shrill and petulant. 'What happens to Tully is the least of it. It's what happens to the rest of us that needs to be considered.'

'The rest of *us*?' Steenman looked at him and shook his head. 'You've no need to worry, Bevan. No one saw you with a gun in your hand.'

'Eh?' Bevan looked puzzled and then shook his head as if to get rid of a tiresome buzzing wasp. 'I'm not worried about that. No one would think I had anything to do with it, or you lot either. We were the *targets*, that's the thing. If they've started shooting at us, then God help us all. Who'll they get next? We won't be safe anywhere.'

'It was an accident,' Steenman said loudly. 'For Christ's sake, man, an accident! You don't think anyone did it deliberately, do you?'

'Oh, of course I do,' Bevan said and sounded more petulant than ever. 'Of course I do, and so should you if you've any sense. Putting guns into those boys' hands – it's madness. If this doesn't put an end to Staveley's nonsense, nothing will.'

'Then they'll try to poison us, do you suppose, Bevan?' It was Sam Chanter, sounding amused. 'Or will it be a secret poison gas developed in the school labs and made of a substance undetectable to modern science?'

'Oh, you can laugh, Chanter,' Bevan cried shrilly. 'You can laugh! You weren't standing next to the bloody man the way I was. You didn't see what it did to him. It's easy for you to scoff when you weren't the target. This time,' he added with a needle of malice sharpening his whine. 'Next time maybe it'll be your turn.'

'This is ridiculous,' Collop said. 'And you've got to stop talking such garbage, Bevan. It was an accident and no one can be –'

The door of the common room opened and swung back against the wall with a little thud as the Headmaster came striding in with a great air of purposefulness. It was a moment before they realized that Staveley was behind him.

'Gentlemen,' he said and then saw Hattie and looked a little puzzled but went straight on. 'Gentlemen, I'm afraid this is a dreadful business we have to deal with. Quite dreadful.'

'How is he?' Sam asked.

'Harry Forster's just come back. Still unconscious, he says. They've put him in intensive care, and he seems to be holding his own. My secretary is seeing to the flowers and so forth.'

Hattie couldn't help it. She let out a little yelp of laughter, and Sam closed one hand unobtrusively over her wrist and she caught her breath and managed to suppress it. Flowers – oh, God, flowers!

'The police are still going over the site. They've checked the kits and the guns.'

'Oh, Christ!' Staveley said loudly and rubbed his face with one hand. He looked much older than he had this morning, Hattie thought, and wanted to go and take his arm and lead him to a chair, he looked so ill. But she stayed where she was. The Headmaster was running on as though Staveley hadn't spoken.

'They say they can see no evidence of anything at all wrong there, and now they're taking the guns to their own people to be checked. To see if the aiming mechanisms were properly aligned ...' He waved one hand in a general sort of way, clearly not knowing anything about guns and how they might be checked. 'But they seem to think it was an unfortunate accident. A ricochet.' He nodded then, liking the word. 'A ricochet.'

'It couldn't be anything else,' Staveley said, and now he seemed to have regained some of his energy. He pushed his way further into the room past the Headmaster and looked round at them. 'How could it be anything else? A dreadful one-in-a-million chance, a ricochet, could have happened to anyone.'

'You were using live ammunition,' Sam said. 'Is that the usual thing?'

'Well, of course it is. Sometimes. I mean it was target practice. A display. We had to do it the right way; no use if they never find out how the real thing works, is it? We're training them, it's a Cadet Training Force, remember, they're learning –'

'Learning to use live ammunition to shoot up people's faces,' Sam said woodenly and Staveley turned upon him, almost whimpering.

'It's all very well for you to go on at me, as though it was my fault. All of you, you're all the same, the police were the same and you, Headmaster, you too, as if it was my fault. I can't be blamed for a ricochet, it could happen to anyone –'

'You sanctioned the use of live ammunition, though, Staveley. I didn't know about that,' the Headmaster said and looked briefly at Hattie as though wanting her to agree with him. 'Had I been consulted I could never have agreed, but there it is. I left all that to you as you were so keen, and I have learned a painful lesson.'

'It could have happened to anyone!' Staveley shouted and the Headmaster patted his arm soothingly and said, 'Yes, of course, my dear chap, we all understand. You've had a dreadful shock, no one understands better than we do, a dreadful shock. Perhaps you could help him to feel better, Mrs Clements, get him to lie down.' And he looked round the cluttered staff common room as though it would suddenly metamorphose into a hospital ward where Hattie could take care of Staveley.

'I'm not shocked! I mean, yes, of course I'm upset, anyone would be, but it wasn't my fault. You could as easily say it was your fault for wanting me to set up a display for Founder's Day! Yes, it could be said to be the Founder's fault – no one can say I had anything to do with it.'

'Of course, Staveley. Do sit down now, relax. You've had a difficult day.' Carefully, the Headmaster didn't look at the old man who stood there and shook his head and muttered again under his breath. 'It wasn't my fault, it wasn't my fault.'

'Well, there it is. We must wait and pray for poor Tully and hope all will be well for him. I have of course cancelled the performance of *The Taming of the Shrew* tonight, Collop. You hadn't, I'm sure –'

'I had expected something of the sort, Headmaster.' Collop

sounded a little sardonic. 'Especially as I saw several of the cast leaving with their parents.' He looked over his shoulder out of the window into the quadrangle where now the last stragglers had vanished and just the two policemen stood at the gate looking tired. 'Am I to keep the production ticking over, as it were, with occasional performances so that we can do it later? Or shall we leave it to bite the dust like poor old Tully?'

'Good gracious, Tully isn't – I mean, the comparison is hardly – really, I can't think of such matters now. We can discuss that tomorrow. I'm leaving now. The police have taken my statement – not that it was of much use, since I was in my office with some of the Councillors at the time – and want to talk to all of you. Then you can go. Goodnight.' And he turned and went with what would have been a scuttle in a man less elegantly made, and left them all standing staring after him.

'If you're ever shipwrecked make sure you do it with our revered boss,' Collop said. 'And make sure you get into the same boat he does. Born survivor if ever I saw one.'

'Police?' Bevan said fretfully. 'Haven't I had enough of a shock today without having police to worry me? Haven't I suffered sufficiently, being a target of these hooligans and –' He stopped then and brightened visibly. 'Protection, that's the thing. They'll have to protect me, won't they? All of us. With homicidal maniacs running around the school.'

'Oh, such stuff!' Harriet said loudly and they all turned and looked at her, a little surprised. They'd forgotten she was there, probably, she thought savagely. 'There are no maniacs in the school any more than there are in here, and to suggest those boys are to blame for what happened this afternoon is outrageous.'

'Oh, yes, the police will protect us.' Bevan was pulling on his coat, ignoring Hattie completely. 'That's the ticket. I'll see them first, explain, they'll see the sense of it, I'm sure –' And he went, and Collop laughed.

'Survivor number two. It'll be a crowded boat, won't it? No room for the rest of us.'

'He has a point,' Wilton said. He looked wretched, his skin damp and sallow, his eyes baggy and mournful. He's had a worse fright than Bevan, Hattie thought, wondering why. What makes him think he's a target? Bevan's just a self-centred pig who only ever thinks of himself, but I thought Wilton had more sense. 'I mean there was a gun and someone fired it and it did hit a master. A bit too coincidental, isn't it? You know how the boys are about us.'

'I thought Tully was rather well liked, actually,' Sam said lightly. 'Just as you are. They think you're a wimp, of course, but they don't dislike you.'

Wilton looked at him and there was a flicker of gratitude in his gaze, and then he looked away, wretched again. It was Collop who answered.

'Tully had a few cronies. A regular collector of Gavestons, was Tully. The ones he liked he liked, and they knew it and hung around him. The others . . .' He shook his head. 'He was as heartily disliked as I am. And you can't say worse than that.' He looked almost proud of his unpopularity.

'Gavestons?' Hattie was diverted and Collop flicked a glance at her.

'Never mind, my dear. Don't you worry your pretty little head over it. Just you stick to your poultices and potions, or whatever it is you dispense. Leave the history and the drama to us.'

'Gaveston was the favourite of King Edward II,' Sam said quietly. 'A highly dubious character and not at all relevant, I'd have said. Unless you have other evidence, Collop?'

Collop shrugged. 'Not to say evidence. But it was common school gossip that Tully liked a lad or two about him of a cold night. Certainly he played favourites.'

'Daniel Spero wasn't one of them,' Hattie said sharply, and then frowned as a confused thought came to her. She remembered Gaveston now, and understood the reference; was Collop suggesting that Tully had been shot at by one of the boys who had a homosexual crush on him, and cause to be jealous? Had Daniel been a boy who'd once been a favourite and then been dropped? Had that been the reason for his desperate behaviour? There was a lot to think about there.

'All this is the most ridiculous nonsense,' Sam said strongly. 'Sitting around conjecturing like this will get no one anywhere. I'm going to see if the police are ready to talk to me. Hattie? What about you? I dare say you're as eager to leave as I am. It hasn't been an exactly agreeable day.'

Gratefully she went with him, pulling on her coat as she went, holding her bag awkwardly under her chin as she did so.

'Sam, do you think it was deliberate?' she said when at last she could speak. They were hurrying along the bottom corridor towards the gatehouse where the police had set up their office for the moment. 'Do you think it was what Collop said?'

'A sex thing? No, I don't. I think it was an accident.'

'But –' Hattie stopped still and made him do so too and he turned to look at her. 'But suppose I tell you that someone – that there had been an intention to – not to do with sex, or not as far as I know, but – Oh, I don't know how to explain this without starting something I don't want to. I mean, I'm not sure I'm right to –'

'You sound like a third-former trying to get out of games or explaining why he hadn't done his prep,' Sam said dispassionately. 'Try again.'

She looked at him and then knew she had to tell someone, and who else was there?

'Arse. Arse and one of my girls. They'd set a trap for the shooters.'

She explained as succinctly as she could and he listened and didn't interrupt, for which she was grateful. And then, when she ended with a rather breathless '. . . and now I don't know what to think. Could it have been they who did this to Tully? Or was it just a ghastly coincidental accident?', stood and thought for a while.

'What do you think is most likely?' he said eventually. 'An accident or a very clever double bluff? Telling you about the pepper so that it looks as though they couldn't have done anything worse than that?'

She thought carefully too, and then said, 'I think it was an accident. I know Arse is a great deal brighter than lots of people think and that he keeps his mind to himself, and I know Dilly's a bright enough girl. But I don't think they're clever enough for that. It's the wrong sort of cleverness, isn't it? Devious and – No. It's not the sort of thing they'd do. The pepper – that was totally believable. I mean, as soon as Dilly said it I knew it was true and they'd done it. It's in character. But real bullets aimed at real heads, even Tully's – I can't see them thinking that way or behaving that way.'

'Neither can I. I've never been one to go for conspiracy theories, and I'm glad you don't seem to either. Last refuge of a foolish mind, always to look for conspiracies. But all the same, there's something a bit odd here.'

'Odd?'

'If they doctored some of the bullets with pepper, how come the police haven't found them? We'd have heard if they had. I doubt there's anything that's happened here this afternoon that wasn't known about by everyone on the premises within a matter of minutes, the way news travels here. So how come no one said anything about pepper this afternoon when the checks and investigations of the Cadets' guns was going on?'

'Perhaps the police kept it a secret?' She tried her thoughts aloud, not evaluating them before she spoke. 'No, that won't do. No need for it, really. Or is there? Do they think it'll be easier to catch the people who did it if they keep quiet?'

'Maybe,' Sam said.

Hattie stared at him. 'Oh, Lord, what do we do then? Tell them or not? If they haven't found it, then –'

'Then Dilly was winding you up with a tall tale and you'll look a complete ass. Is that what you're thinking?'

'Something along those lines.'

'And if they have found it, then you have a civic duty to tell them who did it so that they can be questioned, in case they're involved in what happened to Tully.'

'You've got it again. So what do I do?' She rubbed her face and it felt numb. I'm tired, she thought. Very tired indeed. 'It's hell, this place. Always secrets to keep . . .'

'Oh?' he said. 'What secrets?'

She felt her face go hot. 'Oh, nothing much; it's just that they tell me things, the kids . . .'

'Important things?'

'I can't say.' She managed a sort of laugh. 'I mean, I said it was secret, didn't I?'

'Well, you'd better be careful. Keeping a child's confidence is one thing. Colluding with them in wrong-doing is something else. Don't you think?'

Her face became even hotter and she was very aware of the fact that he was watching her closely. 'Oh, for heaven's sake, Sam! One thing has nothing to do with another. We were talking about pepper in bullets and who put it there and –'

'And you were talking about collecting other facts about some of the things that happen here that might be linked.' He lifted his brows at her. 'Weren't you? If the secrets you mentioned hadn't been in some way similar to this affair, you wouldn't have thought to mention them. They bracketed themselves naturally in your mind.'

'How do you know what goes on in my mind?' She was angry now and encouraged the feeling. It would give her a good reason to be red in the face. 'You're taking a bit much on yourself, aren't you?'

He stood very still and said nothing and then sighed. 'I suppose so. Sorry.'

'That's all right.' She didn't look at him and started to walk again. 'Well, I suppose there's only one thing I can do.'

'Tell the police?'

'No. And neither will you, if you please. It wouldn't be right.'

'Not right? It might be very germane indeed to what happened here this afternoon.'

'I know. But I'm going to talk to Dilly and Arse first. That's the right way to do it, isn't it? Find out from them what happened? They're entitled to that much, I would have thought. And to a warning that the police will be told if I'm not happy with what they say.'

'And Tully's entitled to have the police find out what happened to blow half his face to a pudding,' Sam said mildly, so that his words seemed even uglier than they were. 'And I'm concerned about that. So I'll make a deal with you. You'll have to accept it because now you've told me about what Arse and Dilly did with the ammunition I'm in the same situation you are – with information the police ought to have but without any promise of confidentiality made to them to shackle me. But I'll respect your delicacy about young feelings and wait till you've talked to them. But after that, I claim the right to act as I think I should. You're not the only one with a conscience, Hattie. I can grapple with ethical considerations as well as you. So, when do we speak to them? I'd suggest the sooner the better. You agree?'

Twenty

'Yes,' Dilly said. 'I see.' But she didn't open the door any wider.

'We have to talk about it. Under the circumstances. Don't we?' Hattie heard the note of appeal that had crept into her voice and tried to sound a little more brisk. 'So we thought it best to waste no time, but come to see you. May we come in?'

Dilly looked over her shoulder briefly and then, a little unwillingly, stood back. 'I suppose so.'

They followed her into the hall of the small flat and stood there awkwardly looking at her. There was a smell of elderly cooking oil and fish and French cigarettes and the place looked dull, as though a sheen of dust lay everywhere. Hattie took a deep breath and began to pull off her coat.

'It's warm in here. Very cosy,' she said lightly and looked around for somewhere to hang it. 'May I – ?'

Dilly took it from her a little sulkily and then held out her hand for Sam's coat. He gave it to her and nodded gravely and said, 'I'm sorry about this.'

'Not as sorry as I am,' Dilly said sharply. 'How'd you know Viv would be here?'

'Vivian? He's here?' Hattie felt a weight lift from her back. The thought of persuading Dilly to get him to come to her home, or to allow her and Sam to go to his so that both of them could be quizzed, had been a worrying one. Maybe it would all turn out all right after all, she thought with sudden optimism, seeing good omens about her. 'That's great.'

'Is it? You'd better come in.'

Dilly turned and led them to the end of the narrow hallway, pushed open the door round which a brighter rim of light had been gleaming and led them into the living room. It was cluttered and shabby and stuffy with the smells of food and cigarettes, which were stronger in here. There was an electric fire burning in the grate, and on the rug in front of it the boy Hattie could only think of as Arse was sitting on his heels, staring at the door watchfully.

His face showed no movement but there was a moment of panic in him, Hattie was sure; she could smell it. And she smiled at him as reassuringly as she could, for he looked very young and vulnerable crouched there at her feet.

'Hello, Ar– Vivian,' she said and cursed herself for letting her tongue slip.

'You might as well call me Arse. It's what you're used to. Everyone at school is,' he said and still remained with his buttocks on his heels and his hands folded in front of him. 'What do you want?'

Sam took charge, moving further into the room, pushing a chair forward from the dining table, sitting on it astride and resting his arms on the back. 'Pepper, Arse. It's about pepper. In bullets.'

'Oh, shit!' Arse said.

'No doubt. But all the same, we have to talk about it.'

'Why?'

'Don't be obtuse with me,' Sam said sharply. 'It won't work any better here than it does at school. I know you're a deal brighter than you let on, so let's not waste time. It's getting late and I'd like to have some of this evening to myself before climbing back on to the school treadmill. If you don't mind.'

'So,' Arse said, not looking at him. 'What do you want to know?'

'Did you and Dilly meddle with the ammunition they used for the display this afternoon?'

'She had nothing to do with it.'

He looked at her now, straightening his back like a soldier on parade and Dilly snapped, 'Don't be daft, Viv. Coming the noble protector – it's a load of crap.'

'Well, you didn't.' He looked at her, deflating a little.

'I agreed it was an ace idea. Said it'd be great if you could do it. Kept a watch while you got the guns, ground up the pepper for it. I was up to my ears in it.'

'Now, we make progress,' Sam said. 'Tell me about it.'

'Hasn't *she* told you?' Dilly threw a contemptuous glance at Hattie who reddened.

'After what happened this afternoon I had to talk to someone, for pity's sake. What would you have done, knowing that someone had been meddling with the ammunition with which someone else was later shot? Do be your age, Dilly.'

'Well, I suppose so,' Dilly said after a moment. 'So what's to tell him?' She looked at Sam now. 'It's like I told her. We put pepper in some of the bullets so that they'd explode back in the shooters' faces, make 'em think twice before they picked up guns again.'

'Pavlovian conditioning,' Sam said. 'I like it. It sounds good. Were you sure it'd work?'

'Couldn't be. I tried to get hold of a gun to test a few bullets but they kept them too well locked up. So I had to settle for the best I could do which was to do the bullets and wait for the day to drop them in the kits, so they'd use them. Then no one'd know we had anything to do with it.' He sounded bitter. 'No one would've if Tully hadn't been shot.'

'I'm sure Mr Tully regrets having discommoded you,' Sam said with so heavy an air of irony that the words lost their sting. 'So, what happened?'

'You saw what happened!' Dilly said loudly. 'You were there. Mr Tully got a bullet in his face and I got scared and in the middle of all the fuss around Mr Tully I went and took the bullets we'd done out of the boxes. We chucked 'em down a drain in the Highway. They'll be halfway to the sea by now.'

Hattie stared. 'You just took them out of the boxes with everyone watching?'

'That's the point. No one was. They were all looking at where the fuss was, round Mr Tully. So I just did it. It seemed the best thing.'

'It was marvellous,' Arse said simply and looked at her with a gaze so bright and direct that Hattie couldn't bear to look at him. It was like seeing someone naked who didn't know you were watching. 'Bloody marvellous. There'd be fingerprints on them and everything. I didn't worry about that, didn't wipe them or anything. Just did three bullets, dropped them in three boxes. And she went and took them out.'

'How did you know which were the ones to take?' Sam sounded genuinely curious. 'Didn't they look the same as the rest of the bullets?'

She shook her head. 'You heard what Viv said. They weren't wiped or anything. I could see bits of pepper on them. It was easy.' She giggled then, a little shrilly. There was amusement in it, but there was some hysteria. 'It was bloody daft, it was so easy.'

There was a silence and then Hattie said, 'Well! Now what?'

Sam looked at her. 'How do you mean?'

'Do we involve the police or don't we?' She looked at Dilly then as she heard her sharp intake of breath. 'I'm sorry, Dilly, but you have to see we can't just sit on this. Can we? Tully was badly hurt. Could die.'

'But we did nothing,' Arse said urgently. 'I mean, nothing that could have hurt Mr Tully. It was just the shooters I wanted to get at. They – the way they talk to us, those stinking Cadets, when they've got their uniforms – I could kill them easily. But I never thought of it for Mr Tully.'

'You make it sound as though you'd thought of it for someone else,' Hattie said, and he looked at her sideways and then at Dilly and Hattie could have sworn he'd laughed. But he hadn't, and his face was quite clear of any smile.

'I can't see why you have to tell anyone about this,' Dilly said and her voice was high and tight. 'I mean, no harm's been done, has it? Not by us. We tried a gag and it didn't work, well hard luck, you could say. But we did no harm.'

'That's not entirely the point –' Hattie began and then the door to the living room pushed open and Freddy came in, walking backwards, carrying a bulky load in his arms. He turned and saw them and tried to grin a welcome, though it wasn't easy because he had a flat box held between his teeth; and with some grunting and muttering he set his burden on the table and then bent to pull out the flex attached to it, found the plug and pushed it home into a socket beside the fireplace.

'Hello,' he said then, pulling the box from his mouth, his face wreathed in smiles. 'Well, I'm glad to see you're here! Very sensible of you to think of it. I heard your voices when I was still editing and I thought, Aha! They've realized and they've come to see. Very sensible. Have you given them a drink, Dilly? For heaven's sake, girl, what are you thinking of? Coffee? Tea? Or would you like something a bit better? Got some whisky somewhere around . . .'

'No, no thank you,' Hattie said as Sam shook his head and Freddy went bouncing back to his machine and stood patting it for all the world as though it were a sentient thing, as he chattered at them.

'There it is, all anyone needs to know. I mean, I know it was obvious, wasn't it? Had to be the best way to deal with it, and I thought, Do I call the fuzz, and I didn't fancy that at all, not that I'm anything but law-abiding, ha ha, but you know how it is, no need to get into bed with a dog that's got fleas unless you have to, eh? If you see what I mean. Better to tell the school, I thought. Then we can see where we go from there, and then I hear the doorbell and there you are, and I thought, Now I know why I'm so glad my Dilly's a Foundationer, like I was. Best school there is, intelligence crawling out of the woodwork, eh?'

'I'm sorry, Mr – er –' Sam began.

'Langham,' Hattie murmured.

'Mr Langham, but I'm not quite sure – We came to talk to Dilly. And her friend Vivian, who happened to be here. I'm not sure what –'

Freddy stared at him, his face crumpled with puzzlement. 'You hadn't realized?'

'Realized what?'

'Why, that I've got the evidence!' Freddy cried and slapped his machine triumphantly. 'Evidence about what happened this afternoon! Wasn't I there all day, making my film for Hilary, Mr Roscoe, you know, wasn't I there with my sound properly running and the camera looking everywhere? It had to be the answer, and those stupid police – well, as I say, no need to be nasty, but I speak as I find – those policemen never thought to ask me, did they? But here you are, so naturally I thought –'

'Of course,' Hattie said and laughed. 'You're quite right, of course, Mr Langham. Why didn't we think of it?'

'I was so sure you had.' Freddy looked first crestfallen then triumphant again. 'Not that it matters that you weren't as clever as I thought. I've got the evidence here and that's what's important. After all, I'd have told Hilary tomorrow anyway. I wouldn't leave it to him to sort out –'

'What evidence?' Sam said bluntly.

'Why, all that happened this afternoon at the display!' Freddy seemed to swell a little. 'I was sure to be at that, of course. Very visual part of the day, wasn't it? Of course I was there. I'd covered most of the other bits of Founder's Day so all I had to do was concentrate on the Cadets. Fine body of lads, aren't they? A fine body. I can tell you, I got a lump in the old throat looking at those boys, so intelligent, so hard-working and so steady for the old King and Country bit – or Queen and Country, I should say. It's ridiculous, isn't it, after all these years to –'

'What does your film show, Mr Langham?' Hattie said quickly as Sam took a step forward, clearly driven almost to rage by the man's flood of nonsense. 'Can you see who shot Mr Tully?'

Freddy stared. 'Oh, no. Of course not.'

'Then what's all the fuss about?' Arse got to his feet and moved across to the table to stand beside the machine and stare down at it in some disgust. 'If it doesn't show you who did it –'

'It shows you who didn't!' Freddy said, triumphant again, and now he began to fuss with his machine, peering through the viewfinder, fiddling with the tape feed. 'Look, let me show you. I'll give you a running commentary of what I've got here. Unedited, this is – I wouldn't want to do anything to vital evidence, would I? That'd be tampering with justice, wouldn't it? So, it's the film as taken, wobbles and all.' He laughed merrily. 'A few of those, but never mind, soon get them out when we do the final cut. Now, here we go. Boys and their gun kits, moving up to the butts. Boys setting up the targets – here we are, nice close-up – back to the boys with their boxes, zoom, focus, close-up on box – right, gun is loaded, close-up on breech, bit of a wobble here, but a nice shot otherwise, but here's another, steady as a rock, use that one, gun loaded, cocked, pull camera back, focus on boy as he closes eye and takes aim, there – fires, great recoil, looks fabulous, we cut to the target, bit of wobble again as my camera goes belting over, and we get close-up of target – not bad at all, one ear clipped, very neat, back again to the next shot –'

'Let me see for myself,' Sam said sharply as Freddy lifted his head from the viewfinder and looked up at him, opened his mouth to speak and then thought better of it.

'I'll just rewind,' he said. 'Here you are. Just sit there like that.

Lean forward or you won't see – yes, there you are, jerky because it's just an editing machine, you understand, but the definition's good, isn't it? The definition's good –'

'Let me watch for myself,' Sam said curtly. 'Is there a soundtrack?'

'Oh, there's a soundtrack all right. Here you are.' He fiddled at the side of the machine and then pushed a pair of earphones at Sam. 'Try that for level. OK? Good. If it gets a bit heavy you can always turn it down like this, or up, this way, if you'd rather –'

'Just leave it as it is,' Sam commanded and sat down and fixed the earphones on and Hattie stood and watched as he began to run the machine. She could hear the thin clacking of the soundtrack as it spilled out of the earphones clamped to Sam's head and she ached to see what there was to see; but she said nothing, just stood there and watched.

Beyond Sam, Dilly and Arse stood side by side, not touching but seeming to stand inside the same protective bubble. Between them all, and behind Sam's back, Freddy danced around, clearly yearning to fiddle with his precious machine but not daring to interrupt Sam.

At last it was through and Sam pulled the earphones off and stood up and Freddy hurled himself into the chair and began to fiddle again, this time rewinding.

'He's quite right,' Sam said. 'You can see clearly every shot that's fired. I listened very carefully. There are no shots on the soundtrack that aren't accounted for by what you can see on the screen. There are only four shooters at a time and they all shot at intervals. You can watch each and every one of them. I counted. The Carter boy – I'm not sure which one, but a Carter twin – is diabolical. His shots hardly ever reach the target and God knows where they went. It had to be one of those that ricocheted, I'd say. There's no other answer.'

There was a silence and then suddenly Arse said loudly, 'Yippee.'

'Isn't it great?' Freddy cried, incandescent with delight. 'Isn't it marvellous? To be there when such a thing happens, to get the evidence like that on film –'

'The non-evidence,' Hattie murmured. 'It isn't positive, is it?'

'Non-evidence is the same as hard evidence,' Freddy said. 'Isn't it? I watched and watched and you can do the same. You'll see no one aimed a gun at Mr Tully. I have the next set of tapes inside – the ones I took after he'd been hurt. Didn't get in too close, you know, no need to be ghoulish, not my style, but I got some good shots and you can see easily where he is in relation to the butts, because I got some good long shots in and a few pans. I like the pan shot,' he said ingenuously. 'It sort of makes it all look so important, you know? And there it is on my film, it had to be an accident.'

'An accident,' Dilly said, and began to giggle. 'Oh, Viv, he said it was an accident.'

Arse stood there and slowly his face began to soften, widen and then split into a grin and Hattie watched, fascinated, as the old man who had stood there beside Dilly became a schoolboy, and not just a boy; a merry, happy boy full of joy and youth and excitement. It was a sight she couldn't remember ever seeing before when she'd looked at Arse, and she stared as he turned to Dilly and laughed and then the two of them were clinging to each other and hooting helplessly, Dilly whooping loudly as she tried to catch her breath.

'Listen to her,' Freddy said indulgently as he went to slap her on the back. 'Ever since she was little, she's been like it. It's why we called her Dilly you know, because she sounds just like someone calling their ducks to be killed: whoop, whoop, whoop, there she goes! So it's Dilly instead of Monica which is her real name, not that she'd ever consider using it because she hates it so much. Oh, Tuppence, do stop, there's a good girl. You'll make yourself sick again.'

And indeed Dilly was looking less than well now, still laughing and whooping but her face was pale and set and her eyes seemed to stare and certainly wept copiously.

Hattie came and took her by the shoulders and pushed her down into an armchair beside the fire, and Arse came to stand beside her, leaning over to set one hand protectively on her shoulder.

'It's all right,' he said. 'She'll be all right now.' And indeed Dilly was beginning to relax, leaning back, breathing more deeply to control herself. 'It was just that –' Again his face creased. 'It was just you saying it was an accident, you see. It set us both off. An accident –' And then they were both laughing again and this time they didn't stop.

Twenty-one

The school was buzzing, a low humming sound that seemed to creep into her bones and vibrate there; everybody murmuring and whispering at each other, she thought as she hurried through the soggy fallen leaves in the quadrangle where boys stood about in tight little knots, and across into the main building by the Headmaster's office corridor; everyone on edge, quivering like banjo strings, everyone frightened and excited because of what had happened on Saturday.

It had been the same at home the night before last. She'd been late, of course, because of the visit to Freddy and Dilly's flat, and had found both the girls wide awake and curled up on the sofa next door in Judith's drawing room watching, with wide-eyed concentration, a programme about violence against women, long after they should have been in bed. Judith was sitting with them, looking not much older than the little girls in her pink track suit and trainers, a glass of wine in one hand and a half-eaten apple in the other, watching with as much absorption as the children; and she blinked vaguely at Hattie as she came in breathlessly and then smiled at her disarmingly.

'Thought it best to keep them here with me, ducky,' she said. 'It's the wretched girl's night out. Where *do* all those girls go night after night? I'd forgotten that when you phoned to ask if she could sit in for you, and they didn't want to go to bed in their own room with no one in the house, even though I was next door, did you, my poppets?' Sophie and Jessica stared on at the screen, oblivious of her. 'So I thought you wouldn't be long and fetched them in here with me. Peter's got a late call for a change. What's up at school, ducky? You sounded madly mysterious when you phoned. Just talking about emergencies and not telling a person the gory details is the act of a sadist. I keep telling Peter that. Don't you start it.'

'Not now, Judith,' she said, shepherding the children off the sofa to loud cries of objection on their part. 'I'd really rather they didn't watch stuff like this, you know –'

'Oh, it's terribly educational,' Judith said blithely. 'Then they'll know what sort of chaps not to marry, won't you, sweeties? Yes, of course you will. Now, get them up to bed and come right back. I have to know what all this fuss is.'

She'd had to go back of course, once the children were asleep – and it had taken ages to settle them, because they were so over-excited by the television they'd been watching and so eager to tell her, in gleefully bloody details, all about it – because Judith would have given her no peace if she hadn't; and truth to tell she wanted to anyway. It helped to have someone to talk to. So she rigged up in their bedrooms the old listening device from their baby days, and took the listener end of it with her to go and sit with Judith and tell her of the awfulness of Founder's Day.

Judith listened with a rapt expression on her face and then sighed with deep satisfaction when Hattie finished.

'Marvellous story, sweetie,' she said happily. 'I do like to hear something interesting at the end of a day. Peter's patients are all too boring to give a damn about, though I'm glad so many of them are private and pay well, of course. So, the repellent Mr Tully is dead or damned near it! Well, well. It just shows you what happens to chaps who read nasty sexy magazines and get boys into trouble.'

Hattie stared at her. 'What on earth are you talking about, Judith? David Tully and magazines?'

'Isn't he the chap you found with the boys under the building, smoking pot and reading filthy magazines?'

'Of course not! I just saw boys there – none of the staff –'

'But I could have sworn you said the Tully creature was getting up to no good with the boys and that it was bothering you. I remember perfectly well saying I wouldn't worry if I were you because as far as I can tell, from all I see in the papers and on the telly, everyone's doing that these days. I mean, they've come out with such resounding explosions you wish sometimes they'd go back in again.'

Hattie shook her head in confusion and Judith said, 'But didn't you tell me that? Isn't he the one who was messing about and you thought –'

'Oh, I see!' Hattie shook her head again. 'You've got it all mixed up. Yes, I was bothered but not because of magazines. It was because I saw him kiss one of the boys out in the street, as public as you like. Sam thinks he was just showing off that day, wanted me to see him and be shocked. He says it's not important. But David Tully certainly wasn't with the boys who were smoking pot and who had the magazines –'

'Sam?' Judith said, after the scent like a pointer dog. 'Since when Sam? You usually call them by their surnames, these men you work with.'

Hattie managed somehow to look relaxed and unconcerned. 'Oh, Judith, don't be so silly! He's just one of the masters, Sam Chanter. Biology. And I call lots of them by their first names –'

'Who?'

'Well, Wilton for a start. He's Edward.'

'And when you talk about him here you call him Wilton,' Judith said. 'So it's obvious you couldn't care less about him. But you said Sam as though you were really interested in him –'

'You've got a mind so deep in one rut that one of these days the sides'll fall in on you and choke you,' Hattie said, trying to sound amiable. 'Honestly, Judith, there's nothing in it. He's just a teacher there, and he came with me tonight to Dilly's –'

'Explain, explain,' Judith squealed and Hattie sighed and told her. And she listened carefully and grimaced.

'How dreary.'

'Dreary?' Hattie was amazed; used as she was to Judith's customary inconsequentiality, this was ridiculous.

'No mystery,' Judith said. 'If it's the way you say and this film shows no one could have pointed a gun at the man, it's dull, isn't it? Just a bullet bouncing off a wall or something.' She sighed then, deep in gloom. 'No one could have been sure it would ricochet, could they? I mean, a chap'd have to be a marvellous shot to aim at just the right spot and the right angle to be certain of hitting the bloke he wanted, wouldn't he? So it has to be a real accident, I suppose, which is madly dismal. I'd much rather it was deliberate, someone trying to get rid of the horrible master who had drawn him into a life of unspeakable sliminess down among the sexual perverts ...' She rolled her eyes wickedly as she gave the words all the relish she could muster and Hattie had to laugh.

'You live in a dream world, Judith, honestly you do. The problems we're having at the school aren't out of some TV soap, you know. These are real people having real things to worry about. Maybe characters get hurt when villains ricochet bullets off walls or whatever at them on the box, but they don't at the Foundation. You're making it sound like a cross between the snooker and *Death Wish* umpteen.'

'Well, it could have been,' Judith said with some indignation. 'Some boy madly guilt-ridden by the disgusting things this master has made him do, horrified by the world into which he'd been initiated under threat of – oh, I don't know, threat of something – decides to polish off the source of all his misery, but how to do so and stay out of prison? So he practises and practises and turns himself into a crack shot, a latter-day Robin Hood – or was it William Tell? Anyway, whoever, and on the day sees his mark in the crowd and wham! Gun aimed in opposite direction at correct angle, all worked out by trigonometry because of course the boy's a mathematical genius, and hey presto! Said hateful pervert master hits the dust. Marvellous, that'd be. Your version's much too boring.'

'It might be boring for you, but I can assure you it isn't for the people in the middle of it,' Hattie said. 'The school'll be impossible for the next week or more, you see. Especially if Tully dies. Oh, my God, it'll be awful if he does.'

'Not if he's a wreck for life,' Judith said, brightening. 'Come to think of it, that'd be better revenge than killing him. Marking someone for life with the scars of his evil – fabulous!'

'Fabulous is right.' Hattie got to her feet. 'A tall tale, a thoroughly made-up version. As if anyone could count on ricocheting a bullet off a wall at one person in a crowd he wanted to hit! Ridiculous! It's odds on anyone trying such a trick'd have hit someone else entirely unconnected.'

'I suppose so.' Judith got up too and stretched. 'But it would have been fun if it was like that, wouldn't it? I suppose we'll have to settle for what it really turns out to be, even if it is just a boring old accident. Only be sure to let me know, won't you? *And* about the fascinating Sam. No, I haven't forgotten! Nor will

I. I'll be here when you get back from school on Monday – Oh, no, dammit, I won't. I'm going to a new nail person. Very unusual, straight from LA. Does this nail-wrapping thing, makes even bashed-up talons like mine look terrific.'

And she kept Hattie at the front door for almost half an hour talking on about nail-wrapping and the possibility of having a face-lift, which was the source of her latest campaign to get extra cash out of Peter; but Hattie didn't mind, weary though she was. At least when Judith talked of such matters she wasn't producing ridiculous theories about what was going on at the Foundation.

Yet she lay awake for a long time after she had climbed into bed, thinking about it all. Had it really been an accident? Could there be a germ of something in what Judith had so wildly surmised? There couldn't be, she decided, and then sighed, turned over in bed, and punched her pillow to get it into some semblance of comfort. If only it hadn't been Tully it had happened to; then she'd have no trouble in dismissing Judith's foolish notions, accepting it as a nasty and tragic mishap; but Tully was so eminently suitable to be shot at, that was the thing. She would, she had to admit, have every sympathy with the boy who felt himself driven to do what had been done to that sneering un-pleasant face. Daniel Spero, she thought sleepily, if you were still at school I'd be very worried. So maybe it's just as well you were expelled, or I'd start thinking the way Judith talks and that would be really silly.

Now in the light of a damp and very cold November morning, with the heavy reek of the river and diesel fumes filling her nose, Judith's imaginings of Saturday night were even more obviously nonsense; when looked at in the prosaic light of day they could be seen for what they were. And she went in through the door that led to the Headmaster's office corridor, grateful to get out of the icy dampness to stamp her boots clear of clinging dead leaves on the coconut matting and catch her breath in the warm fug that filled the air of the building.

It was odd how friendly it felt now, when once it had seemed so alien; the smell of ozone from the computer room and the disinfectant the cleaners used in the huge machines that scrubbed the stone floors of the corridors, mixed with the general odour of boy that was so much part of the place, filled her nostrils and helped her relax. This place had a rhythm of its own that it would take a great deal to disturb for very long. It would sort itself out soon, she told herself optimistically. Today's buzz of excitement would give way to the next drama and the waters of school gossip would close over Tully's head and who would remember what had happened this time next term? It would be a bit like the boy Matterson who had died just before she had started here, she thought as she headed along the corridor on her way to the staff common room. Then everyone mentioned him; now no one did. It was as though he'd never existed. So it would be with Tully, and somewhere at the back of her mind a wicked voice murmured, 'And serve him right!' and, filled with guilt at so uncharitable a thought, she quickened her step till she was almost running.

Which was probably why the impact with Freddy, when it came, was so great. He came out of the Headmaster's office door, carrying his machine in his arms, and she was so close to him he was unable either to swerve or stop and she went straight into him. He staggered, slipped and came down with a heavy crump on to his backside, but still clutching his machine firmly.

'Oh, Mr Langham, I'm so sorry!' she cried, horrified, and knelt beside him to help him to his feet. He was red in the face and grimacing in obvious pain, but still clinging to his machine as though it were a lifeline.

She got him to his feet and he stood there swaying a little and blinking. She held on to him and after a moment he caught his breath and peered up at her, for she was a couple of inches taller than he was, and managed a grin.

'Well, that was a fair old purler,' he said, wincing as he took an experimental step. 'Wow, I did do myself a personal there, didn't I? Give me a moment though. I'll be all right.'

'Come back into the Head's office and we'll find you a chair,' she said, but he shook his head.

'No time, really no time. He wants to show the whole school, you see, wants them all to see it.'

Again he winced and she bit her lip and said, 'Well, at least let me take the machine from you. It looks heavy.'

'You have to be very careful,' he said. He let go with regret, and she took it from him, bracing herself to take its weight, which was greater than she'd have expected from its size, and he moved forward, a little experimentally, wincing again as he went.

'I've got to get this to the hall, to set it up to show the school. Assembly day, isn't it? He said it was a Big Assembly day.'

'Yes,' she said, remembering. The whole school, including the sixth, only met twice a week, an odd and old Foundation custom which pleased the sixth immensely. Their freedom from a daily assembly was one of their most jealously guarded privileges. 'Why does he – I mean, I suppose I can see why –'

'To show 'em it was an accident!' He was hobbling along the corridor now, towards the end staircase which led to the gallery above the big hall, and she followed him. 'The boys, they ought to see for themselves. Stop any problems. Gossip, you know. Very wise man, very. Communication's the name of the game, isn't it? And who should know better than I, having worked in media all my life?' He sounded very pleased with himself, proud of his status, and polished it up happily. 'Yes, all my working life I've been in media, mostly movies you know, but some print media along the way –'

'Have the police seen it?' she said hurriedly, more to stop his pontificating than for any other reason, not expecting an affirmative answer. She was surprised when she got it.

'Oh, yes, of course. Saw it last night.' He seemed for a moment to forget his discomfort as he basked in retrospection. 'Very impressed they were, most impressed. Called in senior people to look, showed it to their lawyers, three of them! All sorts of people. Looked again this morning. Not wasting any time, you see. So early too, but they've been and looked again. And gone.' He set his foot on the bottom step of the staircase and began the arduous climb, and she followed him, her muscles shouting protest at the weight of the heavy editing machine. 'No case to answer, they say. If poor Mr Tully should pass on, which of course we all hope he won't, and there has to be an inquest, there'll be no problems, they say, definitely death by misadventure. I'd have to go to court, of course, very material witness, I'd be, the most important witness, in fact.' Again pride blossomed in him. 'The proof would be there, you see, as shown by My Film.'

They had arrived at the top of the stairs and he led the way into the small projection room that had been rigged up at the back of the gallery and gratefully she set down her burden on the table in the middle of it.

'This is the craziest thing I've ever seen.' He looked disapprovingly round at the assorted equipment in the room, some of it clearly very old indeed. That many films had been shown on it over the years was obvious from the battered state it was in. 'Why they couldn't do what other people would have done with such a set-up and fixed up a player and a big video screen down on the stage, I can't imagine, but no, they have to do it differently – it's all rigged up here so we have to use the player here. It's daft. I told the Head and he quite agreed but as I'm sure you know, money's a bit tight. Not enough cash flow at present to improve what they've got. So I'll have to use it as it is.'

'Won't you be using this machine to play the film then?' she asked, and he looked at her and laughed with an air of indulgence that infuriated her.

'Oh, dear me no! That's just an editing machine! That's what I've been showing everyone my film on. Only of course it's not a film as such. It's videotape. I thought you'd have realized that, videotape, not film as such.'

'I'm not an expert in these matters,' she snapped and he looked happier than ever.

'Well, there it is, not everyone can be, can they? But I'm here, so no need to worry. Never fear, Freddy's here!' And he laughed fatly, pleased with himself.

'Well, if you're all right, I'll get on,' she said and turned to the door. 'Sorry I bumped into you that way. Let me know if you have any pain. I'll give you some tablets.'

'I'd be glad of some help if you can manage it,' he said. 'I need that more than pills! I can live with pain. Got to sometimes in my line of business.' He looked very serious for a moment and then became businesslike. 'I can't sort it all out from up here and down there at the same time. If I set it all up here and then go down and fix the screen, will you stay here and let me know if it's working all right? I have to get the focus right, the distance, for everyone to see easily.' He began to fiddle with one of the newer-looking pieces of equipment in the small room. 'I'll set it up. All I need of you is to stay here and watch me through there' – he pointed behind him to an aperture in the wall – 'and then when I give you the word, press the button here, see? If necessary, this is the rewind and this is the fast forward, though I don't think you'll have to bother about that much. Anyway, I hope not. We haven't a lot of time.' He looked at his watch self-importantly. 'Yes, I'll have to hurry.' And he made for the door, holding his back with one hand.

'Are you all right?' she called after him, guilt-riven again. 'Does it hurt much?'

'I'll be all right,' he said bravely. 'Don't you worry about me, I'll go on down and you wait for me to give you the signal to set it going. I'll be about ten minutes. You might like to have a look at the film while you're waiting. You haven't seen it yet, have you? No? Well, there it is. In the editing machine. The earphones are there too. Have a look. I think you'll be most fascinated. Just count the shots you hear as well as the ones you can see and you'll understand why the police have gone away and why the Headmaster wants to show them all my film so that they'll stop worrying and gossiping. It's really not bad, though I say it as perhaps shouldn't. Though as a professional I'd have to be falsely modest if I didn't know when I'd done a good job, don't you think? Yes – and don't worry about my back. I can see my osteopath later if it gets any worse.' With another brave smile he was gone. And as much to batten down her irritation at his behaviour – and at herself for having been so clumsy as to knock him over as for any other reason – she turned to the editing machine and began for the first time to watch the film that was causing everyone so much excitement.

Twenty-two

The first time she saw it she wasn't sure, and she rewound the tape as fast as she could and started to watch it through again, but Freddy signalled wildly from the hall below, bawling for her attention, and she had to do what he wanted. So she set the film going and then peered down through the small window and watched as the picture, greatly enlarged, appeared on the big screen below. Actually it might be clearer there, after all, and easier to watch, she thought, and certainly easier now she knew where to look.

She watched it very carefully this time, listening as best she could, though the sound came rather muffled at this distance, as Freddy, self-important still, fiddled with the screen, setting it at just the point he wanted to get perfect viewing all over the big hall. But she ignored that, concentrating entirely on what she could see on the screen.

And there it was again. Just out of shot, on the left of the picture, what appeared to be the muzzle of a rifle. It hardly showed at all, only an inch or two, and it was obscured by the leaves of a tree that framed the side of the shot, but she was sure it was there, and she kept her eyes fixed on it as the shooting started, listening as carefully as she could. It happened again; as one of the boys in the line-up fired, his gun recoiled and the muzzle there on the left seemed to recoil into the leaves and disappear as though it had been fired at the self-same moment. Had she heard a ghost of an extra shot? Or had that been her imagination? She'd have to watch and listen again . . .

Freddy waved with a wide expansive gesture and, understanding his elaborate signing, she rewound the tape and set it to

'Play' again and was about to start it off when she saw Freddy waving once more. He wanted her to wait and she stood there watching him as he went limping across the hall; clearly he was coming up to the control box.

'It's a bit poor on definition,' he explained, panting as he arrived. 'I haven't edited it and that's why there's some wobbly of course, but I can get it a bit better, I think.'

He fiddled with the controls, muttering under his breath, and then hit the 'Play' button and went to the window to stare down at the screen.

'That's better,' he said after a few minutes, sounding satisfied. 'Better colour. Too much brightness last time.' And he went back to the machine and rewound the tape and grinned widely at her.

'Well, thanks for your help, Mrs Clements. Excellent assistant you were, excellent. If you ever need a job as a PA to a movie-maker, let me know.' He laughed. 'Not that I could afford to pay you what you're worth, of course. You're a treasure. Well now, will you be at the Assembly to see this or have you seen enough? Or do you have to be there anyway, being staff?'

'I'll be there,' she said shortly. She'd had more than enough of his jejune bounce and she wanted time to think before Assembly; and it would be a good thing to see Sam to tell him what she'd seen. Then he could watch too. If they didn't see it now, she thought, that would be that; Freddy would take the tape away with his precious machine and edit it and she'd not get the chance to look again. The scenes showing the shooting of Tully would obviously be cut out; they would hardly enhance a fund-raising video, so it had to be now. Any attempt to see it again later would seem very suspicious.

She thought hard as she made her way into the hall, watching all the time for Sam to arrive, and took her place at the end of the first row where the girls sat, and let the film rerun in her mind's eye.

Had she seen an unexplained extra rifle muzzle after the first couple of shots, or had she been so eager to see something that she had imagined it? She let her memory roll on to what came after that. The camera had cut across to the group of people who had been standing with Tully on the gravelled area, Bevan close to Tully, and on his other side Steenman, Wilton and Collop.

Richard Shuttle from the French department next to Tully on the opposite side, and then someone she hadn't known, probably from the Board of Governors, then Genevieve's father – she'd seen him around on the day several times with some of the Governors – and then George Manson. There had been others but she couldn't remember them, and anyway, they didn't matter. What mattered was just one thing: an extra gun and the angle at which it had been firing. As far as she could tell it hadn't been aimed all that differently from the other guns; certainly not at the wall of the little building by which she'd been standing herself.

And, come to think of it – and now she sat up a little straighter as the idea lit up her mind – that was the only wall around from which a bullet could have ricocheted. Everyone had been saying that was how Tully had been shot, and everyone had accepted it was so, yet no one seemed to have noticed that there wasn't anything the bullet could have bounced from. Not even the police. It was extraordinary.

She saw Sam then, coming in as the boys began to drift in too and she lifted her chin at him, hoping he'd see her unobtrusive signal, and he did, and came across to her, not obviously hurrying, she noticed approvingly, but coming all the same.

'Sam,' she said urgently and very quietly. 'It's the oddest thing. I just realized something. What did the bullet bounce off? I mean, that's what a ricochet is, isn't it? A bounce? Well, the only wall around was on the storage sheds where I was standing and I swear nothing hit them. I'd have heard it, wouldn't I? And I didn't.'

He frowned with the ready understanding that she was coming to value in him so much. She'd always tended to reach conclusions long before Oliver; going, as he used to say sourly, 'from A to Z via nowhere at all,' while she complained at the way he always had to go laboriously through every logical step to reach the same conclusions she did; but Sam was as intuitive and swift as she was herself, and she watched him as he thought about what she said, grateful for his comprehension.

'It must have been the ground, then,' he said. 'There was gravel under the targets, wasn't there?'

She closed her eyes to conjure up a thread of memory of the

field on Saturday afternoon. It wasn't difficult; she suspected she'd never be able to forget it. And he was right. She opened her eyes and said quickly – for the hall was filling rapidly now and he'd have to go soon to his own place further back – 'Yes. But can bullets ricochet off gravel?'

'Don't see why not,' he said and looked over his shoulder as one of the boys in the fifth came and said something to him. 'I'm coming, Richard. Go and start the line, neatly now. Listen, Hattie, I don't think it's significant, you know. A bullet can ricochet off anything, I imagine, even the earth. So why not gravel? It has to have been an accident, whatever it bounced off.'

'I'm not so sure,' she said. 'Watch the left-hand side of the screen where the leaves are, about three minutes in.'

The girls arrived and, nodding politely at Sam, pushed their way past Hattie into their places in the line and she bit her lip, wanting to say more but not able to, and he nodded reassuringly and said, 'I will. The left you say? Fine,' and went back to the fifth.

The Headmaster came sweeping in in his usual elegant style, his gown floating behind him (Did he have it specially weighted to create that effect? she wondered) and stood at the front of the dais, his hands folded on the lectern, looking down at them all with an expression on his face which spelled stern justice tempered with mercy, which Hattie knew now as the one he always assumed for his public Headmasterly appearances, and the big hall with its hundreds of boys and masters sighed to a silence and waited.

'A tragedy,' said the Headmaster in tones about half an octave lower than his usual speaking level, 'occurred at the Foundation on Saturday.'

Silence, except for some shuffling of feet.

'You don't need me to tell you what a loss Mr David Tully is to this school. His flame of talent, his great concern for the truth that is in Art, his care for you, his pupils. All gone.'

The silence became even gloomier and Hattie sank lower in her place, wanting to blush for him. Didn't he know how ridiculous he sounded?

'Not that Mr Tully has died. Glory be. By some miracle his life burns on, albeit dimly.' This is getting worse, Hattie thought, almost in despair. I'll start giggling soon. 'But he lies deep in coma. He is not expected to regain consciousness for some time. If at all. We must weep indeed to have lost so brave a heart.'

Even the shuffling had stopped now.

'And we must pray that by a further miracle his senses will be fully restored to him so that he can be restored to us.' The voice had gone even deeper. 'So although it is not usual to do so for a living person, I ask you to hold a minute's silence to think of Mr David Tully and, if you are so minded – and I trust you are – to pray for his wellbeing. He is one of us but not with us except in thought. Let your thoughts be deep and true.'

He stood there with his head bent and the school descended into a strained and barely contained silence. I'm not the only one who wants to giggle, Hattie thought. God help us all if anyone starts. The whole place'll go up in a conflagration of laughter.

Behind her someone hiccuped and to her right she felt a frisson of giggles move along the line and she caught her breath and looked up at the Headmaster on his dais. He was looking down directly at her with his face carefully set in melancholy lines and she lifted her brows at him, silently begging him to stop the silence at once and get on if he wanted to avoid immediate and appalling embarrassment; and he stared back and then at the girls and finally up at the clock, and to her intense relief coughed and spoke.

'We will now do something I regard as important if unusual under the circumstances. We will watch a film. We will do this for a very important reason. I want no silly gossip around the Foundation, no apportioning of blame, no foolish chatter at all about what happened to Mr Tully. It was an accident, and that's an end of it. But to prove to you all it was indeed just an accident and that no one can be called to fault, I'm going to show you a film that was made here ready for a special fund-raising video by Mr Freddy Langham. It's rather rough and shakes a good deal because it hasn't been cut and edited, but you can see clearly what happened. And you'll see that it puts paid to any hint of reproach attaching to anyone here. It was a sad accident. A live bullet – and the bullets, I'm told, had to be live though I'm not quite sure I comprehend why, but then I'm not an armaments man' – a light musical sound escaped from him – 'a live bullet ricocheted and hit our unfortunate Mr Tully.

Mr Langham will show you the film and afterwards I want to offer no further comment at all about the events of that afternoon. Is that understood? Any talk or conjecture I hear will be swiftly and firmly punished. Be sure of that. All the staff know my feelings on this and, I am sure, share them. There will be *no* gossip. This will put a full stop to the whole matter, except for prayers for Mr Tully of course. Mr Langham?'

He looked up at the small window that led to the projection room and after a moment the light in the small hall dimmed and the window curtains on their tracks clacked jerkily as various boys set to the task by their form masters ran to pull on the cords. The hall shuffled and settled down just like a Saturday night audience at the pictures, Hattie thought, when a particularly gruesome film's on the bill.

The screen lit with the first dancing blank frames of film and then as the Headmaster pulled his lectern out of the way and went to one side of the dais, it started; and she leaned forward, her eyes fixed on the left-hand side of the screen.

The film was getting to be dreadfully familiar. She watched the way Staveley behaved; watched Harry Forster send the shooters off to their places; watched them carry their kits and put them in position; watched Harry go to organize the boys taking charge at the target end; watched as he moved out of shot, carrying the spare boxes; watched as the boys opened their kits. The first one was shown in close-up, reaching into his box, taking the bullets out of the squared-off block with the holes in it which held the bullets as in a rack; then, close-up, moved to the gun, and she watched as he loaded it . . . The film went on in its familiar way and she was getting restless, aching to get to the point when the shooting began, feeling as though it never would. She watched the cutaway as the camera raked round the crowd, homing in on interested watching faces: there was Steenman and Collop, and there was Tully moving towards the gravelled area, still alert and grinning at something someone had said to him; then the party of Governors with Genevieve's father leading them coming into frame; and then, at last, the camera went back to the boys with the guns, closed in on the one taking aim and firing and then cut to the target –

And there it was again. She peered hard at the edge of the

screen, trying to be sure, but it was harder now somehow. The leaves danced and moved as they had on every other occasion she had watched and she could see what it was she had seen before; but this time she couldn't be sure. The muzzle of a rifle or a trick of the light? A bullet being fired at exactly the same moment as another, or a blip of the soundtrack? And then it was too late; the camera had moved, was showing the next shooters loading, cocking, taking aim, hitting their targets, and she leaned back in her seat and bit her lip. Maybe she'd just been looking for something to prove Judith was right? After all, it had been Tully who'd been hit; the horrible Tully who made so many boys so very miserable and who might indeed be part of some sort of sex thing. The fact that Sam had said he thought Tully had kissed the boy in the street just to shock her didn't mean it had to be so; she mustn't take all he said at face value, however agreeable and intelligent he was. She could have ideas of her own, in the matter, after all –

Oh, stop it, she told herself furiously and stood up as, the film over, the Headmaster announced the hymn, *Holy, Holy, Holy*, and a wispy boy from the fifth form began to play the melody on the tired old grand piano in the corner of the dais. You'll drive yourself round the twist this way. Wait and see what Sam saw. That will be soon enough to start deciding what she could do next.

Then Assembly ended in its usual welter of form announcements, details of sports matches arranged and exhortations about the use of the cloakrooms and the way people still insisted on running in the corridors, a highly dangerous activity, and she followed the girls out of the hall towards their form room for the first period of the day, wanting to catch up with Sam to talk to him, and knowing to do so would cause people to gossip. They'd gossip about anything in this school, she thought with some bitterness as Sam disappeared into his own form room and closed the door behind him. Now she'd have to wait till lunchtime. It was an eternity.

It wasn't in fact until after school that she was able to talk to him alone. At lunchtime, the masters' table was occupied from the moment the bell at the end of morning school went until it was time to return to afternoon school again by Bevan, quite ignoring the Headmaster's dictum, expatiating at great length about how much help he'd offered the police about the shooting because of his proximity to Tully, and how little consideration he'd been shown by anyone, least of all the Headmaster who seemed to be totally unconcerned that he, the most senior of the masters, had suffered such a shock. To have attempted to have a private conversation with Sam under those conditions was out of the question and even after lunch, when they generally went to the staffroom for coffee, there was little chance to talk. Sam signalled hopelessness at her with his eyebrows over the heads of the others and she set herself to an afternoon of teaching the youngest forms about personal hygiene as best she could. At least she had her teaching commitments now, for which she had to be grateful. Being so very busy all the time gave her little time to think and today that was a help.

They met at last as they left the school and went together to the underground station to stand on the platform and talk as they waited for their trains. He didn't suggest they should stop off to have a drink as they sometimes did and she was glad of that, she told herself firmly. Very glad. She hadn't the time today, with Judith out at her wretched nail-wrapping session, and her Inge tending to be a little unreliable about looking after Sophie and Jessica when she had her hands full with Petra and Jenny; and if somewhere deep inside Hattie was a little depressed because he hadn't given her the chance to explain all that and say, 'No thank you,' to a drink, she didn't allow herself to think about it.

'Did you see what I meant?' she said. 'You watched the left-hand side where the leaves were?'

'I watched,' he said. 'Though it would have helped to know just what I was watching for.'

'Better you didn't. Then if it wasn't there you wouldn't have seen it because you hadn't been told it was there. If you see what I mean.'

'Yes. You think I might be suggestible. You tell me what to see and I see it.'

'No, of course not! But you have to admit it's strange if you see something without being tipped off. Don't you?'

'I know what you mean,' he said. 'There was that narrow oblong shadow –'

'You thought it was a shadow?' Her spirits dropped like a stone. 'Really?'

'I know what you want me to say. You want me to say I saw a rifle muzzle.'

'Well, the fact that you think that shows you did!' she cried. 'Doesn't it? That's what I thought I saw and if you did too –'

He shook his head. 'I think what I saw was a shadow. An odd trick of the light made a long narrow shadow seem remarkably straight, so that it could have been a human artefact. But I don't think it was anything more than that. A trick of the light. D'you want it to be a gun?'

'What?'

'It seems to me you want to discover something which the police and the man who made the film himself – and who's therefore highly expert at looking at films – didn't see. Do you want this to have been a deliberate act? Isn't it bad enough it was a dreadful accident?'

She bit her lip, staring up at him in the dim light of the underground. Stale cold air whispered around her feet and she could hear the distant rumble of the train. They'd only have another few seconds to talk.

'No, I don't want it to have been deliberate. My God, that would be awful. And yet – I just thought, maybe – he wasn't popular.'

'He's a bastard of the nastiest kind. And the fact that he's now in hospital lying like a vegetable doesn't alter that fact,' Sam said as the rush of air from the tunnel sent scraps of paper and cigarette ends dancing and bouncing along the platform 'I wouldn't blame anyone for taking a pot shot at him. But I don't think anyone did, Hattie. I think that shadow was just that. Don't you believe the police would have seen a gun muzzle if it had been there? They've seen the film several times, I understand.'

The train slid alongside the platform, and squares of yellow light chequered the tiled walls as she nodded, turning to stare up at the indicator. Dammit. It was her train. She'd have to go.

'I suppose you're right, if the police didn't see it. Well, there it is then. I was wrong. All we can do now is wait and see how Tully gets on and hope he doesn't die of his accident. But I still wish I really understood how it happened. Oh, well. Goodnight. See you in the morning.'

'Yes,' he said. 'And let's hope we can get back to normal soon. When you start looking for trouble, then things really are out of step. No more fussing about deliberate shootings?'

'No,' she said as the door closed in front of her, leaving her to wave a little inanely at him as the train slid out of the station on its way westwards. 'No . . .'

But it wouldn't be easy, she told herself as she pushed her way into one of the few seats available. Not easy at all.

'You didn't really think it would make any difference, did you?' the man said and sounded genuinely amazed. 'Why on earth should it?'

He didn't answer, not in words, but he risked looking at him. The man seemed relaxed, amiable, happy even. He smiled when he caught the boy's eye.

'I find it rather amusing, if you must know. That anyone should try such a thing – it's absurd! And having tried, to fail. Well, what can I say? I can't be expected to take such antics seriously, now can I?'

'Might have been you,' the boy mumbled, and the man said sharply, 'What's that? Speak up. I can't stand it when people don't speak up.'

'Might have been you,' the boy said more loudly and this time the man actually laughed.

'Oh, do be your age. Or perhaps you are . . . well, be older than your age. You can be, can't you, when it suits you? As well we know. No one could do anything to me. I'm not at any risk. It's not possible.' He sounded plumply pleased with himself and smoothed one hand over his head. 'No, no risk for me. I make sure of that, don't I?' He laughed again and looked at the boy sharply, but he was brave this time. He didn't laugh back. He just stood there and looked at him.

The man sighed deeply and theatrically. 'I'm getting bored with you,' he said. 'Too tiresome for words, the way you carry on. You're no fun any more. And we used to have fun, didn't we? Lots of fun.'

The boy shifted his gaze and stared at the alabaster figures in the mirrored alcove by the fireplace, flicking his eyes from one to the other. They were his favourite things in this room, such wonderful bodies with their curves and hollows, as deep and green as the sea, beautiful enough to drown in.

'Oh, well,' the man said and got to his feet and began to pull off his jacket. The boy didn't look at him, very aware of what he was doing, but concentrating on the figures in the alcoves. Long legs, small buttocks with a shallow curve at the sides, flat bellies, rounded shoulders and arms –

'So, what's the delay?' the man said. He was down to his underpants now and stood staring down at the boy with an air of quizzical concern on his face. 'Are we shy? Are we unaware of what is expected of us? Are we, heaven save the mark, suffering from an attack of shame? Oh, chastity, chastity, what a cruel goddess you are . . .' And again he laughed and leaned over and began to tickle the boy, running his hands over his chest so that the boy was forced to show a reaction, though he'd promised himself he wouldn't, had been determined to be remote and cool; but he couldn't do anything but giggle helplessly, writhing and twisting and feeling the familiar sensations crawling into him. That was the worst part of it all. That he liked it, that it gave him pleasure, that he wanted it to happen. Oh, God, he said inside his head to a god he knew didn't exist or if it ever had was long since dead; Oh, God, make it quick, let the sickness come. That doesn't feel so bad, the sickness –

Twenty-three

Dilly watched him as carefully he poured milk into her tea cup and then passed it across to her, and nodded her thanks, not taking her eyes off him.

'Are you all right?' she asked abruptly after a long pause during which both of them drank half their tea. He looked up at her, his eyes a little blank. He'd been watching the other people in the café, listening to the loud talk, and he seemed startled when she spoke, almost as though he'd forgotten she was there.

'What?'

'I thought you might still be in a bit of a state over what happened.' Still he stared at her blankly and that made her snap at him. 'Tully, for pity's sake.'

He shrugged. 'What's the use? It's done. It's nothing to do with me any more.'

In spite of herself Dilly shivered a little; he seemed so very insouciant it almost frightened her, and she said sharply, 'Well, it's upset me all right.'

He shook his head at her. 'No need, is there? Why should you be upset?'

'Why should I – ye gods, Viv, the man was bloody shot! He's lying in hospital in a mess of tubes and drips and Christ knows what else and –'

'But you don't like him,' Viv said with a tone of such reasonableness that she suddenly wanted to hit him. 'You said you didn't.'

'I loathed him! But now he's –'

'Whatever's happened to him he's still the same person,' Viv said. He drank the rest of his tea. 'I think I want a Coke now. And some chips. You too?'

'No,' she said shortly, and he smiled at her a little absently and got up and went to the counter, pushing past the knots of black youths who were clustered there laughing and shouting at each other in what were for Dilly impenetrable accents.

She bent her head to stare down at her hands on the red formica table-top, scowling a little. Viv was right in a way, of course; she'd always hated that awful mealy-mouthed thing about being hushed and reverent just because people were ill or dead. If they were bastards they were bastards, no question of that, and it ought to be all right to say so; but he was so very cool – and again she shivered a little and then jumped as a hand landed on her shoulder.

'Well, if it isn't Dilly Dilly come and be killed! What are you doing hanging around in this low joint?'

She twisted her head and looked up into Harry's smooth face and stared at him challengingly.

'I didn't notice it was all that low.'

'It sure ain't no honky hideout,' Harry said and sat down, uninvited. 'You're lucky no one started on you. They don't like people from schools like the Foundation in Watney market and they specially don't like white ones.'

'They've given us no trouble,' Dilly said shortly as Viv came back and pushed wordlessly past Harry to reach for another chair and sit down with his Coke and bag of chips.

'You too, Arse? No trouble from the denizens of this salubrious establishment?'

Viv shook his head, not looking at Harry. 'No. Should there be?'

'You're a cool one, you know.' Harry sounded relaxed and normal now, with none of his usual swagger. 'There aren't many people from the Foundation'd come in here without thinking three times.'

'I know,' Viv said. 'But I'm not them. Was there something you wanted?'

'Mmm?' Harry said and smiled lazily at him. 'You are not, surely, dear fellow, trying to give me my congé, are you? I can't imagine that a man of your breeding would ever commit such a social solecism –'

'Oh, piss off!' Viv said and Harry laughed and got to his feet.

'Piddle away I shall, dear man, piddle away happily. Not to leave you, you must understand. No indeed. I depart to join the person for whom I have been waiting.'

And he bowed with an absurd flourish at them both and then went pushing through the crowd to the café door as several of the tall black boys he passed shouted something cheerful and still, to Dilly, unintelligible at him. They watched him go and then as the crowd parted to let him through saw who was waiting for him by the door, and Dilly was startled.

'Well, who'd have thought it?' she said. 'That one with Harry? Hardly his type I'd imagine. I'd have expected him to go for the sexpot Gillian at the very least.'

Viv sighed and pushed the last of his chips into his mouth.

'Sometimes you're almost as bad as the rest of them,' he said. 'Thinking Harry's some sort of special case. Believe me, there's nothing special about Harry. I know. Nothing special about him at all. So whoever he goes out with it's reasonable. Take it from me, it's perfectly reasonable.'

And he got up and led the way out and Dilly followed and stood on the pavement outside pulling her coat up to her neck, watching Harry and Genevieve walk away through the market, their heads together as they talked with great absorption. It was surprising, of course it was. No matter what Viv said, it was surprising. How could Harry find someone as dismal as Genevieve Barratt interesting?

'What difference does it make to you, anyway?' Genevieve said, pushing out her lower lip in the sulky expression that had always been able to make Stella's belly tighten with anxiety. 'It's my life, not yours. It's my body.'

'I know that, darling! Of course I do! But I'm your mother. You can't expect me not to care . . .'

'You can care as long as you don't fuss,' Genevieve said. 'That's all I ask you to do. It's not so hard *not* to do something, surely? Just don't fuss. You don't understand anyway. It's different nowadays. It was all right when you were young to let yourself go and not care what you looked like but we're a different generation. It matters to us.'

'It mattered to me too,' Stella said, stung. 'But I had more sense than to try to starve myself to a stick. Men don't like sticks. They like women who have shapes, who look like women and not little boys.'

Genevieve laughed quietly, deliberately, as though she were on stage, acting laughter. 'How do you know what all men like?' Where does your experience come from? And you're wrong. You couldn't be more out of date. Men like thin women now. Everyone knows that. Anyway, I don't care what men want; I only care what I want. And I want to be the way I am.'

'Even that would be better than nothing,' Stella said hopelessly, and she let tears show in her eyes, risking it. 'But go on as you are and you'll finish up thinner than ever. You'll look terrible – '

She knew at once she'd gone too far. Every time it happened she knew it was her own fault, that she should have learned from last time; but it was no use, she'd had to do it, had to talk to her, had to let her see her unhappiness, couldn't have sat there at the table beside her and watched her deliberately killing herself without doing something. Could she?

Genevieve opened her mouth and screamed. It was a high-pitched sharp-edged shriek of rage and she had honed it to an intensity that made Stella want to be sick. It seemed to reach down inside her and claw at her and she put her hands to her ears and shrank down towards the table, hunching her shoulders. Anything so that she wouldn't have to hear it in all its hatefulness.

The thumping outside reached her through her legs rather than her ears. She felt the vibration as Gordon came hurtling down the stairs, his feet thudding furiously against the steps as hard as he could and throwing the door open with equal rage, and still Genevieve sat there with her head back, shrieking full blast.

'What the bloody hell's going on in here?' he roared and came in and went over to Genevieve and took her head between his hands and pressed her face against his belly. Stella tried not to look, but she had to, as she always did. There he stood, holding Genevieve's face against his body, his hands cupping her head and slowly Genevieve's shoulders relaxed and the noise stopped.

And then he did it, and Stella, moving slowly, taking her hands away from her ears, setting them on the table, had to watch it and could do nothing to stop him. He bent and nuzzled his nose against Genevieve's hair, murmuring at her and with one hand stroked her back as he whispered into her hair, and Genevieve's own hand came up and her thumb went into her mouth, and it was like ten years ago, when he'd been the only one who could stop little Genevieve's tantrums, when she, Stella, had had to sit and watch as he cradled his little girl, her little girl, in his arms, her arms, and rocked her to peace again. Stella had been a failure then, and she still was. And she sat there dully, her hands on the table in front of her like lumps of dead meat, as slowly Genevieve lifted her head from her father's belly and looked first at him and then at her mother, over her fist, her thumb still in her mouth.

I'll never be any good at anything, Stella shrieked inside her head. I can't be good to anyone ever, not to any of them. It would have been so good to have been able to shriek aloud the way Genevieve had done, to be comforted as Gordon was comforting her, but she knew that could never happen. She just had to sit here at her own kitchen table with dead hands and watch it all for ever.

'My dear chap, why on earth should you let that make any difference?' the Headmaster said. 'Here you are, just a couple of years to your pension – I wouldn't dream of suggesting you shouldn't serve those years and enjoy your just deserts!'

'But the Cadets,' Staveley said again. 'I can't just not do the Cadets.'

The Headmaster sighed, and leaned across his desk, friendly, concerned, infinitely sensible. 'Try to see it my way, my dear fellow. Indeed, try to see it the parents' way. A dreadful thing happened, and though it was entirely accidental, and the police are satisfied of that, the fact remains that one of my staff here lies in Old East Hospital in intensive care, oblivious to the world. It would be a very strange parent who didn't ask himself first of all who was responsible for such an accident happening, and secondly what has been done to safeguard the boys and prevent such an accident occurring again. You must understand that.'

'You're saying it was my fault!' Staveley's voice began to rise in pitch. 'Is that it, telling those parents that it was my fault and that was why you won't let me do the Cadets any more?'

'What else can I do?' the Headmaster said with the same sweet reasonableness. 'I have to make changes in the way the Cadet Corps is run. That has to be obvious. Justice being seen to be done, you know? The natural line is to change the leadership. That isn't to blame you, it's just to bring in new blood, a fresh eye to look for problems, iron out anomalies –'

'Anomalies my arse!' Staveley roared. 'There aren't any bloody anomalies! There was a crazy accident which could have happened to anyone, whoever was in charge. A bullet ricochets and you have to make my life misery? What's the sense in that? It doesn't help anyone. The only thing worth doing in this shithouse is the Cadets and if you think I'm –'

'Oh, dear, oh dear,' the Headmaster said, deep in regret. 'What am I to say to you? When you display such anger and such – forgive me, but I must say it – juvenile profanity, what am I to think but that I have made the best possible decision for the welfare of the boys and the school? If under minimal pressure you descend to such levels, how can we not be certain that it wasn't under pressure on Founder's Day that some important detail missed your eye and contributed to the sad state of David Tully? You must see what I mean.'

'I see you burning me in a sacrifice, that's what I see,' Staveley said passionately but pulling his voice down to a less hysterical level with an obvious effort of control. 'I see you taking away from me the only thing that makes life tolerable in this place and using me as your whipping boy –'

'If you're so unhappy here,' the Headmaster murmured, 'I ask myself if you will be so very disappointed if you miss the last two years of teaching which will ensure your pension.'

Staveley sat and stared at him. The room was quiet; outside the long bleak corridors and the classrooms still cluttered with the day's detritus lay empty, resting in the peaceful hiatus that came between the boys' departure for the day and the arrival of the cleaners, and he sat and looked at the Headmaster who looked limpidly back at him; and took a deep breath.

'Is that it? If I argue, you throw me out and I lose most of my pension?'

'Not most of it,' the Headmaster said, sounding judicious. 'Rather a lot of it though, I fear. They can be so nit-picking, these insurance companies, don't you find?'

'You won't change your mind?'

'Why should I?' Again the picture of sweet reason as the Headmaster spread his hands wide. 'My dear fellow, you must see how I'm placed. If the Foundation is to survive I have to attract new parents to this school and hold on to those we already have. By the skin of our teeth. I must, as they say, explore every avenue.'

'Including the one which is labelled Kick Staveley's Arse Avenue.'

The Headmaster said nothing, and Staveley said savagely, 'And what if the boys refuse to let you do it? What if they show me loyalty and just drop out of the Corps?'

'I'd be delighted,' the Headmaster said promptly. 'It's regarded by many parents as anachronistic anyway. I can well see the lack of such a Corps may be an inducement to some.'

'Most parents want their boys to get the discipline and the training,' Staveley said, his voice rising again. 'It brings out their leadership qualities, helps them to understand the role of author-ity, makes them into better citizens –'

'You have a point. Some parents do think that, I dare say. I shall simply have to take the temperature and see where we go next year. It depends on next year's enrolments, doesn't it? If they're up as I fully intend them to be, then I shall assume the new parents are not put out by the presence of a Cadet Corps here. If they're not . . .' He shook his head then. 'Well, that's a possibility to be considered. I shall get the enrolments up, never fear. And if at the New Parents' meeting I find opposition to a Cadet Corps, well then, this whole conversation becomes purely academic, doesn't it? It would be a pity, then, wouldn't it, if you went off in a huff, just because I was replacing you on the Corps at present? Yes, a pity. Good evening, my dear chap. I'm sure you want to get home. And I have so much work still to do.' And, smiling charmingly, he pressed his bell and the secretary came and hovered at Staveley's side and what else could he do but get to his feet and walk out? Not that there was anything to go out to, he told himself as he shuffled along the lower corridor back to the staffroom. Nothing anywhere, either in front of him or on any side.

'You can't visit in the Intensive Care Unit.' The porter was

scandalized. 'Not without you've got a special permit. You got a permit?'

'No,' the man said. 'But he's a friend of mine, you see. I wanted to see him if I could. Surely I can just see him? I won't disturb him.'

'It's not up to me,' the porter said. 'I get my instructions, and I goes by them. And no one visits the Intensive Care Unit, not without they've got a special permit.'

'Is there some way I can get one of these permits?'

The porter shook his head. 'Not my job, matey. Have to ask the Sister-in-charge.'

'Where is she? How do I find her?'

'She's in the Intensive Care Unit,' the porter said. 'Where else would she be?'

'So how do I get to her to ask for a permit? Can I just go along and –

'Not without you got a permit,' the porter said triumphantly and grinned. 'Daft, 'n't it? But there it is. That's my instructions and I can't go against them, can I? Not and do my job as I should.'

'Oh, it would never do to go against your instructions,' the man said, heavily ironic, and the porter nodded.

'Glad you understand, matey,' he said, 'Not my fault,' and turned away to the next person waiting humbly with a question, and the man wandered off through the Casualty Department and lingered by the exit door, looking around.

It wasn't too busy tonight; there was a drunk sitting with his head in his hands, staring down at the pool of vomit at his feet; the man carefully looked somewhere else. As far as they could get from the drunk and still use the waiting-room seats were a couple with a small child who was asleep on the woman's lap, and a little further along a boy in jeans and sweater leaned back with his head against the wall, his eyes closed. The man looked at him thoughtfully and then went and sat down beside him.

He didn't have to wait long. A nurse came and summoned the couple with the child, who set up a wail as they stood up, and the boy stirred and opened his eyes.

'Hello,' the man said. 'Do you remember me? We met once, a long time ago. At David Tully's flat. Your name's Jeremy, isn't it? I seem to remember you were in the third form.'

The boy blinked and peered at him and then smiled a little uncertainly. 'Oh, yes, I remember. That party –' He looked away then, suddenly, a shifty glance that amused the man very much. He laughed.

'No need to look so worried, my dear boy!' he said. 'It wasn't that wicked, after all! A drink or two, a smoke or two, a magazine or two – no one but the most boring of old farts would fuss over such things. And I'm hardly an old fart, am I? I mean, I may not be a spring chicken, but I was there that evening. And joining in. Hardly the action of an old fart, is it? I was there . . .'

'Yes,' the boy said. 'Yes. You were, weren't you?'

'And what are you doing here now?' the man said with a brisker air, and the boy made a face.

'I wanted to see Mr Tully,' he said. 'You know, after his accident? I s'pose everyone does. Well, I want to see him but they won't let me.'

'I know.' The man sounded sympathetic. 'Got to have a permit to visit the Intensive Care Unit, can only get a permit from the Sister. Where is she? In the Intensive Care Unit. Can I ask her for a permit? No, you can't go to the Intensive Care Unit unless you've got a permit.'

The boy laughed and relaxed and the man settled himself a little more comfortably in the chair beside him. 'It's awful isn't it, when someone you care about is ill and you can't see them?'

The boy went a little pink. 'It isn't that I care about him –' he said quickly, and the man set a hand on his and said, 'Of course. I know what you mean. He's a friend. Just a friend. You'd want to visit any friend who'd had such a terrible accident, wouldn't you?'

'Yes,' the boy said eagerly. 'Yes, of course you would. That's what it is, you see. I like drawing. I do cartoon figures and that and Mr Tully said they were good and he'd help me and he let me go to his parties and all and – well, it's just that he's my friend and I can't tell anyone about – I mean, no one knows he's my friend. He said we have to keep it – well, you know how it is, being at school. You know all about that, don't you?'

'Oh, yes,' the man said. 'I know all about that.'

'So I thought I'd try to see him. I thought if I waited here I might be able to sneak along, you know, just to see if I could get to see him. It's just that –' He looked down at his hands. The

man still had one of his set over them. The boy made no effort to move away. 'It's just that he's my friend,' he ended lamely.

'I know,' the man said and patted his hand and withdrew his own. 'Look, you're not going to get any joy here tonight, are you? And won't your parents be worrying about when you get home?'

Jeremy shook his head, going a little pink. 'They don't know I'm out. They went out first and I'm too old for babysitters now. So they don't know I went out.'

'Well, we'd better get you home in time, then, hadn't we? But I suspect you could use a little something to eat, hmm? And a friend to talk to since you can't visit the one you already have. I know a nice little place we could get a decent bite and you can tell me about your cartoons. I'd be most interested. I might know someone who'd publish them. I've got a lot of contacts, one way and another. Shall we do that?'

There was a little silence and then the boy said, 'Well, yes. That's very kind of you. If you're sure I'd be no trouble.'

'Oh, no,' the man said and stood up and held out one hand invitingly. 'It will be no trouble at all, I do assure you.'

Twenty-four

'She won't talk to me at all,' Hattie said. 'That's why I got in touch with you. Did you tell her you were coming to see me?'

'Oh, no,' Stella said. 'I wouldn't do that. She'd —' She shook her head and looked round for somewhere to sit and Hattie pulled a chair forward invitingly.

'I'm so sorry I've nowhere better to talk to you. This is the nearest thing I have to a room of my own here, and it isn't up to much, I'm afraid.' She looked round at the dismal little classroom with its stained green and cream paint and the few posters she'd found to put up to enliven it, though all they did was highlight the overall shabbiness. 'Do forgive me. But it seemed so important to talk to you. I'd gladly have come to you if —'

'Oh, no! That would never do,' Stella said loudly, and Hattie said quickly, wanting to reassure her, 'I quite understand . . .'

There was a little silence and then Hattie said carefully, 'It's Genevieve and her eating that's bothering me. I told you when I saw you last — at the autumn fair, that time — I had to do something about it, and it's worse than ever, isn't it? She looks thinner now than she did last term, if that were possible. It's such a worry.'

'I know,' Stella said, and looked down at her hands in her lap. 'I worry about it all the time. But what can I do?'

'It's very difficult, I know. If parents interfere they get stick and if they don't interfere they're accused of not caring. It's a dreadful situation to be in.'

'Well, if you know, why ask me to come here and talk about it? You made me come. I didn't want to but you went on and on. I had to.' Stella looked up at her now and her eyes were pinkly accusing. She looked fatter than she had, Hattie thought, with those doughy cheeks and the way her lower lip seemed to droop so heavily. As though she's trying to eat for Genevieve . . .

'I know, I did put some pressure on. And I'm sorry. It's just that – have you tried to get her into hospital? If you're really worried you can – well, it sounds extreme, I know, but sometimes extreme situations demand extreme measures. You could get a psychiatric opinion, have her sectioned –'

'Sectioned?' The woman's voice was flat and dull.

'Admitted to a psychiatric hospital compulsorily, as an emergency. To get some essential refeeding started so that – I mean, she really is at so much risk the way she is. I hate to be so alarmist, but –'

'Do you think I don't know?' Stella's voice was low and Hattie had to lean towards her to hear it, but it was full of anger. 'I know perfectly well how dangerous this starving is, but there's nothing I can *do*. I've tried. If I say anything she gets so mad at me and then she starts to scream and when she screams I have to –' She put both hands up towards her ears as though she could hear Genevieve's screaming now. 'I have to stop. I can't go on then.'

'Is there anyone else who can get through to her?' Hattie asked. 'Her brothers, perhaps?'

Stella seemed to stiffen. 'We don't see much of them.'

'Oh?'

'They don't – they've left home.' Stella slid her gaze across Hattie's face and looked away sharply as Hattie tried to hold her gaze. 'They don't visit.'

'I'm sorry,' Hattie said carefully. 'Family arguments are always painful –'

'Who said anything about arguments?' Stella flared, her face suddenly red. 'I never said there were arguments.'

'I'm sorry. I thought that –'

'Then you thought too much. I just said they don't visit. No hard words, they just don't come any more. It happens. People – they grow away. They get different ideas. Notions. But there were never hard words.'

She seemed to be pleading with Hattie now rather than remonstrating and Hattie, bewildered, but still determined to make her point, said carefully, 'I do understand. I'm sorry I misunderstood. But about Genevieve – perhaps her father could talk to her? Isn't he just as worried?'

Stella seemed to withdraw, and Hattie watched her, puzzled. She was looking down at her gloved hands again. 'He's worried, yes, of course he is. He's worried . . .'

'What does he say about it?'

Stella shrugged. 'I don't see him that much to talk about it. I mean, he's so busy. There's the business of course, but it's all the other things as well. He's a Governor here, you see, and there are the meetings . . .'

'Oh, yes,' Hattie said. 'I'd forgotten.' I must use that, she thought. Maybe I can catch him here when he comes for Governors' meetings, get some sense out of him, get him to do something. She's really too wet to be true. 'Of course, that would keep him busy.'

'That's not all.' Stella warmed to her theme. 'There's the Children's Home at that place in Surrey, he's done the accounts for them for years. And then there's the other things he does. The church and the choir, and things like that. There're a lot of things to take up his time. He's very keen on public service, is Gordon.'

'Yes, I see,' Hattie said. 'It would make it . . . Still, he does see Genevieve, doesn't he?'

'Of course he does! Breakfast's the time. And in the evenings sometimes. And sometimes the weekends though there's always something he has to do. You know how it is. There's always something . . .'

'Yes, I know,' Hattie said. 'But still, if he sees Genevieve he must see how dangerously thin she's getting. And the way she always looks so anxious. You know the look I mean, I'm sure.'

'She is anxious,' Stella said simply. 'All the time. She's got a lot to be anxious about.'

'What?' Hattie said quickly. Too quickly. The woman was looking down at her hands again.

'Oh, her exams, you know, and things like that,' Stella said vaguely and then looked at her watch. 'I really have to be going. Is that all you wanted me for?'

'Isn't it enough?' Hattie said as gently as she could.

'It's important, I know that. You know that. But Genevieve doesn't know it, does she? And until she does I might as well not bother even to think about it for all the good it'll do. So is it all right if I go now?'

'Yes.' Hattie got to her feet. 'Of course. But if I could just impress upon you the need to act soon. To get your GP to arrange a home visit from the psychiatrist, perhaps, so that she can be sectioned. I know it's an extreme action but sometimes –'

'Sometimes you have to do hard things. Yes,' Stella said and stood up. 'Well, thank you.' She went to the door and Hattie watched her, and then as she set her hand on the knob she stopped and half turned back.

'Mrs Clements, sometimes there are things that happen to girls to make them – well, you know what I mean, don't you? They don't want to grow up, that's the thing, isn't it? They don't want to have periods or – or a bust or anything like that. You understand what I'm saying?'

'Of course,' Hattie said carefully, wondering what was to come, hoping for some sort of confidence that would really help, would actually give her something to work on with Genevieve. 'Of course I do. You're very observant to have identified that that's the case with Genevieve, if it is. It's one of the commonest reasons they give in the textbooks for anorexia nervosa, though not the only one, of course.'

'Oh, I know that's the reason, all right.' Stella sounded stronger now and was once again looking her directly in the eye. 'It's just that she doesn't want to grow up. She doesn't like it. And you can't blame her, can you? I mean people like little girls best of all, don't they?'

'Sometimes,' Hattie said, still hopeful, and Stella shook her head vigorously.

'Not sometimes. All the time. That's what it is, you see. She doesn't want to grow up. She likes being a little girl, and if it's what she wants, I don't mind either. I mean, if I could help her stay little, I would.'

'But you can't, can you?' Hattie was disappointed. There was no real insight to come from Stella. This was just chat, words strung in a row for the sake of saying them, nothing new or useful at all. Except for what it told her of Stella's state of mind. It was clear to her now that sick as Genevieve was her mother wasn't too far behind her. She needed a psychiatrist, perhaps could do with some time in hospital herself, being properly as-

sessed. The whole family could do with help, she found herself
thinking, remembering the man with the overpressed suit, the
blindingly white shirt and too-perfect smooth hair. He was as
uptight as anyone could be, getting so agitated when I said
something to Genevieve about her periods.

She sighed then and managed to smile at Stella. 'Well, do
remember I'm here if I can be of any help. Maybe if you talk to
your GP and he wants to know about things here at school, he
can always phone me. I'll be glad to be of any use I can. I do
worry about Genevieve.'

'You needn't,' the woman said with a sudden tartness in her
voice. 'I can worry enough over her for anyone. She doesn't need
more than that.' And she bobbed her head awkwardly and went,
and Hattie collected up her books and odds and ends and, after
giving her time to get herself out of sight, followed her out of the
room. It was still very unsatisfactory but at least she'd spoken to
her. What the next step would have to be she wasn't sure; but at
least she'd spoken to Genevieve's mother.

Which does little more than assuage my conscience, she told
herself then with painful honesty as she went along the corridor
towards the staff common room. It's as much because of being
worried about what would happen to me if Genevieve suddenly
collapsed and I'd done nothing about her that I was so keen to
talk to her mother, admit it. I was just doing a bit of common-
or-garden buck-passing. 'Which can always be invoked if all else
fails,' she murmured aloud, remembering the lectures she had
had in her second year from old Sir Arthur Lancing who had
told them all solemnly that that was the last line of defence for
any surgeon, and could be just as useful for nurses. 'Never stay
with a case you can't help. Shove it on to someone else. It mayn't
help the patient all that much but it won't do him any harm and
it could help you out of trouble.' A dispiriting thought, she told
herself as she pushed open the door of the common room. For all
it's so practical. And I wasn't trying to get rid of Genevieve. I
really am concerned for her –

'You look like a wet weekend,' Edward Wilton said, and she
looked up at him, startled. The room was full of people, most of
them clustered around the coffee tray, and several glanced at her
as Wilton went on. 'It can't be that bad. You don't have exam
results to worry about, after all. Not like the rest of us.'

'I was actually worrying about a pupil's welfare,' she said as she joined the coffee huddle. 'Odd as it may seem, I do think about them as much as about myself.' Liar, she whispered inside her head. Liar. 'But I don't expect you to understand that.'

'It's really remarkable what a coarsening effect this place has on people,' Wilton said. 'Here less than a year and already you're as rude as everyone else in this room. You see, Dinant? Beware of spending too much time in here. You might get as acidulated as Mrs Clements here.'

The man he spoke to looked alarmed. He was tall and remarkably thin and his face was a round pink moon beneath a tangle of absurd yellow curls. He looked rather like a freshly boiled kitten peering out at the world through large pale blue eyes, but his clothes were those of a much older man, a suit of old-fashioned cut with a waistcoat and a singularly dull tie. He looked the epitome of conventionality.

'Oh, I don't think, really, I can't say, perhaps you –' he said and then stopped, looking miserable, and Hattie went to his rescue.

'I'm Hattie,' she said, holding out one hand. 'The new bug before you. I look after the girls in the sixth form.'

'Er – how do you do. I'm Paul Dinant. Art teacher,' the man said, and at once Dr Bevan, who had as usual annexed the armchair nearest to the coffee tray and the biscuit tin, looked up sharply.

'Has something happened to Tully, then?'

'How do you mean, happened?' Steenman said. 'How much more could happen?'

'I mean, has he died?'

'Not to my knowledge. Has he?' Steenman looked sternly at Dinant who blushed and shook his head hastily, denying all knowledge.

'I never knew – I mean, I heard the man before me was off sick – I don't know –'

'There you are then,' Steenman said. 'Nothing else has happened. He remains in the land of the living albeit the Land of Nod.'

'Hmmph,' Bevan said, subsiding into his chair again. 'Thought maybe he'd been replaced because he'd died. But they've had to take a new chap on. Will they still pay Tully? He'll still be on the payroll, won't he? I mean, it's not his fault he's sick.'

The room erupted into a busy chatter about the rights and wrongs of Tully receiving his salary and beneath its cover Hattie said to Dinant, 'Don't mind them. They mean no harm. Well, maybe they do, but they can't do much.'

He glanced at her, scared and grateful. 'I was warned they'd be a bit odd. Seeing what happened to my predecessor.' He brightened. 'I don't know much about it all. Just that there was an accident. Can you tell me? It must have been a very major one.'

Hattie looked at him with her head quirked to one side and then sighed in a slightly exaggerated way. 'Oh, dear, you are definitely going to fit into this common room like a cork into a bottle. Just as nosy as the rest of them.'

He flushed. 'I didn't mean to be pushy,' he said. 'I'm sorry.'

'Oh, that's all right,' she said, relenting. 'You're entitled to ask. It's just that this place is so – it's the most gossipy I was ever in and since I used to work in hospital you'll see just how gossipy that is.'

'It can't be as bad as Art School.'

'Wanna bet? Well, I'll tell you about Tully before someone else comes up with an over-embroidered version. The truth is bad enough.' And she told him as baldly as she could what had happened to Tully and when she'd finished he stared at her, clearly shaken.

'I wouldn't have thought a school could be such a dangerous place.'

'Just you wait and see,' Wilton said darkly, coming to stand behind Hattie. 'This is the original sin bin, the den of iniquity of all times, you take your life in your hands here –'

'And mostly we survive.' Hattie said and patted Paul Dinant's shoulder. 'You will too. The boys are rather sweet.'

'The fourth form sweet?' Wilton said, amazed. 'My God, now I've heard everything.'

'They are to me,' Hattie said serenely, and finished her coffee. She had a free period coming up and there was no hurry. Perhaps, if there was any coffee left, she'd spoil herself with a second cup.

There wasn't. She sighed and found herself a spare chair to sit in and began to tidy the mass of papers she had pushed into a folder in her pile; it was amazing how much assorted bumf could be collected when all she was doing was teaching non-exam subjects, she told herself a little gloomily. Maybe I'm getting as bad as everyone else here, untidy and bad-tempered and sharp-tongued –

The door opened again and she looked up to see Sam Chanter standing there and, as calmly as she could, looked down at her papers again. He'd been behaving so oddly these past three weeks since Founder's Day; cool was the only word she could find to describe him. Where once he'd been ready to chat when they'd met in the common room or in the corridors, now he was always in a hurry to go somewhere else. The suggestions of evenings out never came, and on the one occasion when she had a free evening because Judith had opted to take all the children to the theatre to see *Joseph and The Amazing Technicolor Dreamcoat* and she'd suggested it, he'd pleaded pressure of work as a reason not to accept. She'd been furious with him over that and even more furious with herself for being annoyed. He owed her nothing, after all; he was just someone here where she worked, no more. But it had rankled all the same. She had thought they were friends, and now for some unexplained reason he was anything but friendly, so she made no effort to catch his eye as once she would have done in order to smile at him. She just sat with her head bent over her papers even when he called loudly: 'Listen everyone, there's something I have to tell you.'

The room hiccuped to a silence as one by one they turned to look at him while he repeated his call, and Bevan said sourly, 'Well, now what? Another accident?'

'This is no accident,' Sam said. 'I have to tell you that Staveley's – um, been taken ill.'

'Staveley?' Steenman looked sharply at Sam. 'I saw him yesterday. He didn't look ill. Just his usual self.'

'Thoroughly miserable self,' Bevan said. 'The man's been unfit for human companionship for weeks.'

'He had a nasty shock when the accident happened,' Wilton murmured and Bevan snorted.

'He had a shock? How does he think I feel? Standing there right beside Tully when it happened, how can I be sure it wasn't me the person was after? Whoever shot that bullet wasn't doing it by accident and I'll say as much till my dying day, whether you like it or not. It was deliberate and any one of us could have been the victim and I was the nearest and –'

'Oh, shut up, Bevan,' Sam said wearily and there was a little hoot of laughter from Steenman as Bevan stared at Sam with his face blank with rage.

'Don't you talk to me like that, Chanter. I'm the Senior Master here and just you –'

'Staveley's ill. They found him this morning.'

'Found him?' Hattie looked up and spoke more sharply than she'd meant to.

'You've got it,' Sam said dryly. 'Yes, they found him. In his car.'

'Had he been in a crash or something?' Wilton said, staring, and Sam shook his head and opened his mouth to speak. But Hattie was before him.

'Carbon monoxide?'

'Again, you've got it in one,' Sam said and went on before anyone could interrupt him. 'It's all very clear. He went up to Hampstead Heath, did the usual rig-up from exhaust via a hosepipe into the closed car. He left a note. He's been very depressed, he said, over the loss of the Cadet Force, sees no point in going on, sorry for any trouble he'll be causing – the usual stuff.'

'Is he dead?' Wilton sounded awed, and Sam shook his head.

'No. Poor devil didn't even get that right. The car ran out of petrol and the engine stalled, it seems, before he got too much. He was admitted to the Royal Free and they're transferring him to Epsom. He'll be sorted out there –'

'The loony bin?' Bevan cried shrilly. 'Old Staveley in the bin? Well, I'm not at all surprised. The man's got no stamina! I was nearer to it all than he was, he was miles away, right behind his bloody guns, safe as a house, what's he got to get so agitated about?'

'Sometimes, Bevan, I could cheerfully throttle you,' Sam said and again Steenman let out a snort of laughter. 'The poor bastard's in a terrible state. Deeply miserable. He's been looking like hell ever since it happened and I for one tried to talk to him, but he wouldn't have it, so there it is. He's in hospital in Epsom. I'm collecting for fruit and flowers for him. And I want to make up a rota for visiting the old boy as soon as he's on the mend. He'll need us. He hasn't anyone else.'

'No family?' Hattie asked, and Sam flicked a glance at her.

'No,' he said shortly. 'Lived alone. The classic bachelor existence. He'll need us to visit unless he's to be left completely alone,
and I can't imagine even you, Bevan, would wish that on him.'

'Well, you can do as you wish.' Bevan hauled himself to his
feet from the depths of the old chair. 'I'm not going to be any
hypocrite. Sending Staveley flowers? You must be mad. As for
visiting him, pah!'

The school bell had started to ring and a self-satisfied grin
spread itself across Bevan's face. The news of Staveley's collapse
into depression seemed to have cheered him hugely, for as soon
as the bell stopped its raucous clamour and they could speak and
be heard he said loudly, 'I'm off to class. *My* pupils don't suffer
just because I've got no stuffing. Not like Staveley's lot. Hmmph.
It'll mean more new staff, I dare say.' He threw a withering glare
at Dinant who stood miserably silent at the edge of the group.
'Well, we have to pay for our blessings, I suppose. One way or
another.' And he went stumping off.

'Miserable bastard,' Steenman said, looking after him, but he
was grinning. 'That's set him up for the day, that has. He's
always hated Staveley. How much do you want, Sam? I can
stretch to a couple of quid, I suppose.'

'I want a fiver,' Sam said firmly. 'I want enough to send
something every week for the next two or three, if I can. Poor
old Staveley needs all the support he can get.'

Hattie put her five-pound note in the envelope when he
brought it to her and he said, 'Thanks,' in a colourless voice, and
on an impulse she didn't know she had put her hand on his arm
and said in a low voice, 'There's something I really must talk to
you about, Sam. Can you spare the time tonight after school? In
the usual place. Please. It's important to me.'

He looked at her, and then opened his mouth to speak and
closed it again and finally nodded a little blankly.

'If it's that important,' he said.

'Oh, yes, it is,' she assured him and went out of the room,
hurrying after Bevan and wanting to shout at herself every step
of the way. Now why on earth did I do that? she asked herself.
Why on earth tell him I have to discuss something with him
when I haven't the least idea what I want to talk to him about? I
must be absolutely potty.

Twenty-five

It was awful. He stood there in the street outside the tube station and said coolly, 'Well?' and she stood and stared back at him, not knowing what to say.

He had waited for her outside the school gates and as she emerged he'd nodded curtly to her and then fallen into step beside her as they made for the tube station. And, still not knowing what to say, still hoping some bright idea would come to her, she burbled at him about how awful it was about poor Mr Staveley, and thinking as she did it that she sounded like one of those silly women she used to hear sitting around in Casualty like ghouls, watching the comings and goings of injured people and exclaiming over them with a vast relish that had made her feel sick. Yet here she was doing the self-same thing.

Her speech had faltered to a stop then and she just hurried on beside him, seeking in every corner of her mind for something to say, but nothing came to her and she was scarlet in the face both with embarrassment and exertion when at last they reached the entrance to the tube.

'Well?' he said again and she jumped a little and looked up at him.

'What on earth's the matter with you?' she snapped, not stopping to think at all. 'Biting my head off like that. I – it's – you've been absolutely hateful these past three weeks. What on earth have I done to deserve it?'

He looked at her for a moment and then away, over her head. 'I don't know what you're talking about.'

'Oh, of course you do! We used to – I mean, we'd talk in a civilized fashion. I thought I could regard you as a friend. We were both involved over the business with Dilly and Arse and the pepper, and – and – I thought you were a friend. And now all I get is silence and scowls and –'

What are you doing? a voice shrieked deep in her mind. This isn't what you want to say. You'll make him think you're a complete idiot, a stupid eyelash-fluttering woman who just wants to make up to him and is put out because he won't play her silly flirtation game. You didn't mean to do this, shut up, shut up –

But I did mean to do this, another part of her mind whispered. It was exactly what I meant and she said aloud, trying to sound reasonable, 'Look, whatever I might have said to offend you, I apologize. I want only to be – There are very few people I can be comfortable with here at the Foundation. It matters to me if I've offended you.'

'No, of course you haven't,' he said roughly and now he did look at her, and she thought, He's miserable about something. Now, why should he be miserable? Because I'm angry? I hope so! But that thought had to be pushed away as thoroughly unthinkable.

'I'm glad to hear it,' she said more quietly, and waited.

'I've just been busy,' he said at length. 'There's a lot to think about.'

'I know. I have a fair deal to think about too. I mayn't be teaching A-level courses, but all the same –'

'And there's my book,' he said suddenly and rather loudly. 'Yes. There's my book.'

'Book?'

'I told you. I'm working on a novel. Not easy. I've reached a difficult stage. It – I have to concentrate a lot. That's what it is. I didn't mean to – Oh, this is ridiculous! I really do think you're being a little absurd, you know. I hope I'm friendly enough at school, try to be cooperative, but I'm entitled to my free time and my own – I don't have to explain to people why I choose to be silent, surely?'

'No,' she said, stung. 'You don't have to explain to people. Not that I'd thought of myself entirely as people in the plural, you understand. However, there it is. If my talking to you disturbs your channels of thought over your book so that you can't get on with it in the evenings and weekends, which is, I think, when you told me you work on it, I'll be very careful not to do so again. Goodnight, Mr Chanter.' And she went into the station, fiddling blindly in her bag for her season ticket, enraged at herself for feeling tearful. What on earth was there to be tearful about?

He seemed to her to hesitate for a moment in the entrance and then vanish. She felt his absence more as an increase in light from the entrance than anything else, and she stopped as one or two other people came into the station and then, on an impulse of which she felt ashamed, went back to the entrance, standing carefully at the side out of sight, and peered out to see where he'd gone.

He was on the other side of the road, waiting at the bus stop, and her forehead creased. He could go home to his flat either by train or bus, and once they'd become friendly he had gone out of his way to take the tube to keep her company. Now he was deliberately avoiding her and this time the tears pricked her throat so sharply it was like needles. Damn him to hell and back again, she thought furiously, and went stamping down into the station to wait on the platform, staring down the black hole of the tunnel with eyes smarting and hot and quite unseeing.

She had calmed down a little by the time she got home, which was just as well. It was Judith's birthday and under some pressure she'd agreed to go out with her and Peter and two other couples for dinner.

'I'm having my proper party next month, darling,' Judith had told her jubilantly. 'In Eilat, no less! I crave some sunshine and the only good thing about having your birthday so close to your wedding anniversary is it makes it so hard for husbands not to give you what you want. You can insist on having a very expensive combined anniversary and birthday pressie. Lovely! Right now the only pressie I really want is sunshine, and that's what I'm getting. Now, don't say no to dinner. I've found a darling Thai restaurant on the other side of the Hill, you know, down on Finchley Road, not at all fashionable but totally delicious. I insist you come, you'll have to. I told your two they could sleep over at my house and they're cock-a-hoop. Now, don't look daggers at me. You know they love it and it all works out so well.' At which veiled reference to the important part Judith played in the support system that allowed her to work at all, Hattie had been forced to capitulate.

Not that she had minded unduly; the little girls were indeed excited beyond belief at being allowed to sleep over in Jenny and Petra's house under the indulgent eye of Inge, who played wonderful games with them long after they should have been asleep (and which Hattie couldn't forbid, seeing it was Friday night), and anyway dining out would be agreeable. A welcome change. A chance to think of other things.

So she hurried in and made the girls their supper and listened to them chattering about school and the evening to come as they wolfed it down and she wrapped Judith's present – a couple of pairs of lace-foaming knickers from her favourite shop – marvelling a little at how easy it all was, compared with what she'd feared when she'd taken the job at the Foundation. The children were relaxed and happy, more than content to divide their free time between their own home and Judith's next door; indeed, Hattie thought now, it's as well I'm not the jealous-mother type; I'd be entitled to feel well cut out by Judith, who was adored by the children. But she couldn't mind, because it was so patently good for them. They were much happier than they had been when she'd been a full-time mother, she couldn't deny. Her old intensity must have been a heavy burden for them.

She dressed as carefully as she could, knowing that Judith would of course have produced a spare man for her at her supper party, and she had to go through the motions of being interested, even if she wasn't, so she put on the favourite amethyst dress which suited her so well and wrapped herself in her black woollen shawl and took the children next door.

Her escort for the evening proved to be a surgeon on Peter's firm at the hospital who was clearly much more interested in impressing Peter than Hattie, and that was a comfort, though she thought wryly that the amethyst dress was quite wasted on him; but the other people, a pair of actors who lived further down the same road as her and Judith and Peter and who could be relied on to talk non-stop, and a rather taciturn pair who had something to do with the Arts Council, were pleasant enough and she made up her mind to enjoy the evening.

It started well enough, with much giggling over the contents of Judith's parcels – and since everyone had bought her underwear except Jeffrey Pratt, the house surgeon, who had played safe with bath salts, there was a good deal of ribaldry on the subject of Judith's public image, all of which Judith hugely enjoyed and which made Peter grunt in his usual fashion – which relaxed them all. And the food was fun too, demanding a certain amount of attention in the ordering and then manipulation of chopsticks, and accompanied by surprises that consisted largely of foods that looked innocuous but which were extremely fiery indeed and made people cough and choke.

Judith seemed so absorbed in the general conversation that Hattie relaxed and settled to thinking her own thoughts, which were inevitably of Sam's behaviour that afternoon. To have been so remote in the first place had been bad enough; to have gone out of his way not to travel with her had been even more hurtful. And she stared sightlessly at her food and wondered.

'It can't be that bad, ducky,' Judith murmured in her ear and she started.

'Mmm?'

'You look like you lost a pound and found half a crown, as my old Granny used to say. That sounds odd now, doesn't it? Lost a twenty-pound note and found a fiver, I suppose it ought to be these inflationary days. What on earth's the matter? Not another bit of murder and mayhem at your school?'

'Er – well, not really. I mean, one of the masters attempted suicide.'

'Not really? Ye gods, darling, if that's "not really" what on earth would you say if something bad happened? How do you mean, tried to commit suicide?'

Hattie explained and Judith listened as the rest of their party chattered on, absorbed in each other – the Arts Council couple were being bombarded with complaints by the actors and the two surgeons were conversationally ankles deep in blood and gore – and when she'd finished made a little face.

'You can't be funny about that, can you?' she said a little unexpectedly. 'Poor old sod! Imagine having such a lousy life that losing the chance to order little boys about pretending to be soldiers makes you suicidal. No wonder you look so miserable.'

'Do I? I didn't mean to,' Hattie said. 'I wasn't that upset, I'm afraid. I mean, he's the sort of chap you'd expect it from.'

'Well, if it isn't the poor old sod who has you on the edge of tears, who is it? The divine Sam?'

'I'm not on the edge of tears!'

'Well, a bit near the edge, anyway. This is me, remember, ducks? So tell me, how is the divine Sam, now I think of him? Next time we have an outing like this, we'll have to ask him. Maybe for Peter's birthday next May –'

'No!' Hattie cried hastily. Too hastily, for Judith was on the scent at once.

'Aha! You've had a row!' She pounced. 'Why? When? How?'

'Such stuff!' Hattie said. 'Of course we haven't. There's nothing to row about.'

'Something's happened to upset you,' Judith said. 'More people smoking pot, perhaps?' She giggled, pleased with her alliteration. 'Poor little poppets puffing pot.'

'No, that's all right. I talk to Harry about it fairly often and he's a straight sort of chap. He wouldn't lie to me. It's stopped. Anyway, they were all so shaken by what happened to Tully it's sort of taken the steam out of them. They don't seem, any of them, to have the taste for rule-breaking they used to.' And indeed everyone in the staffroom had noticed and commented favourably on the subdued air the boys were carrying about with them now. Hattie had found it depressing to see such young people feeling so low, but had been glad enough for her own sake; if they had still been hiding away in their basement hole using their drugs she'd have had her bluff called and would have had to do something. As it was, all was well there. She'd been down to look for herself, feeling a little guilty at not taking Harry's word for it, and found the space dusty, cold and clearly abandoned. So now she shook her head. 'I'm not worried about them the way I was.'

'So what else can it be? Is he going to fire you, the ineffable Hilary?'

'Not to my knowledge. The girls are still there so he still needs someone like me, and he seems content enough with what I'm doing. If he didn't fire me over the Daniel Spero affair he's hardly likely to do it now. I've done nothing to upset him.'

'*Ipso facto, quod erat demonstrandum, sine qua non*, and all the rest of it, then!' Judith said. 'It has to be Sam.'

Hattie gave in. 'He's being a little odd,' she admitted.

'Lots of detail, ducky, please! I can't make decisions for you without all the evidence, now can I?'

'Who asked you to make decisions for me?' Hattie managed to laugh. 'Honestly, Judith, I don't know why I put up with you.'

'Because I'm a nice scatty friend who loves you and looks after you and is marvellous with your kids,' Judith said. 'So, details! Lots and lots of luscious details.'

Hattie sighed. 'There aren't any really. He's just been – well, stand-offish, I suppose. We used to gossip so nicely, you know? It was fun going up for coffee in the mornings because he'd be there and we'd natter and –'

'I know,' Judith said. 'It's better than a tangle of legs in a bed sometimes, isn't it? Sex is all right, but a natter over a coffee cup leaves it standing.'

'Sex doesn't come into this equation, damn you,' Hattie said, and Judith laughed.

'Wanna bet? Anyway, there you were, cosy chats over the coffee cups and now – well, now what?'

'I told you. He just isn't there, or if he is, he's already got his coffee and he's sitting in a corner with his head in a book so that I can't disturb him, or he's talking shop with the others. It's all, well, it's like writing in water. Nothing to get hold of but you know it's there. Nothing to point to.'

'And what happened today?'

Hattie told her and it sounded limp in the extreme. 'So there you are,' she finished. 'It's nothing really, is it? He used to see me to the station and share part of my journey home. Now he goes and catches a bus instead.'

Judith was silent, stirring the remains of the noodles on her plate as she thought. Around them the chatter of the others went on and Hattie was grateful for it. Judith might be dreadfully inquisitorial and sometimes tiresome but she was wonderfully comfortable to talk to.

'When did it start?' Judith said abruptly, and Hattie screwed up her eyes, thinking.

'After the film was shown to the school, I think,' she said slowly. 'I told you I thought I saw something and I asked him to look and he did, but he said he didn't think it was anything to worry about.'

'I remember,' Judith said and she sounded unusually sober. 'You thought you saw a gun. He pooh-poohed it.'

'Not exactly pooh-poohed it,' Hattie protested. 'Just didn't think he'd seen what I thought I saw.'

Again Judith was silent and then she looked up at Hattie and her face was unusually unsmiling. 'Did you see him in the film?' she asked.

'What?'

'I said –'

'I heard you. I don't think . . .' Hattie squinted at the wall facing her, not seeing the embroidered pictures of birds and bridges and cherry trees that hung there, but watching the film in her mind's eye. She'd seen it often enough to remember it very well; and then she said slowly, 'No, I don't think I did, to be honest.'

'Oh!' Judith said and that was all.

There was a little silence between them and then Hattie said pugnaciously, 'And what does that "Oh!" mean?'

'Nothing. Just oh.'

'Come off it, Judith, this is me, this time. I know you as well as you think you know me. You do mean something by that. You think there was something odd about not being able to see Sam in the film? There were hordes of other people who weren't in the film! So why make a point of it with Sam?'

'Only because he was so definite about it not being a gun muzzle you saw,' Judith said. 'That was the only reason. It's all settled down, hasn't it? I mean, the police have left it alone. Only if old Tully dies will there be an inquest, and at the moment it's all peaches and cream, isn't it? Everything at the Foundation's lovely.'

'What with suicides and –'

'You know what I mean.'

'I suppose so.'

There was another silence and then Hattie said, 'You think he's involved in the Tully business in some way?'

Judith shrugged. 'How can I know, darling? I just sit here and listen to you talk. It's the things you say that make the ideas come to me. You tell me three things. That Sam's gone funny on you. That he said he didn't see a gun where you saw one on the film. And he wasn't in sight on the film when you watched it. So I can't help thinking, Was he at the other end of that gun you saw, only not on the film? It's a logical thought, after all, ducky, isn't it? It's obviously occurred to you. If it hadn't, how come you put it into my mind?'

Twenty-six

With just two weeks left to the end of term, it wasn't difficult for Hattie to keep herself very busy at school. There were the final rehearsals for the last performance of *The Taming of the Shrew* which was to take place on the last Thursday of term, to replace the cancelled showing on Founder's Day, and that meant most of the girls were heavily occupied with organizing their costumes and arranging their rehearsals round class work. Hattie, in spite of Collop's continuing tendency to produce comments of such biting sarcasm they made her and almost all of the girls want to scratch his eyes out, helped them as much as she could and was very much in evidence in the dressing rooms during the rehearsals, helping the girls reconstruct their costumes there and learning more about make-up. She'd always done the stage make-up for the Old East shows in her student days, and she enjoyed gathering up her old skills as she showed the sixth-formers how to highlight and disguise in the way demanded by the battery of light Collop used for his productions ('We might be amateurs,' he would say. 'But we'll be the most bloody professional amateurs there can be') and generally making them look exceedingly Elizabethan.

All of which made it much easier to keep out of Sam's way. She hardly ever went to the common room at coffee time now, preferring to remain with the girls in their sixth-form room, or busying herself in the props room where a good deal of time was being spent making up what purported to be costly jewellery for some of the cast to wear for this special performance, and she usually went out for lunch, not feeling up to facing them all at the staff table in the dining room. She would walk quickly through the March chill to the market at Watney Street to buy herself something from the delicatessen and coffee in a plastic cup and would eat and drink quickly as she watched the passers-by, concentrating on them in all their winter busyness as a way of not thinking about Sam.

It wasn't easy. She would stare at a woman with a clutch of children wrapped in vivid red and blue woollens (for the people hereabouts favoured strong colour in their clothes) as she haggled with stall-keepers for the cheapest vegetables while cuffing the children indiscriminately if they tried to move an inch from her side, and imagine herself walking over to her, starting to talk to her, finding a way explaining that hitting wasn't the best way to help children grow up happy and successful; would imagine the woman losing her temper and hitting out at her as she did at her children – and then suddenly Sam would arrive in her little fantasy, walking through the hubbub of the market to take her arm and smile and nod at the angry woman and assure her she wouldn't be bothered again by this foolish person –

And then she would crumple her coffee beaker and throw it away and march out of the deli to thread her way through the stalls, sometimes stopping to buy sweet potatoes and plantains – for Sophie and Jessica had learned to like her attempts at West Indian cookery – trying to concentrate on that too; but again Sam would appear in her mind's eye, leaning over her shoulder, pointing out a particularly luscious mango or papaya and telling her to buy it, to try something new –

The truth of it is, she'd told herself bleakly, padding back to school after the lunch hour one day, her arms dragged down and her fingers blanched by an extra load of shopping she hadn't really needed to buy, but which had kept her anxiety at bay while she did it, the truth is, I'm scared and angry, all at the same time. Scared it might be true, that Judith is right and Sam is somehow involved in what happened to David Tully, and angry with myself for caring. If he's the one who hurt Tully I should be a sensible citizen, and a caring one, I should go to the police and tell them what I know, and –

At which point she was stopped short. For what did she know, after all? Nothing. Judith had come up with one of her more ridiculous notions – and Hattie had denied hotly and still did that she had put the idea in Judith's head – and that was all there was. No evidence, not a scintilla of proof that he was anything but what he seemed, a schoolmaster absorbed in his work and his pupils, friendly, agreeable –

'He's not,' she said aloud, stopping in the middle of the pavement, so that other people had to eddy round her as though she were a rock in a stream, and then, catching a curious stare from one of them, plodding on, her head down. He isn't friendly and agreeable, and I hate him for letting me think he was. I was beginning to like him a lot –

'Too much?' her secret voice asked sardonically and she considered that instead of trying to push the thought away. Well, yes. She had to admit it. She had come to regard him very warmly indeed, liking the way he smiled, the shape of his body as he stood there in the common room, the smell of him as she went by, medicated soap and warm skin; and knowing that made her angrier than ever.

What made it all the more difficult was the fact that Sam seemed to have changed. No longer did he try to avoid her. On the contrary. On the rare occasions she came into the common room and he was there he would make for her eagerly, only to be stopped by the way she firmly attached herself to someone else – often Dinant – so that he couldn't talk to her alone. If he saw her in the corridors he would try to catch up with her, or wait till she reached him, and she would deliberately hurry her steps to outstrip him or turn round and go the other way, waiting till he'd gone to complete her errand. He looked tense and angry when she did look at him – which wasn't often, for she was determined to avoid any eye contact – and that he was worried was very clear to her. And she didn't want to think more than she had to about why he was worried and above all didn't want to remember that day in the staffroom when he had attacked Tully so heatedly, telling him he'd cheer if Tully got his throat cut. She most especially didn't want to think about that, or indeed any of it. The possibility that Judith might be right was too awful to contemplate.

It was decided that *The Taming of the Shrew* would manage to get on stage without another full dress rehearsal but a technical one was needed, and she was glad of that. It would make her extra busy and less inclined to silly thinking.

'We'll have a run-through for lights and make-up, but only

principals need wear costume,' Martin Collop said. 'Though I want all props, of course. Half past four sharp, if you please, and I want no time wasted. I've got better things to do than hang around here while you halfwits get your acts together.' As though no one else in the cast had any reason to want to finish on time, Hattie thought wrathfully, and went to phone Judith about coping with the girls.

'I'm sorry to do this so often,' she said. 'But it'll be easier next term. No play, and tomorrow'll be the last late night there'll be for that. We break up next Thursday, glory be.'

'Never give it a thought,' Judith said blithely. 'I like being Mum to four instead of two. Makes me feel useful for a change. Have fun, ducky, and keep out of the wicked Sam's way.'

'Idiot!' Hattie said, ringing off, and went to the school kitchens to see if she could scrounge some sandwiches from the cooks. Collop wouldn't give a second thought to the fact that his cast would get hungry, so she had better deal with it.

She got herself and the trays of sandwiches back to the hall, which was already set out with its rows of chairs for tomorrow's performance, at four o'clock, and found it empty except for the two boys who were rigging lights. They waved to her from the tops of their ladders and she called cheerfully back, then went backstage to set out the food she'd brought. The less Collop knew about it the better, she decided; he might regard stopping for a sandwich as a waste of time and not let the cast eat them; and that would mean a stand-up row, Hattie told herself, because there's no way I'd let him get away with that –

I'm getting positively childish, she told herself then as she set the plastic-film-covered trays on the long trestle table that held the props for the play. Rehearsing conversations and encounters that won't ever take place, getting worked up over things that haven't happened and almost certainly won't. Grow up, woman!

Damn, she thought. I've nothing for them to drink; and she looked at her watch. Should be enough time if she hurried to get to the small corner shop round the corner from the main gates and stock up on lemonade and Cokes. She herself would prefer coffee, but that wouldn't appeal to the cast; and maybe she could get some of them to chip in for the cost of the drinks afterwards? It would make a fair hole in her housekeeping if they didn't.

She got back from the shop with her laden carriers just as

Collop was settling himself in the front row of the seating, and she tried to slip unobtrusively behind the curtains at the side, but he saw her and called, 'What have you got there?'

Bloody man, she thought and looked over her shoulder at him. 'I went to get drinks for them, Cokes and so forth. I thought they'd get hungry and thirsty.'

'Still on watch for the ewe lambs? The boys have the wit to bring their own refreshments —'

'I've got enough for the boys as well,' Hattie retorted. 'And sandwiches.'

'There's generous!' Collop said mockingly. 'Is there even enough for me?'

'Since the school supplied the sandwiches, I see no reason why you shouldn't have your share,' she said. 'Though I'd be glad to have your contribution to the cost of the drinks. I bought these out of my own pocket.'

He grinned, pleased with himself. 'Then more fool you. I've got my own drink, thank you.' He patted the zipped-up bag at his side. 'I'm not used to having a shepherdess take care of me, so I thought of it all on my little own. And I'll need more than Coke to get me through an evening with this lot.' and he scowled up at the boy on top of the ladder nearest to him and bawled, 'You bloody idiot, that'll come down like a hernia if you don't fix it properly! Use your bloody eyes, man! That screw's open!'

'Hadn't forgotten it, sir,' the boy called. 'I had just got it finished.' Obediently he screwed up the bracket that held the lamp and then, after squinting at the way the beam fell on the upstage left area, nodded and came down. 'That's it, sir. You'll see it all works now. Shall I start the run-through?'

'Got your cue sheet?'

The boy pulled a sheet of paper from his pocket and waved it at Collop.

'Then what are you hanging around here for? Get to the lighting board.'

The boy went, taking his ladder with him, and after a few moments called down from the back in a muffled shout, 'Shall we do the music cues at the same time, sir? We could — Johnny Silverman's here and he's got it all ready.'

'Then bloody get on with it,' Collop roared and after another moment the front curtains closed a little jerkily and the lights

that illuminated the hall dimmed slowly. The cast, who had
started to arrive, settled down at the back of the hall to whisper
to each other and watch and listen.

The technical rehearsal went fairly smoothly, with Collop needing to bawl at the hidden lighting and sound engineers only two
or three times and even then on quite minor matters. The music
he'd chosen for the play was unusual, modern jazz with a blues
lilt to it, and it fitted the play remarkably well, once the shock of
the incongruity of it had passed, and the lighting was smooth
and beautifully designed, with pools of light of different colours
appearing at various sites on the stage to focus the audience on
whatever new piece of action was taking place there. You have
to hand it to him, Hattie thought, watching and listening intently.
The man's got a gift for production.

The last chords of the incidental music crashed through the
hall as the curtains closed on the last lighting change, and Collop
shouted, 'Give me all you've got on stage for the calls. I'll rehearse
them now. Well, where are you then? You lot, principals first,
and then the rest of you. In the order I arranged last time. I want
you back stage and in the proper wings right now. Faster, faster
faster!'

They scurried, running across the hall like a tide coming in,
and Hattie stood to one side of the flanking curtain which hung
between the wall and the stage in order to let them into the
wings more quickly, and was amused to see Harry Forster,
resplendent as Petruchio in feathered hat and crimson ruff over
black sweater and tights, waving his sword over his head with
one hand as he came running. His other hand was clasping that of
one of the other principals who ran behind him trying to keep
up, and Hattie had to peer to see who it was, for the stage
curtains were still closed and the house lights were still down,
and then as the pair reached the corner where she was standing
she saw it was Bianca, and was startled. Genevieve? And Harry?

She was looking up at him with her face alight with laughter.
Her eyes were wide and dark in her pale face and for once her
extreme thinness didn't make her look drawn and bony. There
was a glow about her that Hattie had never seen before, and she
looked from Genevieve, who, laughing now, had stopped to
untangle from her feet the train that was attached to her long
white skirt, to Harry, and saw much the same expression on his

face. He was good to look at at the best of times, but now, in his great crimson ruff and with a wide-brimmed feathered hat on his head, he was devastatingly beautiful, and he caught Hattie's eye as she looked at him and grinned widely, a grin full of such bliss and self-satisfaction that it made her blink.

It was over in a moment; he made an elaborate bow to Bianca, who laughed delightedly and swept past him, her skirt held free of her feet in both hands. Harry stretched out one hand and with great skill reached for her bottom and tucked his fingers under it; and Bianca laughed again even more delightedly and then they were gone, into the wings, leaving Hattie staring after them as Collop started roaring again from the front.

Hattie stood there, shaken, and then began to smile, a long slow smile that wreathed her face. For the first time since the accident to Tully she felt a wave of simple pleasure; Genevieve in love? For that was how the child had looked, she thought, staring blankly at the stage as Collop began supervising a series of elaborate tableaux vivants to be used as curtain calls. The girl's in love, and what's better still, it's reciprocated. Harry too had carried the unmistakable air of delight and separateness that goes with that particular state of lunacy. If nothing else gave it away it was the sheer beauty of them both; only when people were wrapped in mutual adoration could they show that sort of glowing glorious face to onlookers, Hattie thought, and hunched her shoulders with delight. To see Genevieve like that was marvellous. There was one problem at least she'd be able to stop fretting about. Because surely, now she had Harry in her life, she'd start to eat again? He wouldn't let her starve herself to illness. I'll see to it he won't, she thought a little grimly as again the stage curtains swished back to show the final tableau of Petruchio standing in a Henry VIII wide-legged pose, arms akimbo, with young Carter, his plump chest suitably bulging over the top of his gown, submissive at his feet, and beside him Bianca standing smiling and chin-tilted in a would-be dream pose, with her suitors equally submissive before her. She looked at them both again, and it was unmistakable. Petruchio was looking sideways at Bianca and Bianca was looking just as slyly at Petruchio and they were like characters in a comic strip rather than a Shakespeare play. Any moment now, Hattie thought, wanting to laugh aloud, plump scarlet hearts with golden highlights on them will bob up around their heads and then plop like bursting bubbles. Oh, yes, the problem of Genevieve is surely solved. I'll speak to Harry, see to it that he persuades her to get help. She'll do anything he tells her, that's for certain.

'OK, that's all for the curtain calls. Just remember them tomorrow and Christ help anyone who moves a muscle until the curtain's well down and the lights are dimmed. Hear me. I'll slay anyone who ruins it, and don't think I don't mean it.'

The curtain rose again and stayed up, and the cast came clattering down from the stage to stand around waiting for further instructions as Collop looked at his watch.

'I have to make a phone call,' he said. 'Before we start the run-through. I'll need ten minutes.' He looked up at Hattie then. 'Nursie here has some sandwiches for all you diddums so now's the time to eat 'em. You won't get a chance later and that's a promise. Go on. I'll be ten minutes, no more.'

He looked at Genevieve then. 'Will he be there at this time?'

Genevieve, her attention dragged from Harry who was standing close beside her, blinked at him.

'What?'

'Are you deaf, girl? I said is he there now? Your father?'

'My father?' Genevieve looked even blanker.

'Ye gods, girl! Who else? He's the Governor, isn't he, the one who deals with the Council applications?'

'Oh,' Genevieve said. 'Oh, yes. He's a Governor. I don't know what he does with the Council though —'

'Forget it,' Collop said. 'I'll sort it out for myself. Got to get an application for a grant for next year's Drama. Now remember, I'll be ten minutes, if that. So get a move on.'

They grabbed for the sandwiches like so many gannets, clearing the trays at an amazing rate, but Hattie rescued one tray and very deliberately took it out to the hall to where Harry and Genevieve were sitting with some of the others, though clearly not with them, since they were still wrapped in their own private bubble.

'I brought you some sandwiches,' she said, looking directly at Genevieve. 'Help yourselves.'

The others did, reaching with alacrity, but Genevieve didn't move and Hattie said more loudly, 'Genevieve?'

'I'm not –' Genevieve began but Harry reached over her shoulder and picked up two.

'We'll share,' he said. 'What's this? Egg and cress. That'll do nicely. Despite our primitive attire, Mistress Clements, we do not choose to sup upon dead creatures, do we, O divine Mistress Bianca.'

'I'm not hungry,' Genevieve said, and Hattie shook her head.

'I think you must be,' she said. 'It's been a long time since lunch. See to it she eats something, Harry.'

Harry lifted his chin, aware now of the emphasis in her tone and then looked at Genevieve, who had her head bent, staring down at her hands. 'What's all this, then?'

'Genevieve doesn't eat enough, Harry,' Hattie said. Her voice was lower now, though the others who were sitting near them were too involved in their own conversations to hear them anyway. 'She's rather thin, don't you think?'

'She's great,' Harry said, and looked at Genevieve and then again at Hattie, and saw the expression on her face, and reached down and picked up one of Genevieve's hands. It lay in his big hand, itself long-fingered and elegant, like a small bag of bleached bones and he closed his fist on it gently and then released it and said, 'But she is too thin. For your health, Bianca of my heart, only for your health.'

She looked at him and then at the sandwich and her face seemed to tighten, so that she made a rictus of a grin and then it smoothed out.

'Are you going to go on at him about me?' she said looking at Hattie. 'The way you do at my mum?'

'Yes,' Hattie said. 'It's important, you see. Even more now that there's Harry, don't you think?'

Genevieve took a deep breath, not quite a sigh and, oddly, smiled, a great wide shimmering grin that lifted her cheeks to a spurious roundness. 'I'll have to, won't I?'

'Yes,' Hattie said simply and again Genevieve took that deep breath that was almost a sigh, and reached for one of the sandwiches in Harry's other hand. She took it, and turned it round once or twice and then very deliberately opened her mouth and took a sizeable bite. And Hattie wanted to cry.

Twenty-seven

———————— ∞∞∞ ————————

Collop, when he came back, looked furious, and Hattie glanced at him as he came crashing in through the main doors and felt her chest tighten. Oh, God, she thought. He was bad enough before; now what's happened?

'What's going on here?' he shouted. 'How much longer do you people intend to tit around? Get yourselves back on stage and ready, for Christ's sake. It's gone six already. Get a move on.'

Quite what possessed Genevieve Hattie couldn't imagine. Perhaps in her besotted state she hadn't noticed the change in Collop's mood, but as he came pushing his way past her back to his chair in the front row she looked up at him and said, 'Was he there, then?'

'What?' Collop snapped.

'You said you wanted my dad. Was he there?'

'What's it got to do with you?' He almost shouted it and she stepped back, startled, and Harry, who had been close beside her, but talking to one of the others, felt her movement and turned at once, lissom as a cat, and looked hard at Collop.

'What's the matter?' he said, not taking his eyes from Collop's face but clearly talking to Genevieve. 'What's up?'

'I don't know,' Genevieve muttered. 'I just asked –'

'And I said it's nothing to do with you.' Collop sounded less fierce now, but he was clearly having to struggle to be calmer. Something had obviously made him very angry indeed. 'I meant, it was Council business, and as such it's private. Nothing to discuss with outsiders, even the Councillor's daughter.' He managed to grin, a somewhat wolfish baring of teeth, and Harry looked down at him from his superior height and said coolly, 'I see.'

'Well, now, are we all ready then?' Collop had clearly decided to change his manner and he rubbed his hands together now in a show of joviality. 'Had your sandwiches? Had your drinks?'

There was a chorused murmur of assent and Collop looked around at them all and said, 'Well, then, where's mine? Hmm? Where's my share?'

There was a shocked silence as someone looked round to where two of the empty trays, bearing no more than a few crumbs and wisps of cress, lay abandoned on chairs, and Collop followed his gaze and grinned, this time with real pleasure.

'Well, well, you are greedy little sods, aren't you? Pigs, every one of you.' The discovery seemed to have completed the overturning of his bad mood. Now he was genuinely delighted to have caused them discomfiture. 'Not so much as a soggy crumb left for the old man? Poor old man, no one to look after me, boo hoo!'

'I've got some KitKat left, sir,' someone volunteered and pushed forward, holding it out, a rather battered chocolate finger in its red wrapping to which much of the chocolate, melted in a trouser pocket, had clung. Collop looked at it and sighed theatrically, 'One half-chewed bit of chocolate. Is that the best you can do? What about a drink, then?'

The Cokes and lemonade had all been finished too, and Hattie, deeply irritated by the man's silliness, lifted her chin and said loudly, 'They're all gone, too. Everyone paid up, of course. You said you had your own, anyway.'

'So I did, so I did!' he said and reached down for his zipped bag. 'And to tell you the truth, dear Mrs Clements, and you, you horrible lot, what I have here is infinitely more interesting than even a whole chocolate biscuit would have been, and certainly beats Coke into a cocked hat.'

He reached in and took out his screw-topped bottle and with an expert twist of the little finger on his right hand undid it, turning the bottle against his other hand with such speed that he cap was off and held inside his palm within a split second, while he held the bottle high in the air in his left hand. It was full of a colourless substance and someone at the back of the crowd, emboldened by being hidden, called, 'Got a drop of vodka in there, have you, sir?'

'No, it's gin and tonic,' someone else said. 'See the bubbles?'

Collop shook his head and laughed and threw back his chin and opened his mouth and began to tip the bottle from its place high above his head, and Hattie thought disgustedly, Boring show-off. He's going to do that stupid trick of his.

Afterwards she tried to remember how it was, how long it had taken, but she couldn't. The event would for always be locked in a sort of time bubble in her head, one in which everything happened at incredible speed and yet so slowly that she was aware of every tiny change in what she saw, as though it were a film being run at impossibly slow speed.

The watery liquid appeared at the neck of the bottle, and began to stream down towards Collop's open mouth. She could actually see space between the leading part of the stream and his mouth; but then it made contact and the sound happened too, a great eldritch shriek that made her head spin, as Collop flung the bottle from him and leapt to his feet, both hands held to his face as the shriek went on; and then he seemed to try to breathe and couldn't, and the sound became a choking silence which was infinitely worse than the scream; and they stood there, all of them frozen into horrified stillness as he stared back at them with slowly bulging eyes over a face that went by smooth stages from red to the deepest purple.

It wasn't until he hit the floor and lay there, his chest heaving and his heels drumming on the wooden boards, that she could move, and she shot forwards to bend over him and then almost reared back, shocking herself, as the fumes caught her, acrid, burning, tear-jerking, and it was as though she were a small inky child again, in a school laboratory, and her teacher was intoning warnings at her about the bottles of acid. Do not touch, dangerous, do not touch –

But that was memory. She was reaching down for his throat, pulling at his shirt and tie to release it and shouting. She didn't know till afterwards what she had shouted, only that she had, but someone went running and then someone else shouted too and more feet were running and she was still pulling at the shirt round Collop's purple throat. He still had his hands at his mouth and she tried to pull them back, but he resisted her, and then at last, with one more heave of his chest, he relaxed and she could pull his hands down and she saw it; the gaping mouth and in it the deep red of the mucous membrane peeling, whitening at the edges, swelling before her eyes, and the acrid fumes came even stronger. Someone pushed in beside her and a long arm came over her shoulder and she saw the black skin and registered – Harry, and then took from him the jug he held in his hand. Water; that must have been what she had asked for, and she pulled on Collop's shoulder, turned him slightly, set his head to one side and began to pour the water into his mouth, watching it run out from the other side, nearest the floor, trying to think what to do next; water to neutralize, alkaline –

'Soda water,' Harry said loudly and pushed a bottle into her hands and she caught the sheer commonsense of it and thought absurdly, Where did that come from? And went on washing out the mouth, unaware of the face above it, just that gaping hole with its fringe of yellowing teeth.

'He's not breathing,' someone said beside her and then began to whimper. 'Is he dead? He isn't breathing. Oh, what's happening? Why isn't he breathing?'

Hattie reached down to the shirt again and pulled it hard, and the buttons burst and she could see his chest at last and the sign was clear: the inwards curving that meant an obstructed airway, and she said aloud, 'Tracheostomy. He needs a tracheostomy.'

'Do you need a knife? A scalpel?' Harry again, on his feet beside her though he'd been kneeling a moment ago. 'I'll get them. Biology lab. Get towels, someone. Cloakroom –'

She went on pouring water in a steady stream into Collop's mouth, reaching for the refills people were bringing, waiting, needing to do something, not sure she was doing anything useful after all, but with acid burns it was what you did. Neutralize the acid.

'How did he get acid in his drink?' she said aloud and then the voice that had whimpered spoke and Hattie turned her head and saw it was Bridget Quinton, one of the sillier sixth-form girls.

'It must have come from Biology. I can smell it. It's the hydro-chloric acid we use in the biology lab. How did he get it in his bottle?'

'I don't know,' Hattie said. 'Has someone thought to call an ambulance?'

'I did.' Arse came pushing out of the crowd to crouch beside her. 'They're on their way. I said it was poison.'

'Arse? What are you doing here?' Hattie said, knowing it was a stupid question, but asking all the same, and still she went on trickling in the water though it seemed pointless now. The acid must be gone, washed away into the floorboards. 'You're not in the play –' And then there was Harry, looming above him and Arse shuffled away and Harry was kneeling in his place.

'Here's a scalpel – will that do? And I found these forceps. A bit rusty, but I thought –'

'Yes,' she said. 'Yes,' and made herself remember. Just by the cricoid cartilage, wasn't it? 'Help me roll him on his back.'

They had him on his back and she reached for the knife, a dull-looking thing in Harry's pale-palmed hand and she said, 'Someone roll up a cloak or something big. I need a hard cushion under his shoulders.'

It was Harry again who responded, swift, deft and unflappable, and she took it from him, a hard little bunch of fabric, and thrust it beneath Collop's shoulders. His head lolled back, the jaw drooping, and she said, 'Harry, hold it up, out of the way.'

She'd never done the job before, had only ever seen it done once and then under controlled circumstances in a hospital operating theatre. But it had to be done so she did it; feeling round the larynx, very aware of the indrawn hollow at the root of his throat just below, choosing a point, pushing the knife along the skin.

Bridget had begun to wail now, and someone was trying to hush her; everyone else was very still, but Hattie was very aware of them all standing there around her as she pushed the knife harder. The skin bowed beneath it but didn't part and almost pettishly she pushed harder on the handle, and this time the point of the scalpel went in. Blood blossomed, deeply crimson, round the point, and there was Harry again, a towel in his hand, a rather grubby cloakroom towel but a towel all the same, dabbing the blood away, and she moved the knife carefully against the cut edge – for all the world, she thought crazily, like cutting a tough-skinned tomato: it won't let you till you make the first break in – and pushed. The hole deepened, opened into a dull red gap and she pushed further, and then it happened; air went whistling past her hand, the hollow beneath the larynx filled as suddenly as though someone had poured flesh into it, and she felt the chest move against her thighs.

'Artificial –' she began, and Harry, still calm, still ahead of her in everything, pushed the forceps he'd been holding into her hand and came round behind her and began to pump on Collop's chest, a rhythmic careful movement that sent the air whistling past her hand again, this time as she set in place the forceps and kept open the hole she'd made.

And there they all stayed, she crouching over Collop, lying on the floor with a pair of old and probably filthy forceps in his windpipe, and Harry leaning forward, then back, steadily beating air into the lungs through the hole she had opened. Silence everywhere except from the creak of Harry's movements against the wooden floor and the breathing of the watching children.

This time she didn't hear the ambulance siren. They were just there, the men with their stretcher and box of equipment, and gladly she handed over to them and sat back on her heels, watching as they moved with immense deftness and set a tube in Collop's throat and tied it in place with a length of bandage, muttering at each other as they worked. 'We'll take him to Old East,' one of them said as she stood up at last and they lifted Collop on to a stretcher. 'He'll be all right, won't you, old man.'

Amazingly Collop's head moved, his hair rumpled against the red blanket-covered pillow, and Hattie moved closer to look down at him. He tried to move his lips, which were now immensely swollen, and she shook her head, hushing him.

'Don't try to talk. You'll be fine. You know where you are? What happened?'

He moved his eyes as though to look around and then at her, and there was an expression in them, knowledge and anger and fear, and she managed a smile of sorts.

'As long as you're fully aware of it all, then you haven't had too much damage. We managed to be quick enough.'

'Bit of a miracle-worker this one, my friend,' the ambulance man said heartily as he bent and unhooked the wheels so that they could push Collop out of the hall. 'If she hadn't done what she done you'd be a goner. Got you fast, she did. Well done. Trained first-aider, are you?'

'I used to be a Sister at Old East,' she said almost absently, still staring down at Collop, and the ambulance man said, 'Ah!' in a sound that carried all the understanding in the world in it.

''Nuff said. Best girls in the world there. You ought to come back. You can do stuff like this, they need you down in A and E, take it from me. They're a dead loss these days. We'll be off, then.'

And they were gone and she was left standing in the hall with a gaggle of frightened children and just a puddle of water on the floor where Collop had lain.

It was later, much later, before she could really think about it all. She'd kept them all there at the school, feeling obscurely it was the right thing to do, but not wanting to call the police, although she felt perhaps she should, and sent instead to the Headmaster, getting Harry to phone him. Harry had become her prop and stay and she was passionately grateful to him, deferring to him in all his suggestions. It was he who shepherded the younger members of the cast off to a form room to settle down to wait, he who found one of the night cleaners to come and tidy up the mess in the hall, especially the water which was bleaching the floor (or was it the acid which had done that? She didn't want to think about that), he who managed to find the makings of hot coffee for her in one of the kitchens.

And after the Headmaster had come and talked to them all, checking on their stories, hushing the anxious younger ones and assuring them all it had just been an accident — a most unfortunate accident — and sent them off to meet the parents who had arrived to collect them after the rehearsal, it was Harry she talked to.

'Isn't he going to call the police?' she said almost fretfully, watching the Headmaster at the other end of the hall, talking soothingly to the girls who stood there waiting to go. 'How can he not call the police?'

'Bad for the school,' Harry said and smiled at Genevieve who was standing close beside him. 'They don't like things getting outside the school here, do they, my dove?'

Genevieve just giggled. She seemed strangely undistressed by it all, happy as long as she was with Harry, and Hattie looked at him curiously and without stopping to think said, 'How long have you two been an item?'

'What an expression, Mrs Clements!' he said and laughed fatly, a happy laugh. It sounded extraordinary after all that had happened in the hall that evening. 'Downright indelicate! Quietly, I think, for some time, since you ask. Now we've decided we can't stay secret any longer. She's my gal, I'm her guy. Ain't that sweet?'

'It is rather,' Hattie said. 'You'll be good for her.'

'She'll be much better for me,' Harry said and there was an intensity in his voice that made it impossible for Hattie to ask any more questions.

'Shouldn't he call the police?' she said then, fretful again, and Harry laughed.

'Ask him,' he said. 'He's coming over.'

She did and Roscoe looked at her, his eyes fixed on her face as she chattered at him about how awful it had been, a dreadful business, it had to be investigated, and then sighed.

'My dear, you were quite, quite wonderful, I've been told. Saved poor Martin's life. I do congratulate and thank you, indeed I do. No need for the police, my dear. Bad enough a prank went wrong. Why further upset?'

'A prank?' Hattie stared at him. 'A – *prank*? How can you say it was – I mean, he could have died, he might still –'

'Prank, a dreadful wicked stupid trick that went wrong,' the Headmaster said firmly. 'We need no further investigation apart from that which I am well able to carry out. And I assure you I shall. Now, my dear, you should go home and recover. You had a dreadful shock.'

'I can't believe it,' Hattie said. 'This was a criminal act, surely?'

'How do we know?' the Headmaster said with all reasonableness. 'Mistakes can be made. The bottle was unlabelled. Foolish Martin kept it in his bag, where no doubt he kept other things. Mistakes can be made.'

'A mistake or a prank?' Hattie said then, sharply. 'It can't be both.'

'Either is bad enough. We don't have to compound it with police meddling, whichever it is. Bad enough we had the other business. We really must be allowed to deal with this matter ourselves. Look, Mrs Clements' – he had taken her to one side and sat down with her to talk earnestly in her ear, holding her shoulder in one warm hand, very avuncular – 'let me suggest this. I'll investigate. If it turns out to be a criminal act, then of course I involve the police. But haven't these children of ours suffered enough already tonight and in past weeks without us bringing further stress to them with police interrogation? We all know the police these days aren't the jolly caring public servants of the dear old Toy Town days! It could do more harm than good to have them marching in here with their heavy boots and even heavier methods. We've all read our *Guardian* articles, surely, we all know the harm that's done when police get involved in matters due to, shall we say, any internal problems. They explode families, damage children deeply, demanding they go into court as witnesses, and to what end? Please, I do beg you, dear Mrs Clements, let me sort this out in house, and then we'll see where we go from there.'

And, tired as she was, she had agreed, and worse still promised faithfully she would say nothing outside the school without the Headmaster's express permission, and had gone home to bed stunned with exhaustion and fit only to fall into bed.

Judith had come in once she'd sent Inge back, obviously anxious, and bursting with questions.

'My God, what's happening? Inge said you came in looking like death, and she's right.'

'I can't tell you,' Hattie said. 'Not tonight. Let me sleep. Just let me sleep. Please. Let me go to bed . . .'

And Judith, silenced for once, helped her shower and put her to bed with a cup of hot chocolate and then went away to let her sleep. And she would have done if she hadn't remembered, suddenly, Arse kneeling in the hall beside her and Collop. And Arse wasn't in the play and had no need to be there, and Arse had put pepper in the Cadets' bullets to hurt them and Arse . . .

After that she slept very little.

Twenty-eight

'Staff meeting,' said Wilton, and stood back from the notice board, peering at the paper he'd just fixed there. 'Five-thirty. Trust him to make us stay late.'

'What's it about?' Dinant looked up from the pile of sketchbooks he was working on, holding them in a precarious pile in his lap, perched on one of the common room's most uncomfortable chairs. 'Do we have to stay? I have a karate class.'

'You'll need it if you don't show. He'll scupper you,' Wilton said. 'No, I don't know what it's about. I just got grabbed by his secretary as I came in.'

Hattie stood at the door and looked at him and then round the room. Bevan was as usual in the big armchair, half asleep, and Steenman was standing in a corner talking to Richard Shuttle; it was just like any other morning and she closed her eyes, which felt hot and sandy, and thought muzzily, Am I still asleep? Did I dream it all?

Wilton caught sight of her and looked at her and his face changed and he pulled a chair forward. 'Heavens, what's up with you? You look awful.'

'I'm sorry,' she said huskily and coughed to clear her throat. 'I'm all right.' But she came and sat down all the same.

'Do you know what the meeting's about?' Dinant persisted. He looked worried. 'I really don't want to miss my class unless I truly have to. I spend a lot of money on them, and they still charge you if you don't go. Do you think I could go and ask the Headmaster to let me off? I'm so new and only Art anyway, so it won't make much difference, I don't suppose.'

'It's important,' she said and her voice was still husky. 'I think you'll find it is important. If it's what I think it is.'

'And what's that?'

She turned her head and looked up to see Sam. She hadn't heard him come in and now he looked at her and his face too changed as he saw her in the clear light from the window. 'Good God, Hattie, what on earth's the matter?'

'You haven't heard?'

'Heard what?'

'I suppose there's no reason why you should have.' She rubbed her face with one hand. It was odd; as though the hand and the face belonged to two different people, neither of them herself. Is the rest of me numb too? she wondered and then shook her head to clear it of woolliness. 'There was an accident last night.'

Sam had pulled a chair forward for himself next to her and he sat down heavily. 'Oh, God. Not another.'

'Yes,' she said. 'Another. Only worse. No, not worse. I mean, he's not badly hurt. Well, he is hurt, of course, but he's not unconscious. He knows who he is and where – I called the hospital you see, first thing this morning.'

They were staring at her in puzzlement and she knew she had to explain but it was extraordinarily difficult to be concise. 'I had to know, and they said he was as comfortable as could be expected but that he'd suffered no brain damage in spite of the anoxia and that –' She stopped and shook her head again. 'I'm not explaining very well, am I?'

'No,' Sam said gently and put one hand on hers. It felt warm and very comfortable there. 'Try again.'

'Sorry.' She took a deep breath. 'It was Martin Collop. Last night at the rehearsal. He did his trick of drinking out of his bottle in mid-air. You know what I mean, the Spanish way. And someone had put – I mean acid had got into it.'

There was a total silence in the room and then Bevan said loudly, 'What was that? What did you say?' He was sitting bolt upright, or as upright as so fat a man could sit, and staring at her in blank amazement. 'What did you say?'

'Someone put acid in Martin's bottle of drink,' Hattie said wearily. 'He tried to drink it, before the rehearsal started. After the technical rehearsal but before – Anyway, he did. And he had to have a tracheostomy and then the ambulance came.'

'Tracheostomy? You mean you did that?' Sam said, and his hand tightened on hers. 'You opened his throat?'

'It had to be done. The acid had blocked his mouth, gone down to the nasopharynx, I imagine. I've been thinking about that, and it must have. I mean he had no airway, not till I put the knife in under his larynx.'

'Good God,' Bevan said shrilly and began to shake. They could see it right across the room, his head trembling on his fat neck, his arms and legs seeming to shimmer with movement. 'Oh, God, they'll get all of us, you see if they don't, every one of us –'

'Give him some coffee, someone,' Sam said firmly. 'Wilton, take care of him. Listen, Bevan, you just stop it right there. We've got enough going on here without you getting hysterical on us. Hattie, tell me, what did the police say?'

Hattie shook her head. 'He won't call them. The Headmaster. I asked, but he said –' She shook her head. 'He won't.'

Again there was a silence and then Steenman said, 'Well, that's a comfort.'

Hattie looked at him, her forehead creased, and he lifted his brows at her.

'Well, isn't is? Bad enough we had to have them last time something went wrong. That was because it was guns, I suppose. At least this time it doesn't have to turn into a public side show. That has to be better.'

Sam ignored him. 'Why not, Hattie? Did he say?'

Hattie lifted one shoulder in a gesture of incomprehension. 'I asked the same thing as you did. But he said it was a prank. Or an accident.'

'A prank? Acid in a bottle of drink? My God!' Sam had closed his eyes and now he opened them and went on. 'Does he mean one of the boys, or one of us, or –'

'Who can say? I just don't know. I imagine that's what the meeting is about.' Hattie lifted her head as the bell began its clamour outside the door, and as soon as it finished got a little shakily to her feet. 'I have a class of sorts. Only the girls, fortunately. They all know about it, most of them are in the cast and were there. They'll need to talk about it. And I'll have to soothe them somehow. One or two were pretty agitated.'

'You look as though you could use some soothing yourself,' Sam said in a low voice and then lifted his head. 'Listen, Wilton, put your head round the fifth-room door, will you? Tell them I'll be there in ten minutes and God help them if they're not already head down in work. They know what they're supposed to be doing. Cut along, will you? Go *on* –' as Wilton showed a tendency to linger. 'You'll be late for your own class.'

The others were going too, Bevan stomping along at Steenman's side; he didn't look at Hattie as he passed her, but Hattie looked up at him and saw the sweat on his cheeks and smelled the rankness of the fear in him and felt a sudden wave of pity as sharp as it was unexpected. The old man was terrified, and she thought, I'll try to talk to him later, see if I can help; and then closed her eyes at her own foolishness. Would she never get rid of this trained reaction those years at Old East had left with her, the knee-jerk desire to get involved with every unhappy or sick person who passed her way? It was ridiculous; she couldn't look after everyone. She'd got enough to do to look after herself and the people she was already worried about. Oh, Arse, she thought somewhere deep in her mind. Arse, did you meddle with that bottle? Did you?

Sam was still sitting beside her as the last of the masters went and his hand was still on hers.

'You had a bad time.' It was a statement, not a question. 'And you're still very upset about it.'

'Wouldn't you be?'

'Of course. It must have been horrific.'

'It wasn't just the accident. Or whatever it was. It wasn't just seeing the damage the acid did, or even doing the tracheostomy. I was a bit high after that, I think. Does that sound awful? I felt, well, pleased with myself.'

The hand tightened even more. 'You're entitled.'

She sat there looking down at his hand and then said abruptly. 'This is a change.'

'A change?'

'To the way we've been.'

'Oh.' He was silent and then said again, 'Oh. Yes.'

'Does Martin Collop have to burn himself with acid before –'

He shook her hand almost angrily. 'Don't say that. It was the way you looked that – Look, I've been wanting to apologize to you. Explain.'

'Explain?' She couldn't look at him.

'I behaved badly. I was rude to you.'

She thought about that. Then she said thoughtfully, 'Yes. I think you were very rude.'

'I'm sorry.'

'Oh? Is that supposed to be the end of it?'

'No. I wanted to explain too.' He sounded annoyed then. 'Not that you gave me the bloody chance. You've been walking around here like a thorn bush!'

'What did you expect? A nice crawling lady coming along and pleading, "Oh, be mean to me again, do, I really like it, you know, that's what women like best, you know, men being hateful . . ."'

'I know better than that, and don't you ever accuse me of anything like that again,' he said sharply, and this time he put both his hands on hers, holding them tightly. 'I had a good reason to behave as I did. I can't explain now. There isn't time. But I'd like the chance.'

She lifted her head and looked at him, examining his face almost dispassionately, looking at the lines round his eyes, the way his hair flopped over his forehead, the somewhat ill-shaven cheeks and the beginnings of jowls. He wasn't at all good-looking, but it was an agreeable face and she liked to look at it. But she had to know first.

'Sam, did you shoot at Tully?' she said and sat looking at him with her eyebrows raised in simple interrogation.

There was a silence as he stared back and then he said stupidly, 'Did I what?'

'Did you shoot at Tully? Was that gun muzzle I saw in the film the other end of you? I mean was it you holding it, but out of shot? Did you shoot at Tully?'

What reaction she had expected, had she thought about it, she didn't know. It wouldn't have been what she got, that was certain. Because he lifted his head and began to laugh. A low fat laugh deep inside to start with and then louder and more uncontrolled, and that it was genuine amusement firing it was undoubted.

'Is that what you've been thinking?' he managed to get out at last, and she stared at him still, just nodding. 'You're potty, you know that? Quite potty.'

She pulled her hand away from him angrily. 'I am not! It was a reasonable question to ask. We'd been friends – Well, I thought so. And then when I tell you I've seen something on the film that looks like a gun aiming at Tully, which would mean it was a deliberate act rather than a ricochet, you suddenly go all cold and distant. And then I remembered' – she swallowed – 'I remembered the time you had a row with Tully, said one day someone'd cut his throat, and when they did, you'd cheer. What would you have thought if you'd been me?'

'Oh, you daft object!' The amusement was still in him. 'Let's think it through, Hattie, shall we? If I were such a deep-dyed villain and thought I'd been spotted by the bright eyes of a clever lady, would I make her angry with me and treat her badly? Or would I suck up to her like all get out and be all sweetness and light so as to convince her I was innocent as the babe unborn and all the rest of it? As for the row with Tully, that was all part of normal staffroom infighting. I loathed the way the man behaved with the boys. I loathed the way he showed off – you saw it yourself! He kissed a boy just to shock you, remember? There was nothing special in that episode in the staffroom to make you cast me as a gunman. Do be sensible!'

She tried to think about that, wrinkling her forehead. It was hard to think clearly. She wished suddenly that she was in bed; now she could sleep. 'I suppose you could be right,' she said eventually. 'I suppose.'

'You're damned right I'm right!' He got to his feet and pulled her up too. 'Look, I have to go to my class, or there'll be all hell let loose, and someone has to go to your girls. But I want you to rest. You need looking after. Let me take you to the Headmaster's office and see if he can arrange something for the girls while you –'

'No!' she said strongly. 'I've got a job to do as much as you have and I'll do it. They need me to talk to. No one else can help them cope as well as I can.'

He looked at her closely and she lifted her chin to look back and suddenly his face folded into a smile of such warmth and approval that she felt herself redden.

'Yes, I'm sure you're right about that. No one else could possibly replace you. And I don't mean just for your girls. All right, I'll see you to your class. Can we meet at lunchtime? I have things to explain to you.'

'No!' she said, not knowing why she was being so captious

when she felt so warm and happy, even excited. To punish him for the way he'd behaved? Perhaps. 'No, I had a dreadful night and at lunchtime I'm going to need a rest. I'll see you after the meeting tonight. Perhaps.'

He looked so cast down that she wanted to laugh aloud. It was a lovely look to see on his face after the past few weeks, and she smiled at him beatifically and said, 'I have to go.'

'You're being rather – Well, all right.' He put one hand on her elbow and steered her to the door and she shook him off.

'I'm not helpless. Tired, yes, and a bit bewildered, but not terminally so. You don't have to treat me like a pre-war Dresden doll.'

'Ouch!' he said and let go of her elbow. 'Reproof taken.'

'Good,' she said, smiling again, even more beatifically, and went away down the corridor to her classroom. He stood and watched her go and she was very aware of his eyes on her back, and enjoyed the feeling. She was exhilarated now, and only pleasantly sleepy. The tension that had filled her when she arrived at school this morning was gone, and she sighed softly, enjoying the sensation of air moving into her lungs. It was good to be alive this morning; and then, remembering Collop as she went past the big doors that led to the assembly hall, she felt a sharp stab of guilt. Wicked to be happy when he was so hurt, but all the same . . .

The girls were there when she reached her room, subdued and murmuring together, and she told them immediately that she'd phoned the hospital that morning and that Mr Collop was all right. He had to heal of course, but he was all right and would do well. And a soft movement of breath seemed to pass over them so that they swayed to it as grass in a field sways to the wind and their shoulders relaxed and some of them smiled.

'That's all right then,' Gillian said. 'So we don't have to go on about it. It was bad enough seeing it. Don't want to go on and on about it.'

They seemed to agree with her, and became more alert, digging in their bags for their books, and then Bridget looked at Hattie and said, 'Please, Mrs Clements, do we have to have a Learning to Live class this morning? It's always very interesting, of course,' she went on hastily, 'but I'm all behind with some of my homework what with the play and all, and it'd be ever such a help if we could have a free period now to catch up.'

Hattie was relieved. The thought of trying to run a class as usual had been daunting, feeling as she did. She needed the time as much as they, and she said so candidly.

'Smashing.' Gillian got to her feet. 'I'm going to the library then. Got the extra books there and bigger tables. Excuse me, Mrs Clements.' And one after the other they followed her, until there were just Dilly and Hattie left in the room.

Hattie sat and looked across the rows of empty chairs at her and Dilly sat with her head down, twiddling with her fingers in her lap and, without having to think about it, Hattie knew what it was she wanted. She said gently, 'Dilly, are you very worried about Ar– Vivian?'

There was a little pause and then Dilly said with a note of insolence in her voice, 'What if I am?'

'I am too,' Hattie said, and Dilly lifted her chin and looked at her.

'He said you would be,' she said. 'It was the first thing he said to me after – when we left last night. "She'll wonder why I was there," he said. "I had no reason to be there, so she'll wonder why and she'll think I put the acid in Mr Collop's bottle." He's clever, isn't he? Always knows . . .'

'I've never doubted his intelligence,' Hattie said.

'You shouldn't. He's a genius, really. You've no idea.'

'You have?'

'Oh, of course I have.' She sounded impatient. 'We're – it's the closeness, you see. Me and him, we're all we've got. I've only got Freddy and – well, I ask you. He's all right, but he's Freddy, isn't he? No good to me at all. And as for my gran and my mum, forget it. I've only got him, and he's only got me.'

'No family?' Hattie was genuinely curious, but she asked as much to delay matters as for any other reason. The question of whether Arse had anything to do with the acid last night still hung unanswered between them. 'He's never said much about his family.'

'Just a mum.' Dilly's lip curled a little. 'One of the stupid sort. Went and had a baby just because – well, because. Viv told me. Said she went on and on about freedom and the way men exploit women and she'd never get married but follow her career and when she was getting older and wanted to fulfil herself, she would. So she did. She was thirty-nine when Viv was born. I ask you!'

'I see what you mean,' Hattie said dryly. 'A great age.'

'It is to have an illegitimate baby on purpose when you don't know anything about looking after babies and when the only reason for having one is to please yourself and not because you care about making a *person*,' Dilly said passionately. 'I hate her for what she did. I'm glad she had Viv, of course I am, but she's – the things she's done to him –'

'Just because she had a career and then wanted to have a baby too? Men can do that.' Hattie was still needing time to think, wanting to keep at arms' length the question of what the boy had been doing in the hall last night. 'I thought you were a feminist.'

'I am,' Dilly said loudly. 'But not a selfish one! If I couldn't make it right for a baby, I wouldn't have one, even if I wanted to. Anyway, she – the way she did it, he's on his own all the time at home. She's always out doing her own thing. It's been like that since he was seven or eight. Never worried about leaving him on his own, because he was so *sensible*, she said. It's like being a lodger, only she pays the bills, he says. Doesn't care where he is or who he's with. I wouldn't do that to a child of mine . . .'

'Because it was a bit like that for you, Dilly?' Hattie said softly, aware now of what was going on, forgetting her own preoccupation, and Dilly's face seemed to crumple.

'It's always been like that,' she said and her voice thinned out and became tight and high as tears moved into it. 'Even when they weren't together it was like I wasn't there, except when they wanted to be sentimental and lovey-dovey and called me Tuppence, and – Oh, what's the point of talking about it? No one gives a shit about us. They have babies just because they feel stupid and randy and want to have someone to shove around and bully and never mind what we might want or we might think. It's like here. No one gives a shit here either, it's all about getting the right number of parents to send their kids here to make money for them, and shoving us through exams just to make themselves look good and how marvellous the teachers are and to hell with you lot, you're just the raw material for us to live our lives on –'

She was frankly crying now. Hattie moved across the room and stood behind her and then, moving carefully, knowing how sensitive and tense Dilly was, bent and put her arms round her and set her face against her hair and began to rock her, very gently, crooning softly at the back of her throat.

'It's all right,' she murmured. 'All right, love. It's all right. We'll sort it out, see if we don't.'

The tears went on in a flood, rose to a choking of sobs and then slowly subsided until she was sniffing and just hiccuping occasionally, and Hattie let go and came round to sit beside her and look at her.

'You're scared too, aren't you?' she said gently and Dilly, mute, nodded.

'Did you ask him why he was there last night?'

Dilly nodded furiously. 'I asked him. I said did he – I said he did the pepper – and I'd have helped him with this like I did with that if he'd asked me to and he got so angry with me – He went off, so angry – Oh, what'll I do if he stays angry, Mrs Clements? What'll I do?'

'I don't know,' Hattie said truthfully. 'I can't know. I can only hope for you that he doesn't. And that he hasn't any reason –'

'That's the awful bit,' Dilly said and looked at her through eyes red-rimmed and still brimming. 'I ought to know. I ought to believe it's all right and I just can't. I keep thinking.'

'You've got a good mind, Dilly. You can't help thinking,' Hattie said. 'It's a gift you're lumbered with.' And she rubbed her face, suddenly aware again of her own fatigue. 'You need some rest.'

Dilly managed a watery smile. 'You mean you do. You look awful.'

'Thanks. Thanks a bunch.' Hattie smiled too. 'A bit better now?'

Dilly nodded. 'It's so corny but I suppose – it's easier when you say it to someone.'

'Yes,' Hattie said. 'It's why I'm here. Listen, go and do some work in the library. You'll feel better if you do.'

'Yes,' Dilly said. 'I suppose so.'

'And –' Hattie hesitated. 'We've got to talk to Viv about this, haven't we?'

'I can't,' Dilly said. 'I can't. I need him – I can't –' And the tears lifted in her voice again.

'It's all right,' Hattie said quickly. 'I'll do it. Leave it to me.'

And Dilly nodded and went away and Hattie sat there staring at the blank door after she'd gone and thought, Here I go again. Always sticking my neck out, always taking on the responsibility. Why do I do it? Why can't I just let people sort themselves out? But there was no answer she could think of.

Twenty-nine

'So there you have it,' the Headmaster said. 'Collop and I both agree that this is as far as the matter goes.'

'He can't agree,' Bevan said shrilly. 'How can he, lying in that hospital and choked with acid? What state is he in to agree to anything?'

'We conversed at length this afternoon,' the Headmaster said smoothly. 'There are more ways to communicate than via speech, you know, Dr Bevan. He wrote down his comments and answers to my points. It wasn't easy, but we managed. And it's agreed that this matter should remain within the school. He is not prepared to seek any police investigation, or make any charges, and the hospital sees no reason to notify them of the accident, so there it remains. A dreadful *accident*. Better care has to be taken of the laboratory keys in future –'

He was careful not to look at Sam, but he reacted anyway, and shook his head firmly. 'Oh, no, Headmaster. I'm not having that,' he said. 'I lock my laboratory very carefully when there are any items that might be a risk of any sort, and dangerous substances are in a locked cupboard anyway. The lab keys are kept by Edwards in his cubbyhole, and when he isn't there, then the cubbyhole's locked. If someone got past that, it's unfortunate, but what more could we have done? We're running a school here, not Fort Knox, and anyway, the boys have to learn how to be reliable with dangerous materials. They handle acids all the time in the lab in class. If someone wanted to steal some it wouldn't be impossible. We're supposed to have intelligent people here, and intelligent people are good at subterfuge. I accept no blame for this mishap and I won't consider it as attaching to any one of the biology staff.'

'Well, point taken, point taken.' The Headmaster sounded conciliatory now. 'As you say, we can't legislate for all the possible villainies of growing boys. And girls of course.' He looked at Hattie and smiled thinly. 'It's hardly just to blame only the boys when we have some girls here.'

'I hardly think any of them would be likely to steal acid for such a purpose,' Hattie snapped, and then caught Sam's eye and subsided. What was the point of getting angry with the man? He was as smooth as a granite wall; anything she threw at him would be deflected back at herself and harm him not at all.

'One more thing,' the Headmaster said and now his voice was creamy with self-satisfaction. 'I will be moving through the school next week with some rather important guests. I have, I may tell you, made excellent progress with the Potemkin Trust –'

'Potemkin?' Sam said. 'I thought they were a right-wing lot.'

'The politics of the Trust are not of significance,' the Headmaster said, his voice richer than ever. 'All we here at the Foundation need concern ourselves with is their interest in education. And they're prepared to put a great deal of money into our school. I can assure you our financial problems could be largely solved. So, be aware, will you, that we have observers in our midst next week. That's all I ask.'

'But how can their politics be ignored?' Sam sounded unusually combative. 'Won't they attach strings to any grant they make?'

'That is not an issue,' the Headmaster said, and then shook his head, looking reproachful. 'I'm surprised at your lukewarm reaction to this excellent news. I've worked extremely hard to bring this injection of much-needed cash into the school. You should all be delighted.'

'I am,' Wilton said loudly.

The Headmaster smiled at him briefly, and then, pointedly ignoring Sam, said, 'Well, then, that's the end of the meeting. Does anyone know where Mr Dinant is?'

'He – he had a toothache,' Hattie said. 'I told him he ought to see his dentist at once. That's why he isn't here. It's my fault, not his.' She reddened as she felt rather than saw Wilton's sardonic stare and then got even hotter as the Headmaster lifted his brows at her.

'Indeed? Well, Mrs Clements, I must say I think you were

being somewhat high-handed. This was an important meeting and you had no right to –'

'Sorry, Headmaster,' she said loudly and got to her feet. 'I intended well.'

'No doubt,' he said frostily, and went to the door. 'Well, see to it that he is told all that transpired here this evening.' And he went, almost slamming the door behind him.

'You're too good to be true,' Wilton murmured as he passed her to follow the Headmaster out and Hattie made a face at him as Sam came across the room to join her.

'You're silly, Hattie, covering up for people, I don't for a moment suppose Dinant had anything at all to do with it, but all the same –'

'He asked me to cover for him and I said I would,' Hattie said wearily. 'Where's the harm? It was a stupid meeting anyway.'

'Not entirely. It showed us even more clearly just how far the Head of this establishment will go to keep it running. Even curling up all cosy with a bunch of people so right wing they ought to wear black shirts. The Potemkin Trust – I ask you! He'll do anything to keep things smooth and quiet to make sure he gets his hands on their moneybags. I wonder, if wholesale slaughter of the staff started, would he go on covering up? It's an extraordinary performance. You have to admire his diligence.'

'Do I? I just see a selfish bastard who doesn't care about anything except the things that matter to him personally.'

'You couldn't be more right. He's after Uppingham, you know.'

'He's what?'

'The gossip is that the Headmastership there'll be up for grabs soon. He wants it. He'll do anything to keep this place smelling sweet until he does.'

'Well, I'm not surprised,' Hattie said. 'I should have expected him to be that way. But can he keep it quiet like this? Won't the kids talk, won't the parents get agitated, take their kids away?'

'He's gambling they won't,' Sam said. 'And you know, the chances are they'll pay no attention. The parents need this school as much as the Headmaster needs them. There aren't that many major public schools in London, and certainly not many for the less capable, like the ones we have here. We get abysmal exam results, you know. It's not that we're bad teachers. It's just that the kids aren't up to scratch in examinations.'

'The ones I meet seem bright enough.'

'It's not intrinsic brightness that matters. It's the ability to jump through hoops that they want in the kids here. Programmed exam-passers, not the sort that do something interesting with their lives after they leave school. And university. Just exam-passers to learn how to make other exam-passers –'

'Like you?'

'*Touché.* Yes, like me. I'm a teacher. And there was a time when I put myself through the hoops. That's how I know about them, and how stupid they are. If I'd known then what I know now I wouldn't be here.'

'I'm glad you are,' she said, without stopping to think, and he smiled down at her.

'Are you? Good.'

'I really must be getting home,' she said then, and got to her feet, as awkwardly as a child. 'The girls'll be wondering where I am. So will Judith.'

'Judith?'

'My friend. Next-door neighbour. Helps amazingly with the children.'

'Oh, yes, I remember,' he said. 'I'd love to see them all.'

'Well, I dare say they'll come to school again some time, like they did for the autumn fair.'

'Why wait till then? Let me come home with you this evening and cook dinner for you. I've got some stuff I picked up at lunchtime. Chicken breasts. Do you have a wok? I'm a dab hand with a wok.'

'Oh, no!' she said, horrified, thinking of Judith. 'I couldn't do that.'

'Oh? Do your children bite? Or is Judith the sort of next-door neighbour who disapproves of followers?'

'No, it's not that. I mean, the children are fine, and she'd love to talk to you.' She made a face then. 'She'd like it a bit too much, to be honest. She's always making guesses about how I get on with people here. No, it's –'

'It's nothing at all but out-of-date girlishness,' he said firmly. 'I have to explain things to you and that'll be the best way to do it. No rush, no interruptions.'

'No interruptions? You don't know my girls!'

'What's wrong with your girls? I doubt they're all that different from other people's kids. I imagine they go to sleep eventually.'

'Well, of course, but . . .'

'But what? Are you scared of me, Hattie? Still thinking I'm a potential gunman?'

'No, of course not,' she said quickly and he shook his head.

'That wasn't a reasoned response. Do you? Is there a little worm of doubt still lingering?'

She shook her head at him. 'I honestly don't know, I truly don't. What you said makes sense, but all the same, someone shot at Tully.'

'You don't believe the ricochet theory either.'

'No, I don't. It's too – too easy. Too convenient.'

'Easier than imagining someone managed to pick out Tully and fire a bullet at him without anyone else noticing?' Sam said.

She grimaced. 'That's what makes it all so complicated. I can't think how it happened and –'

'I think someone did fire at Tully,' Sam said quietly. 'I don't know who and I don't know why. I don't even know if it was Tully who was really his target.'

She lifted her chin, alert at that. 'What?'

'Didn't it occur to you that whoever it was might have been a lousy shot? That maybe he was after someone else who was near Tully, but he missed?'

She was silent for a while and then made a face again. 'I've been rather silly, I think.'

'Not at all. I think you've been the same as everyone else. Knowing Tully was much disliked, you took it for granted that he was the object of someone's loathing, a loathing strong enough to make the someone use a gun on him. But there could be someone else who's just as loathsome.'

'I can't work this out,' she said. 'I'm too tired.'

He was all compunction. 'Oh, hell, I've been thoroughly selfish. Of course you are. And me trying to impose on you for the evening as well. I'm sorry.'

'It's all right,' she said. 'And the evening might have been nice, as long as Judith isn't around.'

'Why not?'

'I told you. Because her favourite exercise is jumping to conclusions,' Hattie said. 'And I'd rather she didn't.'

'Maybe there's a conclusion worth jumping to, when she does it,' Sam said as she made for the door, pulling on her coat as she went, and she shook her head.

'I'm too tired for fencing. Some other time, Sam. I still think there are things to be talked about, but –'

'Yes,' he said and caught up with her at the door, because he'd been collecting her bags and now brought them to her. 'There are. I have to explain why I behaved so badly.'

'There's no compulsion.'

'There is. I feel compelled. It was . . . Can I just say it was because I liked your company too much?'

She looked at him sideways. 'You can certainly say that. It's a compliment, after all.'

'It's the truth,' he said, and his voice was suddenly rough. 'I had it all worked out. Another term at the outside in this dump and I'd have the book finished and then for good or ill, I was going to take the plunge. I believe I can get a publisher and make a living in a way that won't make me feel as lousy as this place does, but even if I can't get published right away, I'm still going to do it. I can get by on what I've saved and my legitimate dole. That was the plan. Then you turned up.'

'Why should that alter your plan?' she said as steadily as she could.

'I like you too much.' He stood there, not attempting to touch her, speaking as though what he was saying was the most ordinary thing in the world, as commonplace as talk of the weather. 'You came in between me and my book, in between me and my work here. I just couldn't think properly. So I thought I'd better try to wean myself.'

She stood there, looking at him very directly, not sure how she felt about what he was saying.

'I see. Wean yourself. It's an odd metaphor.'

'Not at all. You were starting to feel like – well, the stuff of life. I don't like being that dependent. I was once before and when she died it was such hell, I didn't think I could ever cope again. So I started to wean myself away from you.'

'I don't think I could ever cope again,' she said after a long moment.

'No doubt. That's how you feel now. It's how I felt for a long time. I'm just talking about me now, not you. I had to try to break away from what was becoming an uncomfortable dependence. That was why I behaved as I did. I didn't intend rudeness. Oh, God, anything but –'

'There was nothing else it could feel like,' she said, and suddenly yawned hugely. 'But it's all right. I do understand. And I think perhaps . . .'

'Yes?' He was looking very intently at her.

'I think it might be better to go on with the weaning process,' she said steadily. 'I'm not as far along the road as you are, you see. My husband died only a year ago.'

'I've no intention of hurrying you,' he said. 'But I have to stop being rude. Don't I?'

'You can – Oh, please Sam, I'm so tired I can't think straight. Please, leave me be for a while. I really do have to think.'

'Yes,' he said. 'Of course. But I can still take you home. You're in no state to go on your own, are you? I won't be a pest. Not now I've explained.'

'I think I really should try on my own,' she said, and rubbed her face. She was feeling very strange; lightheaded, as though a small part of her were sitting high on a corner of the battered old staffroom staring down at her and jeering softly. 'A taxi, perhaps. It'll be expensive but I think maybe –'

'I'll find one for you,' he said. 'There's a mini-cab firm locally which aren't as costly as a black cab would be. I'll phone for you.'

She was grateful, and let him lead her out and along the corridor towards the stairs. It was very dark there, with only one light burning at each end, and she was glad of his grip on her elbow as he took her along, letting her mind swim comfortably, not bothering to think. She felt agreeably warm inside her weariness and knew at some deep level it was because of what he'd said. She hadn't taken it all in, nor worked out all its implications, but what he had said had been good to hear. She knew that; and listened to the slap of their footsteps along the corridor and down the stairs into the lower corridor. Friday, she found herself thinking absurdly. Poets day, the boys call it: Piss Off Early, Tomorrow's Saturday. I'll think about Sam and what he said tomorrow – me and Scarlett O'Hara. And she wanted to giggle, but was too weary.

'Wait here,' Sam said firmly and pushed her gently into a

chair. They'd reached the Headmaster's office and were in the ante-room. The Head's room was locked, but the secretary's section was always left accessible outside school hours in case anyone needed to use the phone, and anyway no important documents were kept there, being locked safely inside the Headmaster's room.

It was as arid and dull a room as the secretary herself, and Hattie sat staring owlishly round at it, imagining it the way it might look if the secretary was a different sort of woman, one who went in for flowers and pictures, perhaps.

She was staring at the half-open door as Sam, standing with his back to the door, dialled the phone and held on, listening for an answer, and she wasn't sure at first she'd seen anything; she shouldn't have, for the cleaning staff didn't come in on Fridays, leaving the work of preparing for the next working day until Sunday, and with the performance of *Taming of the Shrew* cancelled, of course, there was no cause for any pupil to be about; but then she was out of her chair and halfway across the room before she realized she'd moved. Someone had definitely gone by and she was too alarmed not to find out who it was. The unknown seemed to her suddenly to be infinitely more frightening than whoever might have slipped past the door so silently.

Outside the corridor was dark and cold, and suddenly became even darker as the light at its far end was switched off, and then Sam was behind her, leaving the phone dangling on the desk, and shouting, 'What's the matter?'

'Someone's just gone down the corridor,' she cried. 'I didn't see who it was, he switched off the light. There shouldn't be anyone here, should there?' And Sam was gone in a headlong gallop into the darkness that made her squint in fear after him, almost as though she were the one running full pelt into a barrier she couldn't see.

There was a sudden yelp and then a scuffle and as she peered into the dimness the light at the end of the corridor went on again and she saw Sam had hold of someone by the arm. Someone fairly small and bent over as he struggled to escape Sam's grip.

'Keep still, you bloody fool,' Sam panted, and dragged whoever it was back up the corridor towards Hattie. 'It's all right,' he called. 'Have a look for yourself.'

She looked and then caught her breath. Suddenly the weariness had gone and the sleepiness with it. Her senses were as sharp as she had ever know them to be, and she stared at the bedraggled figure Sam now pulled in front of him, holding him firmly by both shoulders, and said, 'Arse? Not again! Arse, what are you doing here at this time of night? You should have been gone ages ago. Why are you still hanging around?'

Thirty

'But why should you be interested in what went on at a staff meeting?' Sam said. 'That's the most feeble excuse for an explanation I've heard in a hell of a long time! You'll have to do better than that. It makes no sense.'

The boy said nothing, sitting staring down at his outstretched feet which were crossed at the ankles, his hands thrust into his jeans pockets and his hair flopping over his face. Sam made a noise, half snort and half grunt, clearly exasperated beyond speech.

'If you can explain what you needed to hear,' Hattie said reasonably, 'it'll be easier for us to understand. We don't want to make a fuss unless we have to. Just explain why, Viv, can't you?'

He looked up at her then, his chin up. 'Oh, so it's Viv now, is it?'

She bit her lip. 'Oh, hell I'm sorry. I did call you by your nickname before, didn't I? And I shouldn't have done.'

'It's not a nickname,' he said roughly. 'Nicknames are friendly. Picked by your mates. That's an insult they used for me, and he encouraged them. It was his idea in the first place . . .' And then he went red and bent his head again in an attempt to hide it.

'He? What he? Who encouraged them?' Hattie said, and crouched beside him to put one hand on his knee. 'You'll have to explain, you know. It's obvious, isn't it, that we aren't going to let you go just because you won't talk to us? There've been too many unpleasant things happening to make that possible. If you don't talk to us, we'll have to pass the matter on and you'll have to talk to someone else. We'd be more comfortable for you, I think. Don't you?'

He seemed to think about that, then sighed softly and looked up at her. 'All right,' he said. 'If it's the only way I can get out of here, what else can I do? And anyway –' he lifted his chin again but this time there was a sort of exultation in the movement rather than the mulish anger he'd chosen before – 'anyway, it's easier now.'

'Why?' Hattie said, diverted, and sat back on her heels. Her knees were beginning to ache from the posture she was in and Sam, seeming suddenly aware, fetched a chair to her and she sat in it gratefully, smiling up at him.

'Dilly,' the boy said simply, and Hattie, understanding at once, nodded.

'It makes a difference when there's someone else around to share it with?'

'Yes.'

There was a silence and then Sam put a warm hand on Hattie's shoulder and she felt the meaning almost as though he spelled it out. They were sharing now too. 'Well?' Sam said a little roughly, looking at the boy.

Again he sighed. 'I wanted to know what was being said about the acid and him,' he said. 'What you knew. I heard Mr Dinant talking to you about the meeting and I thought – well, that was why I hung around after the rest of the school had gone. I wanted to see if you knew who had put the acid there.'

'I want to know something about the acid and you,' Hattie said, remembering. 'Why were you there that evening? You had nothing to do with the play. Why were you at the rehearsal?'

He pulled his hands out of his pockets and sat up straight. 'It's hard, this. I have to start somewhere at the beginning, don't I? If you're to understand it. And I can't be doing with all this question-and-answer stuff. It's so boring.'

'Well, poor you!' Sam said caustically. 'We, on the other hand, are positively riveted and thoroughly enjoy nagging at you like a pair of third-degree policemen.'

'Well, I dare say it is as tough on you,' he said consideringly, and looked up at Sam and then suddenly grinned. 'Tell you what, I'm flush this week. I'll buy you both a drink and we can talk then. No questions and answers, I'll just tell you all about it. How's that?'

'Are you out of your tiny mind?' Sam roared. 'Do you think we'd –'

'Hey, just a minute,' Hattie said. She got to her feet and put a hand on his arm. 'Listen, Sam, he has a point –'

'A point? This snivelling little –'

'Stop acting like a schoolmaster,' she said, and shook his arm. 'You can do better than that.'

He turned and looked at her and then at the boy. 'What the hell else am I supposed to sound like? We find a boy skulking round here engaged in some sort of villainy – and we've had a fair bit of that already – and you expect me to be all sweetness and light?'

'We could try talking to him like a person instead of as a schoolboy,' she said. 'It'll be easier to do that outside the school. And this room is hardly . . .' And she looked round at it and then at him, her brows raised.

'Thanks,' the boy said and smiled at her and then looked at Sam. 'I'll explain it all, really I will. I want to get rid of it all anyway. I've got better things to do now than deal with the sort of stuff I've had to. Get rid of it all – that'd be good. A drink then? The pub on the next corner's all right. Now *he* isn't around.' And he produced a smile of such happiness that in spite of himself Sam smiled back.

'Oh, well, then,' he said. 'I suppose so. If it's all right with you, Hattie? You're awfully tired.' He put up one hand and touched her face fleetingly.

'I've got my second wind,' she said, and indeed she felt quite different now; tired, yes, aching in bones and muscles, but not exhausted as she had been. She was rather high, if anything, feeling almost as though she'd taken a stimulant. A little more stimulant in the form of alcohol could be very agreeable, she thought, and got to her feet. 'I'll do for a while yet. If we don't hang around. Shall we go then?'

'It's one of the few pubs left in the area that hasn't been tarted up into a juke-boxed game-machined glitter hole,' Vivian said, looking round at the shabby old bar and its dull lights with a judicious air. 'I quite like it. Now.'

'Are you such a connoisseur?' Sam said, unable to keep the irony out of his voice.

'Most people my age are,' the boy said and shot a glance at him. 'It's been a year or two since people of my age didn't use pubs. Now we're the ones who use them most.'

'Not this one,' Hattie said, looking round. There were only a few people there, most of them dispirited-looking men in their forties and older, sitting hunched over pints at grubby tables and muttering at each other, and Vivian nodded.

'That's why I like it,' he said. 'I told you that. All the other pubs where the noise and games are, they're like fourth-form rooms. And a bit younger.'

'Enough chit chat,' Sam said. 'Mrs Clements is tired and I've better things to do than sit here and admire the faded wallpaper and the dirt ground into the floors. What were you doing hanging around the staff common room tonight?'

The boy put down his glass and sighed. 'Yes, well, it's a long story.'

'However long, tell it. But you don't have to string it out for the fun of it. I'm not buying after this round and never you think it.'

'I didn't bring you here to drink,' the boy said with great dignity. 'I promised to explain and I will. It – it starts a long time ago.'

'So, it starts a long time ago. Spit it out.'

The boy was silent for a moment and Sam opened his mouth to speak, but Hattie put a hand on his and he subsided. The boy noticed and looked at her and smiled briefly.

'OK. I was in the third form when it began. Not much good to anyone. Miserable really. So I thought he was being nice to me when it started.'

'Who?'

'Him. Collop.' It was like a swear word in his mouth and Hattie drew back, a little alarmed at the venom in him.

'What did he do?' Sam was very still and not irritable at all now.

'Oh, nothing at first! Not a thing. He was kind. He said he liked my essays, said I could write, said I had a great future. Got me to try my hand at short stories for him. Said they were marvellous. Oh, you never heard such stuff. And I believed every sodding word of it.'

'It could have been true,' Hattie said and he looked at her, his face alight with scorn.

'For Christ's sake, at thirteen? I'd have had to be bloody Tolstoy to merit the sort of things he used to say. But because I was only thirteen and thought myself no end of a magical type, I chose to believe him. It was what I'd always expected, you see.' He looked at Sam then, as though he expected him to understand better. 'When I was very small I'd thought about how it would be later, when I was grown. Somehow I'd get away on my own, and make enough money to have a place of my own to live in, and the only way I could think of doing that was writing books. So I had it all imagined, all ready, and he sort of – he walked in on my imaginings as though he knew what they were, and he took them over. Took them away from me.' He was paler now, and his hands, clenched on the table, showed white patches over the knuckles. 'I believed him because it was what I wanted to hear.'

'And then what happened?'

'It got more. He wanted me to come and see him at his house. Said it'd be easier to talk to me there like a person rather than a child.' He looked a little startled then. 'It was the same as you said but I – it came out different. I only just realized, you know that? It was the same as you said. Only I suppose you said it because you meant it. He didn't.'

'What did he mean?'

There was another silence and Sam said again gently, 'What did he mean?'

'Parties,' the boy said at length. 'Parties. It was – well – incredible . . .'

'In what way?'

'Oh, marvellous. I try to remember how they made me feel, but I can't. I can't make the feelings come back. I can remember what I felt at the time, though. So grown-up – you can't imagine how grown-up! These parties were so – lots of food and drink, of course, and then sometimes other things. Smoked a bit of pot and so on, not that I liked that much.' He laughed then, sounding for the first time like a boy. 'It made me so sleepy, I missed all that was going on. I used to go out like a light and wake up and find the best bits were over. The music and then – Anyway, I stopped doing that. No one minded. That was great too, I thought. No one minded what you did.' He sighed again, softly. 'No one said you had to eat or jeered at you if you didn't, and no one laughed when you went and got a different sort of drink and even if you were sick no one seemed to care. It was all – I wish I could feel all that again.'

He turned his head to look at Hattie. 'That's the awful thing about it. It was all dreadful, I know that now. I was just being – well, softened up, I suppose. But I thought it was wonderful. There'll never be another summer like it.'

'All summer? You were going to parties at Collop's house all summer?'

'Oh, not just that. There were evenings out as well. How very devilish that felt, being in a pub, just turned fourteen! How he got away with it, and so near the school too, I'll never know. But he did. And there were theatres and concerts and – it was like falling asleep and waking up where it was perfect. There was school all day of course, and I had to go back home and see *her* sometimes, you know how it is, but there was always the next party to think of. It was magic, just magic.'

'Who else was at the parties?' Hattie asked, and some of the animation that had filled him went and he lifted his brows and shook his head.

'Oh, I don't know. Different people all the time. Young blokes, people about nineteen or twenty or whatever; actors some of them, and I think there were people from the army. There were a lot of jokes about guardsmen. I remember those. Some of them were a bit – well, creepy. I didn't like them. They were the sort that vanish into the middle of the evening and then everyone would laugh at them when they came back, and me, poor sap, had no notion of what it was all about.'

'What was it all about?' Sam said. 'When did you find out?'

'Look, let's be clear in this,' Viv said, sitting up very straight. 'I wasn't stupid, I sort of knew what it was. I mean, we saw dirty films and I liked that, and there was a lot of mucking about. The older ones and us, we'd – well –' He went brick-red. 'There was kissing and that. But I didn't really *know*, you see. I didn't understand about all of it.'

'I see,' Sam said in a colourless tone, and Hattie sat and stared at the boy, trying to comprehend what it had been like for him, even smaller then than he was now, sitting with older men, watching pornographic films, kissing and that . . .

'But it wasn't *wrong*, do you know what I mean? There was

no harm in any of that. If people did things, went away and did things, it was because they wanted to. No one was ever pushed or anything. If I liked being hugged by someone and kissed a bit and if he liked it if I – if I touched him, well it was me doing it. No one else told me to. It was sort of normal really. Do you know what I mean? Can you understand what I mean?'

'I'm trying to,' Hattie said after a moment. 'It isn't easy.'

'I know. People like you always think it's – You may say you don't care what people do as long as it's in private and you get all upset if anyone says you're prejudiced against gay people, but you'd rather not think about what they really do. You'd rather not know of anything except the romantic parts, the falling-in-love thing. That makes them seem the same as straights. But they're not. Not always.'

'Straight people, as you call them, don't usually involve thirteen-year-olds in their sex lives,' Sam said. 'Do they?'

'Oh, don't they?' Viv said, and laughed, a jeering little sound. 'Going by what I read in the papers more straight people do things to kids than gay ones do.'

'Fair enough,' Sam said. 'But whoever does it, straight or gay, it's regarded as anything but normal.'

'Well, for all that, the parties I went to then were normal. There was nothing really wrong in any of it. It was nice naughty, not wrong naughty; even if there were a few people younger than me – fourteen, I was by then – and a few more a bit older – sixteen or so – there was no harm in it. I thought it was a bit odd there weren't more from school. But I found out later on he was too careful for that. Never had more than one person at a time from the Foundation, except once or twice –'

He faltered, stopped and then started again, a little louder this time. 'But it really was all right there, because it was all normal.'

'I won't argue with you,' Sam said and the boy shook his head and cried, 'But it was!' and someone looked around from the bar to the table in the corner where they were sitting and Sam said quickly, 'Hush!' and he subsided.

'If there'd been anything half wrong about it I'd have felt bad,' Vivian said eventually. 'That's what I'm trying to explain. To start with it was all great. And he kept on saying how I was a good writer –' He took a deep breath. 'And then it all changed.'

Neither of them said anything, just sitting and waiting for him
and he swallowed half the contents of his glass in a gulp and
then set both hands tidily on the table in front of him and started
again.

'He told me there was someone he knew, a friend who could
help me with my writing. Said he had connections in publishing
and that. So I said that was great and he said would I like to
meet him and I said I would so he said he'd fix it. He said he'd
pick me up and take me to his friend's flat ...' His voice
dwindled away, and he sat staring blankly at the facing wall and
then started again, louder now. 'It was halfway through the
autumn term,' he said. 'The first night I thought I needed a coat
to go out because it was cold. It's funny how you remember
things like that.'

Again they were all silent, both knowing without consulting
each other that the time had come to leave him to speak as and
when he chose, and he seemed aware of their patience and was
grateful for it. Because he looked at them both and then smiled
at Hattie, a little shakily.

'The thing is, I didn't know, but he – he was a sort of – well,
fixer for this other bloke. Collop just got people to his parties
and he'd come and keep out of sight and look us over and he'd
choose the ones he wanted and after a while Collop'd fix it up.
And that was it. And the reason I was at the school the night of
the rehearsal – well, he hadn't stopped. I stopped going to the
parties after that first night I went to Limehouse. I was never
asked again. He had done what he was supposed to do, Collop,
getting me there, and that was the end for him. After that he
started laughing at me, said I couldn't write for toffee, said I was
stupid, told the others my name ought to be pronounced Bottom
instead of Botham, the way I say it, the way the cricketer says it,
said they ought to call me Arse to help them remember it ...'

'You're jumping about a bit,' Sam ventured. 'Why were you at
school on the night of the *Shrew* rehearsal, did you say?'

'Because he was still doing it!' Vivian said impatiently. 'Can't
you understand? He was still getting these young ones and having
parties to find people for the other bloke. And there was this boy
in the fourth; well, I found out it was happening to him. He
liked it, of course, just the way I used to, so there was no use
talking to him, trying to get him not to go. He'd think I was

jealous or something, or just a misery. No, I had to tell him –
Collop – that I knew what he was doing and say it had to stop. I
wouldn't let him go on with it. I'd tell someone. That was what I
was going to do. Dilly, you see' – he looked at Hattie, and his
eyes were very bright – 'Dilly's changed things for me. She likes
me. Just me. The way I am. She likes me.'

'She might even love you,' Hattie said, smiling at him, and he
ducked his head, shy suddenly.

'Well, anyway, that was why I was there. And then the acid
happened and I thought, Maybe the kid's done it. The little one, I
mean. Maybe he put the acid in Collop's bottle because he's
already been – because he's hurt him already, and he's not the sort
of wimp I was who just let it go on and on. Maybe, I thought, he's
done something like what I did with the pepper, and that was why
I wanted to hear what happened at the meeting. In case you'd all
found out it was him, the little one – and don't ask me who it is
because I shan't tell you – I thought maybe if he had and you all
knew, I could warn him, cover up for him . . .' He shrugged. 'It all
sounds so stupid now, doesn't it? But I meant well. I was just so – I
wanted it to be better for Jamie – for the other kid. I wanted to do
what I wished someone had done for me, right at the beginning.'

'The panic attack in the lavatory,' Hattie said slowly. 'The day
of the autumn fair when you were ill in the loo and I found you.'

He looked at her and then nodded. 'That was when I found out
about this – the other boy. I saw and I heard – it made me feel so
dreadful I – I was still sort of involved then, you see. And I –
this is hard to explain this bit, because I'm not sure I understand
properly myself – but I didn't want the other kid to get hurt and
at the same time I knew what it was like for him. How there
were good bits as well as the awful part.'

'Let's get this clear,' Sam said, and he leaned forward. 'Forgive
me if I step on your toes at any point, Viv, but believe me it
won't be deliberate. You're saying that Martin Collop procured
you for someone else? Someone who abused you?'

'Yes,' Viv said, and didn't look at him.

'And that abuse went on for a long time. In the man's home.'

'He's got a flat. A fancy flat, down by Limehouse.' The boy's
face cracked in a painful grin. 'I thought it was marvellous, the
first time I saw it. Very fancy. It's filthy really, but I thought it
was marvellous, all black and purple and silver . . .'

'And then you discovered another boy was being put in your place. And you were upset for him. And upset for yourself, because although you hated it, and although you knew you didn't want it to go on there were parts of it you liked . . .'

Viv's face seemed to crumple. 'I didn't like it exactly. It was just that' – his voice dropped to a whisper – 'he was so bloody clever. He knew how to make – to make things happen to me that felt exciting. I felt sick after, but when it was going on it was marvellous. That was the worst thing about it.'

Sam nodded, seeming to understand. 'And then there was Dilly. And with her to help you, you decided to stop it all for good.'

'I knew I could, now there's Dilly. She makes me feel – Oh, it's just knowing she's around, you know? She's Dilly.'

Sam leaned back in his chair and his face fell into shadow. 'Yes,' he said in a flat tone. 'I know what you mean. It's called being in love, you'll find.'

'I know,' the boy said, and looked at Hattie. 'I did try to help the little kid, you know? I did want to. I thought that'd make it a bit better.'

'What would make it really better,' Hattie said very deliberately, 'is telling us who this other man is. The one with the flat in Limehouse.'

He seemed to pull back in his chair, and shook his head hard. 'I can't do that.'

'Why not?'

'I just can't.'

'He can't hurt you,' Sam said. 'Not if you tell us what he did. You were under age when he seduced you. Dammit, you still are. He did seduce you, didn't he? No one will blame you.'

He shook his head, stubborn now. 'I can't say. I don't – I can't.'

'He can't hurt you if he's caught and taken to prison,' Hattie said. 'He's the criminal, not you.'

Again the boy shook his head, angrily this time. 'Shut up! I won't say,' and there was a note of hysteria in his voice, and Hattie put out one hand and held on to him.

'It's all right,' she said. 'It's all right. No more now. Look, Viv, you'd better get home. We'll – Mr Chanter and I'll think about what you've said and decide where we go from here.'

'I'll deny it all,' Viv said, and looked at them with his head up. 'If you go to the police with all this, I'll deny it. I'm only telling you, I'll never tell anyone else.'

'All right,' Sam said unexpectedly, getting to his feet. 'All right. We'll leave it at that. You've kept your side of the deal, told us why you were at school. That you didn't put the acid in the bottle but were afraid someone else had. We'll believe you. There's just one thing I have to ask you, Viv. Was Matterson one of the people Collop procured for his friend?'

Vivian sat very still and stared at him and his face whitened as though an icy wind had blown across it, and he opened his mouth to speak, and then shook his head and got up and, clutching his face with one hand, ran for the lavatory.

'These kids,' the barman said, looking across indulgently as the door flapped behind him. 'Can't 'old their booze, can they? And 'e's only 'ad a pint!'

Thirty-one

There had been a late frost in the night and traces of the purity of it lingered in the quad, and she hurried into the building with her head as far down into her collar as she could manage to get it to protect her ears from the bite of the morning wind, grateful for the gust of stale warm air that greeted her. She felt a great deal better than she would have hoped after the exertions and stresses of the past few days; she had slept dreamlessly last night and felt surprisingly good this morning.

Because of the way Sam was yesterday? Her secret voice murmured in her ear as she brewed a pot of coffee in the corner she'd fitted up in her room for that purpose, and she smiled over the rim of her cup as she sipped, feeling as much warmth from the memory of his words as she did from the scalding liquid.

She wasn't surprised when he appeared in her doorway a few moments later. Already the school was stirring with the early arrivals among the boys, even though there was still more than half an hour to go to the Big Assembly which was due this morning. It would be the last of the term, with the school breaking up on Wednesday for the Easter holidays, and there was already an air of frivolity about, in spite of what had happened to Collop only last week. So seeing Sam with a bunch of sticky chestnut buds clutched in one hand didn't surprise her unduly.

'It's for the dais,' he explained when she looked at it. 'The Head wants us to pay some sort of attention to the fact that it's Easter without being over the top, because of Collop.'

'In equal scale, weighing delight and dole,' Hattie said, and he looked startled.

'A quotation? I'm the one who's supposed to have literary pretensions around here.'

'Then you'll have to look at your laurels,' she said and laughed, and he grinned at her and it was as though they were enclosed just for a moment in a bubble of happiness; but then he came further into the room and said, 'We have to talk about last night, don't we?' and the bubble vanished.

'Yes. I believed him,' she said. 'Did you?' And she poured coffee for him.

'I had to.' He had pulled off his coat and dropped it on the table and now was sitting on the edge, looking at her over folded arms. 'You look much better this morning.'

'I feel it. So what do we do now?'

'I've been trying to work that out. I just don't know. It'll be a waste of time talking to the Headmaster –'

'That goes without saying,' she said bitterly.

'And the police? We can't get anywhere with them unless the boy is willing to talk to them, and you heard what he said about denying it all.'

'But we can't just let it go on! Someone's got to find this man, whoever he is, and deal with him.' She frowned then. 'It was odd. He'd been so upfront about all the rest of it, why should he suddenly get so agitated when we wanted to know the man's name?'

'That wasn't what alarmed him,' Sam said. 'It was Matterson's name that got to him, wasn't it?'

'Not only that. It was asking him who the man in the flat was.' She shook her head. 'I just don't know what we do next.'

'One comfort is that it should stop now.'

'What makes you think that?'

'Collop can hardly give parties for his friend, whoever he is, to pick out his victims, if he's in hospital.'

'But he'll get out,' Hattie said. 'His injuries were dreadful, but they weren't terminal. He isn't like Tully, locked up in a coma for God knows how long. He could be back at work at the start of the summer term. So what do we do? Go to the hospital, tell him we know what he does? Make him tell this other man that the train's hit the buffers?'

'We could try that, but I don't see it'd get us far. He'll deny it, of course. And even if he didn't, how are we to stop him? We can't put a watch on his home.'

'A tip-off to the police, then, anonymously.'

'On what grounds? They have this tiresome preference for evidence.'

She was silent. 'Then we just have to put up with it?' she said at length. 'I couldn't bear that, knowing boys were being damaged this way and not trying to stop it.'

'I wonder who Jamie is? He let that much slip.'

'Even if we quizzed every Jamie in the fourth, what good would that do? It wouldn't stop the man finding other boys to – Oh, God, it makes me so sick!' She was suddenly on the edge of tears. 'I know horrible things happen and I know I can't stop all of them, none of us can do that, but to be this close to someone so wicked and to be stuck this way –'

'Oh, Hattie, don't,' he said, and was off the table and beside her in a second and he put his arms around her and held her close, patting her back comfortingly with one hand.

It was extraordinary. It was the first time anyone had hugged her quite like that since Oliver had, and that had stopped well before the end of his life; to feel it now, a man's arms holding her close, filled her not with pleasure, as she would have expected, but with a great wash of confusion. She had no right to be hugged so, it was wrong, dreadfully wrong; but she liked it and that make the wrongness greater; and she pulled herself into as small a space as she could and slid away from him to stand with her back to the wall, staring at him with her eyes wide and frightened.

He was shocked, so much so that he was left standing with his arms dangling by his sides and his face blank with astonishment, and she felt worse than ever, and knew she had to explain and didn't know if she could. But she had to try.

'That was – it felt all wrong,' she managed. 'I can't cope with – not yet – it doesn't feel right to be – I couldn't manage to –' And then she shook her head and said no more, terrified she was about to weep.

And he understood and took a deep breath and the expression of amazement left his face and he nodded.

'It's all right. I didn't stop to think. It was an instinctive thing, and I do beg your pardon. I promise not to try that again until – I mean, I'll leave it to you, if, that is, you ever – I won't do that again. Please forgive me.'

'Nothing to forgive,' she said, and managed a smile. 'I'm being perfectly absurd. You caught me by surprise. I'm not usually such a wimp.'

'You don't know how raw you are until someone touches you,' Sam said. 'I should have remembered.'

'Were you the same?'

He managed a smile of sorts. 'Oh, indeed I was. I couldn't bear it if people came anywhere near me. It made life very tough for a long time. But it gets better.'

'So I see,' she said, and this time she was able to laugh, albeit a little shakily, and he laughed too, in relief.

'I'm forgiven?'

'I told you, nothing to forgive. I should ask your pardon for being so ridiculous.'

'Believe me, you weren't.'

'Thank you.'

There was a silence, then they both started to speak at the same time and he shook his head and said, 'No, you first,' just as she put up both hands and said, 'I'm sorry, I interrupted.'

'I was just going to say,' he said, 'that there isn't a lot we can do about what Vivian told us. But I'll think about it, and if you do too maybe we'll come up with some sort of answer. Right now I'd better get this damned greenery sorted out.'

'And I have things to do too,' she said and smiled brightly. 'And yes, we'll think about it.'

He nodded and went and then she did allow herself the luxury of tears, only now they were tears of anger at herself and her stupidity, and she kicked the table leg furiously, which only hurt her foot and made her want to weep more. But it was all over almost as soon as it had started, and she blew her nose and dug a little mirror out of her bag and began to repair her make-up. Pink eyes on a cold day were permissible, she told herself, and anyway, she could wear her glasses, even though she only really needed them for very close work.

The door opened again and Harry Forster put his head round. 'Ah! We come not too early on our errand!' he said and came in and stood leaning against the door, smiling down at her. 'I seek succour, good madam.'

'I'm sure you've got all that wrong,' she said, and put away her make-up hurriedly. 'You sound like a bad historical novel rather than the way I imagine the real thing did.'

'That's the whole point of the joke,' Harry said. 'It's meant to be all wrong, like really cheap cloak-and-dagger jobs. Stap me vitals, ma'am, but where's the jest, an none recognize it? I weep for my own ineptitude.'

'You'll weep for better reasons soon if you don't tell me what you want,' she said and he smiled and bowed with a little flourish.

'I seek some advice, ma'am,' he said and then, as she lifted her brows at him, shook his head. 'All right, I'll stop.' And suddenly he was quite different. It was as though someone had switched off one set of gaudy lights and switched on another of a sober colour. He stood quietly with his arms at his sides, looking at her with face so firmly set it could have been carved from wood. It was the most extraordinary transformation and it left her quite speechless.

'It's Genevieve, Mrs Clements,' he said. 'I want to talk to you about Genevieve.'

'Oh.' She was cautious. 'Does she know you do?'

'She knows I'm very concerned about her.'

'But does she know you want to talk to me about her? Because it isn't right to discuss someone else without their knowledge and behind their back.'

'You've talked to her mother about her without her being there,' Harry said, and Hattie reddened. 'She knows you did that. She told me.'

'That was different.'

'Why? Because she was her mother? And I'm only a boy she happens to know?'

'Something like that.'

'Doesn't it occur to you that I might care more for Jenny than her mother does? That I might be better for her than her mother? Who did Jenny eat that sandwich for the other evening? Me or her mother?'

There was a little silence and then Hattie said, 'You've got a point there. But all the same, I'd feel uncomfortable talking about her behind her back.'

'You wouldn't be. She knows I want to talk to you. She'll come herself, maybe, if I tell her the right things about what happens when *we* talk.'

'Bribery?' Hattie said and Harry shook his head. He was still very sober.

'Encouragement.'

She was silent and then nodded. 'All right. I'll talk to you. But I need to ensure that Genevieve herself'll come and see me some time as well. I do care about her, you know.'

'I wouldn't be here if you didn't.'

She smiled. 'Fair enough. Well, what is it you want to talk about?'

'This eating thing. Her periods have stopped.'

She lifted her brows at him. 'Yes, that's a common side effect. An early one. I wouldn't be surprised if it hadn't been like that for a long time.'

'Years and years, she says.'

'Does it worry her?'

'Yes.'

'Then that should be an inducement to start eating properly again. To put on some weight. Her periods won't return until she does have the right body weight.'

'Could she get pregnant before that?' He sounded very intense, suddenly, and she looked at him with a cold spiral of distaste lifting in her.

'Is that why you're so interested? Not because of Genevieve's wellbeing, living as she does on the edge of starvation, but your own worries about making her pregnant? Hardly the attitude of a caring partner –'

'Don't make judgements about me when you've no evidence, madam!' he flared. 'Don't ever make such judgements upon me!'

She took a step back, startled by his vehemence. His eyes were very wide open, so that a faint rim of white showed above the black pupils, and his teeth were very white too, gleaming in his black face, and she was genuinely afraid. He looked the most threatening thing she'd ever been faced with and she wanted to shriek for help. But she bit her tongue and just stood there, looking back at him as steadily as she could.

He seemed to relax and took a deep breath and rubbed his face with both hands.

'I'm sorry. I just got so – I'm not having sex with Genevieve, Mrs Clements. I've got more respect, more – I *love* her. You know what that means? Or haven't you ever really loved anyone properly? Is that what it is, that you make such judgements so quickly?'

'I'm sorry,' she said and her lips felt stiff and hard to move. 'You're right. And, yes, I do know what it's like to love someone almost as desperately as you love Genevieve. I had no right to jump to that conclusion. Though the way you said it –'

'It's someone else who's been – using her,' he said, and his voice was tight. 'I try to push it out of my mind, what she told me, but I can't. It's very difficult when you love someone to know they've been hard-used.'

It seemed to her an odd turn of phrase and she blinked at it. 'Hard-used . . .'

'Ill treated. Bullied. Abused, altered.'

She shook her head, not understanding and he said impatiently, 'She isn't the way she was meant to be! She's been made what she is. Frightened and sick. I know she's killing herself the way she's behaving, and so does she. We have to make it stop. That's why I came to ask questions. I need to know all I can about her state before I can help her get out of it.'

Hattie nodded. 'I understand, and I deeply regret hurting your feelings, Harry. You've got more understanding of it all than I realized. Look, it's called anorexia nervosa, and it's dreadfully common. Usually girls like Genevieve, though it can happen to boys too sometimes. As they get thinner, because they don't eat, they get downy – you must have noticed that – and they lose their secondary sex characteristics. She's got no breasts any more of course, as well as no periods. It's like she was a child. Certainly she's trying to make her body more childlike –'

'Even though having a child's body makes pain for her?' Harry said and Hattie frowned and shook her head.

'I don't understand.'

'It makes it worse for her, being like a child! If only she could be like a woman, could get pregnant, that'd make it all stop, wouldn't it? If she could get pregnant, then she could go to him and make him understand that it was over, that she was grown up, that it had to stop . . .'

He began to move around the little room restlessly, prowling from side to side, and she let her eyes follow him, not sure what to think, not sure if she understood what she thought he was saying, suddenly seeing all the pieces of Genevieve's story fall into place, her mother and her fearfulness, the watchful way both parents had sat and stared at her when she'd talked to them, the way they had been, the three of them, that afternoon at the autumn fair; and she lifted her chin and said softly, 'You'll have to explain more, Harry.'

'It's him, of course,' Harry said savagely. 'It's him! Ever since she can remember, she told me. All those years ... When she was small, a thin child like her brothers, all those years. It's the way he talks to her, holds her, controls her. It's the way he makes her do the things he wants. If she got pregnant, though, and went and showed him, that would stop him, wouldn't it? He'd know the time had come to let go, to let someone else take over and start caring for Genevieve —'

He stopped then and stood and looked at her and for the first time since she had known him he looked his age, tentative, uncertain, yet incandescent with anger and hurt. He was a boy, not a man, and she put out one hand and said gently, 'It isn't as easy as that, Harry. She has to find her own life. She has to control herself. Not just be handed over from one to another strong person —'

'It's too late for that,' he cried impatiently. 'She's already been ruined that way. She'll always have to have people to look after her! And better me than him, with the way he's been.'

'Let me get this very clear,' Hattie said carefully. 'I have to be sure. You say her father has abused her?'

He was standing with his back to her now, stopped short in his prowling. 'Yes.'

'Sexual abuse?'

He lifted his head and almost howled it. 'Yes!'

'Intercourse?' She had to probe however much it hurt him.

He let his head droop now and said in a muffled voice, 'She says not. But I don't believe her. I think he did. Not the normal way though ...'

'How do you mean, Harry?' she persisted, feeling his resistance like a palpable thing.

'Does it matter? Isn't it obvious? Can't you see? How can she eat, how can she find pleasure in putting food in her mouth after — He's done dreadful things to her, and I want to kill him! I want to kill him —'

She came and stood behind him and after a moment risked putting a hand on his back and eventually, after what seemed a pause that lasted minutes, he turned and looked at her. His face was quite smooth again, and he smiled down at her as though none of the things he'd just said had distressed him in the least. The transformation was as complete as the earlier one had been. A chameleon, she thought, or do I mean Proteus? So changeable a thing; how can I trust him?

'So there you have it, Mrs Clements! I want to kill this man, but of course I can't, so I have to find other ways of dealing with him. And I wondered, Genevieve and I wondered, if she goes and tells him she's pregnant and it's my baby, will he know she's not able to get pregnant? Does he have that much knowledge? Do you see my difficulty? I have a better way of hurting him than killing him. If he thinks his little girl's been knocked up by a bloody nigger like me, he'll go through hell, won't he? For the rest of his life. Tell me it'll work. Because Genevieve swears to me she'll do it if it will.'

Thirty-two

'He told me to come and see you,' Genevieve said, standing just inside the door, not looking at her. Hattie sat at her table and didn't move, but she smiled cheerfully and raised one arm to welcome her.

'I'm glad you could come,' she said. 'Harry told you why?'

'He told me. But I can't stay long. I've got a class in ten minutes.'

'Oh well, this near the end of term –'

'I've got a class in ten minutes,' Genevieve said stubbornly. 'I can't stay long.'

'Would it be easier to come back this afternoon at the end of school?'

'No,' Genevieve said, and stared at her with eyes as opaque as pebbles. There was no expression anywhere, except for the aura of stubbornness that surrounded her.

Hattie sighed. 'I'm on your side, you know, Genevieve,' she said. 'I really am.'

'Are you? Then why did you get my mum to come here and go on at her about me?' Genevieve seemed more animated now and Hattie took the chance of standing up. She'd stayed where she was for fear that Genevieve might react like a wild bird and fly as soon as she moved; but remained where she was, still halfway in through the doorway. 'She told me, you know! I do find out things.'

'I wanted to help you,' Hattie said. 'I was afraid for you. I thought you might die if you didn't start eating. I once looked after a girl like you who did die. She didn't mean to, but it happened all the same. She had a heart attack because she was so starved.'

The girl didn't move and Hattie leaned against her table, the picture, she hoped, of casual relaxation. 'I don't want that to happen to you, so I was trying to see if there was any way I could help you. You wouldn't talk to me, so I asked your mum.'

'Well, she can't help, so that was a waste of time.'

'Is there anyone who can help?' Hattie asked softly, trying to hold eye contact with her, but Genevieve slid her gaze away, looking out of the grimy window.

There was a long silence and then she said, 'Harry could.'

'I thought so,' Hattie said, and smiled. 'He's very attractive, isn't he?'

The girl looked at her now. 'Is he?'

'I think so. Don't you?'

She only shrugged and Hattie sighed again, casting around for something to say, and then was startled as the girl's voice cut across, harsh and direct.

'Will it work?'

'Will what work?'

'Telling them I'm pregnant. Will it work?'

'I'm not sure what you mean. What effect do you want it to have?' Hattie said carefully, and the girl made an odd noise through her teeth, full of scorn.

'I want to get away, of course! Out from them for always. I never want to be there ever again. I can do my A levels from somewhere else, Harry says. He's got it all worked out. We can do our A levels together, living at his house. His mum won't mind, she never minds anything, and we don't have to do them here, at school, we can do them from a college, because we're both over sixteen, and then we can get grants and go to university together. It'll be –' She stopped and her face, which had begun to lighten, settled back into its old expressionless mode. 'It'll be very nice.'

'I'm not sure whether telling them you're pregnant would have that effect. They might think you needed more protection, not less. They might try to keep you at home even more,' Hattie said. 'You know them best. What do you think?'

The girl's lips curved and for the first time she looked happy. 'Not when they see Harry. It's him, you see. He hates black people. Always has. He says horrible things about them. If he thinks it's Harry he'll go mad.'

'You expect him to throw you out?'

'Why not? Other fathers do that.'

'But your father isn't like other fathers, is he? Genevieve? Is he?' She persisted because the mulish look had returned. 'Is he, Genevieve?'

'How do I know? I've only got him. I haven't had any others, how can I know?'

'You know. You've lived with him all your life. You've told Harry what he did to you. It isn't what fathers ought to do to their daughters. Is it?'

Genevieve was leaning against the door jamb now, still keeping her exit clear, not risking coming right in. 'If you say so.'

'If *I* say so? Oh, come on, Genevieve! It's not up to me to say it! You're the one who had to put up with it.'

'It wasn't all bad,' she said eventually, not lifting her head. She had both hands in front of her against her white blouse, inspecting her nails minutely, turning her hands over and back, over and back again. 'Not all of it. I told Harry that. He didn't understand. He doesn't know children need lots of cuddling and kissing. His sort of people don't do it.'

'Did your mother ever do it, Genevieve?' Hattie said, and this time the girl seemed to flinch.

'We're not talking about her.'

'Why not?'

'She's the one who ought to be got at, not me!' Genevieve's voice became shrill suddenly. 'It's her, not me, who ought to be sorting it all out, but you can't talk to her, she won't listen, no matter how hard you try she won't listen. I've tried and tried to tell her. I said to her, I can tell you why it's best to be thin, but she wouldn't listen, would she? So don't you go on at me about her. It's her you ought to go on at, not me.'

'I'm not going on at anyone, Genevieve,' Hattie said quietly. 'I wish you'd come in and sit down. It's very difficult talking like this.'

'I don't want to talk,' Genevieve said. 'So there's no need to come in, is there?'

'Well, what do you want?' Hattie went back to her own side of the table. Maybe the girl would feel less threatened if she did that, she thought. Maybe I've come too close to her physically.

But Genevieve didn't move. She stood staring at Hattie and now there was some expression there, a sort of thoughtfulness and then she said, 'I tell you what. You come with us, and tell them.'

'What?' Hattie said blankly. 'You want me to –'

'That's it.' Genevieve began to look positively animated. 'They'll believe you. If you really want to help me, you come and tell them with us, together, that I'm pregnant. That'd do it. They couldn't say it wasn't true if you told them, and they couldn't hurt Harry either. They'd go mad and they couldn't do anything because you were there. I'd be able to go out with Harry and never come back, even take some of my things with me. It'd be great. I should have thought of it before. If you want to help me, that's what you'll do. I'll tell Harry –' and she half turned as though to go.

'Hold on!' Hattie called urgently. 'Not so fast! I haven't said I can do that! It wouldn't be – it wouldn't be true, would it? Or could you be –?'

'No!' The girl sounded disgusted. 'We're not like that, me and Harry. We're different. Of course not. But if you come with us and tell them –'

'Will you start to eat, Genevieve?' Hattie said. 'If I do this, will you go and live with Harry and eat the sort of food I tell him to give you?'

She stood there at the door, still half turned away, and sighed, a long, soft sound. 'It's not as easy as that,' she said, and for the first time she sounded normal, like any other person holding a simple conversation. 'I only wish it were.'

'I know, Genevieve,' Hattie said, and once more risked coming out from behind her table. 'I truly do. I've looked after a lot of people like you. If you'll let me, I think I can get you well again. Make your periods normal . . .'

Genevieve looked at her over her shoulder and Hattie could have wept. There was an expression of longing there, a painful crying need, and she put out a hand and risked setting it on the girl's shoulder. 'It doesn't take too long to do that. Not if we can get your weight up a bit.'

'It's silly, really,' Genevieve said. 'All the others say it's such a nuisance, go on and on about having the curse and how they hate it, but I think it'd be nice. I'd like that. It never happened, you see, not properly.'

'If you began to give up eating early, before your periods were supposed to start, then it would have that effect,' Hattie said. 'We have to reverse it. It can be done.'

Genevieve said, never taking her eyes from Hattie's face, 'You'll come then? With me and Harry? Tell them like we said? And you'll wait till we've got out, so they can't stop me?'

'God help me,' Hattie said helplessly. 'It's the most unprofessional thing I ever heard of in all my life.'

'Yes, but will you do it?' Genevieve was staring at her with eyes wide and dark with hope, and Hattie stared back at her, and thought, When will you stop meddling, woman? When will you learn to let people sort themselves out? Now look what you've gone and done!

'Be careful, Hattie,' Sam said. 'He could be – well, let's not be melodramatic, but he'll be a very threatened man, won't he? Especially if you do what you say you will.'

'I'll do it,' Hattie said sturdily, covering up the trepidation that was filling her. 'I've got to. He's got to feel threatened himself, so much that he's paralysed. If it's not enough, he'll lash out, maybe. If it's really tough stuff he gets chucked at him, then maybe he'll be flattened.'

'And maybe he won't,' Sam said grimly. 'I wish you'd let me come with you.'

'No!' Hattie was scandalized. 'I've been sufficiently out of order telling you about it at all. If they thought I'd done that and then included you on the visit, I'd never get anywhere. They trust me and that means you have to trust me to take care of myself.'

'Oh, God,' he said. 'Phone me as soon as it's all over, will you?'

'Of course I will,' she said. 'And thank you for caring.'

'Don't be such a bloody fool,' he said and managed not to reach out for her. But it was difficult.

'Tomorrow,' Harry said, and came in and closed the door behind him. 'If that's all right with you? I've got it all fixed up with Jenny. She's told her mum she's bringing a friend home, that's all. Just a friend.' He laughed richly. 'She's flapping like a hen, Jenny says. It's the first time she's brought anyone home, she says, since she was in primary school, so her mum's not used to it. Her dad gets in about half past five, so as long as we're there by five we'll be well settled in.'

'Does it have to be this way?' Hattie asked with some distaste. 'Can't we just do the honest thing and say we have to talk to them both and –'

Harry shook his head. 'Jenny says that if he sees a black person on the doorstep he'll slam the door in my face. And I know he'd do that anyway when he sees it's me.' And again he laughed, a fat bubbling sound of pure pleasure. 'I have to be in there and well settled in, as I say. It's the only way. As for cheating on her mother' – his face hardened – 'she's no better than he is. Why care about her feelings?'

Hattie frowned. 'Genevieve didn't say her mother had abused her in any way.'

'It all depends on how you measure it, doesn't it? She knew. She didn't let Jenny tell her about it, but she knew, Jenny says, and that made it worse. She joined in without being joined in.'

'She colluded,' Hattie said a little absently, and Harry made a small bow, sketching his old grand manner.

'Ma'am, I beg to present m'compliments and gratitude for the degree of understanding you display, and –'

'Stop it, Harry,' she said sharply. 'I'm in no mood for that.'

'My apologies,' he said and waited for more.

She frowned and said, 'Why will he do that anyway, when he sees you?'

'I'm sorry?' He looked politely confused.

'You said he'd slam the door in your face as soon as he saw it was you. Does that mean he knows you? Have you already met?'

'He's a Governor of the school, isn't he?' Harry said. 'It's always possible.'

'I suppose so.' She was thinking again, but then she shook her head. 'I'm still not happy about this. You know that.'

'I know it. But you'll do it for me and for Jenny, won't you?'

'I'm doing it for Genevieve herself, not for you,' Hattie snapped. 'Let's get that very clear. We made a deal, she and I. You're part of it, but the deal's between us. She'll eat as I direct if I help this way. It's the only reason I'm doing it, but I can't pretend I like it. It's unprofessional and dishonest.'

'Oh, deary me,' Harry said softly. 'Such crimes to set against people who've only done what they've done.'

She reddened. 'Well, I know, but I'm doing it, aren't I? Just don't push my patience too hard. I've got my own breaking point and never you doubt it.'

'Oh, I don't,' he said, and turned to go, and then held out his hand to shake hers. 'Put it there, Mrs C. I'm grateful to you for coming this far with us, no matter what happens.'

She took his hand automatically and shook it and then looked down. He had several pieces of frayed and grubby sticky plaster applied to his thumb and first two fingers, and she turned his hand over in hers and said, 'What's this?'

He tried to pull his hand away and then, as she held on more firmly, looked at her and his eyes were wide and dark. After a moment he relaxed and laughed.

'I scrubbed 'em too hard against some wood while I was doing some work with the decorations in the hall,' he said easily. 'It'll be OK.'

'Those dressings are disgusting. And if it was wood you've probably got splinters.' She was comfortable again suddenly, back in the role she knew best, a brisk and knowledgeable nurse who understood injuries. 'Come here and I'll deal with it for you. You can get a nasty infection in an injury like that.'

'It's really not important.' He moved towards the door. 'And I have to go. I've got a class soon, and –'

'This won't take more than a few moments,' she said firmly and reached for his hand, and in the small room he couldn't evade her. 'Come and sit down here and let me see what's going on.'

She had already brought out her neat little first-aid and dressing box and had it open on her desk and after another moment of hesitation he came and sat on the table beside it, obediently holding out his hand.

'It's just a graze,' he said again. 'Nothing to fuss over.'

'I'll be the best judge of that,' she said crisply. 'Now, let me see.'

The plasters came off, leaving their sticky residue, and she reached for a swab and cleaned the skin at the edges of the dressing, and then for the first time looked closely at the graze.

And then bent a little nearer and pulled his hand forward so that the light from the centre fitting overhead – not very bright but all she had – was directed straight on to it.

'How did you say you did that, Harry?' she said quietly.

He lifted his head and looked at her. 'A wood graze. I was fixing the dais to take some greenery for Mr Chanter.'

She shook her head and reached for another swab and soaked it in cetrimide, and gently began to clean the injuries. The black skin on the outer part of the fingers shone with the gloss of the soapiness of the cetrimide, and the pallid skin on the inner aspect looked thickened and red in the poor light. She stopped when she'd cleaned it all and then straightened her back.

'You've got some explaining to do, Harry,' she said. 'Those aren't wood grazes, and don't insult me by trying to pretend they are. Those look to me like acid burns. And they're just where they'd be if you'd opened a bottle clumsily and splashed yourself: the thumb and the first two fingers. So, how did you get that? Are you going to tell me?'

Thirty-three

The silence between them seemed to go on for ever; Harry sitting there with his hand held in hers, clear in every detail in the pool of light from the ceiling fitting, and Hattie looking at his face with its beautiful lines and the curve of the downswept lashes that were so thick and curly they could have been a woman's, but for all that the most masculine of faces. It's small wonder that Genevieve is so besotted with him, she thought, and then dragged her mind back to the here and now. She was alone with a person she now firmly believed had tried to kill one of the other members of staff; how could she sit here thinking of what he looked like?

He moved first and looked up at her and there was actual amusement in his eyes. 'I fair mucked that up, didn't I, guv'nor? Should I say, "It's a fair cop, I'll come clean"?'

'This is no time to be funny, Harry.'

'But it is funny! I get everything else right and then I go and give myself away with dirty bandages.' He shook his head. 'And I'm usually so fussy, you know. You never even saw me in dirty trainers.'

'Perhaps you wanted me to find out,' Hattie said. 'That's what some experts say. No such thing as accidents and forgetting, only deliberate actions.'

He sighed softly. 'You could be right. It helps to talk to people. I've no one to talk to.'

'Are you mocking me?' she said sharply, hearing the amused tone still in his voice. 'Because I'm not the pushover you might think I am. I can make mistakes in my judgements but I'm not afraid to say when I have, and if I've made a mistake about you and you ought to be handed over to the police, then handed over you bloody well will be!'

'Oh, I don't doubt it,' he said, shaking his head. 'Please can I have another dressing on this? I don't like looking at it – it's ugly – and then I can sit down comfortably, and so can you.'

The effrontery of it amazed her. This boy was not long past seventeen yet he sat here with the aplomb of a man three times his age, and a man of enormous strength and wisdom, and she marvelled at him; but even more at herself, because she obeyed him and reached in her box for the dressings and the antiseptic.

'Start talking,' she said as she worked with her bandages, fixing a neat clean strip of plaster to each digit. 'And don't play games with me. I want the whole story –'

'And nothing but the story,' he ended. 'I know. And I won't waste my breath or your time any other way. I think you'll have the – heart, I suppose, to see why and what. And after all there's small harm done.'

'Small harm?' she exploded, lifting her head from her work. '*Small?* How can you sit there and say that, with Martin Collop in hospital with a tracheostomy and God knows what damage done to him –'

'You'll see what I mean,' he said, and his voice had hardened. 'Oh, you'll see what I mean when you hear why it was. I suppose the one I do regret a bit is Dave Tully, I wasn't after him.'

'What did you say?' She dropped his hand, the last bandage now in place, and sat down, reaching behind her for the chair, because her legs had suddenly turned to cotton wool. 'Tully? Were you – Was that you who . . .'

'Oh, yes,' he said calmly. 'That was me.'

'Oh, God,' she said and sat and stared at him.

'I'll start at the beginning, shall I?' he said, and smiled at her. 'It's a very good place to start.' And there was a hint of the song in his voice. 'And don't think I'm not taking it seriously, because I'm not beating my breast. I am. But I'm damned if I'll apologize for any of it because it was, well, necessary. You'll see.'

She said nothing, just sitting and looking at him, as the most vivid sense of *déjà vu* she had ever known filled her. She had been in this situation before, listening to a boy starting his story at the beginning. But then she remembered and understood why she felt so; Arse had been as Harry was now, sitting in his grimy pub on that dark evening, contemplative, relaxed, ready to talk. Now Harry was, and she shook her head to clear it of the confusion that had blunted the edges of her awareness and let him speak without interruption.

'Well, where do we begin?' He sighed, a long soft childlike sound. 'I was twelve when I came here first. It was hell. I wasn't like I am now, you know. Oh no. I was your actual ugly duckling. My mum always said I'd get better to look at. Beautiful, she said, and she was right, wasn't she? I know the value of how I am now, and I'm grateful for it. But it wasn't like that five years ago. I was a great lump. Bigger than any other boy in my form and with teeth like tombstones and all out of kilter. The wrong bits had grown, and I was – oh, all over the place. They made my life a complete hell.'

He was sitting a little hunched now, his eyes wide and gazing over her head, far away down into the past. 'I was bullied like no one else was ever bullied. I was spat on and shat on – oh, yes, shat on. They used to collect dog crap and put it on my plate at dinnertime because they knew I wouldn't dare to complain. My mum used to worry, you know, because I was so thin, but how could I not be? I couldn't eat here and at home I was too sick with being scared of the next day and the one after, so I never ate. That's why I understood about my Jenny.' His face softened. 'No one but me could understand Jenny properly. She's suffered as I did, only more quietly, and at home instead of school. It was all right at home for me.'

'Your parents, didn't they know what was happening?'

'My dad's not around much. He's a journalist. White, of course. Spends more of his time abroad than at home. Mum's all right, but she works such odd times.' His face softened. 'She sings. She's Barbara Blossom.'

'Oh!' Hattie said, startled, and he looked at her and his mouth twisted in a wry smile.

'They all say that. Oh, they say, as though no one ever had a well-known mother. Well, I have. And I never told anyone and I don't know why I told you.'

'Didn't she ever come here? Wouldn't the staff have known?'

'I wouldn't let her come here. Nor my father. They did it all by phone and letter, and I've got the same name as my Dad. He'd been a Foundationer when he was a boy, so he thought it'd be OK. And once I started I told them never to come here. Said it was easier for me if they didn't know I had well-known parents, and they were great. They stayed away.' He laughed, an ugly sound in the small quiet room. 'It was such hell here, I didn't want to mix it up with home. Home's good and right. Here's a shithole.'

'And they didn't know you were being bullied and –'

'I told you. I made up my mind they wouldn't. I had to deal with it. I knew I would one day, I just had to wait.'

'Didn't one of the masters –'

'The masters!' His voice was thick with scorn. 'That lot? They knew. They heard the sorts of things that bastard Bevan used to say to me in class, they heard the sorts of things Collop said and chose to forget he'd said when it suited him. But they thought I could handle it. Handle it! As if any kid could handle what I was getting. But I stuck it, and it got better. Oh, the difference it made, growing up!'

'But you aren't –'

'Not yet, you'd say? You don't know the half of of it. I found out how to do it earlier than most. And I'm black, remember. My sort mature younger than your sort.' He laughed at her, enjoying her discomfiture. 'I was having sex with various girls I met in Watney Street, round the market, before I was fourteen. I was shaving by the time I was in the fifth form. You don't know the half of what it's like to be me!'

'You're still not explaining,' she said, needing to take the initiative and get away from the embarrassment his words created in her. 'So you were bullied. But it got better. You solved the problem for yourself and that's very laudable. But why should you think now it's all right to – to do what you did to Martin Collop, and to Tully?'

'Hear me out,' he said, and leaned back in his chair. 'All right, I was OK, and everyone forgot what bastards they'd been. A couple more black kids got into the school and some Asians and suddenly I'm not the peculiar one any more and I'm getting better to look at and clever with it. Getting the work done so well they had to give me good marks. And then Collop got friendly.'

'Oh,' she said and knew what was coming and looked at him and saw Vivian in her mind's eye and tried to understand how

Collop chose his boys. Viv was unprepossessing compared with this glorious creature, and yet Viv had something else, a burning intelligence that of itself was very attractive, and she thought, If Collop had been as good a teacher as he was capable of being with his insight into people, he'd have been a marvel – and felt sick for a moment.

'He asked me to come to his house to a party,' Harry said. 'Only it wasn't just a party.'

'I know,' Hattie said, and he lifted his brows at her.

'You know?'

'Yes. There are – it still goes on. Or did.'

'I see,' he said softly. 'So someone else has confided in you?'

'He had to. I found out things.'

'Just as you did about me?' he said lightly. 'Clever Mrs C. Finding out things about people. It's as well you aren't interested in blackmail, isn't it? You found out about our little den and our comfortable little sessions with a bit of pot, didn't you? Do you always go prying around that way, looking for things that don't do any harm?'

She reddened furiously. 'I did that because I thought it was right! You *could* have done harm! That child Spero nearly burned the school down and himself with it. I had to be concerned about risks with fire and –'

'Phooey!' he said, still softly, not taking his eyes from her face. 'You just hate smoking, whether it's pot or tobacco, even though everyone knows pot doesn't do any harm to people. You went all pompous about it and set out to find out where we smoked and smoked us out.' He smiled then. 'An agreeable pun, isn't it? You smoked us out. But it was all because you were being, shall we say, inquisitive?'

'Say what you like. I did it and I don't care. I'd do it again. And I didn't find out about Collop and his parties in the same way. I was told.'

'Oh? Who's he got hold of now?'

'That's none of your business.'

'No. And it won't be his any longer, will it?'

There was silence and then she said, 'Are you trying to say that you . . .'

'That I put acid in his bottle to stop him getting any more kids the way he got me?' Harry said. 'Yes. That's what I'm saying.'

'But why so suddenly?' She stared at him, nonplussed. 'You said it had gone on for years, the way the staff and the boys here treated you, but that it had stopped. If you'd taken action against them in the beginning, it'd have been – well, not forgivable. It can never be that. But understandable. But to get revengeful now, for other people rather than yourself, is stretching my belief in your altruism a bit thin.'

'But that was before Jenny,' he said, as though that explained everything. 'Wasn't it?'

'You did what you did because of Jenny? But I don't see how what you did would many any difference. I mean, she cares for you, doesn't she? You've only got to wait a while and the world's all yours. Why take acid to Collop now when –'

He sighed again, a little theatrically. 'You've forgotten, like everyone else. I thought better of you, but you've forgotten like everyone else how long it takes to be free. When you're our age, every week, every month is twice as long for people like Jenny and me as it is for you. Longer. And I want to be free *now*. And I thought, I can frighten him off. I can get at Collop and frighten him through him. If Collop gets hurt, then too bad, it's his turn anyway. He'll get over it. But once *he* knows someone's got it in for Collop he'll understand they've got it in for him –'

'Got it in for whom?' she cried, lost now and getting angry. 'What the hell are you talking about?'

Harry lifted his brows. 'Weren't you told properly? About the parties? About how they were so that *he* could come and choose the people he wanted?'

'Yes,' she said. 'I was told that, but not *who* . . .'

'But not the man who came and did the choosing? Oh, I see. No wonder you're so cross. Well, it's no mystery, is it? Gordon. The Ineffable Gordon. Jenny's father.'

She was silent for a long time, sitting and looking at him and trying to see it, trying to see that smooth pallid man with his polished hair and his too-white shirts and overpressed trousers standing behind a door, peering in, choosing the boys he wanted to take away with him – and shook her head.

'He wouldn't tell me,' she whispered. 'He said he wouldn't tell me . . .'

'Now I have to ask who,' Harry said and she looked up at him and shook her head to clear it. There was a lot to get used to here and it wasn't easy.

'Arse. Vivian Botham,' she said. 'He – Oh, Christ! I had no right to tell you that.'

'It's all right. I won't tell a soul. It's as secret with me as it was with you before you told me.' And she believed him.

'But why? I don't understand. Why wouldn't he tell me? How could he not tell me that, when he'd told me so much already about Collop?'

Harry looked at her for a long time. Then he said, 'Do you remember hearing about Matterson?'

'Matterson? The sixth-former who died last year? Before I got here?'

'That's the one. He was Arse's friend.'

It was her turn to be silent now as she tried to fit the information into what she already knew.

'He, Arse – I mean Viv – he was involved in what happened to Matterson?'

'He probably thinks so. He probably thinks it's his fault for showing him how to do what he did.'

'*Arse* showed him?'

'Probably. He used to do that, Gordon. You had to teach your successor his little ways. The man's a bastard, I told you that. Don't you believe me? Arse is too scared of him to give him away, I'd say. How did you find out as much as you did? I imagine you caught Arse in some way? As you did with me? With your technique for nosing around? If you'll forgive me for saying it, Mrs C.'

'I wasn't nosing around! He was ...' And she saw no reason not to tell him how it was that Vivian had been made to talk to her. It was an extraordinary situation. She was sitting here with a boy who by his own admission had done horrendous things to two of his schoolmasters, yet they were talking as comfortably as a pair of very old friends. She felt no unease in his company and no fear at all. And surely she should?

'This is weird,' she said. 'I should be – I don't know, I shouldn't be as calm as I am with you, should I?'

'I don't see why not. I'm a reasonable person. And I'm giving you a reasonable explanation.'

'Are you? What about Tully? You say you hit him – why

Tully? Was he involved in this ring of – I don't know what to call them, they're horrible –'

'Yes,' he said. 'I'm glad you can see that they're horrible. As for Tully' – his face seemed to cloud – 'that was unfortunate.'

'Unfortunate! That's a hell of a word to use for a man who's ended up in Intensive Care.'

'Well, it was. It's just the sort of thing that would happen to a wanker like him. Always showing off, always trying to impress people by being different, wanting to be one of the boys. Too pally by half, he was. We got our pot from him, you know. Really! Don't look at me like that, I've told you nothing but the truth all through. Why stop believing me now? He was a wanker. He shouldn't have been there, that was the thing of it. I was making the best of an unexpected opportunity. There we were with live ammo and the guns and that ass of a man making his film and everyone staring at him as much as at the guns and all I had to do was stroll over to the side and pretend to be cleaning a gun and checking the sights and aim it and fire it. I was shaded by the trees; it was easy in the hubbub. I knew no one'd notice. And what happens? That half-witted wanker spots the camera coming his way and steps out in front to get right into the picture and steps in front of Gordon.'

She took a deep breath. 'You wanted to kill Gordon? I see. That makes some sense.'

He shook his head, almost affronted. 'Of course not! I've no intention of getting myself locked up for life for murder! Accidents are one thing, killing is another. No, I was just going to wing that bastard. Get him in the arm. That'd hurt like hell and limit him a lot. I was aiming at his elbow but because he was further back and because Tully was shorter than he was and stepped in front, it got him in the face. And I'm not that good a shot, to tell the truth. Better than most here, but that doesn't make me good. It's like everything else at the Foundation. The second rate comes out good because there's no first rate to measure it against.'

'So you hit Tully, and you put acid in Collop's bottle –' She stopped then. 'But you were marvellous that evening! You helped me. Without you I don't know what I'd have done. You saved his life.'

'You bet I did,' Harry said loudly. 'I told you, I've no intention of getting myself locked up for life. I wanted to hurt him, that was all. I wanted it to be the sort of accident that could happen. If the bloody cap on the acid bottle in the biology lab hadn't been broken so that the stuff got on to my fingers, I'd have been all right, wouldn't I? Pity about Tully, but there it is. I dare say he'll be all right eventually, too.'

'And if he isn't? Will you confess and –'

'Confess?' He opened his eyes wide. 'Of course not! Why the hell should I? If he hadn't been so bloody vain and stepped in front when he did, it wouldn't have happened. I'd have winged Barratt and that would have been what I wanted. As it was, he had only himself to blame.' His insouciance left her breathless; she could only shake her head at him in disbelief.

'And now,' he said with huge satisfaction, 'now I'm going to get my own back on Gordon Barratt.'

'Your own . . .' she said, filled with a sudden cold fear, and he smiled brilliantly.

'He gave me a bad time,' he said almost dreamily. 'I can't tell you what sort of time it was. He called me nigger and that was the least of it. He rubbed my face in it and worse. He – Oh, it doesn't matter now. But he used me and treated me like – Well, now it's my turn. I didn't know at first that he was Jenny's dad, you see. It was amazing. I fancied her as soon as she came here, as soon as all of you came here. There were the others dribbling after that stupid tart with the boobs and the yellow hair and all the time there was my Jenny, the best thing I'd ever seen. And then when I get to know her and it turns out he's her dad, I thought I'd go mad. I didn't know what to do. I thought she'd love him, you see, the way people do. The way I love my dad. He's – Well, I do. And I thought, If she loves him and I love her . . . It was like the world was coming to an end. That was when I thought of doing something to him and got the gun idea and all that. But then it turned out that she hated him more than I did, that he'd been as bad to her, only he told her he loved her, and –' He took a sudden deep shuddering breath and lifted his head to stare up at the ceiling and there was a long silence and when he brought his chin down and looked at her she saw his eyes were glittering with tears.

'It was like I'd waited all my life for that,' he said and he was a little husky now. 'I just had to find a way to get back at him.

Collop first, only just to hurt him, so that he knew not to do it again, what he's done to me and to the other boys, like poor old Arse, and then I had to get to him.'

'You can't,' she said breathless with her fear. 'Harry, you can't. Murder is the —'

'Who said anything about murder?' He opened his eyes wide again and now the glitter of tears had gone, replaced by the laughter that was usually there. 'When he sees me sitting in his living room, when he's told his girl's my girl and she's pregnant, he'll go mad. He'll lose everything at once, won't he? Because I'll threaten him that if he says a word I'll tell all about what he did to me and other boys. I've got photographs to show him. I'm taking them with me to the meeting when we go there. I hadn't told you about them, but now I can, and that makes it all so much easier. I'm going to show him the photographs, tell him I've got the negatives locked away and I'm going to take away his girl and take away his job and his being Governor, the lot, because if he doesn't do what I tell him to do, then I show the pictures and tell my story. It's all perfect, isn't it? You see? So don't make a fuss about that silly acid, Mrs C., will you? Because it doesn't matter any more, does it? Collop gets better and comes back but he won't hurt any more kids because the bastard's been and had his balls chopped off by me. He won't use Collop any more. Collop won't get whatever it was he got out of it all, and as for Tully, well, I can't say about him. But he was stupid to show off like that and step in front and . . . and well, however you look at it, it's turning out all right, isn't it? So don't spoil it, dear Mrs C., will you? You won't tell anyone what happened, will you? And anyway' – he giggled then – 'if you do, I'll deny it. You've only got my word against yours, but who'd believe such stuff from me? After all, I'm only seventeen. Hardly a villain, am I? With my school record and all.' Again that soft giggle. 'No one'll believe you.'

Thirty-four

There were snowdrops and crocuses pushing against the frozen earth of the little front gardens they passed, and she thought, How absurd! How can they have flowers in their gardens when they have a man like Gordon Barratt living so near them? How can this whole street of mock-Tudor houses with fibre-glass black beams and white plasticized paint and tidy front paths adorned with dripping tired privet hedges actually exist with a creature like Gordon Barratt amongst them? There should be visible signs of the evil that he spread around him, proof to the whole world that Harry had told her the truth. And then she shook her head in an effort to clear it of such stupid thoughts.

But she couldn't. It was like being in a dream; not a nightmare, precisely, but the sort that filled her with uneasiness and confusion. Indeed, she had felt dreamlike all through the long tube journey here, sitting opposite Harry and Genevieve who whispered to each other as they sat with their arms entwined, unable to keep their hands off each other, trying to think what she should do next.

She should of course have told Sam all she knew, she thought mournfully, staring out at the stations that slipped by in all their bright garishness and then at the patterns of house lights as they went through the overland part of the journey, out beyond Wembley far to the north; she should have insisted that he be allowed to come along on this mad expedition. She should have gone to the police and told them what Harry had told her.

But that would have been a waste of time because what had she to say to them? That a boy at the school had told her blithely that he'd deliberately fired a gun at a master and then fed acid to another? As Harry himself said, it would be her word against his, and since the police had convinced themselves the shooting episode was an accident, and had heard nothing from anyone of the acid event, they'd be unlikely to take her hearsay as any real evidence to follow. As for reporting Gordon to them, what after all could she do about him? The only people who could put any pressure on him were sitting opposite her now, giggling and murmuring as lovers always do and always have; and they'd both made it very clear to her that there was no way they would ever make formal charges against him.

'Harry's way's much better,' Genevieve had said, smiling brilliantly when Hattie tried to talk to her about the possibility of making some sort of formal complaint against Gordon. 'He'll sort all that out, you see if he doesn't.' Once she'd been assured by Harry that Mrs C., as he still persisted in calling her, knew all about everything, she'd been a changed girl as far as Hattie was concerned; relaxed, friendly, happy, full of excitement and interest. Her previous self had been like a badly blurred photograph of her in comparison, and Hattie had watched her for the last couple of days at school as the term creaked at last to its end, furtively seeking for signs that she was still ill, needing reassurance that Harry was wrong to be doing what he wanted to do, that she was wrong to allow herself to be used as part of his scheme; but it had been clear that there was no escape that way. Genevieve was totally in accord with Harry and his plans for her future.

Hattie had tried on the last day of term to explain to Genevieve that she was at risk of continuing under the control and manipulation she had always known, only exchanging one jailer for another, but she had looked at her in such incomprehension that Hattie had given up the effort. And anyway who was she to try to push the girl into a different pattern of behaving and feeling? Wouldn't she be being just as manipulative as Harry – almost as bad as the hateful Gordon – by doing so? Let Genevieve make her own choices, Hattie had said to herself, watching the girl hurry away down the corridor to meet Harry at the end of the last afternoon at school for the term; her idea of freedom may have been warped and her choices made for her, but was that so dreadful? Had she, Hattie, been so badly off in those years with Oliver who had been, she could not deny it, rather more masterful than Hattie had liked, and had led her firmly along the roads he wanted her to go? She missed Oliver and his strength still; she couldn't begrudge Genevieve the finding of Harry and his warm protection.

And now she walked alongside the two of them on a dark afternoon in the spring of the year going to meet a man who, if Harry was to be believed, was as evil a person as any she had ever had to deal with. She had to sit and support this boy, now walking rather more silently and with less absorption in his companion than he'd shown all afternoon so far, in his attempts to be a blackmailer. That his blackmail was meant to be benevolent, saving not only Genevieve from the actions of the man being threatened, but also any number of small boys whose future could be destroyed by him, was almost irrelevant. She was going to do things she could never have imagined herself doing.

And she stopped and looked at Harry in the darkness and tried to say, I can't do this, I'm going away! But he looked at her, his eyes wide and glittering a little, and she caught her breath and started to walk again. There was no way out. She had to go through with it all.

Genevieve was, amazingly, the one of them who seemed most calm. She scrabbled in her bag for her front-door key as casually as though she were doing nothing in the least out of the ordinary, unlocked the door and shouted, 'Mum!' in the most normal of voices, and then stood back to usher them into the house; and feeling cold all the way through to her middle, Hattie went in.

The house was chilly. There were radiators in the poorly lit hall, but they must have been turned off, for the air bit at the end of Hattie's nose as she stood and looked about her. The hall was looming and narrow, carpeted but unfurnished except for a small table with a telephone on it, with two doors off to the right and another door at the end beyond the single flight of stairs that ran up to the left. All the doors were closed and there was a smell of disinfectant and floor polish in the air; and Hattie thought, Maternity wards and dead bodies and drains, and shivered a little.

'I'm sorry it's a bit cold,' Genevieve said. 'I should have warned you to wear a sweater. He's mean. Makes a big row when the gas bill comes in, so she keeps it turned down till he gets in. Then she turns it up, because he makes a row over that if she doesn't.'

'I'm all right,' Hattie managed. 'I'm fine.' And Harry caught her eye and grinned. His teeth were very white in his face and he looked happy. His face was alight with laughter.

The door at the end of the hallway opened and she came out: Stella Barratt, in a dress in some dark cloth which she was smoothing over her hips as she came towards them.

'Hello, darling!' she said with a brightness so sharp it set Hattie's teeth on edge. 'So glad you could bring your friends – Oh!'

She had gone very white as she looked over Genevieve's shoulder and saw Harry. She stared at him, her eyes seeming to darken as she looked.

'This is Harry, Mum,' Genevieve said cheerfully, not taking her eyes from her mother's face. She was smiling a little. 'I told you about Harry.' And she slid one hand into the crock of his elbow and squeezed hard and Harry put his other hand over hers and turned his head and kissed her cheek swiftly before smiling at Stella with practised charm.

'Good afternoon, Mrs Barratt,' he said. 'It's very kind of you to invite us to tea. I've been looking forward to this.' His voice sounded more cultured than ever, the sounds rich, the accent precise and the warmth in him self-evident; and when he held out a hand to her she automatically responded and shook it, but when he let go stood looking down at her hand almost in surprise to find it still as it had been before his touch.

'And you remember Mrs Clements, Mum,' Genevieve said. 'We thought we'd ask her to come too. Seeing we've got things to talk about.'

'Things?' Stella said sharply, and looked for a moment at Hattie. 'What sort of things? If you're here to go on again about what she eats and – Well, I'll tell you now, he'll go mad. He won't talk to you. And I'm –' She looked at Harry, opened her mouth to speak to him and then closed it again and looked appealingly at Genevieve.

'Jenny, can I have a quick word?' she said, wheedling a little, and backed away towards the door that Hattie now saw led to the kitchen. 'Just for a moment.'

'No, Mum!' Genevieve said loudly. 'No need to talk on our own at all. It'll all be explained when he gets here.'

'Genevieve!' Stella cried and there was real terror in her voice.

'You can't let him come in and find him here!' And she flicked a glance at Harry and then looked away. 'You can't!'

'I can,' Genevieve said and laughed and hugged Harry's arm even closer and Harry smiled and said ingenuously, 'Why not, Mrs Barratt?'

'Genevieve?' Stella cried again but Genevieve said nothing, looking up into Harry's face.

'Because I'm black, Mrs Barratt? Or because I'm a young man, Mrs Barratt? Or because – well, you tell me why.'

Stella shook her head and said nothing, still looking at Genevieve, who suddenly seemed to be bored by what was going on.

'Come on in,' she said loudly. 'Let's go into the living room. We don't use it nearly enough. Come on in and I'll turn on the fire and to hell with him.' And she pushed open the door that led to the room at the front of the house and reached for the light.

The room opened its eyes, it seemed to Hattie, and stared back at them sulkily. A dull room, over-furnished in the old-fashioned way and with an electric fire standing in the tiled grate. Genevieve shuddered a little and went to switch it on.

'Well, Mum, how about some tea then?' she called, and Stella, who was still hovering in the hallway, looked at Hattie and Harry with a frightened air and then, amazingly, went into the kitchen. Hattie saw her put the kettle on and then turned away to follow Harry into the living room. How feeble could a woman be? she asked herself. If I were she, and my daughter brought two people I didn't want in my home for whatever reason, there's no way I'd be so docile about it. I'd push them out with my own hands. I wouldn't be putting kettles on for them –

'Wouldn't you? whispered her secret voice. But suppose you'd been married for so long to a man who did the sorts of things this man is supposed to have done? How would you be then? And she stared at the fire, at last glowing and beginning to warm the dank room, and deliberately hardened herself against the pity she felt for Stella Barratt. If what Harry said was true this woman was as much a part of it as the man himself. She might have been bullied, might have been brutalized, might have been frightened, but that didn't give her the right to let her children suffer as she had. They deserved better of her than that.

The three of them sat there in the living room as the air warmed, and waited, Hattie in a chair beside the fire, the others side by side on the small sofa that faced it, and none of them said anything until Stella came in with a tray, carefully set and obviously prepared some time ago, for the sandwiches on the plate were curling at the corners and the cake looked tired on its lacy doily.

She dispensed tea, murmuring about milk and sugar and offering food as though this were just an ordinary tea party, and Hattie accepted the cup, needing it to deal with her over-dry mouth, and marvelled. How could this woman be as she was? How could these two children – for that was all they were, after all – be so composed and comfortable? How could she be sitting here like a sacrificial lamb waiting for the butcher?

When he came in it was so unexpected that he was there amongst them almost before they realized he was in the house. The front door had opened in response to a short and sudden scratching at the keyhole and then slammed and there he was standing in the doorway and saying loudly, 'What on earth are all these lights blazing in here for –' And then he stopped, standing staring back at them with his face smooth with amazement.

For a long moment they stared back at him and then Harry leaned forward, set his cup and saucer neatly on the coffee table and smiled up at Gordon Barratt.

'Hello,' he said softly. 'How are you, old friend?'

Barratt looked back at him and still there was no expression on his face. But then his mouth opened and he said carefully through lips that were clearly stiff with control, 'Get out.'

'Oh, come now!' Harry said. 'You don't mean to be so unwelcoming, surely! Not to me, an old friend like me!'

'Old friend!' Stella said in a high voice and Barratt flicked a glance at her.

'Why are they here?' he said, and still his face showed no expression.

Stella said nothing, shrugging helplessly and looking at Genevieve. But she didn't speak either. The self-assurance that had been so much a part of her since they got here seemed to Hattie to have diminished or at least withdrawn somewhere inaccessible inside her, and she sat close beside Harry, her hand once more tucked into his elbow, staring at her father with her eyes dull and her face still and closed.

'Come and have some tea,' Harry invited. 'It's only just made, isn't it, Mrs Barratt? We should have waited for you – how ill mannered of us! But the girls were thirsty. You know how it is with girls and their tea?' And he winked at Barratt, every inch the indulgent male forced to spend time with lesser creatures.

'I told you, get out,' Barratt said and now his control was creaking. 'You stinking nigger, get out of my house –'

'There, what did I tell you?' Harry said in a pleased tone, and looked at Hattie and clapped his hands together in mock applause. 'Now do you believe me? It was all right for him to use me, to torment me, to fuck me, but not all right to call me anything but nigger.' He turned his head and looked at Barratt. 'Sit down. You've got some listening to do. To me. Come and hear what this stinking nigger's got to say to you.'

And amazingly he came in. He stood on his own rug in front of his own fire and after a moment turned and looked down at the fire and its glowing bars and then, with a sudden violent movement, bent and yanked the flex so that the plug came out of its socket and the glowing bars began to die. That seemed to comfort him and to give his some added strength, for when he straightened and looked at them, his face had lost its tension and seemed to bear only a faint sneer as the lips lifted in one corner.

'What do you want?' he said, staring at Hattie. 'Meddling again? I told you once before, you're not wanted here.'

'I may not be welcome,' Hattie said, startled to hear the words come out of her mouth. 'But I think I'm wanted.'

'Attagirl,' Harry said softly. 'Attagirl.'

'And you?' Barratt looked at Genevieve. 'What do you think you're doing bringing this garbage into my home? Do you want street filth ruining it? She's no use. Are you as bad?' And though he didn't look at Stella, they all knew whom he meant.

Genevieve looked at him and lifted her chin. The first time she started to speak no words came, only a breathy croak, and she swallowed convulsively and tried again.

'You're the bad one,' she said and stared at him and for the first time he seemed to show some real emotion. His face crumpled and there was pain there, but it had no sooner appeared than it had gone.

'Bad, me? Not me, honey bun,' he said, and the endearment sounded so incongruous and ugly, hanging in the air of the crowded little room, that the back of Hattie's neck seemed to creep.

'You,' Harry said, and leaned back on the sofa and looked up at Barratt with an air of consideration. 'I wonder if you ever saw this day coming? Ever thought you'd be caught and stopped? Or was it so easy in the early days to frighten the shit out of kids so that they never said a word to anyone about what you did to them that you thought it'd be like that for ever? Well, it isn't. That shit you frightened out of them has hit the fan. That's a saying I rather like and it certainly fits in here. It's hit the fan and it's your turn to get spattered. The worms are turning so fast they're almost giddy with it. Hmm, Jenny?' And Genevieve looked up at him and some of her courage came seeping back into her; Hattie could see it happen and it cheered her enormously. The boy had told her the truth, obviously, and he was going to make it work just the way he said he would. She felt suddenly light-headed with excitement and her pulses began to thicken and thud in her head.

'Shut up,' the man said, but it was just bluster and they all knew it.

'Oh, no. Not any more. I've been shut up for years. My Jenny's been shut up all her life. Now it's got to stop. It has stopped, eh, Jenny?'

'Yes!' Genevieve said loudly and with a suppressed excitement in her voice and Hattie thought, She feels as I do, and smiled at her, and Genevieve smiled back.

'I'm here to tell you my Jenny's coming away with me. We're leaving that school. We'll be doing our exams somewhere else. You won't know where. Either of you. We're going away.'

'Don't leave me, Genevieve! Don't leave me – I never did anything to you, don't leave me!'

It was Stella but her voice was so altered that Hattie wouldn't have known it as hers if she hadn't been looking at her, seeing her lips move. 'Don't leave me! I've done nothing!'

'That's why she's leaving,' Harry said with a sudden note of savagery in his voice, and he turned his head to look at her.

'She's leaving you as well as him, because you did nothing. All those years he's treated her as he treated me and the other boys he got hold of at the Foundation, the way I think he probably treated your other children, your sons. They never come to see you now, do they? You never hear from then, do you? Jenny told me that. Why's that, Mrs Barratt? Because you know he was fucking them the same way he did me? That he was fucking your daughter? And did nothing about it.'

Stella sat and stared at him, her eyes so widely open that a rim of white could be seen above the blue-black darkness at the centre, and she said hoarsely, 'No, that isn't true. He didn't. I never knew. He couldn't, he didn't –'

'He could and he did, and you knew.' Harry's voice was hard and loud in the small room. 'She tried to talk to you, but you didn't want to know. Not ever. Well, now you do know. Your husband, the man you sleep with, that man there – your husband had sex with all your children. Now what are you going to do about that? Keep him here? Or throw him out where he ought to be, in the gutter? You can, you know.'

Stella was staring at him like some mesmerized creature, and he said softly, 'You can throw him out. Right now. Make him go. He can't stop you, can't force you to keep him here –'

'What the hell do you think you're talking about?' Barratt roared. 'You can't come here and say things like that, you –'

'Is it true?' Stella was looking at him now, and her eyes had the same wild look from the visible band of white just below the upper lids. 'Did you – did you do what he said?'

'Oh, shut up,' he said. 'Who gives a shit about you? Shut up, you stupid cow. You' – he whirled on Harry – 'get out, or I –'

'Or you what?' Harry said sweetly and Barratt closed his mouth and looked at him, the old blankness of expression returning. 'You call the police to have me put out? Do that and I tell them all you'd rather I didn't. I show them pictures.' And he reached into his breast pocket, pulling his windcheater aside, and threw the little pile of snapshots down on to the coffee table. And Hattie saw them and made herself close her eyes. She didn't want to see.

There was silence as Gordon stood staring down at the photographs. He didn't pick them up. He didn't need to. They were face up and clearly visible.

'So there you have it,' Harry said in tones of great satisfaction, and he scooped up the pictures. 'I'll take these – No, I won't. You can have them as a memento. A reminder of what happens if you don't do as I say. I've got the negatives, you see. Those are easily reproduced, so you take them when you go. Go on.' And he jerked his head at the door.

'What?' Barratt said stupidly. 'What?'

'You heard me,' Harry said, and smiled benignly. 'Go away. Get out. Take yourself off. You can have – oh, a dozen minutes or so. Just enough to pack a few bits and pieces. We wouldn't want you quite down and out. You'll suffer more if you've got a little something to live on in that foul flat of yours in Limehouse. Then you can sit and remember what you've lost.' He looked at Stella then. 'This house, I suppose it's in his name?'

She looked dully at him, saying nothing, and Genevieve said, 'No,' suddenly and unexpectedly. 'No.'

'Really? You mean she owns it?'

'There was a tax thing, years ago. She told me. It's in her name, because he said it had to be, but she wasn't to get any ideas. She told me that, years ago.' Genevieve giggled suddenly. 'It's your own house, Mum. You've got something of your own for once.'

Stella shifted her head marginally and looked at her. The wildness had gone from her eyes and she looked vague and confused, as though she'd only just woken out of a deep sleep.

'What did you say?'

'I said, this is your house and he's got to get out. He's got to get out of everything, Harry says. The committees and all the things he does, all that. If he doesn't – and his job too, Harry says -- if he doesn't leave them all we're going to the police, aren't we, Harry?'

'Yes,' Harry said cheerfully, and smiled widely at Gordon Barratt. 'You're wasting time, old friend. Now you've only got eight minutes left to pack a few bits. Anything left behind gets thrown out or sold, right, Mrs Barratt?'

Stella shifted her eyes and looked at him. 'Right,' she said and her voice was husky. But there was some expression in it now. 'Right.'

'You can get out, you see,' Harry said gently and leaned forward and reached for her hand. 'It's possible if you try.'

She nodded and looked up at her husband and then, suddenly, smiled, and Hattie felt the crawling sensation that had been in the nape of her neck redouble. She'd never seen anyone look at someone else like that with so much naked loathing.

'Get out,' she said. 'You heard what he said. Get out!'

'But I'm not –' he began but Harry shook his head.

'No time for that, Barratt,' he said. 'Believe me, I'll take you and chuck you out in the street with my own hands. Go and do it. Get your things. You're going. If you don't, we get the police and Genevieve tells them what you've done.'

'You lousy stinking nigger!' Barratt shrieked and lunged across the room, but Harry was too quick for him. As though he'd been watching for the move from the start, he was on his feet and fending off the older man, twisting him, pinning one arm behind his back, holding him as easily as an adult holds a noisy child.

'Don't be such an arsehole, Barratt,' he said. 'You've lost. You're out. It could be worse. We're just making sure your world's ruined. You could have had to go to court and then to prison. You still might if you don't get a move on.'

Barratt pulled himself away and went, running to the door, lurching up the stairs, thudding across the landing, and they listened in silence as the sounds came down to them; scrapes and bangs as drawers were pulled out and doors slammed. And then he was overhead, on the landing, and coming down the stairs as Harry shot to his feet and went to the living-room door to wait for him.

Barratt went across the hall, dragging a case with him. He didn't look at Harry, but as he passed, Harry took his elbow and pulled him round to look him in the face.

'One last thing, Barratt,' he said. 'Just to send you on your way. My Jenny's pregnant. She's going to have another stinking little nigger, just like me. Your grandchild. Isn't that lovely?' And then he dragged him by the elbow and pulled the front door open and pushed him out.

And Hattie sat and listened as Genevieve and Stella jumped up and ran after Harry to stand on the step and watch the man half walking, half running down the quiet mock-Tudor street with its snowdrops and crocuses, his case dragging awkwardly behind him. She began to laugh, softly at first and then more

and more loudly. She hadn't needed to be here at all. She hadn't
had to say more than a few words to the man. Harry had done
it all as he'd said he would, and he'd done it alone. She hadn't
needed to be here at all. It was the funniest thing she had ever
heard of.

Sam was waiting where he said he would be, in the saloon bar of
the pub on the corner opposite the end of the road, and she
walked there, her hands thrust deep into her pockets, her collar
up against the chill. But she didn't feel cold now. There was a
warm centre somewhere deep inside, and it sent a glow all
through her. She could even smell the promise of future summer
in the air, the faint scent of trees trying to burst into leaf, and the
even more delicate fragrance of the snowdrops. It was over.
She'd been a great deal more alarmed at the prospect of meeting
the Barratts on their own territory than she had realized and
now it was all over she was almost giddy with the exhilaration
of it all.

I ought not to feel this way, she told herself. I ought to be
angry still with that man. I ought to be more worried about how
things will be for those children, for Arse and Dilly, Harry and
Genevieve. I ought to be more concerned about Tully and even
Collop . . .

But she was none of those things. She was warm and happy,
and she pushed open the door of the saloon bar of the Orange
Tree and went blinking into the brightly lit fug and its heavy
smell of beer and ham sandwiches and cigarette smoke, looking
for Sam; and saw him waiting, leaning against the bar at the far
end, and his face lit up as he saw her. And she let the door swing
behind her, and pushed her way through the crowd to meet him.